ALICE VS. WONDERLAND

ALICE VS. WONDERLAND

A Chilling Tale Of The Abuse of Power In The Name of Lawyer's Ethics

The Wonderland Castle, Offices of the Kentucky
Ministry of Ethics Near Lexington

STAN BILLINGSLEY

iUniverse, Inc.
Bloomington

Alice vs. Wonderland
A Chilling Tale Of The Abuse of Power In The Name of Lawyer's Ethics

iUniverse books may be ordered through booksellers or by contacting:

iUniverse
1663 Liberty Drive
Bloomington, IN 47403
www.iuniverse.com
1-800-Authors (1-800-288-4677)

ISBN: 978-1-4759-0627-1 (sc)
ISBN: 978-1-4759-0628-8 (ebk)

Printed in the United States of America

iUniverse rev. date: 03/17/2012

About The Author

Stan Billingsley was a Kentucky trial judge for 24 years, serving on the District and Circuit Court bench. Before being elected as a judge, he worked for the U.S. House of Representatives in Washington, D.C., served as an Administrative Assistant to Gov. Edward T. Breathitt, and was elected to the Ky. House of Representatives.

Judge Billingsley served on the Ky. Judicial Conduct Commission representing Kentucky District Judges. In 1995 the Kentucky Bar Association voted him as the Judge of the Year, the only District Judge to ever be so honored.

He is Senior Editor of LawReader, Inc. a legal research site found at www.lawreader.com. LawReader provides a massive legal research site for lawyers and libraries across the state. LawReader contains a national case law data base, and the largest Law Digest on the internet. The site also contains a blog, LawReader News, which is widely read by the legal community.

Judge Billingsley has written books on DUI law in Kentucky, Prosecutorial Misconduct, Small Claims Procedure, and Medical Malpractice Law In Kentucky.

He lives in Carrollton, Kentucky with his wife Gwen, near the Ohio River.

**THIS STORY IS A NOVEL.
ALL CHARACTERS AND EVENTS ARE FICTITIOUS.
ANY SIMILARITY WITH REAL PERSONS OR
EVENTS IS PURELY COINCIDENTAL.**

Nevertheless, the author has worked hard to cite only the correct law and current Supreme Court Ethics Rules.

The Assignment Section of the Kentucky Constitution actually exists. All references to spying technology are technically correct.

The Rabbit Hole Amendments are fictitious but provide a warning on the direction attorney disciplinary procedures appear to be headed.

The proposed ethics reforms proposed by Justice Alice Boone provide suggestions where such rules should be headed.

While this story is based in the Kentucky it is relevant to other states, as most states base their attorney disciplinary rules on the ABA Model Code of Professional Conduct.

Thanks

This work would not have been possible without the advice and encouragement of many people. I particularly thank my editor Jarrett Boyd of Carrollton who liberally used her marking pen on my numerous drafts and false starts.

Courtney and the other young ladies at the Florence, Kentucky Staples print center demonstrated great patience in helping the author to print out numerous working drafts. The assistance of Kelli Harvey at Books On Demand was invaluable.

The paralegals at LawReader.com, Rebecca Kinman and Shelly Chappell, Douglas Milbern, Gwen Billingsley (the CEO of LawReader and my wife), all kindly offered suggestions to keep me on track.

We would like to identify the many lawyers and judges who contributed their thoughts to this book, but I believe there are people who reside in dark places who secretly make long lists and await opportunities to take vengeance against anyone with a law license.

My long held desire to write a novel was encouraged by actress Barbara Billingsley, (Leave it to Beaver, Airplane) a relative by marriage. In 1998 I wrote a short story about a trip to Billingsley England. I shared this story with Ms. Billingsley and she responded by suggesting that I consider writing a novel.

Unfortunately Ms. Billingsley died before this work was published. I thank her for challenging me.

I recently read a book review where the critic accused the author of a crime against literature. I plead in my defense that the message in this novel is so important that hopefully I will be charged by critics with no more than the misdemeanor offense of trespassing against literature, and that parole will be liberally granted.

-The Author-

Prologue

Each state's highest court adopts rules for the conduct of lawyers. Lawyers who violate these rules can be punished. The court may issue fines, public and private reprimands, temporary suspensions and permanent disbarment to attorneys. Any attorneys or judges who are disbarred can no longer practice their profession. These rules are identified as rules to provide for ethical conduct, but many of the rules have little to do with traditional ethics or morality.

Since early in 2017 the ethics rules in Kentucky are enforced by the Ministry of Ethics. This office is under the supervision of the Board of Governors, but in fact it is a creature of the Supreme Court.

No branch of government uses secrecy to such a complete degree as the Judiciary. While this secrecy may be justified when the court is operating in their judicial function of deciding cases, such secrecy is harder to justify in performance of the administrative duties of the Chief Justice and the Court, particularly in the regulation of lawyer's conduct. The Judiciary, unlike Executive and Legislative branches of government, is exempt from Open Records laws and Open Meetings law.

There is no tolling statute on ethics charges. The Ministry can pursue a lawyer for something he may have done more than fifty years before the filing of the complaint. Some cases go on for years. Attorneys have no right to a speedy resolution of the complaint against them. Ethics investigations by the Ministry, even baseless ones, are a modern day parody of the Charles Dicken's novel *Bleak House.* In that book, litigation went on for years without resolution.

There is no minimum standard for what constitutes an offence serious enough to justify permanent disbarment. This lack of a classification system means that even the most insignificant violation has the potential for permanent disbarment. The wide discretion of the Supreme Court in imposing penalties, provides the discipline machine with absolute power over the lives of the lawyers they regulate.

If a lawyer's name appears in the newspaper or on television, he becomes a target of his jealous competitors. Those competitors, like a medieval guild, with the help of the Ministry of Ethics, can decide if a lawyer will be allowed to remain a member of their guild.

Some of the ethics rules adopted by the Court directly contradict one another. One Rule encourages an act and another discourages the same act. While an attorney may seek an ethics opinion in advance of an act, the Court is not bound to honor these advisory opinions. This leaves the members of the Bar with little guidance on what they can or cannot do in many situations. The ambiguity in what the ethics rules require of attorneys, means that the Ministry of Ethics can easily make up the rules as they go along.

The Supreme Court has declared its power to regulate the 'private affairs' of lawyers. Acts which have little relation to the practice of law can be prosecuted by the Ministry. Even the right of free speech, which has been protected by the Bill of Rights of the Constitution, has been limited by the courts, if the speaker is a lawyer.

The Kentucky Ethics Rules and procedures are not unique to the Commonwealth of Kentucky. Forty-seven states, including Kentucky, base their rules on a Model Code of Professional Conduct for lawyers, and a Model Code of Conduct for judges. Both Model Codes are published by the American Bar Association and both Model Codes admit in their language that they are 'general guidelines'. Everyone who reads such a "guideline" is free to interpret it anyway they wish.

Most of the work of the Ministry of Ethics is justified. There are bad lawyers who should be disbarred. Lawyers who steal from their clients, or who by their malpractice injure their clients, should be disbarred or sanctioned. This story focuses on those innocent lawyers who are recklessly lumped in with the ones who should be punished. Those who have been through the process claim that the Ministry presumes their guilt. Such a system appears to focus more on instilling fear, than seeking justice.

In 2007, England and later New Zealand, both fed up with abuses similar to those in this story, took away the lawyer discipline authority of the bar associations, and handed off these duties to an independent consumer protection agency. This agency has more citizen members than attorneys. Their charge is to protect the consumers of legal services. They hope to avoid all the politics found in the ABA style system followed in the United States.

This tale begins when the Chief Justice of the Supreme Court chooses to exercise an existing constitutional provision, in an abusive but legal manner, in order to achieve his goals. No other state official has more unregulated administrative power than does the Chief Justice. The most powerful weapon he wields to enforce his power is the Ministry of Ethics.

Such is the fear of the Ministry of Ethics, that every attorney who receives a letter from it, breaks into a cold sweat, even before opening the envelope. These letters are always stamped in blood red ink with the warning 'CONFIDENTIAL'. Such a letter is a formal notice that the recipients character, and future financial well-being, is at risk. The lawyer is not told who has made a complaint against him, and often the evidence against him is kept secret.

Those who fall into the Rabbit Hole of the ethics discipline machine, find themselves in a strange wonderland, such as the one described by Lewis Carroll in his nineteenth century novel, *Alice in Wonderland.*

Chapter One

The state owned Ford Taurus pulled out of the parking lot of the Ministry of Ethics complex located in a faux castle near Keeneland Race Track between Lexington and Versailles. The castle is called by some 'The Wonderland Castle'. Others call the castle grounds, the Place de la Concorde, after the public square in Paris, where the nobles were beheaded by the Guillotine during the French Revolution.

Twenty minutes later, Heather Regina Hart, the Commissioner of the Ministry of Ethics, dropped down a long hill and crossed the Kentucky river as she drove towards the Kentucky State Capitol Building. The sweet smell of cooking mash from the nearby distilleries was heavy on the November air, as it gently floated through the Kentucky River valley on a light fog.

The Commissioner of the recently formed Ministry of Ethics, was curious as to why she had been summoned to meet Benjamin "Big Cat" Cheshire at his office on Capitol Street near the State Capitol Building.

She couldn't help but feel a sense of caution in any meeting with Cheshire. Others summoned to Cheshire's 's office felt a palpable aura of sleaze surrounding him. She ignored the rumors about him but was intrigued by his wealth and influence. She decided that while she would be careful around Cheshire, she would work with him as long as it would advance her career.

She thought of several reasons why she might have been invited to call on the Commonwealth's most influential lobbyist and power broker. Could it be a discussion of the vacancy on the U.S. District Court caused by the untimely death of Judge McMain who recently went missing in an avalanche while skiing at Gstaad in the Swiss Alps?

She had been an assistant Commonwealth Attorney in Jefferson County for the ten years after her graduation from the University of Louisville Brandeis School of Law. She had compiled an impressive string of convictions on her resume. A nomination to the presumed vacancy on the U.S. District court was a possibility, at least in her mind.

She asked herself, "Perhaps my time has come. Or is this just another request for assistance to silence a troublesome attorney?"

When she was interviewing for the job of Commissioner of the Ministry of Ethics, the Chief Justice had told a number of people that he was impressed by her since she "wasn't a damn social worker". This had been reported to her, and she was proud of what she considered a compliment.

In any event, she did not feel that she could prudently ignore Cheshire's invitation. The Chief Justice had personally told her that she would be wise to make the acquaintance of Cheshire. She was also under the impression that Cheshire had played a significant role in her recent advancement to Commissioner of the Ministry of Ethics. She had been alerted that Cheshire was the Chief Justice's toady.

She parked her car at the curb adjacent to Cheshire's office which was situated in a two-story private home he had renovated on Capitol Street two blocks north of the Capitol Building.

She briefly sat in her car and smoothed her hair. She had timed her arrival to be five minutes early. "*Woody Hayes time.*" she told those in her employ.

Cheshire's secretary invited Commissioner Hart to have a seat while Cheshire finished a call.

As Hart read the waiting room copy of the Wall Street Journal, she heard the phone ring, and overheard the secretary's conversation: "Good Morning Justice Hatter . . . . Yes Sir, Commissioner Hart is here now. Yes Sir . . . I will pass that on to Mr. Cheshire . . . Yes Sir, thank you for calling."

Finally, after responding to a flashing light on her phone console, the secretary invited the Commissioner to enter Cheshire's 's cherry paneled office. She had been cooling her heels in his outer office for twenty minutes, just enough time to demonstrate her lowly position on Cheshire's totem pole, but not so long as to make her angry enough to walk out.

After the receptionist saw the door to Cheshire's office close behind Commissioner Hart, she tweeted to her friend Naomi, that "The Queen of Hearts just came in."

Cheshire's welcoming grin revealed a mouth full of what appeared to be thirty or forty large chemically whitened teeth. His grin was his only distinguishing feature and it lingered in the air long after his mouth had closed.

Cheshire rose from the Queen Anne Desk, which was free of any papers and contained only a telephone console. He rose and directed her to a pair of overstuffed leather Club chairs, where were intimately facing each other.

"So good to see you," he said making the obligatory Dale Carnegie small talk about how things were going at the Ministry and telling her how much he respected her important work.

She noted that Cheshire gave no apology for cooling her in his outer office.

The Commissioner of the Ministry of Ethics thanked the smiling Cheshire for his comments but did not respond with similar inquiries which might extend the meeting. She was not interested in small talk and cautiously played her cards close to her chest.

Cheshire quickly got to the point. "We have a problem, a real outrage, and it's something you should be aware of." He handed her a thick manila envelope. "Your attention to this will be most appreciated." He didn't need to say more. The meeting was over in less time than then she had spent in the waiting room.

She didn't open the envelope to inspect the contents and discover the identity of the Knave of Hearts, whom she would soon be investigating for an ethics violation. Whoever was named in the envelope, would almost certainly be in need of the enlightenment and re-education which could only be properly provided by the Ministry of Ethics. The unspoken message was clear. The CJ wanted something done, and wanted to keep his distance.

The accommodation she made to Cheshire by visiting him, was the third such event in her brief tenure as Commissioner of the Ministry of Ethics through which she had extended her cooperation to the powerful. She knew from a reading of the Rules of Ethics procedure, that she could accept a complaint from anyone. Complainants could even remain anonymous. She saw no problem in allowing her superiors to use the Ministry in this manner. If it advanced her career, so much the better.

The Queen of Hearts was not familiar with the Seventeenth Century fable where the evil little monkey talked the cat into pulling chestnuts out of a fire. As the cat pulled a chestnut out of the fire the monkey would eat it. Only in the end did the cat realize that he had nothing to show for his efforts but singed paws.

The odor from these interventions was noticed by staff attorneys at the Ministry. The Ministry staffers secretly called the special requests for ethics investigations she brought to the Ministry for action, as "FO/HRH's". (Friend of Her Royal Highness.) In internal e-mails and tweets to one another, the Ministry attorneys and paralegals frequently placed the notation of "FO/HRH" in the subject line to emphasize the importance of internal communications concerning the Commissioner's special cases.

While Ministry staffers were unwilling to place their jobs in jeopardy by actually protesting such investigations, most at least tried to avoid being assigned to handle them.

Chapter Two

Madison Hatter had served as a Circuit Judge in Lexington for sixteen years before he was appointed by the Governor to a vacancy on the Kentucky Supreme Court. The vacancy Hatter filled, was created when the prior Justice had been nominated to a position on the Sixth Circuit Court of Appeals by the President. Hatter had a reputation as a generally conservative judge whose orders were well reasoned. He treated all members of the Bar Association who appeared before him with respect.

He spent his first year on the Supreme Court developing friendships with the other Justices and quietly preparing for the special election that he had to endure in order to hold on to the seat for the balance of the term. He narrowly won the special election and was granted an additional eight years on the court. Five years later in 2012, the current Chief Justice unexpectedly retired and took a position with one of the state's largest law firms at a salary three times that of the Chief Justice.

Madison Hatter had been elected Chief Justice on Dec. 21, 2012. His critics noted this as the doomsday date mentioned in the Mayan calendar. His only opponent was Justice Alice Boone. He privately vowed to forever classify her as an enemy. Rumors of questionable promises he was alleged to have made, to add the necessary three votes to his own deciding vote, were numerous.

Upon assuming the office of Chief Justice, his previously good nature morphed into the personality of an army drill sergeant. Some have attributed his personality change to the effects of triple heart bypass surgery. Some called this the Dick Chaney Syndrome. It is not uncommon for survivors of such surgery to become short tempered. In any event power changes some men. It certainly changed Madison Hatter, and not for the better.

The Justices of the Court who served from 2007 through 2014 were called the Gold Court. They were noted for their scholarship and willingness to undo many questionable rulings that had accumulated over the prior decades.

The Gold Court got its name when someone wrote an editorial that said "Their rulings are as good as Gold."

In Hatter's first year as Chief Justice, he appeared to take a ninety degree turn to the right. He quickly earned the nickname 'The Mad Hatter' and the court he served as Chief Justice became known as the 'Mad Court'.

Madison Hatter devoted a great deal of time studying the Constitution and the Supreme Court Rules with the purpose of learning the limits of power he enjoyed as Chief Justice and Administrator of the Judicial Branch of Government. His influence as the Chief Justice was enhanced by the casual attitude of a majority of the other Justices on the court when dealing with the administrative duties of the Court in preparing the judicial budget, overseeing the four thousand employees of the Administration Office of the Courts, and providing oversight on the Ethics rules and procedures. Most justices didn't want to participate in Hatter's little dramas, and preferred to devote themselves to the scholarly duties of the Court.

The Supreme Court under the Gold Court had ended the practice of the prior Court to only schedule one hour a month to review administrative issues of the court. It was said that the attitude of the Old Court was that the Justices were too busy writing decisions to have any interest in overseeing such mundane issues as personnel matters of the four thousand court employees which included clerks, probation officers, bailiffs, and program administrators. They deferred those issues to the Chief Justice.

After a year of the Mad Court, the majority of the Justices once again returned to a policy of benign neglect regarding administrative issues including supervision of the Kentucky Bar Association administration and the 4000 employees of the court system. The prevailing attitude was that they were overworked just writing decisions. They had little interest in the disputes over the battles involved in the doling out of court resources and the hiring and firing of court employees. Chief Justice Hatter realized the opportunity this gave him. By rewarding his friends on the court, he built a solid coalition with three other justices. This coalition, along with the inherent powers granted to the Judicial Branch of Government, made Chief Justice Hatter more powerful than any Chief Justice in memory. His knew the parameters of his constitutional powers, and he pushed his influence to the extreme limits when it suited his needs.

Hatter's turn to the dark side was readily evident in his use of the disciplinary system. He recognized that the Supreme Court made all the rules that regulated the conduct of the state's seventeen thousand lawyers. Hatter paid great attention to this disciplinary machine. He saw the power that taking control of the discipline system would grant him. He was wise enough to never disclose his plans for the discipline system, but soon it functioned as his personal Gestapo. If he had an enemy he could use the ethics system to silence him. His plan to put the management of the Ministry of Ethics in the hands of a person he could control, was his first step in co-opting the ethics machine.

With Heather Hart serving as Commissioner of the Ministry, he could destroy his enemies and never leave a trace of evidence of his involvement at the scene of the crime.

The Constitutional Amendments adopted in 1976 granted the Chief Justice more raw power to take unilateral action than any other official in State Government. The Governor himself, was checked by the legislature. The Governor was a weakling when compared to the Chief Justice. Even the powers of judicial appointment granted to the Governor by the 1976 Constitutional Amendments were watered down by the fact that the Chief Justice was a member of the Judicial Nominating Commissions who nominated candidates for all judicial vacancies. The Governor was required to fill a judicial vacancy from the three nominees selected by the Nominating Commissions which were all Chaired by the Chief Justice. The Chief Justice with the cooperation of the nominating commission could even nominate a candidate who had not requested to be considered. Chief Justice Hatter used this influence to prevent and obstruct the career of any attorney who sought a judicial appointment and whose resume or political bent he didn't like. Those who received his support usually remained tacit allies. Every potential candidate for a judicial appointment, or elevation to a higher court, realized that the Chief Justice could be of great help, or if he disliked them, he could usually block any appointment.

Chief Justice Hatter blocked an effort to make the disciplinary machine subject to the open records laws that hampered the other two branches of government. He observed how the legislature adopted a Legislative Ethics Commission but gutted its intended mission of enforcing Legislative Ethics Rules, by adding a provision of the law which allowed anyone filing a false claim against a legislator to be prosecuted for a felony criminal offense. If the committee found a complaint against a legislator to be frivolous, they could actually seek the complainant's imprisonment. Of course the number of complaints against legislators soon became non-existent.

Hatter refused to consider any penalty for persons who filed ethics complaint against a lawyer, because he wanted to encourage such complaints, otherwise he could not take vengeance on his enemies. He recognized that ethics complaints seeking disbarment could even be filed against Judges, and he was not meek in exercising this power when it suited his purposes.

A judge could be impeached by the Legislature but this was a difficult and messy procedure requiring the intervention of the Legislature. It was much simpler to use the secret process of disbarment. Since all Judges were required to have a law license, they could more easily be removed from office by disbarment than through the impeachment process.

The example of the Legislature in controlling their own ethics review procedures demonstrated to Hatter the importance of the ethics machine. Hatter viewed the lawyers ethic enforcement system as a useful tool while the legislature saw their ethics mechanism as a troublesome institution which should be suppressed.

Hatter noted that anyone could file a complaint against a lawyer or judge and in most situations the complainant's name would remain confidential. Even common criminals enjoyed the right to know who their accusers were, but not lawyers. They could be maligned and accused in secret by unnamed enemies. Hatter had not created the secret complaint, but he learned to use it to maximum effect. At his skillful hands, every attorney and judge in the state was subject to his control.

Chief Justice Hatter trusted few people, but he trusted his old friend Benjamin Big Cat Cheshire. Cheshire had been generous in his campaign donations to Hatter during his contested elections for Circuit Judge and the Supreme Court.

Cheshire marketed his relationship with the Chief Justice when it suited his needs. The large corporations and particularly the state's insurance companies all were aware of the close relationship between Hatter and Cheshire. They relied on Cheshire to do public relations for them and to advise them on pending legislation. Cheshire quickly developed the uncanny ability to predict the outcome of cases pending in the Supreme Court. His predictive powers were shared only with his wealthiest clients and did not come cheap. The only favors that the Chief Justice ever asked of Cheshire was to give him cover in filing ethics complaints with the

Ministry of Ethics when suggested by the Chief Justice and to keep him informed on any potential legislative political changes affecting the courts. He also relied on Cheshire for updates on all the gossip regarding scandals and plots of others in State Government. While Chief Justice Hatter was vaguely aware that Cheshire marketed their close relationship to corporate interests, but he never inquired into this and he never objected.

As a businessman Cheshire was always amazed how public officials would sell their honor for a few hundred dollars or even a tee time at an exclusive golf course. Their small indiscretions could end up costing taxpayers hundreds of millions. He had long ago concluded that a crooked public official was not only a crook, he was a terrible businessman who grossly underpriced the value of his illegal services. This disparity between the cost of a bribe and the benefits to his clients provided a great financial incentive for Cheshire and his clients to dabble in these dark waters.

Madison Hatter's election as Chief Justice gave Cheshire an entirely new opportunity to separate his clients from millions in consulting fees. For the first time he was wired into the highest court in the Commonwealth.

The filing of a secret complaint now and again was a small price to pay. Cheshire was not successful in recruiting Hatter to provide him marketable information. Even though Cheshire had cautiously sought inside information from Hatter, Hatter never crossed the line of sharing truly confidential information regarding pending cases. Soon after Hatter's election as Chief Justice, Cheshire solved this problem by including Hatter and the Supreme Court into his secret program of electronic surveillance.

Chapter Three

After leaving Cheshire's office, Commissioner Hart ordered a sandwich at Starbucks, where she ate alone. She was virtually anonymous in Frankfort. She had made few friends other than professional and staff relationships in her ten months in the Capital City. She lived alone in a condo in Louisville overlooking the Ohio River. She commuted daily to her office at the Ministry. She avoided the publicity that was the lifeblood of almost every other official in Frankfort. The website of the Bar Association did not include any pictures of her. She never appeared at Continuing Legal Education seminars as a speaker. Of the seventeen thousand members of the Kentucky Bar Association, few had every met her. She preferred to keep a low profile and she was successful.

Before returning to her office at the Ministry, she ordered a tall chocolate mocha with whipped cream to go. Back at her office, Commissioner Hart sipped her coffee, as she reviewed mail and phone calls on her I-pad.

A brass plaque on her desk epitomized her dark sense of humor, if not her philosophy, as enforcer of lawyers' morals. It read, "Proverbs 23:14: "Thou shalt beat him with the rod, and shalt deliver his soul from hell."

An autographed photo of Rand Paul with his arm around Hart's shoulder was on the credenza behind her desk.

Although she was certain of the nature of the assignment in the unopened envelope given her by Cheshire, the fact that she was about to destroy the career and reputation of a lawyer was of little concern to her. She had no curiosity as to the identity of the victim. She assumed his guilt in advance. Before she opened the envelope Cheshire had handed her, she reviewed the mail on her desk.

A letter from the Office of the Chief Justice was opened first. The letter informed her of the names of the four new citizen members of the Board of Scrutiny for a two year term appointed by the Chief Justice.

The new citizen appointees included: A nursing home operator from Somerset.

A housewife from Paducah whose husband was a member of the legislature. A nurse from Louisville. A retired executive of Ashland Oil from Ashland.

She made a mental note to do her own vetting of the new 'Scruntineers', (as she derisively called the members of the Board of Scrutiny), beginning with a check of their political registration. She had stolen the term 'Scruntineer' from Walt Disney, who used it to describe his team of fantasy creators. The witticism pleased her and correctly described their work.

The notice contained small portraits of the new appointees. She examined the photos and tried to predict their likelihood for being trouble makers. She hoped that the Chief Justice had done his due diligence in selecting members with a high obedience-to-authority quotient.

She reviewed her calendar and made a phone call scheduling appointments at the exclusive Z Salon & Spa on Shelbyville Road in Louisville. She scheduled a stylist for a touch up on her color, and to have a fill and manicure on her nails.

After she worked through her mail, it finally occurred to her to open the envelope that Big Cat Cheshire had handed her.

The first sheet of paper listed the name of Thomas Jefferson Kenton, Jr. as her next victim. she often called victims of her Ethics prosecutions 'Knave of Hearts'. She was not familiar with the name of Thomas Jefferson Kenton, Jr.

A scanned copy of his Fayette County Bar Association Directory photo revealed a handsome smiling man who appeared ten years younger than his actual age of 70. He had just a touch of gray in his full head of hair. His bar association membership number and office address were listed.

Every lawyer is assigned a bar number when they were first licensed to practice law. This number stayed with them throughout their careers. It occurred to her that it would make sense to make an exception to the 'No Tattoo' policy she applied to her employees, and require that all licensed attorneys should have their Bar membership number permanently tattooed on their forearms. She reasoned this could be in the form of a Bar Code and could be used to confirm attendance at mandatory bar classes.

The brief biography listed Kenton's areas of practice as personal injury, criminal defense, probate, family law, and general practice. His bar status was current, and he was current on his Continuing Education Credits, but just barely. His last CLE had included a seminar on Equine Law which he had attended in Lexington.

Kenton was a widower with two children, Carroll aged 43 and Edward who was 46. He had served two terms in the State Senate some thirty years ago. The report did not state if he had retired or been defeated.

She then turned to the second sheet of paper. It was a photocopy of a newspaper article from the *Lexington Herald-Leader* which listed his name as a potential nominee for the Supreme Court seat currently occupied by the Chief Justice. That explained all the interest in Thomas Jefferson Kenton, Jr.!

The next document included in Cheshire's package was a letter from Thomas Jefferson Kenton. The letter concerned an action of the Legislative Ethics Commission in dismissing a charge against a State Senator against whom a complaint had been filed alleging that he mailed a letter soliciting attendance to a political fundraiser to lobbyists and merit system employees. Solicitation letters of this sort were a clear violation of state law.

The letter from Kenton was addressed to the Chairman of the Legislative Ethics Commission. In the letter, Kenton complained that the Ethics Commission had incorrectly dismissed the ethics complaint against the State Senator. He criticized the Legislative Ethics Commission for justifying the dismissal on a 'non-existent legal theory'.

The original complaint against the Senator, alleged that he had assigned his workers to set up the fundraising event. The Legislative Ethics Commission justified their whitewash by concluding that the state official who had authorized the letter, "could not be held responsible for actions of his subordinates." Even Heather Hart raised an eyebrow when she read the Commission's weak justification for dismissal.

As a former prosecutor she had prosecuted a murder for hire case, and she had certainly argued that the person who ordered the murder was equally responsible. But she had been given Jack Kenton as a special assignment, and she would not question her superiors' motives.

Kenton in his complaint to the Commission Chairman said, "In my opinion this dismissal is shameful and defeated the purpose of the statute which created the Legislative Ethics Commission." Kenton went on to state that he had helped draft the original law that created the Legislative Ethics Commission and, "The Commission by this ruling has ignored the original intent of the law."

The third enclosure in Cheshire's package was a copy of a letter to the Chief Justice from Thomas Jefferson Kenton, Jr. Kenton's second letter discussed his concern "as a citizen" about the conduct of a case by the Ministry of Ethics in which a Notice of Investigation Letter, about a pending investigation regarding a lawyer from Northern Kentucky, was leaked to the press within hours of the Commissioner's decision to launch an investigation.

The leak had occurred the preceding March. The leak was followed by a quick settlement of the Ethic's charge brought by the Ministry of Ethics with the young attorney receiving only a public reprimand.

Public reprimands are published on the Bar Association's website and released to the press. Any ethics sanction has the potential to embarrass the defendant lawyer. Lawyers running for public office can be expected to have such reprimands cited against them.

The young attorney had been under investigation for 'challenging the qualifications or integrity of a judicial official in violation of SCR 3.130 8.2(a).' This rule was increasingly used by the Ministry to silence any criticism of those whom the Ministry chose to protect.

The Ministry of Ethics in its initial meeting with the young attorney, following its policy of intimidation, coerced a settlement by indicating it would be seeking a two year suspension of his right to practice law.

SCR 3.130 8.2 (a) was a rule adopted by the Supreme Court, which prohibited lawyers from challenging the "integrity or qualifications" of judges, prosecutors or other public officials. The Rule, as frequently applied by the Ministry, was a direct challenge to the Kentucky and United States Constitution freedom of speech rights which includes the right of citizens to petition their government for a redress of their grievances. This Rule was in direct contradiction of other Rules in the Code which encouraged lawyers to speak out and question actions of the government including the courts.

The First Amendment right of lawyers to speak out had been chiseled away by court rulings over the years and was justified by the "need for order and decorum." Lawyers, it was explained by the court decisions, had fewer first amendment rights than citizens at large. Those that justified the rule said that lawyers should make "reasonable sacrifices to uphold the dignity of the profession." This interpretation clearly made lawyers second class citizens when it came to free speech issues.

Supreme Court Rule 3.130 8.2(a) rule against free speech, contained a limitation which required the prohibited statement to be 'false'. This wording implies that 'true' statements were authorized by the rule. But this limitation was frequently ignored by the Ministry. Since the Ministry itself determined if any statement was false, and all their actions were protected from public scrutiny by a cloak of secrecy, ignoring this limitation was not difficult.

Ethics procedures are designated as civil proceedings. It therefore does not impose the 'beyond a reasonable doubt' standard of proof upon the state as is applied to criminal violations. The Board of Scrutiny acted as a Grand Jury to formally issue charges. It only needed a majority vote to find sufficient cause to allow a complaint to be brought against a lawyer.

The Ministry readily prosecutes violations of any negative comment made about a judge or prosecutor, executive branch hearing officer and even public advocates, if the judge or official enjoys its support.

Over the years the courts had chiseled away at the Federal and State Bill of Rights regarding free speech. Section 8 of The Kentucky Constitution says that no "branch of government and no law shall ever (. . . limit free speech). Every person may freely and fully speak, write and print on any subject." Section 26 of the Kentucky Constitution declares that ". . . everything in this Bill of Rights is excepted out of the general powers of government, and shall forever remain inviolate; and all laws contrary thereto, or contrary to this Constitution, shall be void."

While the Kentucky Constitution forbids any branch of government from limiting free speech rights, the court which reviews the Rules of the Supreme Court, is the Supreme Court itself.

The Supreme Court rule limiting the free speech of lawyers was interpreted to only apply to statements made about conduct made during currently pending cases which might affect the outcome, and to false statements. Comments made after a proceeding was finalized were allowable under the Rule, but this limitation was ignored by the Ministry whenever they found the limitation troublesome. This broad interpretation of the rule by the Ministry of Ethics greatly expanded the power of the Ministry. Anyone who read the newspaper could find examples of prosecutors, judges and other protected public officials, regularly and freely maligning members of the bar, but these comments by 'the protected class' were overlooked by the Ministry. Clearly the current application of the Rule was to protect those in power or those in favor of the Ministry. Against all others the Rule was strictly applied.

One lawyer's violation of the speech rule involved the indiscretion of publicly speaking out during a seminar of lawyers where recent rulings by judges were being discussed. The lawyer added a comment to the group regarding a ruling by a Judge Johnson by saying: "Judge Johnson is a "redneck," and, "When I have a case assigned to his court I know I'm screwed."

Unfortunately, the crowd contained at least one person who sought to gain favor with Judge Johnson and forwarded the lawyer's comments to the Judge. This was soon made a formal complaint.

Kenton's second letter given to Hart by Big Cat Cheshire, complained that a copy of the official Notice of Investigation letter, which was supposed to be confidential, was received by television stations and newspapers three days before the lawyer being investigated was officially notified. The so called secret investigation was thus a media event before the attorney knew anything about it. Kenton wrote, "This is a hard genie to put back in the bottle".

Kenton ended this letter with a call for an investigation by the Chief Justice to determine if the Ministry purposefully released this information in violation of the Supreme Court Rules of Procedure regarding the conduct of Ministry of Ethics proceedings.

Kenton's letter ended with the suggestion that, "Even if the release of this information was merely an internal security failure, the Commissioner of the Ministry of Ethics should be held publically accountable."

Commissioner Hart's spine involuntarily stiffened as she read this accusation. This often occurred when she was angry, and Kenton's letter made her very angry. She spilled coffee on her white silk blouse. She yelled into her intercom "Jane! Carolyn! Get in here and bring a wet towel!"

Chapter Four

Thomas Jefferson Kenton Jr. was still dressed in his tailored khaki farm clothes as he arrived at his south Lexington law office two hours late.

"Midge!" he called over the intercom to his blond secretary after he sat at his desk. He began reviewing the twenty phone call notes which were arranged neatly in four rows with five messages in each row. He started reviewing the phone calls and messages with the upper left hand row first. Erin always arranged them from left to right, top to bottom, in the order in which they were received. He always responded promptly to every call.

As Midge entered the office she asked what had kept him so long. He smiled at her and reported that Kenton Stables had a new foal, and he was in perfect condition. Midge shook her head in mock disapproval as she commented dryly that he was dressed like a stable mucker and he had a lunch meeting with Justice Boone in an hour.

She sat down and began taking shorthand notes, as he quickly reviewed the phone messages, and gave instructions for responses. In the middle of the last row he noted a "Please return call-Urgent" message from Williston Stafford.

"What did Will want?" he asked.

"Says it's important that he sees you right away but he refused to say why."

"Get him on the phone."

"Good morning Will. Sorry I missed your call what's up?" Kenton inquired.

Midge heard Kenton twice say "Interesting", during the mostly one-sided conversation with Williston Stafford. He ended the call by inviting Stafford to meet him at the Kenton farm at 5:30 to continue their conversation in depth.

He ignored Midge's raised eyebrow which invited an explanation about the call. He resumed dictating responses to the last phone messages he deemed urgent enough to review at the moment. He placed the message from Williston Stafford in his wallet.

After Midge left his office, he quickly changed into his tailored Tom James Italian wool suit which had just been delivered by his personal tailor Jordan Yocum. Before leaving he announced into the intercom, "I'm gone."

He left by the private entrance to avoid the lobby full of clients waiting to see other lawyers in his firm.

He maneuvered his Porsche Carrera convertible nimbly through the heavy post-Thanksgiving traffic towards the nearby Champions Trace Country Club just south of the Fayette County line. He glanced at his Rolex chronograph and determined that he would be on time for his meeting with Justice Alice Boone.

Chapter Five

Immediately after he read the anonymous letter and document delivered to his office in the morning mail, Williston Stafford had called Jack Kenton to see if he knew anything about the plan mentioned in the document included in the unsigned letter. He then began to examine in detail the issues raised by the anonymous letter.

The plan titled "The Rabbit Hole Amendment," if adopted would give unparalleled power to an already powerful Chief Justice of the Kentucky Supreme Court, and would further increase the virtually unlimited powers of the Ministry of Ethics to regulate the conduct of attorneys.

The plan appeared to have been developed by the Ministry of Ethics at the request of Chief Justice Madison Hatter. It bore a confidentiality warning which threatened dire consequences to anyone other than the Chief Justice who read it. Stafford doubted the authority of the Chief Justice to punish anyone for reading such a document.

The authors of such letters usually lacked the spine to reveal their identify and were seeking a third party to do their dirty work. As a blogger, Stafford's writings focused on topics related to the law and lawyers. His articles were frequently published on LawReader.com. This made Stafford a natural target for such letters. He was aware of the falsehoods such letters often contained, but he also was aware that 75% of all rumors had an element of truth in them.

In his phone call to Jack Kenton, Stafford briefly outlined the content of the document from the Ministry of Ethics. Jack had not sounded surprised with the revelation but apparently did not want to discuss it over the phone.

Stafford returned to his workstation, surrounded by a TV tuned to MSNBC on his left, a computer monitor in the middle and another computer monitor on the right. The window next to his workstation looked over the front yard of his antebellum home in Carrollton, near the Ohio River. A louvered window shade shielded him from view of the Jehovah's Witnesses and other visitors who might interrupt his work if they saw him in the front window as they walked down the busy sidewalk in front of his home.

One monitor at his work station displayed an article he was writing and the other was connected to LawReader.com. With access to LawReader he could live in a small town and still have access to a full sized online law library, essential to any lawyer or legal researcher.

His workstation configuration allowed him to view both the document he was writing, and at the same time view the legal references that are essential to write authoritatively about any legal topic. A small sign taped to his desk proclaimed, "Knowledge is power."

He took great delight in publishing detailed legal arguments which often took the hot air out of lawsuits and legal opinions mentioned in the press. Most journalists lacked a legal background and their articles relating to legal topics never gave the reader the proper balance, since they didn't express conclusions about the merits of legal arguments raised in their stories.

Stafford enjoyed exposing bogus legal arguments in his missives. This outspokenness made him a hero to some and a crackpot to others. He belonged to that group of men and women who were retired and no longer actively practiced law. There weren't many options for those in power to threaten or silence him. Stafford thought of himself as being like a Eunuch in the Forbidden City of the last Chinese Emperor. The Emperor's Eunuchs were the only people he could trust and they were considered harmless by the public. The Emperor's Eunuchs wielded great influence over the Emperor.

The Ministry of Ethics document directed to Chief Justice Hatter sparked his interest. Stafford's curiosity impelled him to see what Hatter and The Ministry of Ethics were planning. He began by reviewing past legal rulings made by the Chief Justice.

He absent mindedly chewed, but never lit, a cheap cigar as he entered the search phrase, "Justice Madison Hatter" and "ethics," into the LawReader case law search engine. He clicked on the search button, directing the computer to review two hundred years of Kentucky appellate court decisions, and to provide him a list of every decision in which Chief Justice Madison Hatter had been named.

The search engine read through a digitized library, which if printed in hardbound books and placed in library stacks would cover six and a half basketball courts, and within three seconds a list of 54 decisions were posted on his screen. This was the place to start in order to review Hatter's professional thoughts.

He then clicked the date button on the search engine screen and rearranged the cases in chronological order with the most current decision on the top of the list and the oldest case at the bottom. He scanned the case names and synopsis of each case on his screen until he found a case titled McCollum v. Garrett.

Stafford clicked the search engine tool that took him to the paragraph in the long appellate decision which displayed his search terms. He found the dissent written by then Justice Madison Hatter. The date of the decision indicated that it must have been decided just after Hatter was first elected to the Supreme Court and well before he had been elevated to the office of Chief Justice. The dissent stated Justice Hatter's legal philosophy:

". . . the public interest in the unflinching enforcement of the law must prevail over the private interest of a wronged citizen."

Stafford then searched an online legal dictionary and found the definition of Fascism;

"Fascism: a form of totalitarianism which emphasizes the subordination of the individual to advance the interests of the state."

He chewed his unlit cigar almost in two as he read the two quotes over and over. He was not one to use a word like 'Fascist' without great justification. He could not come to any other conclusion. Chief Justice Madison Hatter was a Fascist at heart. Anyone who felt so strongly that the interest of the state must override the interest of individual rights had to be, by definition, a Fascist. Anyone who gave immunity for prosecutors to withhold exculpatory evidence needed by defendants to defend themselves in court, was a Fascist in Stafford's view.

In his forty years as a student of the law, he had never found a more shocking statement of the law actually written by an American appellate judge. He read the case again to confirm that Hatter had actually made that statement, and had allowed his name to be identified as the author.

Slowly he realized that the anonymous confidential Rabbit Hole Amendments which he had just received, was consistent with Hatter's harsh view of the law.

Stafford believed if a public official wasn't subject to redress for his abuse of power, then he could violate the rights of a citizen at will. From the language used by Justice Hatter in the McCollum case, one had to conclude that Hatter and others believed that they belonged to a privileged class of officials who could violate the law at will, and justify their misuse of power in the name of law and order.

For 102 years before the McCollum decision, a defendant wronged by a malicious prosecution, could sue the prosecutor for civil damages. That possibility kept some prosecutors in line. But when the Supreme Court granted prosecutors "absolute immunity" the only remedy left was for the court to grant a new trial. When a defendant obtained a new trial it often did little to remedy the wrong. The defendant granted a new trial had to figure out a way to finance a second trial, and was frequently held in jail until the new trial was conducted. Stafford concluded that the courts had became complicit in denying defendants their constitutional rights by not vigorously slamming prosecutors who played such games.

Stafford noted the comments of Justices Charles Leibson, Sara Combs, and Donald Wintersheimer who ruled against Justice Hatter (who was then serving as a special Court of Appeals Judge) where they dissented and held that the 'absolute immunity doctrine' that Hatter advanced was novel to Kentucky law.

Stafford noted from his reading of recent rulings that the Harmless Error Rule was frequently cited by Chief Justice Madison Hatter to excuse virtually any error committed by a prosecutor or by the police.

The conservative court members lead by Hatter, even expanded this Rule to forgive prosecutors and police for violation of basic constitutional rights.

Under the Harmless Error Rule, as interpreted by Hatter and his group, the appellate courts could ignore serious trail errors by prosecutors or the police. If a majority of the appellate panel personally believed that "the defendant would have been convicted by the jury anyway," the error could be declared harmless by the appellate court, and therefore, the errors at trial were forgiven. While misconduct by prosecutors and the police was frowned upon by the courts, such infractions were almost never punished. This clearly sent the message that such infractions were like a father scolding his son for getting in a fight on the school ground, and then patting the spunky son on the back and gave him money to get an ice cream cone.

This Harmless Error doctrine as advanced by Hatter and his cohorts, infringed on the traditional power of the jury to decide the facts of a case. This new interpretation of the doctrine granted the appellate court, the power to virtually retry the case and base their ruling on their interpretation of the facts in the case record. For hundreds of years the doctrine was used to ignore truly insignificant trial errors. The modern interpretation allowed the doctrine to be used to ignore serious trial errors. Such an expansion of the doctrine, allowed the appellate court to decide the facts of a case on appeal. Traditionally appellate courts were only authorized to consider questions of law in their appeal process. The harmless error rule was hundreds of years old, but was only applied to very minor errors in a trial. But in recent application of the rule the court often justified a new definition of the rule in applying the catch-all harmless error rule by concluding, "The jury would have convicted the defendant even if the prosecutor's error had not occurred." This assumption allowed the appellate court to place themselves inside the juries mind.

Stafford and all who informed themselves on such matters, discerned a continuing direction in the criminal law to limit the rights of citizens brought before the bar of justice, to limit the power of the jury panel to make informed decisions, while increasing the power of appellate courts to overlook violations of a defendant's rights.

Stafford had long felt that this movement endangered the entire legal system. "Why," he wrote in his draft document, "would the court give unlimited immunity to prosecutors, when they were already the most powerful officials in the criminal justice system?"

Justice Hatter and others didn't trust juries, and their pro-prosecution bias was evident.

The unwitting public had the illusion that trial Judges controlled everything that happened in the courtroom. If that allusion was every true, it certainly ended in 1976 when the Judicial provisions of the Kentucky Constitution were amended by a constitutional referendum. This amendment granted the Chief Justice broad administrative powers over the lower courts and over judges and lawyers.

Stafford found examples in his research where every Chief Justice who had served since 1976 had found some way to enhance and consolidate his personal power over the courts. Most of these accretions of power had been beneficial, and had enhanced the independence of the judiciary, but some assertions of judicial power were questionable.

Stafford concluded that Chief Justice Hatter was planning to expand the power of the courts to further regulate the conduct of lawyers by limiting their ability to even speak about perceived inequities.

He then went back to the LawReader home page and clicked on the link to Rules of the Supreme Court. These rules are adopted by the Supreme Court to regulate the conduct of attorneys in the practice of the law. These Rules were identified as "Ethics Rules" but many dealt with issues that a non-lawyer would have trouble identifying as having anything to do with morality or ethics. He clicked through several topics listed until he found "SCR 3.130 Kentucky Rules of Professional Conduct—Preamble: A Lawyer's Responsibilities"

The Code of Professional Conduct, written by the Supreme Court, provided a justification for the Court's regulation of the conduct of lawyers and judges. He found the heart of the Code to be contained in Paragraph VI.:

"VI. A lawyer's conduct shall conform to the requirements of the law, both in professional service to clients and in the lawyer's business and personal affairs. "A lawyer shall use the law's procedures only for legitimate purposes and not to harass or intimidate others. A lawyer shall demonstrate respect for the legal system and for those who serve it, including judges, other lawyers and public officials."

He read the words 'personal affairs' in the Code and raised an eyebrow. He could readily see how Ethics officials could use that phrase to terrorize every attorney in the state.

This Rule was one of the justifications advanced for the creation of the Ministry of Ethics.

The following sentence in Rule VI, which weakly attempted to preserve free speech for attorneys was simply ignored by Hatter's colleagues:

"While it is a lawyer's duty, when necessary, to challenge the rectitude of official action, it is also a lawyer's duty to uphold legal process."

Stafford asked himself, "Does that mean a lawyer can challenge a ruling or does it say he can't?"

The Rules were full of such language. The first section of the rule authorized an action, and the second section made it unethical.

Even lawyers had trouble understanding such vague and conflicting language. It was obvious to Stafford that the Rules were written to allow the ethics machine to interpret them to mean anything the Bar wanted them to mean.

He copied and pasted that Preamble Rule into his draft article.

He paused for a moment and considered why the Supreme Court would extend the disciplinary process to regulate the 'personal affairs' of lawyers. The law abhors vague generalities, in laws and rules, which may be so broadly interpreted as to negate basic constitutional rights at the discretion of the reader. The right to regulate a lawyer's 'private affairs' could be read to include anything from private sexual conduct, business dealings, political thought, writings, public or private comments and who knows what else. Was it improper for a lawyer to speak harshly to his wife? Was it an ethical violation for a lawyer to spank his child for misbehaving?

He then read Preamble XII which included the comment: "An independent legal profession is an important force in preserving government under law, for abuse of legal authority is more readily challenged by a profession whose members are not dependent on government for the right to practice."

He compared Preamble rule VI to Preamble rule XII. Rule VI says that a lawyer's business and private life outside the practice of law can be regulated by the Supreme Court. The second rule conflicts with the first, and recognizes the importance of assuring the independence of a lawyer from government regulation.

Stafford concluded that this conflicting language was a typical example of what happens when the Supreme Court delegates their rule making powers to a committee. Stafford, recalled the old witticism that "a camel is a horse created by a committee'.

Stafford, found more Rules which had what he called "whiplash" language. One who tried to understand the Rule could suffer whiplash with the rapid reversal of the language in permitting and denying the same act, all in one sentence.

He then returned to the anonymous letter he had just received. The post mark on the letter was "Frankfort, Kentucky." There was no return address.

The anonymous letter briefly stated: "Someone should look at this."

Instead of a signature, it ended with the words, "A Friend".

Attached with the letter was a copy of a document from Heather Regina Hart to the Chief Justice. The document was titled, "Rabbit Hole" with a letterhead identifying it as a document from the Ministry of Ethics to be considered by Chief Justice Hatter.

Stafford wondered who would have access to this document. Was it someone in the office of the Commissioner of the Ministry of Ethics or was it someone from the Chief Justice's office?

Was the leaker a secretary? A staff lawyer with a conscience? A paralegal? He wasn't sure of the answer. It almost certainly had to be an inside source in one of the two offices.

"Was it authentic?" he asked himself, "Was it a hoax hoping to create a comment from him which could be easily discredited to his embarrassment? Was he being set up by the Ministry or perhaps the Chief Justice?" Or was it a reckless excess by Heather Regina Hart, the Queen of Hearts, expressing her philosophy of interpreting every rule to allow her to say 'Off with their heads?'"

He couldn't ignore the large red letters on the Rabbit Hole Amendments which said, "CONFIDENTIAL WORKING DOCUMENT".

He reviewed the rules regarding confidentiality. It appeared that the confidentially rule was designed only to protect the defendant, not to protect the Ministry of Truth. He noted that the person charged with an ethical violation could waive confidentiality.

Any leaker who held a law license was subject to severe sanction for releasing ethics proceeding documents such as a warning letter, without the permission of the defendant lawyer. It was only later that Stafford, found the obscure Rule that allowed a "victim" of unethical conduct by a lawyer, to go public on his complaint. This was interpreted by the Ministry to allow an attorney who filed a complaint to go public with his charges against another lawyer.

He found no authority for the Chief Justice to enforce any penalty for releasing an administrative planning document such as the "Rabbit Hole Amendment". Such a document did not involve a currently pending case before the court.

He recalled a prior incident where a lawyer claimed that a Notice of Investigation letter had been released to two television stations and a newspaper days before the lawyer received the official notice letter. He noted that no action was ever taken about this leak, at least to his knowledge.

In any event, Stafford was certain that someone at the Ministry, or perhaps someone on the Board of Scrutiny, was not above leaking information when it served their purpose. He wondered how many others had received copies of the two documents.

Stafford realized that caution was required before doing anything with this letter. He was unsure if the Squeal Rule adopted by the Supreme Court in 2009 applied to this situation. The so called Squeal Rule required that all lawyers who had knowledge of an ethics violation turn in any lawyer whom he had reason to suspect.

Stafford concluded that the Squeal Rule was an example of the old saying that "widows and orphans make bad law."

Widows and orphans laws sound good in dealing with a problem of a widow or orphan in hard circumstances, but when broadly applied to the rest of the world, it usually works great injustice.

Stafford recalled a ruling of a Planning and Zoning agency which allowed a widow whose home had burnt down, to have an exception to the law that forbade the placement of mobile homes on her lot. They felt compassion for her, and granted her permission to violate the mobile home zoning law. Good for the widow, but disastrous to the zoning laws applying to everyone else.

The Squeal Rule was adopted as a reaction to the Fen Phen disaster which brought the bar into serious disrepute when three lawyers from Lexington were alleged to have overpaid themselves in a class action lawsuit.

This new rule sounded good when applied to the defendants in the Fen Phen case, but when applied to all other conduct of lawyers had harsh results. No one dared to come forward to protest the Squeal Rule.

Such rules are a favored technique of despots who control their minions by making it a legal duty for everyone to report everything to the government. In Nazi Germany, Communist China and the Soviet Union, children were encouraged to turn in their parents. Since 2009, the rule was applied by order of the Supreme Court to make all lawyers snitches for the Ministry of Ethics.

Stafford smiled to himself when he noted the documents claim of confidentiality. No agency of state government used the word "confidential" more recklessly, or more improperly, than the Ministry of Ethics.

Stafford used LawReader to examine historical comments on the use of secrecy by government agencies. He found a speech by John F. Kennedy.

> "The very word "secrecy" is repugnant in a free and open society; and we are as a people inherently and historically opposed to secret societies, to secret oaths and to secret proceedings. We decided long ago that the dangers of excessive and unwarranted concealment of pertinent facts far outweighed the dangers which are cited to justify it." President John F. Kennedy-April 27, 1961

He added to his working document a quote from George Orwell's novel 1984, which described the messages carved in stone over the entrance of Orwell's fictional "Ministry of Truth" which proclaimed: "War is Peace, Freedom is Slavery, Ignorance is Strength."

Stafford was amused at the thought that "Perhaps Orwell wrote the Rules of Professional Conduct. The practice of writing something with the intent of meaning just the opposite was the hallmark of the Rules of Professional Conduct and of Orwell's Ministry of Truth.

He added to his working draft an additional message which he felt should be carved over the door of the Ministry of Ethics under the administration of Commissioner Hart. "Confidentiality Is What We Say It Is"

He knew from prior research regarding the Ministry of Ethics, that the actual rules regarding confidentiality were almost always misapplied to protect the Ministry. Only through secrecy could they hide their misdeeds and shady dealing.

The only rule regarding "confidentiality" which Stafford could find was Supreme Court Rule 3.150. It was created to protect the defendant from embarrassment in Ministry prosecutions during the investigatory phase of their actions. The right to confidentiality as applied by the Ministry, shielded the Ministry from scrutiny of their actions by the media, the bar, and even from their masters at the Supreme Court.

The Catch 22 of this rule, which often made it so effective, was that a lawyer notified of a pending investigation by the Ministry of Ethics was usually too frightened and embarrassed to assert his right to waive confidentiality.

Most defendants were afraid to further anger the Ministry under the delusion that it was still possible that the Ministry might drop the investigation and not proceed to a formal charge. Even in cases where the defendant lawyer waived his right of confidentiality, the Ministry still applied the confidentiality rule to their own actions.

Stafford could find absolutely no justification for the Ministry to hide behind a confidentiality rule that had been waived by the defendant lawyer.

More than once, the Ministry had intimidated and silenced an outspoken lawyer by merely sending him a one page letter notifying him that he was under investigation and then kept the investigation open for years without dismissing it or proceeding to a formal charge and a hearing.

As Stafford reviewed the Code of Professional Conduct he found that the rules regulating the actions of the Ministry of Ethics strangely failed to place a time limit on their investigations. Most civil rules have a time limit in which a complaint must be brought. These are called Statutes of Limitation.

If a complaint is filed after the designated statutory period has expired, then it will be dismissed as being stale. But there was no time limit on any type of ethics complaint against lawyers.

The Ministry of Ethics could start an investigation and never end it. Sometimes when challenged they would formally dismiss the ethics charges before it was appealed by the defendant, and therefore, there was nothing to appeal. In these instances, the Supreme Court never heard of, or had an opportunity to review the actions of the Ministry, and the overreaching of the Ministry was hidden from the Supreme Court.

One could only speculate as to whether this insulation of the Supreme Court was the intended result of the Rules for Proceedings of the Ministry of Ethics adopted by the Supreme Court. In any event, it was effective, and the media never pierced this protective wall of insulation.

Stafford returned to the LawReader search engine and quickly called up a case that he had read many times. He then pasted a quote from the case in his working draft.

". . . an attorney, just as any citizen, has the right to criticize the courts and their decisions . . ." Kentucky Bar Ass'n v. Heleringer, 602 S.W.2d 165 (Ky., 1980)."

Stafford reread the documents which detailed the Rabbit Hole Amendments and which appeared to be designed to negate the rights of an attorney to criticize any public official. He printed out a copy of his working draft, placed it in an envelope, and then closed down his computer.

He then went upstairs to shower and change from his sweat pants and UK tee shirt to prepare for his meeting with Jack Kenton. As the razor cleaned the two day's stubble from his face, he wondered just how far the Chief Justice and his lacky, The Queen of Hearts, would go in silencing their enemies. Before leaving to meet Jack Kenton, Williston made a photo copy of the document he had received to take to Kenton.

(**Author's Note: The Rabbit Hole Amendments may be found in the Appendix to this book.**)

Chapter Six

As Jack Kenton entered the nearly vacant Members Grill in the clubhouse of Champions Trace Country Club, he saw that Supreme Court Justice Alice Boone was already sitting at a table overlooking the eighteenth fairway.

He had selected this out of the way meeting place due to the small patronage suffered by golf course clubhouses after the golf season ended.

She greeted him as he took a seat across the table from her.

"I appreciate your taking the time to meet me" he said.

"That's no problem", the Justice said. "I was on my way to Frankfort and this really wasn't much out of the way." They made small talk until the waiter took their orders.

He got to the point, "Justice, I hope I'm not imposing on you, but I have heard an interesting tale that I wanted to run by you and see if you can add anything to my understanding."

She looked at him intently but said nothing.

"Have you heard of a project called Operation Rabbit Hole? It is supposedly being advanced by the Chief Justice."

The Justice showed no emotion or acknowledgment of such a plan. He continued, "I understand that it is a project authorized by the Chief Justice and assigned to the Ministry of Ethics to flesh out."

"How do you know about this?"

"Someone has been anonymously sending out copies of this project. For some reason a copy was mailed to me last week. I know of one other person who also received a copy and I would assume others must have received copies."

Kenton took a copy of the Rabbit Hole document and slid it across the table to Justice Boone. The corners of her mouth gave the slightest hint of a grimace, but he couldn't be sure, as she was very good at maintaining her judge face, developed from years of trying to appear impartial as opponents argued their cases before her.

"Jack," she said quietly and distinctly, "I have heard rumblings about a project and this may be it. I haven't seen anything on paper and the Chief Justice hasn't said anything to me."

They sat quietly for a moment as she perused the document while they worked on their salads. Her face reddened as she read the Rabbit Hole Amendments.

Kenton took another approach, "Let me ask a hypothetical question. Let's suppose that someone was actually proposing a major change in Supreme Court Rules, would they be able to slide this through without ever disclosing it to the members of the Bar?"

Justice Boone hesitated for a moment, "I suggest you look at SCR 1.010. That rule discusses the authority of the Supreme Court to make policy." She emphasized the word "court".

"While the Chief Justice is designated as the Executive of the Judicial Branch, he cannot make rule changes without approval of a majority of the justices. The practice of the Supreme Court has always been to invite comment from the members of the bar, but it is not required to inform the Bar in advance and the Court is not bound to follow the Bar's recommendations."

Kenton asked, "Is it possible for the Chief Justice to get this plan passed by the court?"

Justice Boone's face darkened. She placed her napkin on the table and said, "I won't speculate on what other justices might rule on any specific issue, but as I've said, the usual procedure is to disclose any Rules changes to the Bar and invite their comment. You will have to form your own opinion as to whether or not the members of the Court would support a plan such as the Rabbit Hole plan.

"You are asking if it would be possible for such a plan to be adopted by the court. My answer is that to my knowledge no rule has ever been adopted without running it by the Bar Association for comment. I know for a fact that no such plan has been submitted to the Board of Governors. You should read the Supreme Court rule regarding adoption of rules.

"My reading of the Constitution leads me to believe that the entire Court makes policy for the judicial branch of government, and that suggests that a new Supreme Court Rule can be adopted by the Chief Justice but only if he can obtain three votes that would give him a majority.

"I know of no requirement other than tradition, that requires input from the Bar Association."

She sensed his frustration and tried another tack. "I will hypothetically say, that if there is such a plan as Rabbit Hole, and if such a plan attempts to make radical changes in the Supreme Court Rules without complete disclosure to the public and with an opportunity for the Bar to comment on it, then I can't see how it would be possible for the Chief Justice to obtain a majority for passage.

"It just won't happen. But, I admit, Stranger things have happened. Hatter is not likely to even bring such an issue before the court unless he is damn sure that he has the votes to get it passed."

Kenton interjected, "If he did call up such a plan for passage and if it was adopted by the court in secret, there is no method for an appeal to a higher court since the jurisdiction of the Federal Courts generally does not extend to state procedural rules."

She nodded her agreement with his conclusion.

Having made his point, he then asked her directly, "Have you been informed of a plan to extend the authority of the Ministry of Ethics?"

She lowered her voice, "I admit I haven't heard anything about this. In fact I have been working on a number of Supreme Court Ethics amendments that are quite different from those contained in this document you have given me."

He changed the subject and expressed his concern about the Ministry and its ever expanding power. "Justice, the Supreme Court has created a monster. They have created an ethics enforcement system that denies due process rights to 17,000 lawyers.

The judiciary is exempt from the Open Records laws that apply to the rest of State Government. They are further shielded from public view by confidentiality rules that they violate whenever it suits their needs. If they really don't like a lawyer they leak information before any official action allows the release of such information.

They are a secret cell inside the most secretive branch of government. The Supreme Court conducts all of its administrative business in secret. They hold all their votes in secret. The Chief Justice appoints the "grand jury" or Board of Scrutiny that votes approval of charges. He then appoints the Trial Commissioners who try ethics complaints without a jury. The procedure that calls for input by the Board of Governors in ethics prosecutions is useless since the Ministry may appeal dismissals to the Supreme Court. As you know in criminal cases, when a defendant is acquitted, the Commonwealth cannot appeal the verdict.

But the Supreme Court has defined an ethics procedure as a civil procedure, and therefore allows an attorney to be placed in double jeopardy. If he is acquitted by the Board of Governors he can be retried by the Supreme Court."

Justice Boone listened quietly as Kenton carried on, "Further, an attorney is denied the right to remain silent. The ruse of using the Board of Governors as a reviewing body is a charade. The final judgment is made by the Supreme Court, and the Board's rulings really has no binding effect."

Kenton took a drink of water and went on, "Having declared these ethics procedures as civil procedures, the charged attorney is treated like a criminal. Of the cases I have reviewed it appears to me that the burden of proving his innocence is borne by the attorney and not by the charging agency.

The Ministry only has to prove their case by a "preponderance of the evidence" and not by the "beyond a reasonable doubt" standard. The bottom line is that this system provides little justice to an attorney charged with an ethical violation.

The Chief Justice is given superpowers of appointment of all the important participants in the process. The system is rigged against an attorney who falls into the disfavor of the Chief Justice or his Ministry of Ethics. The idea of new rules to further expand the powers of the ethics machine are provocative and dangerous, and must be stopped!"

Justice Boone did not defend the system. "Jack, I am working on a new set of Ethics Rules. We are about to submit these to the Bar for their consideration. It is the opinion of several members of the Court that the Ministry of Ethics has seriously abused their authority.

"As some of us see it, we can only return the Ministry to its correct function by amending a number of rules. I can't tell you who is supporting my efforts, but I can tell you that I would not submit them if I didn't feel confident that my rules would be adopted. This Rabbit Hole thing is a complete surprise to me. Let me look at these. You don't have a problem with me sharing these with other court members do you?"

Kenton readily gave his consent for her to pass the document around.

"Jack" she continued, "I'll keep your name out of this."

Kenton changed the subject and inquired about Commissioner Heather Hart. "Justice I have never met the Commissioner. Frankly, I don't know anyone who knows much about her. What can you tell me about her?"

Justice Boone smiled before replying, "That is a good question. No one knows much about her. She is from Louisville. She was an assistant Commonwealth Attorney for about ten years before being hired for the Ministry of Ethics job. She has a reputation as a hardnosed prosecutor.

She almost never plea bargained down any cases. I've heard that the Commonwealth Attorney was glad to see her leave Louisville. She had a reputation of being very controlling. It is said that once the Commonwealth Attorney suggested she back off on a weak case, and she threatened to resign and go to the press if she was ordered to dismiss the case. I believe it dealt with some sexual 'he said/she said' type claim against a UofL basketball player."

"Do you know anything about her personal life?"

"I know she had a younger sister that was a cheerleader at Bellarmine College. They say that she never speaks to her sister. One of our staff attorneys went to High School with her. She says that Hart was the eldest child and felt that after her younger sister was born that her parents ignored her.

Her mother idolized the younger child who is said to have been much prettier than her older sister. Her father died when she was a child and her mother made her run the house and do most of the baby sitting. She apparently never had much of a social life, but was good student.

"She never married. She seems to have devoted herself to her studies and to her work. She is not known to have much of a sense of humor. I met her once and she is pretty much a cold fish."

Kenton asked one more thing, "Justice would you mind sending me a draft of your proposed Rules Amendments?"

She readily agreed but asked him not to disclose them to anyone else as they weren't finalized.

As he paid the bill, Jack concluded that she didn't know about the Rabbit Hole plan before today. But she certainly knew about it now. He was encouraged that she had taken his copy of the Rabbit Hole Amendments.

That part of his mission had been accomplished. The leaked Rabbit Hole plan would almost certainly be ridiculed by anyone who read it. Now all members of the Supreme Court would be brought into the loop.

If they were questioned by the press and others when it became public this information could be useful.

Anyone who told the press they hadn't seen it, would be revealing themselves as one of the Chief Justice's toadies.

Chapter Seven

Big Cat Cheshire locked the door to his office at 3:00 o'clock and told his secretary that he was taking no calls, and not to disturb him.

He then entered the private stairway from his office and ascended to the darkened room on the second floor that was illuminated by dozens of LCD lights on the numerous computers and servers which encircled the room. He flipped on the switch to the infrared camera and the laser listening device which were both aimed at the Governor's Office on the south side of the Capitol on the first floor.

He then took a seat at the small desk and watched the monitor flicker to life. The Governor's office on the first floor of the Capitol building, was swept for listening devices at least once a week, a practice that had been followed for many years.

Fortunately for Cheshire, the Governor's staff and the Courts, had not kept current on new technology and were unaware of infrared and laser spying techniques. The infrared camera showed the heat signature of the Governor's Office, and revealed any movement around the Governor's desk. The figures displayed on his monitor were gauzy red, yellow, green and blue, but clearly defined the shape of a human.

The monitor revealed a heat signature of someone rising from the Governor's chair and shaking hands with an apparent guest. He felt confident that the dark red figure was the Governor since no one else would dare sit in his chair. From the Governor's printed schedule for the day, which was widely distributed in advance, he knew that Chief Justice Hatter was scheduled to meet with the Governor at 3:00 p.m.

He then switched on the laser mike, a vibration detection device, aimed at the window of the Governor's office. The laser microphone picked up vibrations via the doppler effect and turned them back into sound. This device detected the delicate vibrations of the window pane caused by the inhabitants of the room as they spoke. It then converted those vibrations into the words of the occupants of the room.

The software converted the vibrations into printed words on a second monitor on Cheshire's desk and these were preserved in a digital format on the hard drive.

One new addition to his spying technology was a digital video camera with a long range telephoto lens. When used with the Laser Microphone he could now capture video and audio of meetings held in the targeted rooms of the Capitol Building. Unfortunately the Governor's Office had heavy drapes covering the office windows which prevented any effective use of the video cameras. His office was the only Capitol building office protected by heavy drapes.

It had taken Cheshire a month to set up his new laser microphone voice detection system. He had two locations for his laser equipment. One site was on the roof of a stucco home on Shelby Street and was directed at the window in the Governor's Office on the south side of the Capitol building.

His video equipment was more difficult to use since the camera had to be much closer to the targeted room. He accomplished this by parking an unmarked van close to the Capitol Building when he wished to capture video. This was mostly used to tape Supreme Court deliberations held in the court's conference room on the second floor of the Capitol. Its windows were on the north side of the Capitol Building. Occasionally, he used the mobile unit in his van to bug other meetings.

The second laser site was the more important of his devices. The state government had made his spying mission easy since all of the other regular targets of his laser bug were on the north side of the Capitol building.

He had tried several sites before finding a perfect location for this second laser site. It was placed on the roof of the Armory Museum on a hill just north of the Kentucky River. This location provided sufficient elevation that it passed over the intervening trees and buildings and provided a clear view of the north side of the capitol. This height also aided his telephoto video cameras.

From this one site he was able to clearly scan the entire north front of the Capitol building and could monitor conversations in the office of the President of the Senate, and one floor below the Office of the Chief Justice.

On the left front of the Capitol building, he was able to scan the office of the Speaker of the House and the Supreme Court conference room where the court met in secret to vote on cases.

Cheshire had lately found that his most valuable resource was this conference room. Once a vote was taken in this room, the case was assigned to one of the Justices in the majority for final editing before it was published and released to the public. This allowed Cheshire several weeks of advance notice of important decisions. He had paid special attention to the Supreme Court since he realized that he could learn of rulings of the court weeks before they were announced to the public, and this information had great market value. In one case he advised a party that they had lost their appeal and a multi-million dollar lawsuit was going to be reinstated. They quickly settled the case before the unfavorable decision was entered.

Since the case was settled, the Supreme Court withdrew their decision and dismissed the appeal.

Occasionally he got lucky and was tipped off to a ruling that affected the stock of a corporation. The normal delay in the Court actually publishing their decision to the public, provided him with plenty of time to play the stock market. This advance information had proven to be very profitable for Cheshire.

His two laser sites were joined to a wireless transmitter which broadcast all the encoded signals back to the secret room in his office. If someone discovered either of his transmitters, they would still have no idea where in Frankfort the signals were being gathered. Each unit was no larger than a cigar box, and was marked "Property of U.S. Environmental Protection Agency—Do not Disturb—$10,000 fine."

The meeting between the Chief Justice and the Governor ended at 3:45. It revealed to Cheshire only an uninteresting discussion of the proposed Judicial Budget being requested by the Chief Justice for consideration in the upcoming session of the General Assembly.

As soon as the Chief Justice left the Governor's Office, he heard the Governor's side of a phone call dealing with a plant opening ceremony to which the Governor had been invited.

He stood up and readjusted his device to the office of the President of the Senate to see what was going on. He waited for a few moments and saw no motion on the infrared monitor. He then aimed his equipment at the office of the Speaker of the House but he was also absent.

He smiled to himself, and concluded that the money he had spent on his equipment had made him many times that much in "lobbying" fees over the last two years. His equipment was old technology and had been in existence for decades. Much of it was actually second-hand. But like other things, the State Government just didn't keep up with private industry and failed to recognize the dangers of existing surveillance technology.

By knowing in advance which legislation was going to be favorably considered, he was able to approach clients who would be affected by such legislation and offer his inside knowledge and assistance to the client at great cost. He was so often right in predicting the future of legislation, that he was called "The Grinning Oracle" by his grateful clients.

Chapter Eight

After returning to his law office and meeting with several clients, Kenton finally arrived at Kenton Farms, situated four miles east of Georgetown in Scott County, half an hour before his scheduled meeting with Williston Stafford.

He went immediately to the breeding barn, and spoke with the handlers about the new colt that had arrived earlier in the day. They confirmed that everything was fine. The colt was nursing with his prize brood mare, "September Morn" when he visited the spotlessly clean stall.

He heard the resident dog bark and turned to see Williston Stafford entering the barn with a cigar in his mouth. He warned, his visitor not to light the cigar even though he knew that Stafford had ceased lighting up his cigars years ago.

Stafford, realizing how seriously horse people considered the danger of barn fires, and with more important thoughts on his mind, did not defend himself, but dutifully took the cigar from his mouth and placed it in his pocket. At $1.50 a pop he wasn't about to throw it away.

The two lawyers stepped into a small office in the barn. Kenton found a bottle of blended Chivas Regal and two Dixie cups in one of the cabinets and poured a double shot for each of them as Stafford took a seat at the small table.

"Are you still drinking this blended crap?" Stafford asked, in retaliation for the "don't smoke" warning.

Kenton, properly chastised and the score evened, changed the subject and thanked Stafford for driving down to the farm for the meeting.

They discussed the Rabbit Hole letter that Stafford had called about earlier in the day. Kenton brought Stafford up to speed by explaining, "I've had a copy for about a week.

It was sent to me by some would be whistleblower, I guess. I suppose that if it's authentic, that someone at the Ministry of Justice has gone whistle blower on their boss."

Stafford nursed his drink while Kenton continued, "I've tried to verify if it was a real document or just a hoax. I talked with a Justice of the Supreme Court about it, and he seemed surprised. If it was a hoax I would have expected him to have quickly told me. But as soon as I brought it up he was eager to read it. If it was a hoax and they knew about it I believe they would have said so. I believe it's the real thing, but if it is, then the Chief Justice is obviously aware of it and apparently the Ministry is carrying water for him on this."

Stafford probed, "Who did you meet with?"

Kenton smiled, and said, "You don't need to know just yet, and I gave a blood oath of silence just to get the meeting."

Stafford watched Kenton's face for a tell as he knowingly responded, "I understand why you would want to protect Alice Boone."

Kenton took a long drink from the Dixie cup, "You have six more Justices to guess, but Ol' Tar Baby, he don't say nothin'."

Stafford concluded that he had hit the bull's eye and went for the kill, "It would sure seem strange for a hound like you to wear that thousand dollar suit and a pair of $500 shoes to meet with old man Hatter!"

Kenton kept his poker face, but it was hard, very hard to do so.

"Jack," Stafford continued, "I've looked at some decisions by Hatter and I believe that he has been waiting a long time to pull off a coup like this. I think he has become intoxicated by the power of his office."

Kenton agreed, "He pushed through the Rules creating the Ministry of Ethics, and that went easily for him. The Rabbit Hole Amendments would appear to be the next logical step. He brought in the Queen of Hearts to run the Ministry, and she seems to be dancing to his tune".

Stafford said, "The Rabbit Hole document has some fatal flaws in it. Hart has gone over the line with her suggestions. She has to be the most clueless politician in Frankfort if she thanks this power grab will stand."

"You are assuming several things, that may not be true. The majority of the members of the bar don't know what the Hatter and the Queen are doing, and generally believes that ethics rules don't apply to them. The other half have an idea of what they are doing but don't have the courage to speak up. And anyone who has appeared before the Ministry and who might actually have witnessed their conduct is easily discredited as an angry litigant who was prosecuted for ethics violations and is not to be trusted."

Stafford cleared his throat, "I drove down here over these damn narrow roads because I believe that something must be done about this, and you are my personal nominee for the person to start the revolution. And when you tell me that you have already been checking on this with one of the Justices, I believe that you agree with me."

Kenton cocked his head, "Where would you start such a fool's errand?"

Stafford took out a piece of folded paper from his jacket pocket and began his lecture in the analytical way that a well organized legal mind is trained.

"We must expose their plan to the public.

"We must assess if he can get three more votes on the Supreme Court, and determine who they are. Then we work on them.

"We must come up with a clear explanation why this plan is so dangerous, and show how the public will be damaged by it.

"We need to give cover to the Justices who might be inclined to fight Hatter, and we must be able to punish at the polls any Justice who is inclined to help him.

"We start by printing out a thousand copies of the Rabbit Hole plan and nailing it to every courthouse door in the state. We can inform the Blackberry and Twitter crowd by going viral on the internet.

"Attacking the Chief Justice personally will be tough, but we have the benefit of the Queen of Hearts. She has made no friends, and she scares the hell out of anyone who knows what she has been doing. So we have to expose her megalomania. Her only real supporter is the Chief Justice. He found her and he will figure out a way to dismiss her if she becomes a liability. There is already a good chance that someone in her army is already setting her up or we wouldn't have a copy of the Rabbit Hole plan.

"I've called about a dozen of her victims and have discovered a growing list of her tricks. One thing they have told me is that these people are just plain mean. They treat every lawyer coming before them like a child molester. Sometimes she even refuses to meet with a defendant's lawyer, but if the caller is influential she will take his calls and play nice.

Her number one tactic is intimidation. Her practice is to hit everyone low and hard, even those with minor offenses and strong defenses. She overcharges them, and if they fight back, she delays and delays, letting her victims twist slowly in the wind as their wallets are drained. She plays the

Board of Scrutiny like a cheap fiddle and blocks discovery requests and controls most evidence rulings of the Board. Due Process is an orphan in her prosecutions unless it benefits the Ministry. Her most important tool is the secrecy she hides behind.

"She prevents the Supreme Court and the Board of Governors from learning what she is doing by hiding behind the confidentiality rule. When she sees any chance that the victim might appeal to the court, she makes a plea bargain deal in such a way that the Supreme Court never has a chance to review her actions. This means that the Supreme Court may actually be unaware of her most egregious actions. So we have to be sure they learn what's going on out at the Castle."

Stafford concluded his thoughts, "The whole set up of the Ministry of Ethics is a labyrinth of conflicts of interest. The Ministry is charged with being the legal counsel for the Board of Governors, but is also hired by the Board, and their actions are to be reviewed by the Board.

"So the Board who is supposed to monitor the acts of the Ministry also relies on the Ministry for legal advice. How likely is it that the Ministry as their counsel is going to advise the Board that the Ministry has exceeded its authority? If that isn't a conflict of interest then I don't know what is. But the plot thickens. The Ministry can hide its misdeeds from the Board and from the Supreme Court by a number of tricks they pull. Not every action of the Ministry is subject to any appellate review. There just is no other example in state government for a prosecutorial type agency to be free of appellate review."

Kenton was smiling at Stafford's detailed accusations. As he finished off his Scotch he responded, "We can expect that Hart will fight back like a cornered badger." If she can find the slightest hint of impropriety on our part, she will turn the Ministry's guns on us in a heartbeat. Stafford nodded his agreement.

Chapter Nine

The afternoon meeting of the Ministry staff was quickly assembled at the order of Commissioner Hart. The legal staff had recently doubled to sixteen lawyers, twelve paralegals and a dozen clerks and secretaries. All attorneys but one were present. The missing person had called in ill. The Commissioner and the attorneys sat around the long conference table, and the paralegals sat in chairs behind them around the wall.

She called the meeting to order merely by sitting in her chair at the head of the table. She began by saying, "We need to provide our full attention to this case" as she waved a handful of papers above her head.

"The respondent is Thomas Jefferson Kenton, Jr. of Scott County. Does anyone know him?" she asked.

Two of the young lawyers (who were only a year out of law school and happy to be employed in a steady job) raised their hands as if in competition to curry the favor of the Commissioner.

The first one who answered was Bill Lizarde, who said, "He's a horse breeder from near Georgetown."

The other young lawyer, Dicky Dormouse, added, "He's said to be considering a run for the Supreme Court seat occupied by the Chief Justice. He has a general practice but does some personal injury work in Lexington."

A third lawyer who was a decade older than most of the rest, making her almost 40 years old, broke in and said, "He comes from a highly respected family and is said to be wealthy."

The Commissioner was not impressed with these disclosures as Cheshire had reported most of them to her already.

"This appears to be a case where SCR 3.130 8.2 (a) has been violated. He has clearly attacked the qualifications and integrity of a state official," she concluded.

With this group of mostly inexperienced lawyers, most of whom had not tried a case before a jury, and whose legal careers only preceded the creation of the Ministry of Ethics by a few months, her conclusions were final. If she said he was guilty, they were not about to speak out and question her further. No one said Amen, but their silent acceptance of her conclusion of Kenton's guilt served the same purpose.

The Commissioner read to them a copy of the letter that Kenton had mailed to the Legislative Ethics Commission.

Eight of the fifteen lawyers felt they must have missed something, as they failed to immediately see where any ethical rule had been violated. Five of the attorneys, simply didn't care one way or another if the Commissioner had described an ethics violation. They defined their job as something in the nature of a clerk who organized and filled out forms. They were only "following orders".

The two remaining lawyers looked at one another with that here-she-goes-again look but prudently said nothing.

The Commissioner, not feeling the need to discuss the merits of the case, commenced handing out assignments.

"Dormouse," she ordered, "do a criminal records check and I mean a real check as far as the records go, and if he went to school out of state, check those states."

"Lizarde," she continued, "You will work on his Continuing Legal Education records.

Go back ten years and verify his attendance and the certification of all courses he has reported attending."

"Duchess, you and Loretta will do a credit check. I want to know everything about every recorded deed or mortgage or credit card expenditure for the last five years."

"Gryphon, you and Mallard check with the Racing Commission and see if he has ever had any complaints regarding his trainer's or breeder's license."

"Turtle," she derisively called at the one who was violating the office dress code by wearing a Mock Turtleneck sweater to the office, "You and Cathy Piller will draft the warning letter. I want it on Bunny White's desk in the morning."

"Bunny, review it and then see that it goes out in tomorrow's mail."

She passed out a copy of the Kenton letter to the Ethics Commission to Turtle, but withheld the second letter that mentioned her name. She didn't intend to let her staff know that she had been one of Kenton's targets. While it meant ignoring one potential charge she concluded that they could give Kenton a very nice "Tea Party Trial" with the one charge, and if she were to pursue a compliant in her own behalf, she would have to recuse herself from the Kenton prosecution since it would be disclosed that she was a target of his loose pen, making her an interested party.

Turtle and Cathy Pillar both cringed as they had drawn the short end of the straw. Pillar as the senior staff attorney would be the one to sign her name to the warning letter to be mailed to the Respondent. Fisher, being the youngest attorney in the Ministry, was assigned to prosecute the complaint. No one in the office expected Jack Kenton to do anything but negotiate a plea.

Only a small number of lawyers charged by the Ministry ever fought back. Fisher asked Bunny White about the chances for a plea, and she was assured that this case would never be tried.

The Commissioner continued the meeting for another hour and went through the reports of all the staff attorneys on the progress of their other cases. Several motions regarding demands for discovery of the facts relied on by the Ministry had been filed by charged attorneys. The Commissioner discussed methods to avoid providing discovery and authorized new charges to be filed against those trouble makers.

Commissioner Hart finally dismissed the others but signaled with her index finger that she wanted Dodo Anderson and Marion Marchharre' to stay in the room. "Find out if Kenton's horse farm employs any illegal aliens," she directed. She then rose and left the conference room.

They looked at one another and realized that had never seen that trick pulled before. They had no idea where to find such information without violating about a dozen federal immigration laws.

Dodo Anderson whispered to Marchharre' after they were dismissed from the meeting, "Ours is not to question why . . ."

One of the paralegals tweeted the others, "FO/HRH!!!"

The following day was a Tuesday. The notice letter was written and delivered to Bunny White as directed. It informed Kenton that he was under investigation by the Ministry of Ethics for having violated the Rules of Professional Conduct by writing a letter to the Legislative Ethics Commission and accusing them of doing their jobs in "an inappropriate manner" while knowing that said statement was false. The Notice of Investigation letter did not explain the Ministry's conclusion that Kenton's statement was false. The letter warned him not to discuss this investigation with any member of the Court of Appeals or the Supreme Court.

The warning letter provided few factual details. This ambiguity was designed to allow the Ministry the maximum amount of flexibility to change or expand the charges at will. This lack of factual details was a tactic of the Ministry to keep the actual details of the alleged offense secret from the defendant lawyer. If he wanted to obtain that information, he would have to work to get it.

The official Notice of Investigation letter, which would cause large ripples in many ponds, was properly addressed and mailed by Bunny White to the "Hon. Thomas Jefferson Kenton, Jr.". It arrived at his Lexington law office on Wednesday morning.

The Ministry staffers, most of whom were former prosecutors, and more experienced in criminal law than civil proceedings such as the ethics process, assumed anyone receiving a Notice of Investigation letter was guilty. They had been trained as prosecutors and found it natural to treat the lawyers they investigated as criminals.

The Board of Governors had stood by without comment when Commissioner Heather Hart staffed the Ministry with ex-prosecutors. No one on the Board of Governors demanded that the Ministry employ any former Public Advocates who might have been able to explain the concept of due process to the other prosecutors.

Bunny White, while herself a former prosecutor, often wondered how the Bar and the Supreme Court justified creation of a discipline machine clothed in secrecy and charged with the duty to seek out and punish its own members. She once told a friend, that she couldn't imagine a corporation ever hiring a dozen ex-FBI agents and turning them loose on the corporate shareholders.

Chapter Ten

Erin had placed Jack Kenton's mail on his desk. When he read the return address a small chill came over him. Every lawyer who received mail from the Bar Association experienced a similar reaction.

He thought to himself, "The Bar Association never writes to tell you that you have done a good job on a case. They never write to tell you that they want to recognize your excellent work over many years. The Bar Association only writes to tell you bad news". The letter justified Kenton's apprehension when he read its terse message accusing him of unethical conduct.

Thomas Jefferson Kenton, Jr. had been a licensed lawyer for over forty years and had never had his ethics challenged. Both his father and his grandfather had been lawyers. The ethics complaint charged in the Warning Letter was the first filed against a Kenton in three generations.

The letter represented a threat to his livelihood, to his honor, and to his family's long and distinguished record of service to the community.

The Notice of Investigation Letter meant that he would be subjected to an investigation of the most intimate details of his personal life. It meant that he needed to employ a lawyer for his defense, and he had heard tales where a lengthy ethics defense might cost $40,000 to $50,000. A failure to defend himself against the charge meant almost certain conviction and possible disbarment.

The disbarment, or even a thirty day suspension, meant that he would have to write all of his current clients and inform them of his suspension. Years of trust he had earned from his clients would be destroyed. The trial judges who were sitting on the twelve pending lawsuits he was currently handling, would be notified of a suspension. The judges would be ordered to deny him access to the courtroom during the suspension. The black cloud caused by a suspension, would be infectious enough to even affect the partners in his law firm.

The first call Kenton made was to his legal malpractice insurance carrier. Ethics prosecutions had become so common since the creation of the Ministry of Ethics, the malpractice insurance carriers had recently added a rider to their standard malpractice insurance policies which covered the first $20,000 of a lawyer's legal expenses in defending ethics complaints

The malpractice insurance carrier representative asked him to copy them on all the correspondence and confirmed that they would provide him an attorney experienced in defending ethics charges by the Ministry.

Since the creation of the Ministry of Ethics, and its new emphasis on regulation of the comments of lawyers and investigation into their private affairs, many lawyers had read the tea leaves. Many law firms had wisely added an ethics coverage clause to their malpractice insurance policies.

He next called Williston Stafford. He read the letter to Stafford and said, "The balloon has gone up!"

Stafford replied, "I'll get the Eunuchs together at Summit Hills, Saturday morning at 12:00 o'clock."

Chapter Eleven

Kenton pulled into the parking lot of Summit Hills Country Club, next to Thomas Moore College in Northern Kentucky, shortly before noon. He walked through the club's bar, and found the stairs leading up to the Men's Grill. Stafford had pushed together three card tables, and had assembled eight other lawyers and one retired judge.

Stafford called the attendees "Eunuchs", since all of them were retired from the practice of law, and were not likely to be subject to actual financial damage if a counter-attack by the Ministry was launched against them. The secrecy of the meeting evidenced everyone's mutual belief that a counter-attack by the Ministry was a very real possibility.

Each of the invitees had been geographically selected to represent the seven Supreme Court districts of the state.

No other people were in the Grill, save the bartender who professionally ignored their conversation and busied himself washing glasses.

As Kenton approached the table, Stafford directed him to the empty chair at the head of the table. All but Judge Kennedy were drinking coffee. He was already on his second whisky.

Stafford began, "I would like to ask Judge Kennedy to share his thoughts with us about why you were invited here."

Judge Kennedy stood up with all the solemnity he usually reserved for speaking at a wake. The white haired Irishman said, "Chief Justice Hatter has used the virtually unlimited powers of his office to control the conduct of lawyers by his expansion of the Supreme Court discipline rules. He influenced the hiring of Heather Hart, a former prosecutor. She has no appreciation for the delicacy of her position as enforcer of ethics. She treats her job as if she was still a criminal prosecutor."

He paused for a moment and took a long sip on his whisky, and continued. "It has always scratched me the wrong way, that the investigators for the Ministry of Ethics are called prosecutors. Ethics discipline hearings are civil matters. Why in God's name do we call administrative investigators 'prosecutors'? Is it any wonder they treat lawyers like criminals?

"But I digress. I believe we have all sat by silently and allowed the Bar Association discipline process to take control of the Bar Association. People like Heather Hart have never really practiced law. She has never run a law office. She doesn't understand the difficulties of actually practicing law. Since her first day as a lawyer she has been a prosecutor and now has been advanced to her position as Minister of the Ministry of Ethics. Is it any wonder that she and her staff have failed to understand what it is like to be a real lawyer who scrambles to make a buck and to keep body and soul together?

Stafford chuckled when Floyd Bowling shouted out, "Give her hell Judge!"

Judge Kennedy ignored Bowling and continued. "It's time for the members of the legal profession to start a revolution. The Supreme Court and it's Ministry of Ethics have become predators seeking to destroy our rights.

"This Lawyer's Revolution is necessary if we are to achieve the righting of the many wrongs against our profession by our own masters. I don't suggest violence, I suggest the exercise of our rights to use the ballot box to remove those who oppress us. If we are to stop this little dog and pony show in Frankfort, we are going to have to change some faces."

Rosenwald raised his hand and worked in a comment. "Judge you must admit that this problem exists because there is an almost total lack of interest of the 17,000 members of the Bar Association about how the Bar is operated. Who operates the Bar Association, and how it is operated, are issues which most lawyers consider to be a game of inside baseball. This lack of attention or concern by the bar members of this state has allowed all of this to bring us to the current crisis."

Judge Kennedy replied, "Rosy, you are exactly right. Everyone has found it unpleasant to deal with the Bar Association, and most don't know what is going on with the discipline machine. But we can inform them. If we show them that there are others willing to stand up to Hatter and Hart, and if we show them that there is a chance for success, our call to arms will be heard.

"We should all recognize that the 17,000 members of the Kentucky Bar Association represent hundreds of thousands of clients every year. If the attorneys are motivated on an issue of public concern, they have the potential to influence their clients to march to the ballot box and remove from office those who would limit the ability of the legal profession to be advocates in the public's behalf."

Kennedy ended his speech by turning the floor over to Stafford who stated, "The straw that broke the camel's back is the prosecution against Jack Kenton. All he did was to write a letter to the Legislative Ethics Commission. I have read that letter and it was merely an analysis of the law and it said they made a mistake in the legal conclusion that a state official who allows his underlings to break the law in making solicitations for campaign contributions from lobbyists is not responsible for their acts. This exercise of free speech began a scheme to retaliate against Jack Kenton. But in reality, it is an attack against every lawyer.

"Someone at the Legislative Ethics Commission issued a fatwa and the Ministry heard the call. You all will recall that Sir Thomas Beckett, the Arch Bishop of Canterbury, was murdered by the minions of Henry II who had pleaded to them, 'Who will rid me of this troublesome priest?'

"Jack Kenton had the right to write his letter. It was temperate and respectful. But the Legislative Ethics Commission sought revenge by filing an ethics complaint against Kenton with the Bar Association.

"I understand their anger. He angered them. They had the right to file their complaint, but the Ministry of Ethics had the duty to filter out that complaint.

"The Bar Counsel in an unexplainable decision chose to carry water for the Legislative Ethics Commission. She has interpreted SCR 3.130 8.2(a) to limit the first amendment rights that lawyers have enjoyed since time immemorial. It is one thing for the Bar to regulate the conduct of lawyers with their clients and in the courtroom, but he wrote his letter merely as private citizen. He did not need a law license to do this, and he didn't give up this right when he became a lawyer.

"It's a stretch for the Ministry of Ethics to protect legislators from public criticism as they are doing in their case against Jack Kenton."

Judge Kennedy interjected, "Not only are they limiting the free speech rights of lawyers, they have begun an attack on the Judicial Conduct Commission. They are prosecuting Judge Natrona Clay for a ruling he made on the bench. If they are allowed to expand their authority to remove judges, then the members of the Bar who are angered by a Judge's ruling can file an anonymous complaint against him.

"The conduct of Judges is supposed to be handled by the Judicial Conduct Commission, not by the Ministry of Ethics. This review of a judge's rulings by the Ministry makes it more powerful than the Court of Appeals or the Supreme Court.

"As you may know, the existing rules prohibit the Judicial Conduct Commission from reviewing a judge's rulings. Review of a judge's decisions is an issue that should be addressed by the appellate courts. Otherwise judicial independence will be left in the hands of secret committees of lawyers and unelected ethics officials.

"By investigating and bringing ethics charges against a trial judge for his rulings, they have demonstrated that they see no limits to their powers. The Judicial Conduct Commission was set up to be the exclusive agency to regulate the conduct of Judges. Now the Bar is horning in on the JCC's jurisdiction. The power to punish a judge for a ruling he made on the bench, is denied to the Judicial Conduct Commission, but the Ministry is doing an end run by assuming such a power.

"Will any judge be willing to make rulings which the Ministry finds controversial? Will judges stand up to the public mob that every once in a while calls for punishment of a defendant even though the state can't prove his guilt?

"Today, we are confronted by the Ministry of Ethics, whose very name has an Orwellian tone. I personally believe they want all lawyers to fear them like citizens feared the Ministry of Truth in Orwell's 1984. They want to scare the hell out of all members of the bar. I assure you they have already succeeded in scaring the hell out of trial judges.

Stafford changed the subject. "It appears that the Chief Justice has now directed the Commissioner of the Ministry of Ethics to come up with a plan to further expand their control over the personal lives of bar members.

"For the life of me I can't understand why all of these Supreme Court rules that deal with the required conduct by lawyers are not submitted for a vote by the members of the bar who have to live under these rules.

"In the packet before you, you will find a copy of a proposal, prepared by the Ministry of Ethics, for rules changes. They now seek to infringe even further on lawyers' free speech rights. They now seek to control your wardrobe, your personal habits, and to limit your political thoughts to an unprecedented degree. They are spying on lawyers with hidden cameras at seminars held by the Bar Association.

"If adopted, these rules changes will forever make all lawyers who disagree with the Ministry of Ethics, speechless serfs.

Judge Kennedy spoke again after taking another long sip of whisky. "The thing that upsets me the most is the message they have sent us is that no one should mess with their friends. We don't know the name of the person who filed the complaint against Jack Kenton. That information has not been revealed by the Ministry and may never be.

"But we know the State Senator benefited from the Legislative Ethics Commission dismissal of the complaint against him which alleged he had illegally solicited campaign contributions from lobbyists and merit system workers. Of course, we don't know for sure who filed the complaint against Jack Kenton. These people operate in a dark world of secrecy.

Stafford continued, "They seek to make two classes of lawyers. We cite in your packet examples where members of the SCR 3.130 'protected class' have committed acts and said things without action by the Ministry, while ordinary lawyers have been prosecuted for ethics violations for doing the same thing.

"Today their focus is on Jack Kenton. It shames me to think they would single out one of the best among us.

"Today they go after Jack. Tomorrow their focus will be on you, unless you duct tape your mouth, censor your letters, restrain your thoughts, and tread meekly through life, bow and divert your subservient eyes in their exalted presence.

"We have all been guilty of sitting back and watching them pick off the stragglers and the mavericks. We have felt safe in the anonymity of the herd. Today, I say they have gone too far and it is time we speak up."

The group applauded in unison and Adkins, Huddleston and Judge Horner shouted, "Hear! Hear!"

Stafford, said "The sun is over the yardarm," and he motioned the bartender to the table.

Stafford told the group of a complaint pending in the Ministry where they cited a lawyer for charging an excessive fee, "The client without asking, handed the lawyer a check for $1500 and told him to delay a foreclosure action as long as he could. The lawyer accepted the employment and filed an answer on the foreclosure action. Later the client became unhappy with the lawyer and filed an ethics complaint against him. The attorney offered to go to fee arbitration but the Ministry refused the offer. He even offered to return the entire $1500 if the Ministry would drop the charge, but they refused. But the kicker here is that the client hired another lawyer to continue with the case. The replacement lawyer charged him $25,000.

"And hold on, both the Trial Commissioner and the replacement lawyer practice in the same law firm!

"When the lawyer filed a motion to ask the Trial Commissioner to recuse himself from the ethics hearing, the Trial Commissioner refused. A judicial officer subject to the Judicial Conduct Code such as the Trial Commissioner, should have informed himself on his law firms conflict. He had the ethical duty to unilaterally recuse himself from the case.

"The attorney filed his recusal affidavit with Chief Justice Hatter, but Hatter ignored the statute that says he must "immediately consider the facts" of the recusal motion. I'm told that the Clerk sent the recusal affidavit back to the attorney and the Chief Justice never even considered it. I've been advised that Hatter never told the other members of the Supreme Court of his refusal to obey the recusal statute, but there was no requirement that he tell them.

Red Horner added, "Don't hold your breath waiting to see if the Ministry prosecutes the Trial Commissioner for this violation which happened right in front of their eyes. This is just another example of the Ministry not applying the rules against themselves that they apply with vengeance against others."

One of the Eunuchs from far western Kentucky sarcastically joined in, "I'm unaware of any rule that says large law firms are exempt from the rules regarding conflicts of interest."

Janie Shaw added, "How is it possible for the Ministry to allow a Trial Commissioner to hear a case when his law partner is the complainant's attorney of record? If a private attorney did such a thing the Ministry would be on him like flies on scat."

Most of the heads in the group nodded in agreement with the obvious impropriety of such an occurrence.

A representative from Calloway County held up his hand and gave his opinion, "The process before the Board of Scrutiny does not permit the charged attorney to be heard. He can only send the Board a letter explaining his defense. His testimony is not allowed. He is not provided with the name of his accuser. He is not allowed to see the evidence against him. He is not even allowed to take the deposition of his accuser. The Board issues no findings revealing the facts and law the Board relied upon to justify the issuance of a formal complaint. They allow ex parte motions before the trial commissioner by their prosecutors, and don't allow that right to the defendant.

"There simply is no due process. The Board of Scrutiny meets in secret and the charged attorney can't look his accuser in the eye. He can't even speak in person to the Board of Scrutiny.

"We have the finest court system in the world. Why has the Supreme Court taken such proceedings away from the court system? The courts used to hear these claims and used rules that are regularly used in civil proceedings. Rights were enforced. Decisions were made by impartial judges and not by political appointees. Their decisions were subject to an appeal by an impartial panel. The burden of proof was on the state not on the defendant.

"Why have they imposed a George Orwell type of committee on the legal profession?" Stafford seeking to focus the debate changed the subject to a positive solution to the problem, "It appears that once again the Ministry takes care of its own, and sanctions the rest.

"If the Supreme Court continues to allow these abuses, then our only remedy is to use the ballot box to change some faces on the Court."

Wiley from Bowling Green asked Kenton to discuss the investigation pending against him.

Kenton passed out copies of the letter he had written to the Legislative Ethics Committee which the Ministry had charged was inappropriate.

He summarized his reason for sending the letter. "I was not picking a fight with them. I helped write the legislation which created the Legislative Ethics Commission. I not only had the right to express my thoughts, I believe I had the duty to speak up."

Kenton concluded, "I look forward to our day in court." He placed heavy emphasis on the word *our.*"

Stafford explained how to organize additional members throughout the Commonwealth to help in the cause. He explained the procedures of the Ministry of Ethics and gave tips on how to avoid their attention. The small group continued their discussion and planning during a lunch of the club's famous fried Halibut on Rye with Cole Slaw, which was ordered for all by Stafford.

After lunch Stafford concluded by warning the members that once the Ministry learned of their identities that they might be subject to retaliation. "So, you should be cautious, and for god's sake keep yourself out of any ethical troubles."

As the discussion went around the table each Eunuch detailed some reason why they felt compelled to do something about Hatter and his Ministry of Ethics.

One spoke of his complaint that "the Ministry is full of lawyers wet behind the ears. Most have never practiced law and have no idea what the practice of law is like in a real courtroom."

A Eunuch from Ashland said, "What gets me is how damn mean they are. They ignore the Code of Professional Courtesy, and they treat lawyers who appear before them and their defense attorneys, as if they are criminals.

"One of my former associates was called in to defend himself for being an hour short of the CLE hours and they accused him of lying when he tried to prove to them he had sufficient hours. You'd have thought he'd kidnapped Lindberg's baby!"

Stafford added, "Don't forget the case where the attorney checked his CLE hours on the Bar Association web site which indicated he was current. The Ministry admitted the web site showed he was current with his CLE hours. Nevertheless, while they conceded that the Bar Associations web site web site was incorrect, they cited him anyway. They said he should not have relied on the Bar Association records. They actually fined and sanctioned him. Shockingly the Supreme Court upheld the sanction.

"Now they have a policy where they don't send you a notice each year informing you of the CLE hours you have earned during the preceding year. They now just post your status on the Kentucky Bar Association web site. Have they forgotten that the Ministry has argued successfully before the Supreme Court that it's no defense for a lawyer to rely on the Bar Association web site to determine his CLE status?"

Combs from Harlan commented, "My son represented a respondent and asked to meet with the staff prosecutor, and the prosecutor refused to even discuss the case with him. My son then brought in a former President of the Bar Association who requested a meeting with that same staff attorney on the same issue, and the meeting was readily granted. They seem to grant special privileges to those they fear, and screw everyone else."

Morgan from Louisville laughed and said, "There is an old saying in the Army, "RHIP"—rank has its privileges." Another added, "And I say FTA!" to the knowing chuckles of the veterans among them.

A fourth added, "The current set-up allows them to avoid discovery. I am aware of an instance where a defense attorney asked for discovery and the Ministry quashed the request by getting a pro se protective order from the Chairman of the Board of Scrutiny. They never served the motion on the defense. His lawyer just got a protective order denying his discovery out of the blue. He wasn't even granted the due process right to be present and to argue his motion." Several nodded their heads and agreed they had heard that trick pulled several times.

A fifth Eunuch added his thoughts, "They are paid by our dues, and they treat us like common criminals. They keep all specific details of their caseload secret. There is no way to accurately determine their actual caseload. I bet a dollar to a dime that 90% of their actual case load consists of anonymous complaints written in crayon on the back of envelopes.

"I served on the ethics board ten years ago, and most of the complaints we received clearly failed to state a legal claim. Most of the complaints filed are nothing more than allegations that the lawyer lost their case, or the lawyer sued them. I suspect that most of the claimed complaints handled by the Ministry are likewise written on an envelope with crayon and state no valid claim.

"Further, when the Ministry releases statistics on its caseload, it considers each count of a charge against an attorney as a separate case. So it's possible that the claimed case load of 70 to 80 per staff lawyer, really works out to 70 to 80 counts against only 35 to 40 lawyers, and they take years to clear their cases."

Rosenwald joined in, "We have absolutely no way to evaluate how much work they are actually doing under the present set-up, and the Chief Justice is ignoring his administrative duties in letting them run their shop in secret. We hear complaints that the Chief Justice is permitting the Queen of Hearts to nominate the Trial Commissioners who hear ethics cases. If that is happening then the entire Supreme Court is complicit because the rules require the Supreme Court to give their consent to the selection of Trial Commissioners.

"The Ministry of Ethics has a staff full of attorneys, paralegals and clerks, which costs the bar members well over a million dollars a year in salaries and office expenses. This is all paid by our dues, and all of this just to handle some 100 real cases a year! My grandson is a Public Advocate in Somerset, and he handles a caseload of 525 cases a year! And those cases are real cases. Criminal cases with real consequences!"

Jones from Owensboro added, "The vast majority of the Ministry's case load is handling complaints about insufficient CLE credits, failure of lawyers to stay in touch with their clients, and the occasional case regarding mishandling of client's money. Most of the cases they handle are open and shut cases and their suggestion that they handle 1000 cases a year is really misleading. It would be more accurate to say they get 1000 pieces of mail a year, and this adds up in reality to only about 100 real complaints a year.

"They must be worried about their low case loads. They now have a proactive policy of going out of their way to sleuth around and dig up cases that clients would never have filed on their own.

"Once they latch on to a lawyer, if they have a weak case, they won't admit it, they just keep it in the investigative phase for years. This keeps the lawyer on the hook, and this indicates to me that they often don't have much of a case, otherwise they would submit their claims for speedy hearings and let the chips fall where they may.

"They make the best use of the fact that the Supreme Court rules don't impose a statute of limitations or a speedy trial privilege to the members of the Bar Association. A real court would never allow them to get away with that crap!"

Combs jumped back in, "I suppose they are trying to justify their existence by expanding their mission to police our public comments. If they get away with controlling our speech today, tomorrow they will extend their inquisition to examine and correct our thoughts."

"Well," another Eunuch interjected, "Everything they wish to hide they declare secret. If you ask me, the Taliban could take lessons from these guys!"

Stafford was surprised by how angry the Eunuchs were. He was encouraged that they were highly motivated and eager to do something about the overreaching Ministry of Ethics.

Stafford voiced his thoughts to the group, "Abraham Lincoln never had to join a bar association. He practiced law morally and correctly without the benefit of a Ministry of Ethics to monitor his every move.

"The State Bar Association may have made its most effective power grab in the middle of the Twentieth Century, when it took away from individual trial judges the right to discipline lawyers in their district. This new disciplinary power, like all government power, is not static. It widens its breadth every year.

"The State Bar Association in recent years has enacted rules regarding the handling of legal fees which were paid in advance as a deposit against future work by the lawyer. The rules require the lawyer to take these advance fee deposits and place them in a strictly regulated trust fund. The lawyer can only disburse to himself an amount equal to the fee earned at any particular time. If an attorney is holding his client's fee in trust, he is subject to review by the Ministry to prove that he has only withdrawn a fee justified by the amount of work performed. Client's didn't ask for this and only want the job completed. But the Ministry can now make you justify every dollar you disburse to yourself.

"When the trust fund requirements were first adopted, lawyers were encouraged to voluntarily donate the interest earned from these trust fund bank accounts to the State Bar Association. That program represented only the camel's nose under the tent. In 2009 the voluntary program became mandatory. Strangely only small trust fund accounts are subject to the seizure of interest earned.

If there is a really large trust fund account, it is exempt from the Bar's seizure of interest. I would suspect that the large law firms got that provision written in to the rule.

"At first the trust fund rules allowed the attorney to maintain these trust funds in a bank of his choosing. The next step in the accretion of power by the State Bar Association may be to require all client fees to be paid directly to the State Bar Association and held in a centralized Attorney's Fee Trust Fund controlled by the Bar Association.

"I can hear their justification now, *'By accumulating these funds, we can negotiate a better interest rate then individual attorneys could negotiate.*"

"And this will save the children and support our troops!" one wag chimed in.

Stafford continued, "If the Rabbit Hole plan is enacted, one provision will require imposition of a system where each attorney wishing to draw on his fees as they are earned, will have to file an invoice supported by a sworn affidavit with the State Bar Association.

"The lawyer would have to justify his fee demand, and of course this procedure will put the burden on the lawyer to justify these claims. If the State Bar Association or the client is not satisfied with the fee claim, the attorney will be entitled to an administrative hearing, and the right to appeal to the Supreme Court. Such a process will, of course, be so expensive and time-consuming that fee disbursements would be subject to arbitration. This will allow the State Bar Association to hold on to the lawyer's rightfully earned fees for years if they wished.

"If the attorney complains too loudly, the Ministry of Ethics can be used to temper his outrage and to reason with him. Twenty-five years ago the Federal Government sued the Kentucky Bar Association which then had a Minimum Fee Schedule written into the Code of Conduct. A lawyer who charged less than the Minimum Fee Schedule could be sanctioned with an ethics violation. The Federal Courts threw out that rule.

"We will just have to see if this new attempt by the Bar Association to set attorney fees will withstand a Federal Court challenge. It appears that they are now setting a Maximum Fee Schedule, but that it only applies to small law firms."

The Eunuchs clearly distrusted the ever growing inclination of the courts and the State Bar Association, to control the professional and privates affairs of lawyers.

Rosenwald told the increasingly outspoken group, "If you have any doubt about how far Hatter is planning to go, then let me read to you Rule VI of the Preamble to the Code of Professional Conduct." He placed heavy emphasis on the last two words,

"Preamble Rule VI. A lawyer's conduct shall conform to the requirements of the law, both in professional service to clients and in the lawyer's business and *personal affairs*."

Wiley spoke up, "First they enacted ever increasing discipline authority over us, and now they will seize our purses. The next step the State Bar will take will be to increase "Bar Dues" from a fixed annual fee, to a graduated tax on all fees earned by lawyers. The imposition of a tax on lawyers by the judicial branch of government, an act usually reserved for the legislature, is probably on their long range agenda."

Stafford concluded the meeting with the statement, "We have to build a statewide coalition who will be willing to express their thoughts at the ballot box. That is the only thing we can do to seek a redress of our grievances. You each have your assignments!"

He then placed his right hand palm down towards the center of the group, and each member stood and placed their hands on top of another in a man pledge of group loyalty to the project.

As Stafford walked back to the parking lot with Jack Kenton, he commented, "I would be more impressed with the Eunuchs if they had been more outraged by the infringement of the First Amendment than on their wallets."

Before Kenton and Stafford parted, Kenton asked, "Williston. Can we motivate enough lawyers to join together to change the makeup of the Supreme Court and the Board of Governors?"

Stafford thought for a moment, and answered, "Yes. But we can't make one mistake!"

CHAPTER TWELVE

Chief Justice Hatter took out a pen and began to make a list on his yellow legal pad. He wrote down the names of all seven Justices on the Court. He placed a check mark by his name, indicating a secure vote for the Rabbit Hole Amendments. He then added a check mark beside the names of two other Justices from whom he had secured pledges at no small cost. One Justice had bargained for his pledge to assign him the right to write the opinion in a case of great concern to the coal industry which held great influence in the Supreme Court district from which he was elected. The other had merely sought an agreement to obtain employment of two of the Justice's otherwise unemployable relatives in some sinecure in the massive Administrative Office of the Courts of which the Chief Justice was the Executive Officer.

Three committed votes. That left him one vote short of the required four. He drew a circle around Justice Boone's name and counted her as his main obstacle.

He knew he could never turn her around. She had emphatically criticized him for the consensus building methods which he had used to defeat her in the election by the other Justices which had elevated him to the office of Chief Justice.

"That leaves me with three votes for adoption, one definitely against, and three who will be greatly influenced by Justice Boone." he said to himself.

He had gone over these numbers for a month, and couldn't seem to break the coalition against him. He had one option left which he hesitated to implement. He called this option, 'Dribble Drive' after the aggressive offense brought to Kentucky basketball by Coach Calipari back in 2009.

He had read and reread the provisions of the state constitution which in 1976 had been amended to modernize the Judicial Branch of government. The antique system created by the 1892 constitution had said little about the administrative functioning of the judicial branch of government.

The Judicial Amendment of 1976 granted broad administrative powers to the Chief Justice. He not only maintained the traditional powers of a Chief Justice on the Supreme Court, he now was granted administrative control over the four thousand employees of the Administrative Office of the Courts. This included the powerful Circuit Clerks in all 120 counties.

In his studies of the current Kentucky constitution he ran across a troubling section which he realized might some day present him or a succeeding Chief Justice with a problem.

For some reason the 1976 Judicial Amendments failed to transfer the listing of the Circuit Clerks from the Executive Branch to the Judicial Branch. It presented a legal argument that the Chief Justice had no administrative control over the office of the Circuit Court Clerk. Since 1976 every Chief Justice had assumed that the Circuit Court Clerks were under his control, but strangely the constitution continues to identify that office as a part of the Executive Branch of government.

Section 114 of the Constitution allowed the Chief Justice to remove a Circuit Clerk "for good cause", but Section 97 of the Constitution still listed the office of Circuit Clerk as an Executive Branch office. Chief Justice Hatter was troubled by the conflicting sections which apparently gives the head of the Judicial Branch the right to remove an official of the Executive Branch. He saw the apparent conflict of the separation of powers doctrine.

The Circuit Clerks were a powerful force to deal with. They personally met with every voter who had to go to the Circuit Clerk's office every four years to renew their driver's licenses. He feared a fight with the Clerks, and certainly was not going to educate them on this potential error in the new Judicial Article. Since 1976 the Clerks had not raised this issue, and he feared doing anything to arouse them.

He had successfully taken steps to control the discipline mechanism of the Bar Association. He had pushed through the creation of the Ministry of Ethics under the ruse of modernizing the discipline process. He had waved the bloody shirt of the Fen Phen scandal and cited the need for a better organized ethics machine, "If we are to maintain the respect given our profession by the public, we must adopt the Rabbit Hole Amendments."

He had intimidated the Board of Governors into placing Heather Hart in control of the new Ministry of Ethics. While she was sometimes too enthusiastic, she was safely under his control.

Madison Hatter had explained to Heather Hart the possibility of an expansion of the Ministry's powers so that they could sanction a trial judge for a bad ruling. He was interested in setting a precedent of limiting the traditional powers of trial judges to call their shots as they saw them. He believed such a precedent could be applied to appellate judges, but recognized that this might be opposed if it were recklessly applied. Nevertheless, he would keep this option in his trick bag.

Such a precedent would effectively bypass the limitations imposed on the Judicial Conduct Commission. This limitation of the Judicial Conduct Commission prevented them from sanctioning judges for legal but unpopular rulings.

The Hatter plan allowed the Ministry of Ethics to bypass the Judicial Conduct Commission and assume powers that were never envisioned by the American Bar Association or the original Supreme Court rules. The Judicial Conduct Commission was based on the theory that only Judges should review the ethical actions of other judges.

If such a precedent was established, the Judicial Conduct Commission was effectively gutted, and anyone sanctioned by the Judicial Conduct Commission thereafter could be sanctioned by both commissions for the same offense. The Ministry had selected Judge Natrona Clay for the first shot at establishing their right to review judicial rulings.

The Judicial Conduct Commission amazed the few people in the state who happened to pay attention, by failing to defend their turf. Hatter laughed to himself at the idea that the members of the Judicial Conduct Commission were still walking around thinking they were still alive.

Hatter thought of an old case that had come before his court when he was a Circuit Judge in Lexington. A man was stabbed in the back and was so drunk he was unaware that there was a butcher knife sticking in his back. He went to a bar and sat down on a stool.

Another patron of the bar noticed the knife and called an ambulance. The drunk felt nothing when he was stabbed in the back by his angry lover. He was amused by the idea that the Judicial Conduct Commission members all have knives in their backs and are still walking around unaware that they were the victims of a jurisdictional assault.

He concluded that since he had failed to break up Justice Boone's coalition, his only recourse seemed to be using the Assignment Section of the Judicial Article of the Kentucky Constitution to replace an appellate judge. This aggressive Dribble-Drive strategy did not require a new rule. It didn't require a new law. And the part he liked best, was that if he applied Dribble-Drive, there wasn't a damn thing the other Justices could do about it.

He picked up a copy of the 1976 Judicial Amendment to the Kentucky constitution, and found Section 110 (4)(b).

"The Chief Justice can assign temporarily any_justice or judge of the Commonwealth, to sit in any court other than the Supreme Court when he deems such assignment necessary."

He noted that Section 110(4)(b) had included the word "justice" and not just the word "judge". This meant that he could assign Justice Boone and her chief ally Allgood anywhere in the state, and the only condition was that the Chief Justice found the assignment to be 'necessary'. The more he thought about it, this section was written so carelessly that he could assign the entire court to duty elsewhere, and the Governor would replace them with Special Justices. If he only needed to remove one Justice, he didn't need to fill the vacancy by requesting a gubernatorial appointment. The court could do business with only six justices present.

Chief Justice Hatter sat back in his leather chair for a moment and thought about a potential coalition between a Governor and the Chief Justice. If such an alliance were ever formed, the two officials could create their own Supreme Court, made up of Special Justices who would be amenable to do their will. This had the potential of allowing such a coalition to repeal any statute by ruling it unconstitutional, or by siding with some powerful corporation to provide them relief that the elected court might have denied. The potential for abuse of the assignment section was a sobering thought.

Only members of the Kentucky Supreme Court were classified as Justices and all other judicial officers including Court of Appeals were called judges. This section of the constitution was a awesome error due to loose draftsmanship. The four Chief Justices that had preceded Madison Hatter had either been ignorant of this section's evil potential or had had enough character never to abuse it.

Hatter smiled to himself, and imagined someone trying to challenge his clear constitutional power to assign opposing Justices to some obscure assignment at the far ends of the Commonwealth whenever he wanted them to be unavailable to vote on Supreme Court business. No Justice had ever been assigned away to other duties for such a purpose, but the constitution placed no limitation on his exercise of this option.

The Chief Justice had to suppress his glee upon finding this section of the constitution. He wanted to call a press conference and tell the world of his discovery. But reason prevailed and he kept this treasure to himself until the day he would need it. And that day was approaching.

It was one thing to use the assignment section on minor administrative issues coming before the court. Who would notice? Who would care? He took time to speculate on what he could do by obtaining the Governor's support in a plan to control future court rulings on substantive issues. If the Governor wanted the Supreme Court to rule a certain way on a future case, he would only have to work out an arrangement where the Chief Justice would reassign two opposing justices, and the Governor could replace them with "friendly" special justices.

He was actually fearful of the reaction of the public to such a ploy, but he figured it was only a matter of time before another Chief Justice and another Governor would figure this out and attempt to get it accomplished. He recalled that Governor Ernie Fletcher had nakedly granted a blanket pardon to every member of his administration. Who would have thought that a Governor would ever have done such a thing?

If Governor Fletcher got away with pardoning dozens if not hundreds of his friends and prevented their conviction and punishment, was it too much of a stretch to consider a Governor conspiring with a Chief Justice to control rulings on important criminal or civil cases?

He was amazed that that this scheme was actually authorized by the Kentucky Constitution when the 1976 Judicial Article Amendments were approved by the public and the assignment section was adopted. "How could they have missed this?" he asked himself.

While this assignment power had never been exercised in this manner by any other Chief Justice, Madison Hatter concluded that he would make the most of the opportunity to at least influence an administrative task such as changing the Supreme Court rules. Only a few lawyers would be concerned or even know what the issues were. He realized that this must be done secretly and there would be no time for public protest to become organized until it was a fait accompli.

He looked for loopholes in his plan, and concluded that as long as his two committed votes stuck with him, all he would have to do to get his fourth vote was to fill one vacancy. He would need the Governor's cooperation in appointing Special Justices who were reliable. He reviewed Fletcher v. Graham, the famous case in which Governor Fletcher appointed two Special Justices to hear a case involving the Governor's actions in issuing his blanket pardons to his administration officials.

Governor Fletcher's participation in the selection of two justices to hear a case concerning his own powers was like having a person charged with a crime having the right to appoint four of his friends as jurors on the panel which would determine his guilt or innocence.

Hatter already had a half a dozen candidates in mind that he would ask the Governor to appoint. Most attorneys would love to pump up their resume by being appointed as a Special Justice even if for only one day.

"How would the press react to such a blatant power play?" he wondered. He concluded that it would be at worst a one day's news story on page three, and perhaps a editorial opinion or two which would not be read by anyone but the editorial boards.

The public was rarely concerned with the technical application of arcane constitutional provisions that did not interfere with their personal lives. If some lawyer got burned, the public would probably cheer Hatter's clever move.

Hatter tried to envision the reaction of the legal community and the Judiciary to the implementation of Dribble-Drive.

"First," he argued to himself, "they wouldn't be able to reverse anything I do."

"Secondly" he continued, "the increased control the Chief Justice would receive from adoption of Rabbit Hole would give him even more power to silence his opposition. The other Justices on the Court would be faced with a fait accompli clearly authorized by the constitution!"

Without additional thought, he picked up his telephone and set Dribble Drive in motion by calling Nathan Smith.

Smith was just leaving his office when the phone rang. He was greeted by the Chief Justice who in a cheerful voice ordered, "Nathan, I'm going to need you in Frankfort on Friday morning. Can I count on you to stand in as a Special Justice?"

Nathan Smith, was instantly flattered and readily replied, "Mr. Chief Justice I will be glad to be of service to the Supreme Court at your discretion."

The Chief Justice then told him, "The special session of the court meets at 9:00 a.m. I'd appreciate it if you could be in my office by 8:45. It's on the second floor. This is just a session to consider some minor rules changes which I think are necessary, but we will certainly call on you in the future with something that has a little more meat to it. You should stand by for my call, I will have to get this approved by the Governor but that should be no problem.

"Thank you, Sir," Smith said, "You can count on my support. I'll be there on time."

Hatter ended by warning, "Don't say anything about this. Confidentiality is the watchword of all our proceedings."

The Chief Justice made a second call to his second prospective nominee Jim Stewart from Mayfield. They were old friends and he also readily agreed to accept such a gubernatorial appointment if asked.

Hatter then went to his secretary's desk, which being Saturday was unoccupied, and typed out a brief order directed to Justice Alice Boone and Justice Allgood. He was going to keep Dribble Drive close to his vest.

The order from the Chief Justice, citing the authority of Section 110 (4)(b) of the constitution, assigned Justice Boone, a graduate of Harvard Law School, to sit in Division One of the Gallatin District Court, to handle the Small Claims docket on the coming Friday. Justice Allgood was assigned to similar duty in Robertson County, a county so small that it averaged only two Small Claims cases in a year.

He had carefully checked the online dockets of trial courts posted on the Courts web site to confirm that the Gallatin District court had a Small Claims docket for that date. He had read in the day's newspaper that the regular District Judge of Division One of the Gallatin District Court was in the hospital recovering from injuries received in a traffic accident.

He noted from the court's internet docket, that Robertson County Small Claims Court had only one case pending.

He prepared another order scheduling a meeting of the Supreme Court for Friday.

The third document was a certification to the Governor stating that there were two vacancies on the Supreme Court and requesting two appointments of Special Justices.

He personally walked this document down to the Governor's Office and was admitted immediately. He presented the Governor with the order and discussed the urgency of the appointments. He did not reveal the details of his plan.

The Governor reviewed the document, and having previously signed such orders readily consented but with one change. The Governor explained, "Chief Justice, my son-in-law practices in Lexington, I believe he would benefit from such an appointment, and I'm going to add his name to this order. Which one do you want him to replace?"

Chief Justice Hatter only needed Nathan Smith so he recommended that his suggested nominee James Stewart of Mayfield, be replaced with the Governor's son-in-law. The Governor was delighted to give his son-at-law a career boost, and signed the order after adding the correct name.

Nathan Smith was a former Commonwealth Attorney from Lexington. He was noted for his law and order bloodlust. Smith had once campaigned by attacking his opponent, who was a highly respected public defender, by heavily broadcasting a video of himself, saying, "I have never represented a criminal, and my opponent has made his living at the service of murderers and child molesters." Hatter admired Smith's creativity, and so did the voters.

Of the lot considered by Hatter for appointment as a Special Justice, Nathan Smith was clearly the most likely candidate to keep his commitment to the Chief Justice. Smith's law firm frequently had cases on appeal before the court, and often relied on the Chief Justices' coalition to limit the liability of Smith's insurance company clients whenever possible.

The Chief Justice in his interview with Smith, made it clear that Smith owed part of his soul to the Chief Justice. Smith seeing the benefits of cooperation, and the downside to opposition, had readily agreed to be a proxy for the Chief Justice's will.

As Hatter thought about the loyalty he had imposed on Nathan Smith, he recalled General William Westmoreland who had famously said, "Grab them by the balls and their hearts and minds will follow."

The Chief Justice went back to his office and reviewed the orders and personally prepared envelopes for them.

He then called in a bailiff and directed him to personally deliver the reassignment orders to the two Justices who would be lending their talents to the Commonwealth's two smallest counties. He directed the bailiff to serve these orders no sooner than Thursday at 5:00 p.m., preceding the special meeting of the Supreme Court he had called for Friday morning.

Chapter Thirteen

The infra-red detector in Big Cat Cheshire's office picked up motion in the Chief Justice's office the moment he entered his office. The infra-red device can detect human movement through six inches of concrete. The devices triggered the laser voice detection devices, and the digital coding and recoding tools kicked into operation. While Cheshire's technology could not detect the thoughts of the Chief Justice, it was able to register the phone number he dialed, and it picked up his side of the conversation.

Cheshire's technology guru, Matt Simons, had been able to install some spyware on the computer of the Chief Justice's secretary. He planted a Trojan Horse called Echo Bug in an e-mail which was routed by his software to appear to be from another Justice.

When the secretary opened the e-mail it allowed the bug to migrate to the hard drive where it would sleep until someone started using the keyboard. Periodically the entire content of the computer was compressed and transmitted to Cheshire. On Monday morning, Cheshire reviewed the weekend logs and noticed that the Chief Justice had been in his office on Saturday morning. That was unusual, he noted.

He opened the laser recordings which had been translated into text, and read the report on the phone call to Nathan Smith that had been picked up by the laser mike. The software was able to interpret the phone number of Nathan Smith that had been dialed by the Chief Justice.

He noted the keywords from the message. There was to be a "special administrative session of the Supreme Court on Friday", and that someone named "Nathan" was going to be appointed as a Special Justice. He also noted the comment about confidentiality.

His curiosity was whetted, and he accessed the e-mailed keystrokes from the court computer on Hatter's secretary's desk. The printout displayed a number of legal documents prepared between the hours of 10:35 a.m. and 12:15 on Saturday morning.

Cheshire then logged on to the AOC website and called up the Supreme Court calendar, and could find no mention of a special session for Friday.

He checked the infra red motion detector log and found that only one person had been in Hatter's office on Saturday.

This information confirmed that whatever the Chief Justice was doing he did without the assistance of his secretary, on a Saturday morning, and demanded confidentiality from a fellow named Nathan. Something was obviously afoot.

Cheshire found the phone number from his laser detector report, and logged on to a reverse phone directory on the internet, and quickly found that the phone number was registered to a law office in Lexington.

He then Googled the law firm, and found that a Nathan Smith was listed. Cheshire then Googled the name Nathan Smith, and found numerous news stories about his years as a prosecutor. Cheshire noted that Ivan's (Nathan Smith's blogger name) old web site had preached hell fire and damnation and the virtues of the death penalty.

On the web site pages Cheshire viewed, he found no articles revealing Smith's losses, or any mention of the times his errors were overruled by the courts.

Cheshire, then went back to LawReader.com and found the pathway to the court's online information which provides information about pending cases in the Court of Appeals and the Supreme Court. He directed the search engine to call up all cases in which Smith's law firm was listed for the Court of Appeals as reported by the web site of the Administration Office of the Court's web site. He was shown a list of twelve cases currently pending in the Court of Appeals. Eight of the twelve appeals involved insurance companies who were represented by Smith's firm.

A check of cases currently pending in the Supreme Court on discretionary review revealed that Smith's law firm was involved in three pending cases.

While Cheshire was not a lawyer, he knew that Smith would not be permitted to sit on a case which involved one of his firm's clients, but the news that he was to sit on the Supreme Court must have thrilled his clients.

"And increased the fees he was charging them!" Cheshire said to himself.

Cheshire spent most of an hour reading and analyzing the documents the Chief Justice had personally typed. He wasn't able to figure out what the CJ was planning to do on Friday, but it was clear that he was replacing Justice Boone on Friday with a flaming right-wing ex-prosecutor.

He concluded that he needed to find out what merited such special efforts by the Chief Justice. Cheshire was a master of turning knowledge into money.

Chapter Fourteen

The eight Eunuchs Williston Stafford had recruited went back to their homes and began their work. Phone calls were made. Mid-week dinner meetings were arranged. By Wednesday evening the brotherhood of the Eunuchs had grown to over one hundred members.

On Thursday copies of the RABBIT HOLE plan were leaked to investigative and editorial reporters of the *Courier-Journal*, *Herald-Leader*, *Kentucky Enquirer*, *Owensboro Messenger*, and six other newspapers. A dozen television stations were also the recipients of the plan. A number of political bloggers received copies on Thursday. The universal response of the media was to review the report, but to question its authenticity. Two reporters called the office of the Chief Justice seeking his comment, but he wasn't taking any calls. Several other reporters were simply busy on other stories, and didn't see much urgency in addressing an issue that seemed to only apply to lawyers. As a result no story made the news during the Friday morning news cycle.

Late Thursday afternoon, the Chief Justice's order was personally delivered to Justice Boone just as she was preparing to leave for the day. She was in her regional office in Salyersville when she received the assignment order.

The Chief Justice had addressed his written order calling for a special meeting of the court to the Justices' offices in the Capitol building. He had followed up his notices with a phone call to all the Justices, except Allgood and Boone, informing them of the special meeting. He was prepared to defend this decision in not calling Justice Boone, by reasoning that since Justice Boone would be busy in Gallatin County, he was not required to notify her of the special meeting in Frankfort.

Justice Boone read the order assigning her to duty on the District Court in Gallatin County after the bailiff left her office. She was incensed. She had been on the court for many years and had never heard of a Supreme Court justice being assigned to such duty. She was particularly upset about the brief period of time she would have to travel to Gallatin

County. She wasn't even sure the assignment was legal. She quickly looked up Constitutional "Section 110 (4)(b)" which was cited in the Chief's order. It clearly said the Chief Justice could assign a Justice or a Judge to any court in the state, on his own finding of necessity.

As she read the authority cited in the order, she realized that Jack Kenton had warned her that something like this could happen. "Still," she thought, "It has_never been done." She had only seen this rule applied to permit a retired Justice to serve on the Court of Appeals. The provision was commonly used to assign trial judges with light caseloads to help other trial judges who were wrestling with a back log of cases on their docket.

Justice Boone immediately called the Chief Justice's office, but he was not in the office and his cell-phone was off line.

She left a message with the Chief Justice's secretary asking him to call her back and said it was Urgent.

The Chief Justice was rarely unavailable to take a call from another Justice. Her political antenna told her that Hatter was up to something and was intentionally unavailable.

She reviewed the monthly calendar showing the schedule of cases to be heard, and found no meetings in Frankfort were scheduled. Nothing was on the calendar for Friday.

She reviewed her options, and concluded that unless she could talk the CJ into rescinding his assignment order, that she would have to comply. If she refused to honor the assignment, she would be subject to a contempt citation for violating a court order. She could imagine that he would jump on a chance to humiliate her for violating a lawful court order. If she blew off the assignment, she could also be criticized for not respecting the important work of the District Court.

She saw no option but to honor the assignment. She would be a good soldier, but she sure as hell was going to privately express her displeasure with the Chief Justice to his face.

The trip from Salyersville to Warsaw in Gallatin County would take about three hours. She decided to leave immediately and spend the night at Belterra Casino across the Ohio River from Gallatin County.

As Justice Boone passed through Winchester she finally decided that Jack Kenton must know something about this. He had raised the possibility of the CJ playing some kind of game like this.

There were strict rules which limited the types of conversations that could be held between judges and lawyers. They could talk with one another about some things, but conversations about a pending case, or a case likely to come before the judge, were strictly forbidden. Such conversations were called "Ex Parte" discussions. Some judges freely ignored this rule assured that they could control their own moral conduct.

Lawyers were far more careful in attempting to discuss a pending issue as it could result in serious consequences for the lawyer, and could force the judge to recuse himself from the case discussed.

Discussions over the water cooler might be a useful method to share institutional knowledge, but between a lawyer and a judge, casual discussions had to be carefully controlled.

A conversation between a lawyer and a judge were, in most instances, a careful ballet in which the participants might dance close to a line but never cross it. Most lawyers formed their evaluation of a judge on the judge's compliance with this rule. It was obvious to most lawyers that a judge who would improperly talk to them about a case, and perhaps give an advantage to them, were just as likely to violate this rule at their expense. Judges who followed the rule strictly were respected by the bar.

This rule against Ex Parte conversations was strictly practiced by Justice Boone and by Jack Kenton.

She pulled to the side of the road as she entered Fayette County, and dialed Jack Kenton's phone number. Kenton promptly answered.

She briefly related the court assignment she had received. She admitted that she had ignored his warning about the CJ making use of Section 110 (4)(b) to make an assignment of a Justice at his discretion.

She asked him, "How could you possibly have foreseen the use of this obscure rule? It has never been applied to a Justice of the Supreme Court."

Kenton, replied, "Justice, I can't have this conversation with you."

She was surprised by his response. "Why?" she asked, as she was unaware of any pending case which would implicate the Ex Parte rule.

Kenton spoke in carefully measured words, "Don't misunderstand me. I would love to talk with you. There are a number of issues which should be discussed, but I have been ordered not to speak with you."

"Who could order you not to speak to me?" she demanded.

"I probably can't even tell you that, as it might be construed as a violation of the order I have received. He paused before repeating his statement, this time emphasizing the words "the order I received from the Ministry of Ethics."

She was speechless for a moment before asking, "What's going on?"

Kenton responded, "Please don't question my friendship. I'll be able to explain this to you later and you'll understand. In the meantime, I am ordered not to approach you. I feel obligated to honor that order."

He coyly suggested a source of information to her, "Now that order does not apply to everyone. For example Williston Stafford can talk with anyone he wishes."

He thanked her for her call, told her to drive safely and said he must hang up the phone, and he did. She understood the message. She should call Williston Stafford.

She entered the highway again, and analyzed who could order an attorney not to speak to a Judge?

Justice Boone considered why Kenton couldn't talk with her, there was no statute which would prevent such a conversation. That left only a judicial order or ethical conflict. There was no appeal pending before the court in which Kenton or his firm was involved as far as she could recall.

It then occurred to her that while Kenton might not currently have something pending in her court, he might be involved in something that *could* be heard by the Supreme Court. She realized that Kenton's reluctance to discuss the matter was as much for her protection as for his own.

Ten minutes later, she pulled into the convenience store near the Cracker Barrel Restaurant just off I-75 on the north side of Lexington to gas up her car. As she filled her tank, she dialed the number of Williston Stafford. It was pretty obvious that Kenton was suggesting that Stafford would not be subject to the Ex Parte restrictions.

She told Stafford of her call to Jack Kenton and his unwillingness to speak with her. Stafford spoke cautiously and said, "While I am not under a court order to prevent me from talking with you, and I don't anticipate being a party or an attorney in any matter coming before your court, I also don't want to be in the position of being accused of helping someone skirt a lawful order, and I don't want to get you in trouble."

What he said to her made sense, but she probed further, "Jack said you could talk to me. That's why I called you."

Stafford relented, "Justice, I would just hypothetically observe that Supreme Court Rules that have been adopted by your court (with a touch of sarcasm emphasizing the word "your") may apply here. One of those rules forbids anyone who has been officially notified that they are being investigated by the Ministry of Ethics to discuss the matter with a member of the court."

She ignored his jab and questioned him, "Are you saying Jack is being investigated?"

"I haven't said any such thing. I am just hypothetically citing your own rule to you," Stafford replied. "Okay," she said, "I understand. I won't ask anything about Jack".

"But," she continued, "there is another issue. Jack had recently asked me about Section 110 (4)(b) of the Constitution. Are you familiar with that Section of the Constitution?"

Stafford said, "No but I can look it up."

She interrupted him, "That's not necessary. Basically it grants the CJ the authority to assign any judge or justice to sit on any court anywhere in the state at his discretion. Prior Chief Justices' have used this rule to shift Circuit and District judges around to help balance case loads.

"There was a big backlog of DUI cases in East Kentucky counties during the 90's and Chief Justice Robert Stephens assigned judges from around the state to work off that backlog. On occasion some circuit judges have been assigned to help out on the Court of Appeals.

"When the Senior Judge program was in effect, the CJ assigned those judges to courts around the state. So that power of the CJ is well known. But recently Jack asked me if I was aware that the Constitution allowed the CJ to assign Justices of the Supreme Court in the same manner he could assign retired judges.

"Here's why this is important," she continued, "Hatter has ordered me to Warsaw to hear the Small Claims docket tomorrow morning!"

Stafford seemed incredulous, "How did he justify this to you?"

Boone replied, "Williston, he didn't explain it to me. He sent a bailiff to my office this afternoon, with the order of assignment. I tried to call him but he hasn't returned my call. This is completely out of the blue."

"Is there something on the Supreme Court docket tomorrow?"

"No," she said, but added, "I have checked the official calendar and nothing is scheduled for tomorrow."

"Williston," she continued, "Jack Kenton asked me, some weeks ago, if I had heard anything about a plan to change the Rules of Professional Conduct. I believe he said it was called, ""Operation Rabbit Hole?"

Stafford paused before saying, "Justice, I receive a lot of anonymous mail. I have heard mention of such a project. I am told that it has been ordered by the Chief Justice to be confidential. While I doubt his authority to legally declare something like that confidential, I don't want to pick a fight with a man who can sic a Pit-Bull like Heather Hart on anyone who challenges his authority."

"Further, If such a document actually exists, I wouldn't be able to prove it was authentic. It could be a hoax. I would feel a lot better about talking of such a document if someone like yourself could confirm it was authentic."

Justice Boone realized he was fishing for confirmation.

She conceded to Stafford, "I don't discuss internal court business as a rule. But I confronted the Chief Justice on this after I received a copy of the so-called Rabbit Hole Amendments. The CJ asked me to keep this confidential since it was an unjustified embarrassment to him. He said that document was just a rookie error by Commissioner Hart."

Williston accepted this statement as confirmation that the Rabbit Hole plan actually existed.

Justice Boone continued, "He said that he had asked Commissioner Hart to make suggestions for any housekeeping that might be needed on the Rules of Professional Conduct from her organizations point of view, and she came up with this silly over-the-top report".

"And you actually believed him?" Stafford asked.

After dinner at Jeff Ruby's Steak House at the Belterra Casino, she decided to visit the casino which is a river boat that no longer travels on the Ohio River. It is now moored permanently in a small bay which shelters it from the Ohio River. A road over Markland Dam connects the casino to Kentucky and it is only six miles from I-71.

Justice Boone loved to play the slots, and found a machine that attracted her attention. She placed a $50 bill into the Penny machine and watched her money disappear in exchange for nothing more than a display of flashing lights, bells and whistles. After an hour she decided to enter the room where the high dollar slot machines were displayed. She placed a $100 bill into the $10 machine and promised herself that when this money was gone she would retire for the evening.

After her third spin of the wheels, she noticed Bulldog Louden was playing a $5 machine on the other side of the room. Bulldog was the Kentucky legislature's most vigorous opponent of casino gambling.

His Chairmanship of the Senate Judiciary Committee allowed him to block all efforts to authorize casino gambling in Kentucky. He was a frequent visitor to Belterra which was on the Indiana side of the Ohio river.

She recalled news stories about the millions of dollars that Indiana received from casino gambling most of which was paid for by the Kentuckian's who crossed the state line to fund Indiana state government.

The casino interests had invested hundreds of millions in construction of four casinos on the Ohio River to service Kentucky gamblers and would be financially ruined if the Kentucky legislature enacted legislation allowing gambling in the Bluegrass State. Louden had fiercely fought a law allowing a public vote on gambling in Kentucky, thereby costing the state hundreds of millions in tax revenues.

Louden was a frequent and appreciated guest at the Belterra Casino. His long time efforts to prevent casino style gambling in Kentucky preserved the millions of dollars a year earned by Indiana casinos from Kentucky residents who crossed the river to enjoy their vice.

His natural sense of entitlement caused him to never question why he always seemed to leave this Casino as a winner. It never occurred to him that his complimentary room, complimentary meals, complimentary drinks, and unusual good luck was a reward for his anti-gambling sentiments. After all, other high rollers were comped all the time. He never mentioned the uncommon luck that he had at Indiana Casinos. He much preferred the Casinos bordering Kentucky over the Casino's in Vegas, where he never seemed to win anything.

Justice Boone didn't believe that Senator Louden had noticed her and she decided to avoid him. Before leaving she gave the machine one more spin. Her last spin was a winner. She had aligned some bars and a multiplier and as a result won $600. "Not bad!" she said, as she pushed the Cash Out button and received a ticket for her winnings.

Chapter Fifteen

As Justice Alice Boone entered the Gallatin District Courtroom in Warsaw, Kentucky to consider a Small Claims case filed by a landlord seeking to collect a rent payment from his unemployed tenant, the Kentucky Supreme Court was meeting in Frankfort, to consider new rules which would diminish the civil rights of every licensed attorney and judge in the state.

At nine o'clock all the Justices of the Supreme Court, save Justice Alice Boone and Justice Allgood, entered the conference room on the second floor of the state capitol building. Special Justice Nathan Smith was seated in the leather chair at the long conference table where Justice Boone usually sat.

The bailiff whispered to Special Justice Smith he must turn off his cell phone until the session was completed. The bailiff then checked the room to assure that no one but authorized Justices and Special Justices were present before locking the door behind him assuring that they would not be interrupted and that their deliberations would be in secret.

The bailiff in charge of security was unaware of the invisible laser beam bouncing off the window of the conference room. Likewise he had no idea that a small pin hole video camera was planted in the conference room and was sending video signals to a receiver being monitored by Cheshire's henchmen.

Chief Justice Hatter began the session by welcoming the Special Justices, and without giving any details, advised the court that "Justices Boone and Allgood, are otherwise occupied today and the Governor had appointed two Special Justices to take their place."

Wasting no time, he passed out a resolution adopting a list of changes to the Supreme Court Rules regarding professional conduct required of all lawyers. This was the first time that three of the Justices had seen the proposed rule changes.

Justice Anderson raised his hand and was recognized by the Chief Justice. Anderson moved for adoption of the rules amendments. His motion was seconded by Justice Smith who was barely able to hide his eagerness to call his daughter and share the good news that her thirty year old son would soon have a steady job at AOC and could move out of her house.

Justice Hatter commented that he had appointed a special committee to make recommendations to update the rules, and that he approved of their work. He didn't disclose who was on the special committee and no one pressed him.

Justice Van Buren interrupted and objected, "Just why are these rules changes needed?"

The CJ, certain that he had the required votes to pass the amendments, was unconcerned about Van Buren's question. He calmly defended the motion, "These rules basically codify several precedents already recognized by prior rulings of the court. The committee has worked long and hard on these suggestions, and I believe we owe them due consideration.

"We believe that these amendments will correct the situation we found ourselves in during the Fen Phen scandal. That was a black eye to the court and we can't let that happen again."

He didn't spell out exactly what he meant by this.

Van Buren protested, "We are not bound by the recommendations of any committee!"

Special Justice Smith ignored the unofficial rule that Special Justices should be seen but not heard, interrupted Van Buren and spoke in favor of the amendments.

Justices Collins and Zevely glared at the Special Justice, but he ignored their displeasure. Anderson said, "I move for a vote on the question." Before anyone could protest the Chief Justice raised his hand and voted in favor of adoption. The Chief Justice and his coalition all were recognized in favor of adoption of the rules amendments.

The Chief Justice, announced that the amendments were adopted by the vote of four in favor and three opposed.

Anderson, then moved to adjourn the session. Justices Zevely and Collins protested, but the Chief Justice ignored them and recognized four votes for adjournment, and announced the session was adjourned.

The Chief Justice looked at his gold Rolex and noted that the session had taken only fourteen minutes to radically change the ethics rules of the Supreme Court and to vastly increase his power to regulate the conduct of lawyers and judges.

Within half an hour, the amended rules were formally published in an order signed by the Chief Justice. A press release was promptly e-mailed to the journalists and newspapers and media outlets on the courts media list. At 1:30 p.m. a notice was posted on the Courts web site with the comment that the new rules would be effective immediately.

Chapter Sixteen

As Justice Boone was half-way home from Warsaw, her cell phone rang, and a reporter for the *Courier-Journal* reported the adoption of the new Supreme Court rules, and sought an analysis. She said she had not attended the meeting, as the Chief Justice had assigned her to Gallatin District Court, and she was not aware of the called meeting of the Supreme Court, and she knew nothing of any rules under consideration, but would be glad to comment after she was more informed.

A reporter for the *Herald Leader*, called Justice Boone within minutes, and likewise inquired about the new rules. The reporter added to her knowledge of the situation by asking her to comment on the reason why Nathan Smith had been appointed to take her place at the special meeting.

The news of Nathan Smith being appointed to replace her hit her like Tartarus's mythical bronze anvil falling from the heavens.

As her face reddened in anger, she lost her sense of judicial restraint, and replied, "If Nathan Smith was appointed by the Chief Justice to take my place at this meeting then it was the most unethical power grab by a Chief Justice in the history of the Court! It's totally without precedent and may justify an impeachment inquiry."

By Saturday morning, 500,000 newspapers were delivered on the doorsteps of readers across the state carrying her comments. "*Justice Boone calls for Impeachment of Chief Justice!*" Fifteen television stations carried stories about the special meeting and the allegations of wrong doing by the Chief Justice made by Justice Alice Boone.

By 11:00 a.m., three copies of the news stories quoting Justice Boone had been mailed to the Ministry of Ethics.

On Sunday morning the *Courier-Journal* reported that in an apparent protest a copy of the new rules had been taped to the doors of the Jefferson Hall of Justice in Louisville with the word "SHAME!" written over them in red ink.

Over the next week copies of the new rules had been taped to the doors of court houses in 12 counties.

The Chief Justice was quoted in a news release, "On Friday the Supreme Court adopted several housekeeping rules which merely reflected prior court rulings and which recognized court precedent going back to 2009."

The press release continued, "I am saddened by the intemperate comments of Justice Alice Boone. Her ill considered comments questioning the constitutional authority of the office of Chief Justice were improper. If Justice Boone will take the time to review the Judicial Article of the Kentucky Constitution she will surely modify her unfortunate and ill advised comments which question the integrity of the Judiciary."

Chapter Seventeen

Big Cat Cheshire, followed the growing brouhaha over the following days. He was beside himself in trying to figure out how to use his information to his financial benefit.

He read from his electronic notes the comment by the Governor to his press secretary, "They are ripping out each other's throats, and for once I am enjoying sitting back and watching someone else being eviscerated."

The President of the State Senate was recorded calling the Chief Justice congratulating him on his comments in "standing up to Alice Boone, who was clearly uninformed on the applicable constitutional law."

The Speaker of the House of Representatives, a close friend of Alice Boone, had left a voice mail on Justice Boone's office phone in Salyersville, "Justice, call me if you need to talk."

Cheshire took out a notepad and tried to make a list of possible beneficiaries of his inside knowledge.

"State Prosecutors? No law had been violated, just the traditional rules of the court, and only the court would be interested in that.

Federal Prosecutors? They would love this, but still I don't need anything from them and I don't trust working with them. They might ask how I got my information.

Lawyers? This argument concerned their personal freedom, but most of them would not dare enter the fray if it took them away from adding up their billable hours, or unless someone paid them to get involved.

Judges? Judges earned only a moderate salary by Cheshire's terms, so there was no monetary potential there. Besides they were so tightly controlled by the Chief Justice and the Ministry of Ethics, that they would not get within ten miles of Alice Boone or the CJ.

The Press? They didn't have any money, and no interest in paying for information anyway."

Cheshire realized the beauty of the Chief Justice's power move. He was seizing absolute power over the judiciary and the state's lawyers. This was a masterful plan, and it apparently was based on constitutional law.

Not only had he created a situation where he now had three votes on any issue coming before the court, he could banish any Justice who dissented to service anywhere from Paducah to Pikeville. Since the Supreme Court was the highest court in the State, there was no other court to which his opponents could appeal.

If one of the Justices moved to reconsider the rule amendments, the CJ could just banish that Justice and seek appointment of another pliable Special Justice to assure his four vote majority in the event there was a counterattack implemented to repeal the rules changes. His evaluation of the Chief Justice's ruthlessness factor increased tenfold.

Cheshire continued on his list:

"Chief Justice Hatter? Right now he didn't need any help from Cheshire, and there wasn't any secret information he could use to blackmail the Chief Justice. By acting so publically he had removed himself as a blackmail target."

Chapter Eighteen

By Tuesday the Commissioner of the Ministry of Ethics was considering the problem presented by the complaints filed against Justice Boone. Commissioner Hart called in three of her staff prosecutors and actually sought out their advice.

She explained, "The Rules give initial jurisdiction over the conduct of Judges to the Judicial Conduct Commission. The only times the old Inquiry Commission (which preceded the Ministry of Ethics) intervened with a judge, was after the Judicial Conduct Commission had completed its review and had voted to refer the matter to the Inquiry Commission." She concluded by asking, "How can we justify action against Justice Boone without waiting for the JCC?"

Bunny White, a platinum blond and the most senior of the prosecutors, opined, "The JCC can't disbar a Judge. They can only recommend the removal of a Judge, or Justice from office. That recommendation goes directly to the Supreme Court for approval. However, my reading of the rules convinces me that the Ministry retains the ultimate power to suspend Boone's license to practice law.

"The Rules permit the Judicial Conduct Commission to recommend to us the further sanction of a license suspension or disbarment. I believe this shows that we have the jurisdiction to do this. The provision in the Rules for the Conduct Commission are so vague they don't prevent us from intervening even without a recommendation from the JCC.

Commissioner Hart asked, "Is there anything in the Rules which prevent the Ministry from directly proceeding against the Judge without waiting for the JCC to act?"

White wiggled her nose, as she did when she was nervous, and carefully responded with the answer desired by the Queen, "There is no language in the Supreme Court Rules that strictly forbids the Ministry from going after a judge's law license.

"I have always been an advocate of the so called 'Dattilo Theorem'. Tom Dattilo was a lawyer from Indiana who frequently argued, and sometimes successfully, that "You can do anything not specifically prohibited by the rules."

Bunny White paused and continued, "And there is nothing in the rules that specifically prohibit the Ministry from unilaterally going after a judge's law license. Nothing specifically says we have to wait for permission from the Judicial Conduct Commission."

She paused again before adding, "Since a judge is also an attorney, I see no problem. Just because Alice Boone is a Justice, she is not immune from SCR 3.130 8.2(a)."

The Commissioner asked, "So we can do anything to a judge that we can do to a lawyer. Our only limitation under this interpretation is that we can't directly remove a judge from office, but we can cancel their law license, and by doing so we accomplish the same thing, since they can't serve as a judge without a law license."

White answered, "I agree. Since the rules don't specifically prohibit us from doing that, then we can do that."

Commissioner Hart said, "But appellant judges criticize trial judges all the time and the JCC never does anything about it!"

The Commissioner flashed a smile, something rarely seen by her staff, and gleefully commented, "A Judge criticizing another Judge! If all judges are under our jurisdiction we could justify doubling our staff! I love this Datillo Theorem!" She clapped her hands and said, "Mr. Lizarde engrave an invitation to Alice to be our guest at a Tea Party in her honor."

Several staffers looked at each other in amazement as they realized that the legal question of whether or not the Ministry could bypass the Judicial Conduct Commission had been casually decided on the basis of one Indiana attorney's theory.

This interpretation, if upheld, would grant the Ministry of Ethics the power to remove a judge from office, a power reserved by the Code of Judicial Conduct to the Judicial Conduct Commission. Since a Judge was required to be a licensed attorney, by revoking his license, the Ministry could unseat a judge.

While the staffers questioned this move they knew when to keep quiet. One did not interfere with the Queen of Heart's plans. After the meeting most of the Ministry staffers indicated in tweets to one another that they were going to keep as far away from this case as possible.

Chapter Nineteen

It took all of two days before the report from the Ministry of Ethics found its way to the Chief Justice to inform him that the Ministry had issued an official notice of investigation letter to Justice Boone.

The notice informed Justice Boone that she was being investigated for bringing into question the integrity of the Chief Justice, and for "questioning his qualifications to remain in office."

It took less than an hour for the Chief Justice's secretary to mail a letter to the other members of the Court advising them that Justice Boone, "pursuant to the Rules, was forbidden from approaching any of the other members of the court to discuss the ethics complaint being investigated by the Ministry of Ethics."

The keystrokes on the secretary's computer were forwarded automatically to Big Cat Cheshire. Before Cheshire could decide how to use this information, two Supreme Court law clerks and one Justice, had leaked the news to LawReader, several political blogs and the state's two largest newspapers.

Williston Stafford had received three phone calls, and several e-mails, by noon of the following day. The reports informed him that the Ministry of Ethics had issued a warning letter to Justice Boone. He shook his head in disgust at the leaks.

He spent the afternoon calling the various Eunuchs across the state to discuss the escalation. After he had finished his calls, the Eunuchs had agreed to create a fund raising organization to collect money for the legal expenses of Justice Boone and Jack Kenton. The fund named "Free Speech for Lawyers," was formally set up within two days. Stafford selected non-lawyers to manage the fund to shield them from the jurisdiction of the Ministry.

Stafford then wrote an article which was published on LawReader and shortly e-mailed to thousands of lawyers via their weekly newsletter. Google and four other search engines picked up the story within hours and the article was soon available on every continent on the globe.

The Stafford article didn't mention the names of Justice Boone or of Jack Kenton. It focused on the adoption of new rules of conduct for Kentucky lawyers, which imposed a dress code, a make-up code, a no-smoking rule, and stringent sanctions for questioning the actions of any public official.

The *BBC* headlined the story on their international news under the headline, "Blue Noses in the Blue Grass." Fox News airhead commentators predictably praised the Chief Justice for bringing out of control lawyers under control. *The New York Times* wrote an editorial that supported the right of free speech, "even for lawyers." The editorial questioned whether "someone had put something in the Bourbon made in Kentucky".

Jon Stewart did a skit on his Comedy show in which one of the correspondents wore a sign on his jacket with a six sided star of David and the words "Lawyer—Verboten." The speechless correspondent was wearing duct tape over his mouth and couldn't answer such innocuous questions such as "Are you a lawyer?" All he could do was waive his arms and nod his head.

Within a week, a bar near the Hall of Justice in Lexington, had changed its name from Bubbas to 'The Silent Lawyer' and displayed a sign of a man carrying a brief case with duct tape over his mouth. Another sign inside said, "What's said here stays here."

Throughout the next month, comics and commentators enlarged on the story. Legislators in five Red states introduced legislation calling for the adoption of what became known as the "Kentucky Rule."

A half dozen skits were posted on YouTube. A new Jib Jab cartoon had a character in a blue suit carrying a brief case using sign language to argue his client's case. The Judge in the cartoon and all the bailiffs and attorneys had duct tape over their mouths. The cartoon featured the jockey riding in the Kentucky Derby with duct tape over his mouth, and therefore, unable to urge his mount on to victory.

U.S. Supreme Court Justice Scalia was asked by a law student at a seminar if his originalist legal philosophy found any support for a precedent for the government to limit a lawyers speech under a sedition theory. Scalia announced that he expected that this issue might find its way to his court and he couldn't comment further. Nevertheless he allowed himself to be photographed standing amidst a dozen Yale law students who were all wearing duct tape over their mouths. That picture appeared on the cover of Time Magazine.

Within six weeks the Free Speech for Lawyers Fund had raised $500,000 dollars. The Avon corporation donated $10,000 to the free speech fund and ran an ad in half a dozen women's magazines showing a female judge wearing duct tape, with big red lips painted over the duct tape, with the tag line, "Don't Hide Your Avon."

Altria, the parent company of Phillip Morris Tobacco Company, quietly donated $25,000 to the "Free Speech Fund". They apparently didn't approve the No Smoking rule in the Rabbit Hole plan.

Chapter Twenty

Both Justice Boone and Jack Kenton quickly secured separate legal representation.

Jack Kenton waived the confidentiality of the proceedings against him, but Justice Boone did not exercise that right.

While there were no leaks from the Boone defense team, there were numerous leaks from the Chief Justice and the Ministry of Ethics. No leaks came from Kenton's defense team. There was no doubt by anyone that Justice Boone was under investigation. The newspapers frequently cited unnamed sources naming both Justice Boone and Jack Kenton and gave a running account of both investigations.

Both groups of lawyers received offers for the volunteer services of several major law firms from across the nation.

In June at the state bar convention, lawyers stood at the doors to the Convention Center, and passed out pieces of duct tape which some attorneys wore over their mouths, and others placed on their sleeves. When Chief Justice Hatter took the stage to give his annual update on the Supreme Court, half a dozen of the participants at the back of the room starting hissing. Hissing is an old law school tradition. Such raspberrys are given when a student has given an incorrect answer to a question by the professor.

The "hissing" swelled through the gathering of 1,280 lawyers and became loud enough that the Chief Justice, unable to quiet the derision, cut his speech in half and angrily left the stage before completing his remarks.

The Commissioner of the Ministry of Ethics was not in attendance at the state bar convention, but that practice was not unusual. Her picture had never been posted on the Bar's web site, and her face was seldom recognized when she was in public. She had never sought to form any relationships with members of the bar except official ones.

Her isolation preserved her private life, but left her without a base of allies from which to draw support for the vigorous implementation of her programs, such as her hated dress code and make-up code, and her hated anti-smoking code.

Pursuant to the new Rabbit Hole rules, four of the Ministry's prosecutors had been assigned to monitor the CLE classes to observe lawyers who left the mandatory classes early. The Ministry had posted video cameras at the exits to the conference center and made a record of all lawyers who left early. The video had a time stamp, which allowed the Ministry to determine from the CLE affidavits those miscreants who had later filed affidavits claiming to have attended all sessions of the seminar. The Ministry was testing new software that allowed video tape surveillance of the lawyers and could analyze any suspicious behavior. The software created by Perceptrak would allow all bar members behavior to be predicted so that the Ministry could study the need for what they called, "preventive ethics review".

The four Ministry staffers present at the CLE event, were sleuthing to find attorneys who might be in violation of the various habit and dress codes. They were overwhelmed by the number of violators.

The rules amendments had been successful in silencing public criticism of public officials but private criticism was widespread. It was later determined by the Ministry that the habit and dress codes were being almost completely ignored at the seminar, but compliance around courthouses was much improved.

Six members of the Fayette County Bar Association attended a UK basketball game wearing blue suits and had placed duct tape over their mouths. An ESPN camera man got a clip of the group, and Dick Vitale worked a comment into his description of the loud UK crowd, "Lawyers are usually the loudest people in the room, but not in Kentucky Babe!" Within hours another $55,000 was donated to the lawyers Free Speech Fund.

Throughout the winter and spring it was almost impossible to attend any gathering of lawyers without observing someone wearing a duct tape arm band as a badge of honor.

Administrators of the state's largest law firms quietly ceased enforcing the personal habit codes when they had negative feedback while recruiting new associates.

The Ministry had mailed reporting forms to all the state's trial judges with the warning that the Squeal Rule applied to judges. They were told they should honor their duty to report any violations of the dress code they observed. Seymore Love, a paralegal from the Ministry was assigned to randomly subpoena courtroom video tapes to review compliance with the dress codes across the state.

Williston Stafford was never publically identified as the leader of the Lawyer's Revolution. He was asked on a number of occasions if he was the leader but he always blew off the question with the comment, "A tidal wave needs no leader." Nevertheless, no one doubted that he was the nominal leader of the Lawyer's Revolution.

Chapter Twenty-One

Cheshire continued to gather intelligence on the Lawyer's Revolution. His equipment had picked up a question by a visitor to the office of the Speaker of the House. They asked the Speaker if impeachment of the CJ was being considered. The Speaker did not shoot down the idea. He evasively replied, "In the fullness of time, all things are possible."

The Governor had at first removed himself from the controversy. Even though he was a lawyer, he found no benefit in being a public leader in this fight.

Two of the Governor's aides were picked up on Cheshire's surveillance discussing the matter. One of the aides speculated, "This is clearly a scheme by the CJ to enhance his conservative creds before launching his campaign for the Governorship."

The best information about the so-called Lawyer's Revolution was now being provided by Cheshire's laser mike listening detector which had been placed on a telephone pole at the rear of the grounds of the Ministry of Justice to monitor conversations in Commissioner Hart's office.

There was so much data coming in that Cheshire hired two retired Kentucky State Police detectives to help sort it out. He had not yet found a use for this information, but the data was so interesting that he was compelled by his curiosity to continue his efforts.

His diligence was encouraged in late May when the Commissioner had a conference with the prosecutor assigned to the Kenton investigation. He learned that the prosecutor had been ready since the first week the complaint was given to Commissioner Hart to file the charges with the Board of Scrutiny.

Bill Lizarde summarized the case to the Commissioner, "The case is very simple, we give the Scruntineer's Board a copy of SCR3.130. We introduce a copy of Kenton's letter to the State Ethics Commission. He has already admitted that he authored the letter. The only thing left for the Board of Scrutiny to do is to vote out a charge."

"Have you found anything on the credit investigation," the Commissioner asked.

"Nothing there," the prosecutor responded. "He inherited at least four million dollars from his father, and he is not indebted to any banks. Hell, he owns half interest in a bank! And we can confirm from his state income tax statements that he is doing well in his law practice. The horse farm is one of the few that is in the black."

The Commissioner asked "How did you get access to his state income tax records?"

"Chief, You don't want to know. But I will say that the lawyer at Revenue was a "friend" of ours." She knew that he meant that the lawyer was under investigation by the Ministry, and probably received a favor for his illegal act.

The Commissioner, aware that tax records were highly confidential and were not available even to her office, stepped to the office door to see if anyone could have heard that comment.

"Bill, let's forget that you told me that. It never happened, and you will lose any such information that can be traced back to the Department of Revenue."

When Cheshire read the transcript he nearly wet his pants. This was a major league mistake by the Commissioner of Ethics. "Her office commits a felony by looking at a lawyer's tax records and I have an audio tape of her authorizing the destruction of evidence!"

The Commissioner changed the subject and told the prosecutor, "He has been twisting in the wind for five months. Let's let him twist a little longer. Have you noticed how silent he's been lately?" She fired one of her witticisms at the staff prosecutor, "No whine before its time!"

She made no mention of her desire to delay the investigation long enough to poison Kenton's option of filing for election to the Supreme Court in opposition to Madison Hatter. Since there were no speedy trial obligation imposed on the Ministry, the investigation could be held over Kenton's head indefinitely. They'd had several cases which had been pending for over five years, and one case had been under investigation for nine years.

Lizarde continued the meeting with reports of the criminal check, the immigration check, and other checks they had conducted, "Nothing there, he's clean." he said.

A week later Cheshire got a transcript from Justice Boone's office. She'd held a meeting with two of the lawyers representing her. The attorneys reported on their motion to take the deposition of the Chief Justice.

Boone's lawyers wanted to document any conversations CJ Hatter may have had with the other Justices in his coalition. The Chief Justice had refused to voluntarily attend a deposition. The Chief Justice's staff attorney had filed a motion to dismiss the deposition notice that had been served on him. Being Chief Justice, there was no one who could order the Chief Justice to appear for a deposition where he could be cross-examined. He held sway over the Ministry of Ethics and they were not foolish enough to question his authority.

Boone's lawyers had filed a notice to take Nathan Smith's deposition. Smith filed a motion to quash the notice alleging judicial immunity.

The attorney reported to Boone, "We have asked for a hearing before the Board of Scrutiny to rule on those motions but they have been sitting on them for three months. We can't get them to rule on anything. We filed your response to the Investigation Notice, but things are just in limbo. They won't tell us who made the formal complaint against you, and they won't give us a time table for their proceedings."

Justice Boone gave the lawyers her thoughts about the proceeding. "If the complainant was the Chief Justice he would have to recuse himself from hearing any appeal we might need to make in the future. So he will never be disclosed as the complainant."

Justice Boone continued, "Hatter has great influence in the appointment of the Ministry's Commissioner and he appoints the members of the Board of Scrutiny. He surely found a stand—in stooge to file the complaint. Credit him with the good sense to avoid the mistake of being personally involved. He plans to backstop any complaint issued by the Board of Scrutiny with a Supreme Court stacked to uphold the sanctions against me if I am convicted. And he plans to be able to vote in support of my conviction.

She changed the subject, "Here is where I want you to look."

She pulled out some documents and handed them to the lawyers and said "Check out this docket calendar of upcoming court cases. This could explain their foot dragging. Check and see if Nathan Smith or his firm would benefit from a delay of the Ministry's prosecution."

Cheshire's listening devices could not detect what these documents revealed. "Which cases?" Cheshire mused.

Chapter Twenty-Two

Williston Stafford eyed the pictures of former Presidents of the Idle Hour Country Club on the wall as he walked to the dining room to meet Jack Kenton. The pictures revealed successful businessmen from the Bluegrass who were mainly known to the public as the men who had denied the membership application of Garvice Kincaid, who before his death in 1975, was one of the state's wealthiest men.

All pictures on the wall were white and male. Kincaid had lived across the street from the country club but was intentionally never invited to join the private club made up of Bluegrass Bluebloods.

Stafford found Kenton seated near a window overlooking the eighteenth green. They discussed in hushed tones, the civil disobedience occurring around the state by lawyers who were uncomfortable with the yoke of heavy regulation imposed by the Rabbit Hole rules. After they had finished lunch, Kenton handed Stafford an envelope, and said, "Our friend has been busy."

The note which Stafford, took from the envelope, contained no identification. The message stated briefly:

"HRH exercising discretion to delay reference of Boone and Kenton complaints to the Inquisition Clerk. HRH received complaints without supporting affidavits, but has subsequently secured affidavits. Names of affiants not revealed to staff. HRH waiting for next rotation of Board of Scrutiny hearing subcommittee to advance to next step."

Stafford explained to Kenton, "The full Board of Scrutiny does not hear the complaint, they have rotating panels of three members each. One of the panels is appointed as Chief Inquisitor. It sounds like Hart, and perhaps the CJ, don't trust the current hearing panel that would receive the two complaints. I believe they are waiting till a more favorable panel rotates. We have no idea as to the rotation schedule. It could be days, it could be months."

Kenton asked, "Who is the presiding officer in such a procedure?"

"One of the Board members is appointed to be the hearing officer. He's granted powers that a trial judge would envy. He rules on all evidentiary questions, and is in total control of all procedure. He has the role of a prosecutor and the role of a judge. The procedure is set up to act like a Grand Jury which votes for an indictment. And the hearing officer is appointed by the Chief Justice and is absolutely immune from any civil misdeeds he might commit. In fact, the Commissioner and everyone involved in the prosecution has civil immunity even from unlawful acts they commit."

Stafford, sat back in his leather chair, and shook his head in disgust, "Jack, are you sure you want to do this thing? They are getting ready to crucify you, and if you so much as complain about it, they can do it over and over again until they make their point."

Stafford, after a pause, asked, "Have you thought about apologizing and asking them to call off the hounds?"

Kenton, smiled and answered, "My father would turn over in his grave if I surrendered."

Stafford added, "It's worse than I had imagined. I can't imagine how the deck could be more stacked against you."

Kenton ignoring the obvious said, "If there is one thing I have learned about the practice of law, it's that your enemy always makes at least one mistake, and so will Hart. We just have to be ready for her mistake."

Chapter Twenty-Three

After returning to his office, Williston Stafford, once again researched the procedures for the handling of an Ethics Complaint before the Ministry of Ethics. He made a list of each step in the process through which a complaint travels before a final decision is made by the Supreme Court. He placed the citation of the Supreme Court Rule next to the steps to be taken.

(1) When a complaint of professional misconduct comes to the Ministry of Ethics, the gears of the disciplinary proceedings are set in motion.
(2) The Ministry of Ethics reviews the complaint, has it reduced to a sworn written statement (SCR 3.160) and files it with the Inquisition Clerk.
(3) The Inquisition Clerk (or deputy) notifies the attorney by certified mail, etc. that he is under investigation. He is asked for his or her response, and given a couple of weeks to reply in writing. SCR 3.160.
(4) The Ministry of Ethics prosecutor investigates the complaint and presents the case to the Board of Scrutiny. SCR 3.170.
(5) The Board of Scrutiny consists of nine persons (six attorneys, and three non-attorneys) appointed by the Chief Justice with consent of the Court. The Board of Scrutiny meets in panels of three, with two attorneys and one non-attorney on each panel. SCR 3.140.
(6) The Board of Scrutiny reviews the investigative evidence from the Chief Prosecutor and any response from the accused attorney (Respondent) and determines whether the complaint should be dismissed or a charge filed. SCR 3.170.
(7) If the Board of Scrutiny determines that probable cause exists for a charge to be filed, it drafts the formal charges which are filed with the Inquisition Clerk. SCR 3.190.

(8) The Inquisition Clerk appoints the next available Trial Commissioner to serve as a hearing officer. SCR 3.230. Trial Commissioners are also appointed by the Chief Justice, subject to approval of the Supreme Court. SCR 3.225.
(9) The Trial Commissioner sets the matter for a hearing.
(10) All charges, pleadings, motions, notices, briefs, orders, etc. shall be filed with the Inquisition Clerk. SCR 3.290.
(11) After a hearing, in which he has received evidence, briefs, and oral arguments, the Trial Commissioner must decide the case by a preponderance of the evidence. SCR 3.330.
(12) Upon submission of the case, the Trial Commissioner files a written report with the Inquisition Clerk. SCR 3.360.
(13) The written report sets forth the findings of fact, conclusions of law, whether or not a violation occurred, and if so, the proposed sanction.
(14) Either party may file a timely "Notice of Appeal" with the Inquisition Clerk (SCR 3.365) which transfers jurisdiction to the Board of Governors.
(15) The Board may review the record or grant a de novo hearing. SCR 3.370.
(16) The Board's decision may be appealed to the Supreme Court by either party. SCR 3.370(8). Notices, pleadings, briefs, etc. before the Board are all filed with the Inquisition Clerk and upon filing of the "Notice of Review" of the Board's decision, the record is transferred to the Supreme Court Clerk.
(17) After the parties file briefs, the case is considered submitted to the Supreme Court for a decision. SCR 3.370."

Stafford searched articles on the internet, and determined that the Ministry of Ethics receives about 1,000 complaints a year but only about 100 are actually subjected to complete inquisition review process. Most complaints filed against attorneys are dismissed for lack of cause, as they don't even allege an ethics violation.

Many violations merely express the outrage of a complainant that an opposing attorney said something mean about them, or that their own attorney lost the case. Most charges which actually state valid claims of ethical violations are settled. This leaves only a small fraction of cases of serious attorney misconduct.

Stafford recalled anecdotal comments at the last meeting of the Eunuchs to the effect that the Ministry was now investigating, of their own volition, activities of attorneys who are active in politics. He was unable to find any examples of such activity other than the claim against Jack Kenton.

It was widely believed that anytime a jury awarded a large verdict that someone at the Ministry raised an eyebrow and sought out potential evidence of wrongdoing.

Stafford was aware of the practice of many prosecutors who piled up criminal counts on a defendant, thereby giving the Commonwealth something to use to plea bargain with and to coerce guilty pleas. This practice was mirrored by the Ministry of Ethics prosecutors.

In the plea process used by the Ministry, the defendant attorney admits to some wrong even when he is innocent, and is slapped on the wrist and warned not to repeat the act. This plea negotiation process works due to the power of intimidation. Sometimes threats are made to include other members of a lawyers firm.

Some prosecutors intimidate the defendant attorney by threatening to add additional charges if the plea bargain isn't accepted. The prosecutor who plays the intimidation game gets a high conviction rate and doesn't have to be bothered by all the work necessary to take a complaint through all seventeen steps of the Inquisition process.

The hard nose plea bargain process adopted as a Modus Operandi of the Ministry of Ethics is thought by some to be draconian, considering the complexity of practicing law. It is easy for an attorney to unknowingly commit a violation of one of the often indecipherable and often conflicting ethics rules.

The idea of applying plea bargaining intimidation to free speech issues is a new use of power introduced by the Ministry of Ethics. Understandably, few lawyers have the courage to challenge the Ministry.

Stafford rechecked the number of cases filed before the Ministry of Ethics, and then found the number of attorneys, paralegals and clerks employed by the Ministry. The actual case load of meritorious complaints worked out to a work load per attorney of about 8 to 10 cases a year. When he added in the paralegals, who often did much of the actual work, the case load came down to 4 to 5 cases per year per lawyer/paralegal.

No other legal department in State Government came close to such a small case load per attorney. Stafford was aware of caseloads carried by

Public Defenders who typically handled 300 to 500 cases per year. The Ministry of Ethics was really scraping the bottom of the barrel in trying to justify its existence by filing ethical complaints about what Justice Boone had said, and what Jack Kenton had said. If they were going to monitor everyone's speech they could easily increase their work load statistics to justify their excessive staff.

Each Ministry attorney handles only a few cases a year. "How tough could it be to prove that Jack Kenton wrote a letter?" Stafford asked himself. "How hard could it be to prove that Justice Boone made a comment to the media?"

"Why is there a lengthy prosecution when both defendants admitted the only issue that needed to be proven?"

He sat back in his chair and mused. "The only procedural step left for the Ministry is to argue that the statements made were in violation of the Code of Professional Conduct.

"It's not as if the Ministry was having to uncover hidden funds or solve a mystery. There was no he-said / she-said type of conflicts to be proven or disproven. In both cases the defendants admitted their statements. Yet both of these free speech offenders would be subjected to a 17 step discipline process that would cost them tens of thousands of dollars to defend, unless they admitted their guilt and surrendered their free speech rights."

Stafford compared the workload of Public Advocates. Most of the cases handled by the Public Advocates were serious felonies. The work required to defend a man facing 20 years to life was certainly a more important public interest than the investigation of lawyers who criticized public officials. Those Public Defenders worked their buns off in defending real criminals.

The work of Public Defenders was subject to public view. The work of the attorneys for the Ministry of Ethics was hidden behind faux castle walls. The public and most officials in state government were kept in the dark about the small case loads carried by the Ministry.

Stafford could not recall if a member of the legislature, during consideration of the Judicial Branch budget, had ever inquired about the caseload of Ministry lawyers. He noted that Chief Justices had set the precedent of allocating the funding of judicial offices. Unlike the Executive Branch agencies, the specific budget allocations for each department were determined by the Chief Justice and not by the Legislature.

Once the Legislature approved the total judicial budget request, the Chief Justice had the power to decided which programs received cuts and which programs received increases. If the Chief Justice favored the Ministry of Ethics, it was not likely to face any budget cuts or questions. The Ministry answered to no one but the Chief Justice in budgetary matters.

With the new rules, particularly the adoption of the tax on attorney's fee trust funds, the Chief Justice now had an income source that was unregulated by the legislature.

Before the adoption of the Rabbit Hole Amendments the Ministry received $1,500,000 dollars a year in funding, the largest expenditure of the Bar Association. After the new amendments were adopted, the Ministry's budget would be doubled.

Stafford did some math and concluded that the administrative cost for each of the real cases handled by the Ministry cost came to $15,000. He was shocked by this high cost for handling civil matters.

It was obvious to Stafford, that the CJ was actively building the Ministry of Ethics into his private government by firmly placing his hands around the neck of every lawyer or judge in the Commonwealth.

His assignment of Justice Boone to the Gallatin District Court, to keep her from voting on the adoption of his new rules, demonstrated that even other members of the Supreme Court were not immune to his ambition.

The Senate President and the Speaker of the House both envied the power of the Chief Justice to temporally remove judges who disagreed with him during important votes.

"How nice it would be," the Speaker of the House once said to the Senate President, "If I could order a difficult House member to go sit on the City Council of his home town during an important vote."

If he had resided in any one of the other 49 states, Stafford would have been permitted to write a letter-to-the editor complaining about the Ministry, and the misuse of its expanded authority. In Kentucky, he would be placing his law license at risk if he stood on a soap box and expressed his thoughts about a judge or prosecutor.

Something flashed in Stafford's brain, "There is only one place in which a lawyer could challenge the authority of the Ministry."

He remembered Kenton's comment about "every opponent always makes one mistake." It occurred to him that perhaps the Ministry's mistake was overlooking the Judicial Proceeding Immunity rule. That doctrine protected attorneys and witnesses from punishment for statements they made in a judicial proceeding. The only place that Jack Kenton could openly counter-attack the Ministry and expose the truth of their misdeeds was in a real courtroom. A state courtroom would allow Chief Justice Hatter to influence the final decision. But the Federal Courts provided an alternative route.

Stafford accessed several articles on LawReader.com and found out the jurisdiction of the Federal Court might be available if the issue was framed in a constitutional right such as a violation of the Fourteenth Amendment's requirement of Due Process of Law or the First Amendment Right to Free Speech.

He read one of the articles that indicated that the Federal Courts would restrict such a claim against a state ethics body only to cases which had been completed and had no more access to state appellate relief.

If Kenton filed a Federal lawsuit against the Ministry, his comments about the Ministry would be protected by the Judicial Proceeding Immunity rule. He immediately e-mailed Jack Kenton with that thought and attached the articles he had found on LawReader.com.

Chapter Twenty-Four

Supreme Court Justice Alice Boone stepped off the express elevator to the top floor of the Riverview Center in Covington and was shown by the hostess to the walnut paneled Governor's Room of the Metropolitan Club. Stafford was standing in front of the large picture windows looking at the river traffic on the Ohio River. Visitors could view the Roebling Bridge below them, and could see the nearby Great American Ball Park home to the Cincinnati Reds.

He turned and smiled as the Justice commented, "The Reds are playing the Los Angeles Dodgers."

"So you know your baseball?" he asked. She grinned and said, "Chad Billingsley is pitching today, he is currently 9-4 for the season with a 3.14 ERA."

Stafford was impressed with her knowledge of baseball.

The waiter appeared in the room and served Williston, a 21 year old Glenlivet on the rocks, and a glass of Jackie's Pinot Noir to Justice Boone.

"I may know baseball, but you know the way to a woman's heart, the Justice said as she tipped her glass to Stafford after sipping the delicate red wine that had a hint of cherries.

The waiter left the private dining room and closed the door. The table was large enough to serve 20 people but today served only two.

Stafford pulled out the chair at the head of the table for Justice Boone, then sat to her left so he could continue to view the Ohio River and the Ball Park.

Justice Boone got to the point quickly. "Thanks for meeting me. I want to run something by you. You know I respect your opinion."

Stafford smiled the same smile he made when an automobile salesman told him that he "had a great deal for him on a used car" but he was nevertheless flattered.

The Justice pulled a folder from her Louis Vuitton briefcase and slid it to Stafford. "You have been a critic of the way the Supreme Court Ethics

Rules are written, and I would like you to review some changes that are being discussed. Go ahead and read these. She ordered in her judicial tone that didn't invite a response other than compliance.

The papers she handed him consisted of a three page outline of a proposal to amend the current ethics rules. He nursed the mellow whisky as he digested the outline.

When he finished, he asked, "Do you really think the Board of Governors will ever approve the repeal of the secrecy rules?"

Justice Boone looked him in the eye and stated purposefully, "The Supreme Court adopts the Rules not the Board of Governors."

Her eyes flashed as she continued, "Secrecy is the nuclear fuel of tyranny! The reason the system is in the ditch with the Ministry of Ethics is that they use secrecy to instill fear. The Supreme Court Rules have delegated to the Ministry of Ethics the power to sanction and even disbar any lawyer who criticizes them or their Rules.

"Most of their prosecutions are correctly based. But they shouldn't get a blue ribbon for those cases, we expect them to do *all* their work in a fair manner.

"But occasionally they cross the line and deny due process to those they cite. They have been allowed to hide their overreaching conduct behind the rules regarding secrecy. That secrecy allows them to cover their tracks. To me that pretty well defines tyranny.

"I don't agree with much that Ayn Rand wrote, but I agree with her comment that 'individual rights are not subject to a public vote.' The Ministry of Ethics has been granted the right to determine what rights that lawyers may enjoy. If they like you, you get a pass.

"If they don't like what you do or say, they sprinkle some mushroom dust around the room and 'poof' your rights are deemed an ethics violation and it's off with your head. We should be aware from recent history that when the public believes the government has taken away their First Amendment rights, there are always some crazies who resort to the Second Amendment!"

Stafford was stunned by the passion of her language.

Justice Boone drained her glass, and continued what had become a lecture, "We went wrong in the incremental adoption of Ethics Rules over a period of years. No one really stood back and shot an azimuth to see where those rules were taking us. There is no unified code.

"It used to be that the local Circuit Judge was empowered to issue ethics sanctions against lawyers who acted out. Their ethics inquiries focused on three areas. Did they steal from a client or did they poorly represent a client? Or Did they disrupt the court in an attempt to influence the outcome of a pending case.

"The prosecution of such actions was by the local Commonwealth Attorney. The virtue of that system was that everything had to be done in public. There was maximum transparency. If the judge or prosecutor went too far they could be removed from office at the next election.

"The vice of that system was that a local attorney was often granted more slack than a visiting attorney, and this 'home cooking' was one justification for setting up a system where the Bar Association was solely entrusted with the responsibility for prosecution ethics violations of attorneys."

She asked Stafford for another glass of wine, and when he returned to the room, she continued, "Using the Bar Association to enforce ethics rules has its merit, but they really screwed up the administrative setup to accomplish this. The Board of Governors selects the Bar Counsel. The Bar Counsel is the in-house attorney for the Bar Association. But when the Supreme Court assigned ethics enforcement to the Bar, they added this job to the legal advisor's role played by the Bar Counsel. The Bar Counsel then became the ethics prosecutor.

"They then really screwed up when they allowed all ethics complaints to be shielded by the secrecy or confidentiality rules.

"The Bar thought the secrecy rules would protect the accused lawyer from the embarrassment of having a frivolous complaint filed against them. But then the new Ministry of Ethics learned to use those secrecy rules to hide complaints against their friends, to terrorize their enemies, and to cover their due process violations under Harry Potter's cloak of Invisibility.

"No one took the time to understand the setup they created. The Bar Counsel is supposed to be the legal counsel for the Board of Governors. But as the ethics prosecutor, he is supposed to be monitored by the Board of Governors. The Board of Governors was set up as the reviewing agency for ethics findings of the Board of Scrutiny and the Trial Commissioner.

"Since the Board of Governors is a reviewing body serving an appellate function regarding actions of the Ministry of Ethics, they are required by due process to not be involved in the actual prosecution. This dual role prevents the Bar Counsel from reporting to the Board of Governors the day to day happenings of the Ministry.

"These dual functions imposed on the Ministry are highly inconsistent. As legal advisor the Commissioner of the Ministry is required to tell the Board of Governors everything that is happening in their agency, but when the Commissioner serves as a prosecutor, the secrecy rules forbid the Commissioner to tell her 'employer' anything. Therefore oversight of the actions of the Ministry are virtually impossible.

Justice Boone continued her exposition, "The Board of Governors can't really intervene in ethics prosecutions, it can only review them as an appellate body before dismissing or upholding the findings of the Ministry and the Board of Scrutiny.

"The accused attorney has the right to appeal to the Supreme Court. This is construed to give the defendant attorney two appeals. The second appeal emasculates the first appeal by definition."

Justice Boone added, "the weirdest rule is that the Ministry is supposedly under the administration of the Board of Governors, but if the Board of Governors dismisses a complaint against an attorney, the Ministry can appeal the Board's ruling. Think about that. If the subordinate can appeal over the head of their boss, who really is the boss?

"If the Board of Governors needs legal advice regarding the actions of the Ministry they must rely on the Bar Counsel who runs the Ministry of Ethics to advise them about any claims of wrongdoing. That presents a terrible conflict of interest for the Bar Counsel. The Bar Counsel is hardly a disinterested party when he advises the Board of Governors about the legality of conduct by the Ministry for which he himself is responsible.

"This Gordian Knot of conflict has been covered up by all the institutional secrecy. The Supreme Court has abdicated any direct responsibility for the management of the Bar Counsel or the Board of Scrutiny, in the same manner that Pontius Pilate washed his hands.

"The Board of Governors can fire the Commissioner of the Ministry of Ethics, but can't inquire about their actions during an investigation. Go figure!"

The white coated waiter knocked on the door before he brought in a silver tray with a Cobb salad for Justice Boone and a Club sandwich for Williston Stafford.

As they ate, Williston responded to the lecture, "Justice, you are preaching to the choir!"

The Justice's voice softened as she continued, "I'm about ready to present my amendments to the Supreme Court. I propose that we recognize our duties to the consumers of legal services, and to make all ethics complaints completely transparent.

"If a lawyer gets charged with DUI, its immediately disclosed to the public and printed in the newspaper. I see no reason why a complaint alleging a lawyer has stolen from a client, shouldn't likewise be immediately disclosed to the public. There is no moral or practical justification for ethics investigations to be hidden from the public. After all, the Ethics Rules are for the protection of the public.

"Under my proposal, the legal counsel for the Board of Governors will have only one job. That's to be the legal advisor to the Board of Governors. That will be the Bar Counsel's only function. The Bar Counsel will continue to be subject to being hired and fired by the Board of Governors at will.

"The ethics prosecution role of the Bar Counsel will be assigned to persons not under the influence of the Ministry. The President of the Bar Association will select a prosecutor for each complaint. The prosecutors will not work for the Ministry of Ethics. All prosecutors will have to have the qualifications of a Circuit Judge, which is a minimum requirement of a law license and eight years of legal experience.

"The trial of all ethics complaints will be heard by a panel of three retired judges selected by the Chief Justice with the approval of the Supreme Court."

Justice Boone rested her presentation and focused on the Cobb salad.

Williston Stafford, broke the silence, "Why are you telling me this?"

"Because, you are going to get this passed."

At that moment Joey Votto hit a home run over the center field fence of the Great American Ball Park and $500 worth of fireworks, paid for by the Kroger supermarket chain, exploded into the sky.

The loud noise was a perfect punctuation to Justice Boone's pronouncement assigning Stafford a major role in getting the new rules passed. A large cloud of smoke from the fireworks slowly dissipated over the Ohio River.

"And how am I supposed to do that?" Stafford asked.

"You are going to write an article for the Bar Association Magazine endorsing these rules amendments, and you are going to use some of that money you have collected to publicize the need for these reforms, and you are going to travel to every village and hamlet from the Breaks of the Big Sandy to the Mississippi River to spread the word and to sell the plan.

"You are going to recruit candidates to run against Madison Hatter and his gang. Then you are going to recruit candidates for every vacancy on the Board of Governors."

The color drained from Stafford's face as he sat mute.

"Now," she continued, "the basic work you must do only involves three justices. Use your resources and focus on them. This is a task that I can't do in the way that you can. You and your Eunuchs will know what to do. I have to keep my distance from you. The only legal way we can turn this lost ship around is to use the democratic process. The ballot box is the only legal tool we have."

Williston Stafford knew what it felt like to be 'tethered prey'. He had heard that this term was frequently used by the Commissioner of the Ministry of Ethics to describe those unfortunate attorneys who came before her predatory ethics machine.

He was glad that he was in agreement with Justice Boone because it would have been difficult to refuse her.

Justice Boone rose from her chair signaling the completion of the meeting. She gathered her briefcase and gave Williston a hug.

He walked with her to her car in the lower level parking garage. She thanked him for meeting with her. Before leaving she pulled an envelope from her bag and placed it in his hand before entering her SUV and driving away.

After she was out of sight, he opened the envelope. It contained a piece of paper which was blank except for the names of three Justices of the Supreme Court and the words "FOCUS ON THESE".

Tweedledum turned off the acoustic laser mike that had been aimed at the window of the Governor's Room at the Metropolitan Club. He then encoded the electronic recording and sent it via his Verizon wireless card to the computer in his office in Frankfort.

Before he had arrived back in Frankfort and hour and a half later, Matthew Simons had decoded the recording, and had sent a copy to his home computer to add to his growing list of purloined recordings.

Matt Simons rarely visited Cheshire's office during the day, but today he had good reason. He had finally secured a piece of prized software that he had long sought.

The software would allow his boss's eavesdropping to be expanded from the limits of the laser detectors which could only listen in to fixed locations. If the subject of the surveillance was not accessible to their laser mikes, they subjects of their surveillance were immune to Cheshire's spying. Simons showed Cheshire the disk and the small black box in his hand and explained that the system was called 'Hot Mike'.

The software allowed the user to dial a subject's cell phone and remotely turn on the microphone which each cell phone contains. The microphone picked up any conversations conducted within seven or eight feet of the cell phone. The Hot Mike equipment could turn a subject's microphone on and off at will. It then encrypted any conversations and transmitted them to the listener who could be anywhere in the world. The victim of the system had no indication that his phone had been turned on.

Cheshire was impressed by Simon's new tool and quickly authorized it to be set up after he was assured that the transmitted signals could not be traced. Cheshire called up the address book on his computer and printed out a list of cell phone numbers of twenty-five officials in state government whom he desired to reach out to with the Hot Mike. He gave the list to Simons with directions to enter them into the new system and get back to him as soon as the system was operational and could be tested.

After Cheshire left the office, Simons went to a work station usually occupied by Tweedledee to enter the cell phone numbers in the computer's watch list.

He finished the cup of coffee he had poured into a paper cup, and reached under the desk to pull out the trash can in order to dispose of the cup. On the top of the trash he noticed a handwritten note in Cheshire's unique bold handwriting.

He picked out the note and read a work assignment that Cheshire had made to Tweedledee. "Prepare to monitor all communications to and from the home of Rebecca Kinman to her lawyer **Ward Bourne."**

Both Bourne's office phone number and Kinman's were listed. The note ended with the message, "Bill to Goliath Insurance account."

Simons recognized the name of Rebecca Kinman. She had been one of his teachers in high school. He had read in the paper almost a year ago that she had lost a leg in an automobile crash. Simons did a file search on Tweedledee's computer and found a file named Goliath. He opened it and learned that she had sued Kyota Motors and that Kyota was insured by Goliath. Bourne was listed as her attorney.

Simons had always liked Mrs. Kinman. He quickly installed a worm on Tweedledee's computer directing it to forward all files to his personal computer. The worm would search the computer's files once a day and in seconds forward all new files to Simons.

Chapter Twenty-Five

The Free Speech for Lawyers Fund Board Members met at Williston Stafford's invitation for a luncheon at the Pendennis Club in downtown Louisville on West Muhammad Ali Boulevard. The club has provided a private meeting place for the city's most prosperous businessmen for more than a hundred years. The members were seated at a table in the Grill Room.

The construction of the current club building was overseen in 1927 by Club President Owsley Brown, President of Brown Forman distilleries. The Brown family remains a major force in Louisville politics.

In honor of the famed distiller, Stafford had directed the bartender to serve each of the Board members a shot of Woodford Reserve bourbon with a glass of branch on the side.

The board received a financial report from the treasurer who accounted for donations of $574,510. He noted that donations had been received from thirty-seven different states and from five foreign countries.

The Chairman, then asked Stafford to address the board.

Stafford stood and presented the board his observation that they had two things they could do. First, they should help fund the legal expenses of Justice Boone and Jack Kenton.

"We believe that Justice Boone will need $50,000 for her legal defense since most judges do not maintain malpractice insurance."

He reported that Kenton's malpractice insurance carrier would pay for the first $20,000 of his legal expenses. Therefore he suggested an award to the Kenton defense fund of up to $20,000 in the event the insurance coverage did not take care of the final cost of Kenton's defense.

The board chairman dutifully complied and called for a motion. The $70,000 expenditure was approved.

Stafford continued with his presentation, "The second thing the board can do is to try to prevent this attack on lawyers from continuing, and to seek repeal of the onerous Rabbit Hole rules. Our only legitimate remedy it to take at the ballot box. We need to recruit candidates to run against

Chief Justice Madison Hatter, and Justices Anderson and Wilkerson. If any one of those three are defeated, then there will be a majority of four Justices who can set aside the Rules Amendments and rein in the Ministry of Ethics."

One board member expressed her support for Stafford's suggestion and added, "Let's not overlook the fact that whatever happens, Justice Boone will be damaged by this event, and if she runs again, we should be prepared to support her. You can't expect the public to understand how a judge can be subjected to a claim of an ethic's violation and still deserve to be retained."

Another board member spoke up, "We should let Van Buren and the other Justices who oppose Hatter also benefit from the fund."

The board chairman, suggested a motion to approve Stafford's suggestions and to immediately employ a public relations agency to provide advice on how best to conduct the campaigns. The motion was made, seconded and adopted.

Stafford concluded the meeting with the comment, "In the meantime we should focus our attention on the two justices who are wavering, or at least I believe they may be wavering. We need to educate them on how serious the members of the Bar are about the need to repeal the Rabbit Hole amendments and to rein in the Ministry of Ethics."

Stafford pulled a half dozen envelopes from his folder and handed them out to the named persons. "I have a specific assignment for each of you" he said as he passed the envelopes out.

In celebration of the successful meeting, Stafford ordered another round of Woodford Reserve.

Chapter Twenty-Six

Cheshire sat alone in his office reviewing the weekly intelligence reports prepared for him by the two retired state troopers who were now in his employ. He called them Tweedledee and Tweedledum. They had prepared separate files on the Speaker of the House, the President of the Senate, the Governor, the Chief Justice and Heather Regina Hart.

He began with the file on Chief Justice Madison Hatter. The surveillance revealed comments he made critical of the number of lawyers being graduated by the state's three law schools. He had told another Justice of the Supreme Court, "They are graduating 450 to 500 lawyers a year, and that's far too many.

"We can't close any law schools, because they all have their own constituency. They would never allow such a bill to be passed by the legislature. In 1970 there were only 3,000 lawyers in Kentucky and now there are over 17,000. Lawyers are being bred faster than rabbits.

"We only have a need for maybe 10,000 lawyers. We never should have exceeded that level. More than that and half of them are starving to death and have to panhandle for clients. While we can't close the law school breeding barns, we can sure as hell lift some law licenses and let them go sell insurance, teach school or work on their daddy's tobacco farm. In the end they will benefit from this and the lawyers remaining will be able to make a decent living.

"At the very least we must achieve some equilibrium and have as many lawyers leaving the profession as are entering it. This will leave us with a Bar which is lean and mean."

Cheshire realized that the Rabbit Hole Amendments the CJ had pushed through had created dozens of new grounds for the disbarment of attorneys. The news that he was advocating the disbarment of thousands of lawyers would explain his excessive funding for the Ministry of Justice. If they graduated 450 new lawyers a year, and if only a 100 or so lawyers were retiring or dying off annually, then Hatter needed to disbar 400 lawyers a year just to curtail future growth.

If he disbarred 1,000 lawyers a year, then in four years he would come close to reaching his goal of only having 10,000 licensed lawyers chasing dollars.

Another report on Chief Justice Hatter was a phone conversation with Heather Hart. She gave him an update on the video tapes made at the bar convention where he had been hissed by some of the lawyers. "We have identified ten lawyers who were clearly hissing while you spoke. There were two dozen who left the seminar early but filed CLE reports reporting they had added the full day of lectures. We have also identified over 100 lawyers who were not wearing suits to the convention. We have issued unofficial warning notices to those attorneys who we were able to identify."

The Chief Justice commented, "I don't suggest that you pursue the dress code and hissing violations too actively, just scare them and let them know we are watching, and keep it discrete. At this time, I don't want a public discussion of this as it might reflect negatively on the Court.

"Just keep them on the meat hook for at least a year or two, and that will silence them. As long as you have them tied up they will be as silent as church mice. But the ones who violated the CLE reporting requirements, should be vigorously pursued. And go for permanent suspensions!"

Commissioner Hart continued, "We have reports of five judges who were seen smoking in their offices, and about seventy lawyers who were videotaped smoking on courthouse grounds."

The Chief Justice gave his blessing to the project with a curt, "Burn them!"

Commissioner Hart replied, "We are on that!" Our Perceptrak software has been field tested at oral arguments held by the Supreme Court last month. We have found a 72% ability to predict a Justice's vote on a pending case. If you wish we can continue this monitoring and provide you with a monthly report on each Justice."

Hatter responded, "Great. I would like that, but I want it delivered to me personally at my home. Never send it to the court. I want it placed only in my hands. Is that clear?"

"Yes sir, I understand."

Cheshire, after reviewing a recording of the conversation, made a note to check with Matt Simons about the Perceptrak software, that sounded useful.

The next report was a request from Commissioner Hart. "Have you thought any more about my request for approval of an investigative branch for the Ministry? Back in 2005 Attorney General Stumbo created a similar investigative branch for the Attorney General's Office. He called it the Kentucky Bureau of Investigation. His successor Jack Conway changed the name to The Department of Criminal Investigations (DCI). At the present we are severely handicapped in our ability to find ethics offenders. By relying only on the squeal rule and after the fact reports, we are unable to do any preventive ethics work. I believe we could be far more pro active if we had our own detectives.

"I would propose calling it the Bar Association Bureau of Ethics Law. (BABEL). It would certainly get minds right if we could lead attorneys from their offices for a perp walk."

"Regina, I know the idea of a perp walk would be effective, but we can't actually arrest someone for an ethics violation. You could send the detectives into courtrooms or their country club and have them personally served with their warning letter. Your men could flash their badges and embarrass the hell out of them."

Commissioner Hart interjected, "Sir I think you miss the point. With an investigative department who are sworn peace officers, we can investigate criminal acts by lawyers. We would no longer be limited just to ethics violations.

"For example in the Fen Phen case, just think how much more effective it would have been if those lawyers had been arrested by the Ministry under your direction.

We could then have turned them over to the Justice Department for prosecution. This would have avoided the black eye that the court received in that disaster. If we are to adequately enforce the mandatory IOLTA tax on lawyer's trust accounts, we need to be able to investigate lawyers banking practices."

The Commissioner added, "You have the authority to hire additional staff and assign them to the Ministry as Bailiffs. I would like to start out with five bailiffs. Section 110-4-b of the Constitution allows you to 'hire such administrative assistants as you deem necessary'. Call them 'administrative assistants' or call them 'bailiffs', it doesn't matter."

Chief Justice Hatter ended with a comment, "I like this, but I don't think I can fund it until next year. I really don't see the need for that many investigators when we only have about one or two criminal complaints actually filed against lawyers. They are a pretty law abiding group. Study this further and keep in touch."

The report regarding the two legislative leaders only concerned upcoming bookkeeping legislation regarding the courts and was of little interest to Cheshire.

The report on the Governor was more interesting. A cell phone microphone had picked up a Hot Mike conversation the Governor had with Justice Alice Boone. Thankfully the Governor faithfully carried his Blackberry with him at all times. The Governor and Justice Boone discussed the Chief Justice. The Governor wanted to understand what Hatter was up to with his Rabbit Hole amendments.

The Governor said, "I couldn't believe he assigned you to the Gallatin District Court so he could ram through his Rabbit Hole Amendments. That was beyond the pale."

The Governor explained his actions in making the two appointments. "The Chief Justice never mentioned that he had created the two vacancies on the court by assigning you and Justice Allgood to other duty. I was negligent in not inquiring about that, but nothing like this has ever happened to put me on notice. I apologize to you and Justice Allgood. But all I had before me was a certification of two vacancies and a constitutional duty to fill the vacancies. Everything appeared above board. I won't soon forget this little trick by Hatter!"

Justice Boone said, "It has certainly placed a dark cloud over the whole court. I would not be the least bit surprised if there isn't some kind of payback in the works. Smith's law firm represents a lot of insurance companies and they almost always have something on the appellate docket."

"Alice do me a favor. Keep me informed if Hatter pulls another trick like this one."

He gave her a business card which his private cell phone number, and reminded her emphatically, "Call me immediately if the CJ appears like he might try to reassign a Justice."

Chapter Twenty-Seven

Jack Kenton had been looking forward to dinner with his son Edward, and daughter Carroll at the family residence at Kenton Farms. It had taken a half dozen phone calls to arrange this infrequent reunion. While he had a close relationship with his children, and they with each other, they seemed to rarely be able to visit him at the same time. He was resigned to the realization that when he was their age he had also been lax in spending time with his father. This was an oversight he now regretted. There was hardly a day that went by that he didn't think of an issue he would have liked to discuss with his deceased father. While they disagreed on many issues, his father's advice could always be trusted.

The only other guests were Williston Stafford and his wife Edith. They were considered family.

After dinner they retired to the Trophy Room. In this room the many silver plaques and gold trophies earned by thoroughbreds raised at Kenton Farms were displayed.

A fire in the massive stone fireplace warmed the room. A picture window overlooked a large pond which was covered with a thin layer of ice. Kenton opened an ancient bottle of single malt for the men, and poured each two fingers of straight heaven. Carol requested a glass of Chardonnay as did Edith. The group sat around the fireplace in four leather club chairs and discussed the current crop of horses being trained at Kenton Farms.

Edward, having been warmed by the Scotch, interrupted the small talk and asked his father about the ethics investigation being advanced by the Ministry of Ethics.

"Why did you take on those people Dad? Didn't you know that they would strike back?"

Williston was surprised but delighted by the question. He suppressed a smile as he and the two Kenton offspring looked at him in anticipation of his response.

Jack paused as he sipped the Scotch, and looking into the depths of the roaring fire said, "At my age one begins to review his life and to measure his accomplishments and his failures. I have been blessed with two wonderful children, a lovely wife, God bless her soul, an inheritance from your grandfather which gave me this farm, and success in my practice of law.

"I have been privileged, perhaps too privileged. Life has been easy for me as compared to many others. One who is so fortunate should ask himself what has he done to pay back all the good things he has enjoyed. Losing your mother was a great loss, but I weigh that against the two wonderful children she left me. I had many good years with her."

He paused as he took another sip of whisky.

"I have thought about the question you ask. What I did was a reaction to who I am. We all become a part of what has inspired us over the years. From your Grandfather, I learned that you had to work hard to achieve anything worthwhile. He believed that a man's word was his bond. While that phrase is often used, your Grandfather really believed it and lived it.

"He also beat into my head the responsibility we have to look after our family, our employees and our community. I think I have inherited that, and I'm sure that both of you have the same inspiration.

"When I was just out of college your Grandfather helped me to score a summer internship with Congressman Stubblefield in his Washington office. That was 1963.

"During that summer I got to participate in the White House Summer Internship program for college students who were in Washington. We attended joint sessions of Congress and attended speeches by Senators, Ambassadors and Justices of the Supreme Court. I once saw Attorney General Bobby Kennedy drive by the Longworth Office Building in a beat up Ford Falcon convertible with his hair flying in the wind. I saw Everett Dirkson, Sargent Shriver, Robert McNamara, Gerald Ford, Lyndon Johnson and other luminaries as I roved around Capitol Hill.

"I saw many other high officials and political stars that summer. The lesson I learned from that was that they were human just as I was. They were within arms reach literally.

But the highlight of the summer was a invitation given to about 1,000 students to attend a speech by President John F. Kennedy on the south lawn of the White House. I remember that day like it was yesterday. It was a hot sunny August day.

"It's hard to explain a time like 1963, the world was quite different then. My generation had seen the election of a young President who was handsome, rich, and literate. He had written books, had attended Harvard, and had a beautiful wife. We all wanted to be like Jack Kennedy.

"He had told my generation on many occasions that we were special, that we would run this country some day, and that we had a obligation to serve our country. Harper Lee's book To *Kill a Mockingbird* was made into a movie in 1960, the same year that Kennedy was elected president. The tone of that book fit in nicely with Kennedy's concept of duty and social fairness. Every lawyer should see that movie.

"On that day, I believe it was in early August, they had erected a platform on the south lawn of the White House. I heard the Marine Band play 'Ruffles and Flourishes' and then as JFK walked out on the platform, they played 'Hail to The Chief'. I still feel chills on the back of my neck when I think of that moment.

"Kennedy's hair was almost red. His skin was far more weathered then I have ever seen in any pictures of him. He had a million watt smile that said 'I'm loving this, and I'm really glad you are here with me'. He quoted Bismark, Shakesphere and Burns. His message was to tell us that the responsibility for running the country was a responsibility we all bore. He pointed out that there was no higher calling than public service.

"After the speech we were given a tour of the White House. Among the college students present were Republicans as well as Democrats. Even Republicans were won over by Kennedy.

"Three months later, when I was in law school, he was assassinated in Dallas. I was sitting in a Constitutional Law class taught by Professor Thompson, when someone opened the class room door and shouted, "The President has been shot!"

"The only sense we could make out of the comment was that the President of the University had been shot. Upon leaving the classroom I heard a radio on someone's office desk, and ran over to hear the announcer say that President Kennedy was dead.

"When I graduated from law school at the University of Kentucky, I took a year off and worked on Capitol Hill before going to law school. The glamour of Washington had dimmed after Kennedy's death.

"The country took an even darker turn as the war in Viet Nam took more and more lives of my generation.

"In April of1968 they killed Martin Luther King, and in June they killed Bobby Kennedy. In May 1970 the National Guard killed four students at Kent State, and my generation took the massacre as a message that our government was more than willing to kill us if we disagreed with it.

"JFK told us that our generation was a force to be reckoned with. Sometimes that promise seemed in doubt in the dark years that followed his death. His call for us to dedicate ourselves to public service was a message that my generation took to heart. I wasn't the only one inspired by Kennedy and his words. My whole generation was inspired. We really believed we could make a difference.

"They had killed our Prince but they could not kill the dream. I worry sometimes that your generation has no such heroes."

He looked at Williston and saw a moistness in his eyes. They looked at each other in mutual understanding.

"After law school I had to build a practice. I met your mother and soon you two came along. I served a couple of terms in the State Senate, but just enough to enhance my resume without besmirching my reputation too badly.

"There were some thoughts of higher office, in those years, but the stars just never aligned correctly. I often wonder if I should have tried harder.

"I guess I credit JFK for the idea that government must serve the public. I surely got from him the idea that we all have a responsibility to serve our country in some way. The practice of law seemed to be the place for me.

"Every once in a while you get a case where someone is getting screwed over by the system, and you intervene and see that justice is applied. When that happens, I get a little bit of the old excitement I got when I was at the White House listening to JFK.

"I no longer have a vote in the legislature but I do have a pen. When I saw what the Legislative Ethics Commission was doing, I wrote my letter. I didn't have to think about it, and I certainly don't regret it. When they bend the rules they are corrupting the Kennedy dream and they will always get away with this kind of thing if no one speaks up in protest.

"Government shouldn't be used merely to protect the powerful. What these people are doing is wrong, and perhaps I was foolish to think that I could make a difference. I wasn't trying to advance any interest on my part. There is nothing I can gain from this but the knowledge that I still believe the dream and in some small way have kept the faith. This was a small act on my part, but I can't tell you how satisfying it was to me, no matter what the outcome happens to be.

"I'm not the only one in this fight. There's Williston and any number of others.

"Bobby Kennedy used to quote Dante. He said that the hottest places in hell are reserved for those who remain neutral in times of moral crisis. I am fortunate that I don't have to remain neutral."

Williston placed another log on the fire. Carroll came to her father's chair in front of the roaring fire. She sat on the floor and laid her head against his knee, as the rejuvenated fire warmed the room.

Chapter Twenty-Eight

Commissioner Hart entered the weekly Monday morning staff meeting in the ornate conference room of the Ministry of Ethics. Walter Walrus, the newest hire and therefore the designated flunky, marched behind her carrying the tall latte' he had purchased at her direction, and for which he would not be compensated. Walrus placed the latte' next to the Queen, and placed three napkins (never more, never less) alongside the steaming caffeine he had reheated for 46 seconds on the office microwave as directed.

"White," the Queen barked, "Begin!"

Bunny White gave her weekly report consisting of statistics regarding the number of cases pending.

"We have five cases which have been pending for four years, ten cases which have been pending for three years, fifteen which have been pending for two years, and one hundred twelve which have been pending for more than a year.

"We have seventy-one new cases in which investigation letters have been served this week.

"Since the adoption of the Rabbit Hole amendments we have increased our case load by 300%, and now have 320 investigations underway."

White, then broke down the type of cases that were pending.

"We have one hundred fifteen cases involving dress code violations, seventy two cases involving smoking (five of those by judges), thirty eight cases involving criticism of prosecutors, judges, and administrative law judges in violation of SCR 3.130-(8.2), (Seventy nine of those cases involved criticism of the Ministry), 52 cases involving questionable CLE certifications (Forty nine of those were confirmed by our monitoring of the state convention), ten cases involving failure to pay dues, three cases involving failure to maintain required CLE hours, three cases involving fee disputes, twelve cases where attorneys failed to communicate with their clients, three cases involving theft of client funds, one case involving false statements made to trial judges, one case involving conviction of a felony, five cases involving past domestic violence claims, four cases involving misdemeanor conviction of a lawyer, (one is a DUI and three are traffic offenses), we have no cases involving felonies by attorneys, and fifty three cases involving improper decisions by trial judges."

White continued her detailed report, "We have thirty six complaints pending for violations of the Squeal Rule. Over the next three months these numbers should increase as we now are making inquiries, whenever we receive a complaint, about others close to the offending attorney, who might have known of his improper conduct and yet failed to comply with their duty to report the violation.

"Our early experience indicates that there may be as many as three or four attorneys who are aware of an offending attorneys bad conduct, and did not report the violation themselves in violation of the new Squeal Rule adopted by the Supreme Court in 2009.

"One of the side effects of the Squeal Rule is that those close to an offending attorney will be less likely to come forward and provide a defense for him, since this may subject them to sanctions under this rule."

The Queen smiled at that observation.

Bunny White then detailed the statistics on closed cases.

"In the last week we disposed of 35 cases by pleas, and 2 cases by final decision of the Board of Scrutiny. We have dismissed 27 complaints which did not state a violation, most of which were totally indecipherable. Eleven cases are pending in the Supreme Court."

The Queen reviewed her copy of the weekly report, and commented, "At this rate we will not reach our goal of 1,000 pending cases for another four or five months. That is unsatisfactory!"

The room was silent as she continued, "I want you all to review those twenty seven dismissed cases. We will not reach our target goals if you are careless in dismissing so many complaints. From now on, no cases will be dismissed until I personally sign off on them. I want a written justification for any recommendation for a dismissal.

"I want you all to understand, that the Chief Justice has announced a goal of reducing the number of lawyers by 38% within ten years. The budget for the Ministry of Ethics has increased from $1.5 million dollars in 2010, to $3 million dollars in the current year.

"We have to justify that increase by providing Chief Justice Hatter with at least five hundred suspensions a year. We are not even beginning to achieve that goal."

The Queen, sipped her scalding latte' and continued, "If any of you are not up to this, raise your hand!"

No hands were raised.

She further warned, "Your beginning salary is now equal to that of a District Judge. If any of you want to test the market for your skills, then have at it. I won't tolerate any slackers. I have gone to bat for you, and it's time we see some appreciation from you."

"White," she continued, "Do you have the individual caseload reports on each staff attorney?"

Bunny White called to her secretary Sandra to bring in the reports which were always placed in a black envelope.

The Commissioner made a small drama at her weekly meetings of having all negative observations she had made about staffers, placed in the hated black envelopes. They all knew that it was not a good thing to have your name placed on such an envelope.

Sandra shortly entered the conference room and handed Bunny the envelopes. Every male attorney in the room was momentarily distracted as they noticed the tight low-cut yellow sweater that Sandra was wearing. As soon as she left the room, they again focused on the potential bad news that might be in the Black Envelope delivered by the well endowed secretary. The Queen noticed their distraction and sighed in hopeless contempt. She expressed her negative thoughts about her male staffers, "Men are idiots, you are standing on the gallows and you are distracted by a tight sweater!"

The Commissioner reviewed the report for five minutes, but it seemed like an hour on the rack for the assembled attorneys.

"Turtle," she began in a low voice, "You disappoint me."

"Hare," "Disgusting."

"Seymore, Do you like your work here?"

Seymore Love did not reply until the Commissioner raised her eyes from the report and looked directly at him. "Yes, Commissioner!" he shouted as if the Commissioner was Chef Gordon Ramsey on Hell's Kitchen.

The Queen went down the list and made a derogatory comment to everyone except for Salamander Samuels.

"Salamander, You seem to be specializing in finding trial judges who make improper decisions. You will go far. That is ripe ground."

The Queen laid the reports on the table, and in a low voice addressed the staff.

"In case you don't understand we need one hundred suspensions a month. The Bible says that he who is without sin should cast the first stone. Well, we are without sin and it is okay for us to throw stones. So let's get on it!"

She paused and put on her best motherly face. Then in her best Valley Girl cheerleader voice asked loudly, "How many suspensions do we need a month?"

The staff replied in unison, "One hundred Commissioner!!"

"I can't hear you!" The staff in unison replied loudly, "One hundred Commissioner!"

She concluded the meeting by stating, "These reports are unacceptable. We'll have another meeting next Monday, and I want to see some results or heads will roll."

The Commissioner motioned for White to stay while the other staff members were dismissed.

"As I understand your report, the Squeal Rule might be a way to multiply the number of citations?"

White nodded her head in the affirmative, and said as she pulled a note from her file, "No question about it. The Squeal Rule, SCR 3.130(8.3), reads: "(a) A lawyer who knows that another lawyer has committed a violation of the Rules of Professional Conduct that raises a substantial question as to the lawyer's honesty, trustworthiness or fitness as a lawyer in other respects, shall inform the Association's Ministry of Ethics.

She went on, "As we read this, the Ministry gets to determine the existence of sufficient facts to bring a charge. We believe it's a factual question as to whether any violation 'raises a substantial question as to a lawyer's honesty, trustworthiness or fitness'.

That is worded so broadly, that we can nail almost anyone."

"I like that," the Commissioner responded, "we could quickly turn three hundred complaints into one thousand complaints with a little footwork and a little creativity. I will issue a directive to the staff, to implement this new rule and to work it hard."

"One other thing Bunny, the Chief Justice says he is considering our request for funding for up to three new bailiffs. With that thought in mind, I have come up with a design for their uniforms, and I believe uniforms are essential to show the public and the bar who they are dealing with, when we serve papers on attorneys."

Commissioner Hart, pushed an artist's rending of the proposed uniform for the new Ministry of Ethics bailiff uniforms in front of White.

Bunny White suppressed a gasp as she recognized that the black plastic shako hats with a black feather plume and white tunics covered with brass buttons, were identical to the uniforms designed by Nixon's chief henchman, H.R. Halderman on orders from President Nixon.

Halderman's uniforms for the White House Police Force were announced in 1970. They were never actually worn by the White House Police as the entire nation had a good laugh at the ridiculous uniforms. The plan was quickly cancelled. The uniforms ended up being donated to an appreciative high school in Utah for their marching band.

White wanted to say that the uniform design looked like those worn by Austrian police in the 1800's, but she knew her place, and responded, "Delightful, really spiffy!!"

Chapter Twenty-Nine

Chief Justice Hatter rose from his chair as Yuvonne Rhodes, his Executive Assistant entered his office suite in the Capitol building. "Did you bring your report?"

Yuvonne tossed her long blond hair over her shoulder as she pulled out her report and began.

"As you are well aware the Rabbit Hole plan adopted last year contained fourteen provisions recommended by Commissioner Hart. Several of those suggestions were not adopted as they cannot be adopted by an amendment of Supreme Court Rules. One suggested requires a constitutional amendment, and several probably require legislative action.

"The proposal to extend absolute immunity to all actions of a prosecutor could face a court challenge due to its conflict with the jural doctrine. Civil law suits against prosecutors were allowed before the adoption of the current Kentucky Constitution which was adopted in 1892.

"There is a legitimate legal question as to whether or not the Supreme Court can use a Supreme Court Rule to overrule a long standing doctrine of the common law. That appears to be a problem area that may be raised by someone in the future. I recommend that the best way to impose this new rule is to do so in the framework of a real case being heard on appeal.

"As good fortune would have it, a Fayette County case, involving the Commonwealth Attorney, has finally been decided by the Court of Appeals. That court upheld the current law, and denied absolute immunity extension to the investigatory phase of the prosecutor's work.

"The Commonwealth Attorney has requested discretionary review, so if the Court agrees to hear that appeal, you will be able to reconsider the current law. I believe that if this case is fast tracked we can get it to the full court for consideration in less than six months."

The Chief Justice chuckled as he commented to his assistant, "The Queen of Hearts feels that as a prosecutor, she needs this added protection if she is going to reach our goal of 100 suspensions a month. In any event, draft an order accepting discretionary review, and advance it for the earliest consideration."

"Consider it done!", Yuvonne made a note of this assignment on her legal pad before continuing.

"Item number two concerns the Commissioner's suggestion that the Court issue a ruling that any prosecutor is immune from criminal prosecution for official acts. We are stuck on this one as it will take either an act of the legislature or a court decision to implement this rule.

Yuvonne leaned forward. "There is just no jurisdiction for the Court to ignore a criminal statute that was meant to apply to regular citizens. We have found no justification for creating immunity for anyone from criminal prosecution short of an act of the legislature. Even legislative action on this remains questionable.

"We tried to get the legislature to adopt a new statute on this topic, and got as far as getting the bill introduced in the Senate. The House Judiciary Committee Chairman refused to bring it up for a vote.

"The Chairman of the Senate Judiciary Committee, Bull Dog Louden, called me and told me in no uncertain terms that it was dead and would never be allowed to be voted on by the full Senate. He said if we would send him a bill that said that legislators couldn't be convicted for criminal acts, he might change his mind."

The Chief Justice mumbled, "I never liked that SOB."

Yuvonne continued, "We have no cases pending where a prosecutor has been criminally prosecuted so it isn't likely to come up for consideration by the court." The Chief Justice surrendered, "This one is kind of dangerous anyway, so let's just put it at the bottom of the list."

Yuvonne's tone of voice became more upbeat, "Since the old court made participation in IOLTA mandatory, and the Rabbit Hole amendments assigned 10% of the interest collected on client funds deposited with members of the bar, we have collected a lot more than anyone anticipated.

"The new amendment requires that those funds be awarded to the Ministry of Ethics. We have collected over a quarter of a million dollars for the Ministry."

She produced an order, "You just need to put your John Henry on this order and we can distribute the funds to the Ministry of Ethics."

The Chief Justice was obviously delighted, "Draft an order authorizing the Ministry of Ethics to hire five bailiffs. Call the Queen and tell her to send me some names."

Yuvonne went to the next topic, "The Rabbit Hole amendment that requires attorneys to report monthly on how much money they are holding for their clients has certainly surprised me. I don't believe anyone thought that attorneys were holding that much client money in trust."

Yuvonne regressed, "Forgive me for asking, but what in the devil does the Ministry need with bailiffs?"

Hatter smiled broadly, "Give the Queen credit. She is going to use them to serve ethics complaint notices on attorneys. Back in 1986 the court ordered the arrest of an attorney for contempt. The case was the Conley case, (709 S.W.2d 434 (Ky., 1986). Nothing gets their attention like ninety days in the Franklin County jail. I suppose the Queen could use the bailiffs to serve contempt orders and haul the attorneys off to jail. This will be great public relations!

"Commissioner Hart believes, and she is absolutely correct, that when an attorney is confronted at motion day in his local Circuit Court with a uniformed bailiff serving him the official notice of an ethics investigation, he will soil his linens and everyone in the courtroom will be on notice not to mess with us."

His toothy smile became a loud laugh, "She even has designed come crackpot dress uniform with feathers and brass buttons so everyone will know who the bailiff represents."

Yuvonne had seen the uniform and was not impressed, nevertheless she forced a smile.

She continued with her report, "The provision of the Rabbit Hole amendments limiting the exclusive jurisdiction of the Judicial Conduct Commission to sanction judges, was not protested by the JCC. While there was talk of litigation, nothing ever came from that. You told me that they were spineless and you would take care of that and I guess you have indeed solved that problem."

The Chief Justice did not respond other to motion with his hand for her to continue. He didn't like the Judicial Conduct Commission as he had no control over it. The members of the JCC were mostly elected by other judges or appointed by the Governor. They owed little loyalty to the Chief Justice.

Yuvonne dutifully plowed down her list, "The amendment that requires attorneys to be licensed to practice ethics cases before the Ministry also required that they attend special classes to qualify for a license to practice such cases. We had the AOC conduct training classes, and the forty nine attorneys who signed up and attended will graduate next week. The Ministry of Ethics had all their attorneys attend, and there were thirty four private attorneys who attended. They have asked you to speak at their graduation ceremony next Wednesday and to deliver their licenses."

She handled the Chief Justice the forty nine licenses for his signature. As he began to sign them he nodded his head and said, "Good, I will be glad to speak to them."

She returned to her report, "The program to require all attorneys to file annual reports stating any ethics violations they suspected was a rousing success. The deadline was last Friday.

"The Clerk of the Supreme Court says that they received over l5,111 reports. About 13,000 reported no ethics violations and the other two thousand or so, reported a total of 3251 potential counts of violations of ethics rules. That means that about two thousand attorneys didn't file a report.

"They will be contacted shortly with a warning letter. The Commissioner will have about 3200 new investigations, since the new rule makes failure to report an ethics violation itself a violation."

"Damn, that's a lot of investigations! I expect the Queen will be asking for more money to hire more lackeys."

Every word spoken during the meeting was accurately recorded via Yuvonne Rhode's cell phone microphone which had been switched on by Big Cat Cheshire's henchmen Tweedledee and Tweedledum.

The eavesdropping of the Chief Justice's meeting with his secretary was delivered to Matt Simons and he fed the audio obtained in the eavesdropping into a software program converted it digitally into a typed report that was sealed and later placed in a locked drawer in Cheshire's desk awaiting his review.

Before completely erasing the report from his computer, Simons e-mailed a copy of the report to himself. His home computer's hard drive was full of similar reports which he was saving for a rainy day.

Chapter Thirty

Matt Simons was a tall lanky former submariner. He had served on a nuclear submarine after being trained as an electronic technician. The work he did for Cheshire was simple compared to the crypto work he did for the Navy.

He was aware that eavesdropping was highly illegal, but he comforted himself with the thought that he just set up the equipment, and as far as anyone in Cheshire's employ knew, he left the actual eavesdropping to others. He had envisioned that this would be his defense to the FBI in the event Cheshire was ever caught.

He had long realized that the information he was handling for Big Cat Cheshire might have great value to the right people. He had concluded that Cheshire wasn't paying him enough when Cheshire appeared at the office one day driving a new Bentley Azure T convertible. He looked up the value of the car on the internet and was stunned to see that the price exceeded $400,000.

He rapidly concluded that $400,000 exceeded ten years of his salary and then some. He roughly calculated that if you financed such a car the monthly payment would exceed $10,000 a month. "You didn't get that type of car loan from the state employees credit union!"

Cheshire's method of financing his ill gotten gain presented an opportunity for Simons to *Carpe Diem.* Simons had spent many evenings sitting in his one bedroom garden apartment on the north side of Frankfort, trying to rough out a plan for turning his information into cash.

It was easy to deliver the information by the internet, but it was much more difficult to collect the money paid by the purchaser. He concluded that he would have to study how to have money wired out of the country, and then wired back. Such a method he concluded was the best way to hide his money trail and to conceal his identity. That was something they hadn't taught him in the Navy.

Simons spent several weeks surfing the internet until he came up with a plan. Within ten days Simons had a forged social security card, an Arizona driver's license, and a green card to boot.

Simons had easily obtained a new identity, and had devised a method to safely receive the money he hoped to earn by selling the eavesdropping material. He was beginning to believe that he might be able to pull this off.

Now all he needed was to find some marketable intelligence to steal from his boss. Then he would need to find a deep pocket buyer for his stolen eavesdropping library.

Chapter Thirty-One

Chief Justice Madison Hatter seldom gave press interviews but after having been booed and hissed at the CLE event in Louisville, and tired of being made to look like a buffoon for his passage of the Rabbit Hole amendments, he finally concluded it was time to publically justify and defend his position.

When he learned that Williston Stafford's group had raised over half a million dollars, and reportedly planned to use it to finance candidates to challenge the Justices who voted for the amendments, he knew the game was on and action was required.

His press officer had called Sherrill "Scoop" Wayne of the *Louisville Courier-Journal* and arranged the meeting in Office of the Chief Justice on the second floor of the Capitol building.

Scoop began the interview with a hard ball. "Justice, What do you say to your critics who claim you have abused your constitutional duties by passage of the Rabbit Hole amendments which are being used to disbar and sanction attorneys at an unprecedented level.

"They say your dress code rule, the no-smoking rule, the new control over client security funds, and the requirement for annual reports under the squeal rule, have interfered with the constitutional rights of bar members."

The Justice had anticipated the question, and hit it out of the ballpark. "First you should remember that the Rabbit Hole amendments were adopted by the Supreme Court, I just had one vote.

"Mr. Wayne, as you know the bar suffered a severe blow during the Fen Phen scandal back in 2007. Our Rule Amendments were instituted to bring the conduct of the members of the bar into line with what the public expects of the legal profession. In the Fen Phen case clients were defrauded of some $200 million dollars. I can't begin to tell you how detrimental that was to the bar. These amendments to the Supreme Court Rules were a necessary response to the public's demand for more control over lawyer's conduct."

The reporter did not challenge the Chief Justice on the incorrect claim that the Fen Phen lawyers stole $200 million dollars.

He took a drink from a bottle of imported Pellegrino water and continued, "We believe that the law schools have gone too far in creating new lawyers. In 1970 there were only 3,000 lawyers in Kentucky, and now there are more than 17,000. We have so many lawyers that many of them can no longer make a decent living, and the temptation to misdeal with client funds has become more of a problem. We can run a first class legal system with 10,000 lawyers. The entire country of Japan has only 22,000 lawyers and the U.S. has more than one million.

Sometimes we must do things we would rather not do, but bringing some discipline and order to the bar is my pledge to the public. We needed those rules to begin to weed out those lawyers who do not comply with the high standards of conduct expected by the public."

Scoop intervened, "Do you mean to say that you are going to suspend 7,000 lawyers?"

The Chief Justice, ignoring his recent memo to the Ministry of Ethics, lied and responded, "There is no set number. I would hope that an acceptable number will be far less than that, but we have no set number. The number will be determined by the conduct of the lawyers, we will not arbitrarily remove lawyers." He emphasized again, "They will remove themselves by their conduct."

Scoop added, "Justice, you say you just had one vote, but wasn't it unusual for you to assign Justice Boone and Justice Allgood to another court the day the Amendments were adopted."

The Chief Justice smiled and replied, "I resent your implication that I had control over the votes of the appointed Special Justices. The Governor appointed two outstanding lawyers and certainly I had no influence over his appointments. You disrespect me and the Special Justices with such a question. Those amendments were adopted because they had great merit."

The reporter pressed, "But what do you say to critics who say your use of the rule allowing you to assign Justices to other courts was never intended to be used to interfere with another Justice's vote?"

Justice Hatter sighed and said, "Read the rule. The constitution clearly permits the Chief Justice to assign other Justices to any court in the state. There was no misuse in my exercise of that clearly stated Rule. The public approved the Judicial Amendments in 1976, and every word of that provision was in the Amendments. I didn't write that provision, I am just using it as it was obviously intended."

The reporter changed the subject, "The cost of the judicial system has increased from under a $100 million dollars a year in 1980 to over $350 million dollars in the current year. The Administrative Office of the Courts now has close to 4,000 employees. Will the removal of 7,000 lawyers have any effect on the judicial budget requirements?"

"Well, let me say," the Justice replied, "the number of lawyers has little to do with the budget requirements of the judiciary. We hear well over a million cases a year in the Kentucky court system, but that caseload can be handled as well by 10,000 lawyers as by 17,000.

"It has been reported to me that only one-third of the graduates of our states' three law schools have found jobs by the time they graduate. Law Schools are oversupplying the marketplace with lawyers.

"A typical law school has increased their tuition to astronomical levels. They have a student to professor ratio of about 1 to 60. No other college is as profitable for the universities then their law schools. If they won't reduce their number of graduates, we will have to tighten up the Bar Exam standards and reduce the number of lawyers being admitted to the Bar.

"The lawyers who remain will have to work a little harder, but they will be rewarded for their extra work, and we believe this will improve the incentive to adhere to the conduct rules mandated by the court. I believe that idle hands are the Devil's playground."

The reporter accepted the offer of a bottle of Kroger brand water and continued his questioning, "The Ministry of Ethics is funded by the Kentucky Bar Association, which is funded by members' dues. The budget for this ethics committee represents the largest expenditure of the Bar Association, I believe it was $1.5 million in 2010, and now exceeds $3 million dollars a year.

"The Ministry of Ethics staff is now larger than 90% of the private law firms in the state. When the number of lawyers who pay dues is reduced, where will the funding come from to support the growing cost of the Ministry?"

The Chief Justice, had not expected that question. He replied, "We have recently ordered that 10% of the funds derived from the interest income on client trust funds will be assigned to the Ministry. The added protection provided by the Ministry to clients, justifies the use of interest of client trust funds to pay for this service.

"We have a philosophy that the Judicial system should be as self-funding as possible. We have ordered an increase in the application fee required of all law school graduates who seek admission to the Bar. That application fee will in the next year be increased to $5,000. This will raise an additional $2 million dollars and maybe as much as $2.5 million dollars. This increase will make the Ministry of Ethics self-funding. The current funding comes from lawyers dues and not from the legislature. No taxpayer funds are expended for the Ministry of Ethics operations, except for the cost of their office rent."

Scoop inquired, "Justice, we have learned that the Ministry of Ethics is pursuing an ethical complaint against Jack Kenton for his criticism of the Legislative Ethics Commission. Your critics are suggesting that you have encouraged this investigation in order to discourage Kenton from running against you in the next Supreme Court election. Have you had anything to do with that investigation?"

Justice Hatter, looked directly at the reporter and replied, "Mr. Wayne, I don't interfere with the Ministry of Ethics. I see that they have the support and funding that they need, but the Commissioner is selected by the Bar Association Board of Governors. I have never advised Commissioner Hart regarding any investigation.

"Further, I cannot discuss any pending investigation as it is possible that an appeal from any Ministry ruling may be appealed to the Supreme Court. Further let me say, that I am not in any way confirming any investigation of Jack Kenton or anyone else by answering your question.

"If Jack Kenton or anyone else wishes to run against me, that is their right, and I respect that.

I will let the voters decide if they want me to continue on the court."

The Chief Justice rose from his desk, and thanked the reporter for his time, ending the interview.

Chapter Thirty-Two

Williston Stafford carried a bag of White Castle hamburgers to the noon meeting with Tim Stein a member of the Kentucky Bar Association Board of Governors.

Stein had directed Stafford to meet him in one of his law firms twelve conference rooms on the twenty-first floor of the PNC bank building in downtown Louisville.

Stein asked Stafford if he wanted a soft drink, water or coffee, all of which were available in the Walnut paneled conference room. Stafford divided the Rectal Rockets and napkins and took a seat next to Stein at the end of the long table. "I love these things!" Stein said, "How did you know?"

Stafford ignored the question and thanked Stein for seeing him. "I have been denied a meeting with several Board members, and your willingness to talk with me is really appreciated. I assure you that anything you say here will be confidential."

He then began the interview. "Tim, I am trying to understand the relationship of the Board of Governors of the Bar Association to the Ministry of Ethics. I have read and reread the Supreme Court Rules concerning the Ministry. I have tried to make up an organization and flow chart and just can't make heads or tails of this beast. Can you educate me on how the Board of Governors and the Ministry of Ethics relate to one another?"

Stein swallowed his third hamburger and wiped his chin before beginning. "The Board is as confused as you are. The Rules have been adopted over many years and many of the Rules are conflicting. The Supreme Court makes the Rules, and sometimes asks for our input, but that usually is just a courtesy. They often ignore our input.

"The end result is that the Board of Governors, which is made up of two representatives from each of the seven Supreme Court jurisdictions, has the authority to hire the Commissioner of the Ministry of Justice, and I suppose we have the authority to fire her, even though that is not clearly stated in the Supreme Court Rules. But there is precedent where the Board actually fired a Bar Counsel."

Stein continued, "The Rules mandate that the Board relies on the Ministry for legal advice. So if we ask a legal question about any errors or improprieties of the Ministry we must rely on the Commissioner of the Ministry for legal advice. The Commissioner has the dual role of being the Legal Counsel for the Board of Governors, but she also functions as the Prosecutor of cases on which we seek procedural advice. If we ask if a certain action of the Ministry was in error, we get a biased and self-serving legal opinion that is unreliable. We have no authority to spend funds to hire an outside counsel to represent the Board. Further, the Board of Scrutiny decides which charges to dismiss and which charges to approve, Think of them as the Grand Jury. Then the Ministry completes their investigation and if the approve a complaint they present the case to the Trial Commissioner appointed for the case for a hearing.

"Due to their application of Confidentiality rules we never hear about anything they are doing unless there is an appeal to the Board. Since we are an appellate body, we can't inquire into the actions of the Ministry unless there is an appeal to us.

"There are more than a few cases where the Ministry and its predecessor have filed ethics charges against an attorney and kept them pending for years. The never ending pendency of an investigation is a special trick which keeps the victim in perpetual stress. If the Ministry has a weak case they can just keep it pending forever. If they choose, they never have to admit that a case they want to prosecute has no merit. There are no Speedy Trial rights in these Ethics prosecutions. The only rule regarding a time frame in which the Ministry must complete their investigations and prosecutions, merely requires them to do their work 'promptly'. There is no definition in the Rules or advisory commentary of what is meant by the word 'promptly.'

"I am told of some cases which alleged pretty serious ethics violations were buried by the Ministry and never saw the light of day. They hide their misdeed behind the secrecy and confidentiality rules. The Board has no control over the Ministry's investigations. We only get the case if the Trial Commissioner finds the attorney guilty or if the Board of Scrutiny appeals to the Board of Governors.

"There are always rumors about the Ministry which suggest that friends of the Ministry are cut a lot of slack, while their enemies are aggressively investigated and prosecuted. I can't prove that, but there is enough smoke hanging over the Ministry Castle, that there just might be a fire somewhere.

"There is no statute of limitations for ethics violations. They are, therefore, allowed to extend a case indefinitely. The Ministry prosecutions aren't subject to double jeopardy rules.

Stafford was making copious notes in his notebook as Stein continued.

"Technically ethics prosecutions are civil cases. While Ministry officials act like criminal prosecutors, and treat lawyers like criminal defendants, they are not limited by the double jeopardy rules which only apply to criminal cases. When they see a charge is not panning out in their investigation, they have been known to just keep adding new charges until the defendant is worn down or financially ruined by the costs of litigation.

"The message they send is pretty clear. "If you piss us off we will add to your misery! If we don't like you, we will screw you, but if you cooperate and humbly confess to whatever violation we charge, we might cut a deal with you.

"This type of hardnosed plea bargaining might be justified for murderers or in criminal court, but it raises a lot of eyebrows when applied to minor "ethics" offenses such as having failed to obtain the necessary Continuing Legal Education Hours. There was one poor fellow who checked the KBA web site to find out how many CLE hours he had earned for the required continuing legal education updates lawyers are required to obtain each year. The web site reported that he had completed the required hours. The Ministry however, disagreed with the posted CLE hours and found he was half an hour short.

"They responded that he was in error in relying on the KBA web site even though the KBA admitted their error. They cited him of course, and unbelievably the Supreme Court upheld the complaint. That incident smelled worse than my breath after eating your hamburgers. One would have thought that since the KBA web site had incorrectly reported the attorney as being in compliance, that they could have just ordered him to obtain the necessary hours and let the matter slide.

"Then there was the Jack Nelson case several years ago where he was called out of a CLE class by the Judge for whom he clerked, to attend to some court business.

This made Nelson twenty minutes short on his CLE hours for the year, and he was cited. The Board of Governors thought that this could have been handled as a 'good cause' exception, by assigning an additional twenty minutes of CLE, but the Ministry was inflexible. They insisted on a public reprimand and a fine. It is hard to believe that 20 minutes of actual courtroom work wasn't as valuable as sitting in a lecture hall for the same period of time.

"The Judicial Conduct Commission once entertained a complaint against a sitting Chief Justice, and in doing so showed some real back bone. The matter was dealt with privately, but at least they confronted the Chief Justice. They stood up to a sitting Chief Justice who had served as an honored guest at a charity event fundraiser. Apparently this violated some obscure rule for judges. But I have never seen the Ministry go after a Supreme Court Justice, until the Boone case."

Stafford started to speak, but Stein cut him off and continued, "The largest budget item of the KBA is now the Ministry of Ethics. They have hired more and more attorneys. They have made little effort to hire their lawyers from across the state, and they only seem to recruit from Lexington, Frankfort and Louisville. I personally believe there is a central Kentucky bias against rural attorneys.

"The Ministry of Ethics now has more lawyers and staff than the average Kentucky law firm. Chief Justice Hatter is creating new fees and recently approved funding to hire bailiffs for the Ministry. What in the hell do they need bailiffs for? They don't prosecute criminal laws, they only deal with ethics violations the most of which are technical violations of the confusing Supreme Court Rules.

Stein wiped his hands and accurately threw the bag from White Castle hamburgers fifteen feet across the room into the center of the trash can and continued without reference to his athletic feat, "We have been looking at their creation of their own rules of procedure, and one member on the Board commented, 'They are making up Rules as if they're Harry Potter's Ministry of Magic.'

Stafford interjected, "Are you familiar with their expansion of their jurisdiction over Judges?"

Stein paused briefly and commented, "I am aware anecdotally that they are testing their authority to supersede the Judicial Conduct Commission and to sanction one judge for what they allege is a "bad decision" he made in a ruling. We are aware of that case, and we are aware that the Judicial Code of Conduct prohibits the sanctioning of a judge for an mistaken ruling. This is a very basic rule protecting the independence of the Judiciary. You appeal bad decisions, you don't take the judges law license just because you disagree with his ruling. But that case is still pending before the Ministry and it certainly hasn't come before the Board of Governors.

"The Rules are so unclear I can't say if will ever come before the Board. So I don't know all the details and really should not comment on what might happen. But yes, we are aware that they are apparently trying to expand their jurisdiction to nail a judge for a ruling he made which was based on perjured evidence presented to him.

"We have been waiting for the last three years for a ruling in that case, but the Ministry certainly has shown no respect for the 'Promptness Rule'. For some reason they seem stuck in neutral. Nevertheless this complaint against the trial judge has sent a warning to the judiciary. I believe the message they are sending by going after a trial judge, is that henceforth, any judge's ruling will be subject to popularity review by the Ministry, most of whom are former prosecutors."

Stafford commented, "I bet the lawyers representing the judge don't have their hourly fee clocks in neutral."

Stein smiled and said, "You can be sure of that. That just demonstrates the Ministry's attitude that 'if we can't convict you, we can at least financially ruin you'. There really should be a rule that allows acquitted lawyers to have their attorney's fee reimbursed as in done in Federal Civil Rights actions."

He continued, "In all seriousness, if they do sanction the trial judge for his ruling, this is sure to go before the Supreme Court for review. Since the Supreme Court adopted the Rabbit Hole amendments, God only knows what they will do.

"Williston, there is one other thing you should be aware of. As you know the criminal code has a structure where the penalty for each offense is spelled out. Some offenses are designated as misdemeanors, and some are designated as felonies. But the Rules of the Supreme Court have no structure setting a level of seriousness of offenses. Even the most minor offense can warrant the ultimate "death penalty" sanction of disbarment.

"The Supreme Court in 2010, in one of their rulings, sent a message to the ethics prosecutors that they should ease up and try to work out alternative sanctions and remedial acts to deal with minor offenses. But in that decision the Supreme Court did not mandate such a rational theory. It only asked the Ministry to consider that practice. So far the Ministry has chosen to ignore that suggestion by the Supreme Court."

Stafford asked his final question, "You have an enlightened sense of fairness and reason, but how does the rest of the Board of Governors feel about the expansion of the Ministry's hardnosed policies?"

Stein looked at his hands as if they had blood on them, and replied in a soft voice, "I see about a 50-50 split. I just can't predict whether they will ever stand up and start representing the members of the Bar or if they will continue to be the Chief Justice's rubber stamp.

"We do have some authority over the Ministry's budget, but have almost never turned down any of their requests. The Chief Justice is a strong supporter of the Ministry. Many Board of Governors members are strong supporters of the Chief Justice. Not many attorneys want to take him on. Remember, most of us will from time to time have to appear before the Supreme Court for our clients.

"Then there is the fear that all of us have, that the Ministry, if displeased by our actions, may turn their guns on us. We are lawyers too, and our license to practice is our most valuable asset.

I just don't know what the Board of Governors will do in the future to rein in the Ministry. I don't have a good feeling about the future.

Williston rose and gathered up his notepad, but Stein continued.

"I have a good life. I earn over $300,000 a year. I have two children in expensive colleges and another wanting to go to an Ivy League school. I will admit that I am afraid of the Ministry. If they place their cross-hairs on me I could lose everything. It's far safer for Board members to ignore the Ministry's abuses, and hope the Supreme Court will clean up the mess. I honestly don't know if I have the backbone to take them on . . . ."

Stafford looked at him for a moment and said in a hushed voice, "You'll do the right thing," before showing himself out.

Stein remained silently seated in his $1,000 dollar Aeron Executive Chair looking at the nearby river.

Chapter Thirty-Three

Williston Stafford arrived at Kenton Farms Saturday morning at 11:30 and was greeted by Jack Kenton at the front door. Stafford carried his briefcase with him as he was shown into the dining room, where a dish of apple cobbler and ice cream was waiting.

After pleasantries were extended and the dessert was finished, the table was cleared off, and the two lawyers began their work.

Stafford began, "Justice Boone has suggested that we focus on the education of three justices." He showed the list to Jack Kenton.

Kenton reviewed the list, "I've drafted some letters for you and they should be distributed to the Eunuch Commander in the Supreme Court District of each of the three Justices. Ideally we should request that they should ask their local attorneys to reword the letters to personalize them but to maintain the central theme.

"We must caution everyone mailing a letter to carefully refrain from being too aggressive. They should not make any demands for action, but should express a tone of concern and request consideration of the requested action."

Stafford nodded his head in agreement, as Kenton continued, "I've prepared a list of the addresses of all local newspapers in the three Supreme Court Districts. I would suggest that you solicit local attorneys in each county in these three districts to write a Letter to their local newspaper.

"The newspaper letters should be followed by personal letters to each of the three Justices. We should aim for at least two dozen letters coming from each of the Justices' District. They will be more likely to be influenced by letters from local attorneys. I have heard judges say that they try to take care of their local lawyers, because they are the only ones eligible to run against a judge."

Stafford interjected, "I have put together a list of speakers for a Speakers Bureau made up of Retired Judges. I would suggest that each service club in these Districts be notified that we have a speaker who would like to attend their meeting and speak on the evils of secrecy as being applied in the discipline of lawyers. The local Rotary, Lions and Optimist clubs are always eager to latch on to a luncheon speaker."

Stafford then handed Kenton a draft of a fifteen minute speech prepared for delivery to the various service clubs. The theme, crafted by Stafford, briefly discussed how the secrecy of ethics investigations was a consumer protection issue.

The speech focused on the impossible standards being set by the Ministry of Ethics and how that was going to reduce the number of lawyers in rural areas and more importantly would reduce the ability of their lawyers to adequately represent the businessmen members of the service clubs.

The draft speech pointed out that their locally elected Supreme Court Justice could rein in the excesses of the Ministry of Ethics, and suggested they all personally express any concerns they might have to the Justice representing their district.

Kenton read the draft letter and responded, "This is good. Be sure to have each speaker send a copy of their speeches to each Justice with the date and name of each group that heard the speech. We want them to be aware that their local voters are being engaged."

Stafford, went on, "We have compiled a list from public records of every campaign donation made to each of the Justices in the last election. We are well into the effort of getting as many of them to write their district's Justice as possible."

Stafford then pulled a half dozen display ad mockups from his briefcase. "Our ad agency in Louisville has prepared a series of small newspaper cartoon ads which will be published in each Supreme Court District which has a contested race."

Kenton' eye caught one ad which showed a lawyer standing in front of a judge in a courtroom. The cartoon lawyer had a gag over his mouth. A statute of Lady Justice sitting on the judge's bench had the blind fold traditionally found on the statute of justice falling down to become a gag over her mouth. The copy read, "Your lawyer's voice is your voice. When he is silenced, You are silenced."

Kenton reviewed the other cartoons, and nodded his approval. "When will these start running?"

"We need about a month for the letters to be sent to each Justice, about another month for the Service Club speeches to be conducted, and then we will start the Letters-to-the Editor campaign, shortly after that the cartoons will be published throughout the state. This will all be completed in the sixty days before the next Supreme Court election.

"Justice Boone is agreeable to this time frame and won't submit her Amendments until the time is ripe."

Stafford replaced the draft speech and the cartoon display ads in his briefcase. He concluded the meeting with a final request. "Jack, there is a special assignment for you. We have talked it over and have concluded that you are the best person to speak to Chief Justice Chappell. He has been retired for twenty years but he still is highly respected by Bar members and the public.

"We want to use him in an ad campaign endorsing Justice Boone's Rules Amendments. We know you are close to him, and your mutual interest in the breeding industry gives you an entree' that none of the rest of us have."

Jack Kenton made a face of mock despair and said, "Boy, that's a difficult assignment. He hates publicity."

"But he loves the Court. He was one of the main authors of the Judicial Amendment to the Constitution back in 1976. The Rabbit Hole Amendments and the creation of the Ministry of Ethics surely are contrary to the system he worked so hard to implement. If we can get him to issue a call to the public to repeal the Rabbit Hole amendments with adoption of Justice Boone's Amendments, we will gain a degree of credibility that we just can't get otherwise."

Kenton walked Stafford back to his car. Stafford sat in his car and rolled the window down, and asked, "How about it Jack? Will you recruit Justice Chappell?"

Kenton couldn't hide a broad smile as he said, "Do you have any idea what this will likely cost me? He has been trying to get a breeding right with Morning Thunder, but he refuses to pay the full $50,000 fee. I know if I ask him to do this he will demand an expensive consideration."

Stafford laughed and shouted out the window as he drove off, "Which is it Jack, $50,000 or the end of civilization as we know it? After all ole' Morning Thunder will be doing all the work!"

Chapter Thirty-Four

The Queen of Hearts entered the Ministry of Ethics conference room and called the weekly meeting to order. Every prosecutor who wasn't scheduled for hearings outside of Frankfort was by the Commissioner's policy present at 9:00 a.m. every Monday morning.

The Queen sat silently taking notes as the prosecutors took turns giving updates of their current assignments with a report on how many new complaints they had approved during the last week and the total number of investigations in their portfolio. She nodded her head in approval but said nothing.

When the last prosecutor had finished, Commissioner Hart asked Bunny White to report on the new applicants seeking a position with the Ministry. Bunny read the names of seven applicants. Commissioner Hart asked the assembled if any of them knew any of the applicants. Salamander and Turtle both raised their hands.

Salamander went first. "I know Art Petrov, he was a classmate of mine at Chase Law School. He originally was from Buffalo. He has been working for the Attorney General's office in their criminal appeals branch."

The Commissioner looked at Salamander, "Do you recommend him for the Ministry?"

He was not used to the Commissioner asking for his opinion on anything and concluded this could be a trap. A small bead of cold sweat crept down the back of his neck as he realized that he would be vouching for Petrov, and if he was hired and screwed up, it would be a black mark for which he would pay dearly. Salamander was aware that Queen often looked for someone to blame when something went wrong.

He recalled Lewis Carroll's Alice in Wonderland story where the Queen of Hearts was very unhappy when she found that someone had painted the roses red. The order to paint the roses was given by the Queen herself, but when the worker defended himself by foolishly answering, "You ordered us to paint the roses red." Her response was "Off with his head!"

Salamander lied and said, "Well I really didn't know him that well. He was a pretty good student but I don't know about his work for the A.G."

The Commissioner then turned her eyes on Turtle. He responded before weighing the potential consequences as had Salamander, "I know Claudia Smithson and I think she would be a great addition to the team. She was on the Law Journal at U of L. I thought she was working for the Commonwealth Attorney in Lexington."

"Bunny", the Commissioner ordered, "Get them and that Bradford kid in here this afternoon."

Of the seven applicants, she had decided to add Petrov, Smithson, Carolyn Cockle and Edward Bradford to her team. While their employment was her decision, the four had been strongly recommended by Chief Justice Madison Hatter.

At 4:00 p.m. she met with the job seekers in her office. She noted that Claudia Smithson was appropriately dressed. She wore closed toe shoes with a modest one inch heel. Petrov had the build of a weight lifter and his imposing physique might be useful in intimidating those who needed to be intimidated. Bradford wore an expensive black suit, but had an inappropriate head of long curly black hair.

"Edward," she said to Bradford, "we have an appearance code we adhere to around here, and I would suggest that if you want to make it around here, when you show up tomorrow, be sure you have visited a good barber. We want you to look like a prosecutor, not a procurer."

She continued, "Petrov and Smithson and Cockle, you will be working together as Ethics Monitors."

Smithson and Petrov glanced at one another briefly. "Your job will be to visit law firms around the state and to issue warnings to people who may not have actually violated any Ethics Rules but who are seen as potential violators. We want to focus on any lawyer who advertises on television. You will also do consumer interviews. We watch the press for trials which receive publicity, we want you to interview the clients in those cases to be sure they are happy with their lawyer's conduct."

Bunny White has a list you will begin working on immediately."

Petrov who was of Russian heritage, was familiar with the concept of the state having monitors of potential conduct. In the old Soviet Union there was a division of the KGB that did the same kind of thing.

The Commissioner continued, "At the top of the list are those attorneys who advertise on television. The Bar Association has never approved of their ilk, but the Courts have restricted our right to regulate them. We have a check list of potential violations that you can ask them about, starting with in inquiry of any ethics violations they may have witnessed.

"The most effective tool you will have is the Squeal Rule. We want you to be on the lookout for those who have learned of potential ethics violations and have not reported them. I would suspect that every lawyer knows of something they should have disclosed.

"We don't expect you will find any violations but your visit will let them know they are being watched. See Salamander. He has a copy of the checklist speech you will need when you drop in to do your Ethics Audits. Any problem with that?"

They answered in unison, "NO, COMMISSIONER HART!"

The Commissioner turned her attention to Bradford. "Bradford, assuming you get that head of hair under control, you will be assigned to our Consumer Protection Office. Petrov will help out. You will also work with Turtle to review the Bar Magazine articles and advertisements for correctness. The magazine is published every other month and you will be responsible for reviewing all ads and feature stories. Since the Magazine is mailed to all licensed lawyers we want to be sure that our message requiring strict compliance with the Ethics Rules and policies are followed. You will have the title of Legal Editor of the Bench & Bar magazine. I want you to encourage them not to take ads or articles from anyone who doesn't share our mission."

The Executive Director of the Bar Association was livid when he heard of this interference with his managerial duties, but he said nothing.

After the Commissioner had dismissed the four new employees, they met briefly with their assigned mentors and completed the required personnel papers including their Oath of Confidentiality which had been written personally by Commissioner Hart. They each were required to sign a contract with the Ministry waiving any rights to ever publish or disclose any of their activities regarding their work at the Ministry.

Chapter Thirty-Five

Big Cat Cheshire reviewed the report of Justice Alice Boone's meeting with Williston Stafford at the Metropolitan Club in Covington. He called in his secretary and directed her to write a memo which outlined Alice's proposed Rules Amendments. "Leave out the date and parties to the conversation. Just detail a checklist of the proposed Rules Amendments."

He then picked up his phone and personally called Commissioner Hart. It was time for a sales meeting.

Within an hour his driver had pulled Cheshire's limousine onto the grounds of the Ministry of Ethics. As suggested by Cheshire, Commissioner Hart met him on the grounds of the Ministry castle. As they walked on the grounds inside the high stone walls, protected from sight and hearing of the world, he made his pitch.

"Commissioner, in my work I come across a great deal of information. I'm a businessman and that information is expensive to pursue. We do surveys and studies, and of course keep our ear to the ground. In the course of our work we have detected a potential challenge to you and the Ministry itself. If we thought this was just Frankfort gossip we would ignore it and I wouldn't be bothering you with this."

"What kind of challenge?"

Cheshire smiled a toothy smile and continued, "There is a plot to repeal the new rules you call Rabbit Hole Amendments. Of course that plans are aimed at you and if they actually succeed you might be out of a job." Commissioner Hart's dour expression did not change. She remained silent as they walked around the grounds of the castle.

"I don't have it all nailed down, but we believe that there is enough credibility to our research that suggests this should be pursued for more details."

"Who is involved?".

Cheshire flashed an even broader smile, "Now Commissioner, that is where the value of our lobbying services is involved. We don't just pass on rumors in my business. We check out the rumors and ignore the gossip and look for real action plans. We then evaluate their credibility and suggest to our clients a course of action to neutralize the plan. And this information is our stock in trade."

The Commissioner stopped and faced Cheshire and asked, "And just how much does your service cost?"

Cheshire's smile vanished as he informed the Commissioner, "Our minimum fee is $10,000 a month."

He softened his voice and continued, "I make my clients a guarantee. If after the first month they are not completely satisfied with our services then we will refund their $10,000 and the contract will be torn up. No one has ever asked for a refund."

The Commissioner felt her knees weaken as she realized that $120,000 a year could never be hidden in her budget request to the Board of Governors.

In her best Queen voice she raised her eyebrows and asked, "And just how do you suggest I raise $120,000 a year for this service?"

"Good question," he commented, "We have looked at this issue for some time and we suggest a method somewhat like the method used by the SoberMoms Association. They accept donations from prosecutors who enter into to pre-trial diversion pleas with drunk drivers. Pre-trial diversion of DUI cases is clearly against the law, but no one seems to care. The SoberMoms ignore the diversion program, but they have their hand out every year for the donations paid by the prosecutors from funds they collect from defendants who must pay a hefty fee to enter the diversion program. Everyone is happy.

What we suggest will be an improvement over the SoberMoms scheme. We believe you could do the same thing by allowing lawyer's charged with minor offenses to be diverted to a rehabilitation program."

"But is this scheme legal?"

"It will be perfectly legal."

Cheshire had prepared well for this question, "We are aware of a case several years ago where the Supreme Court suggested that the old Inquiry Commission, which of course was replaced by the Ministry, look for efforts to plea bargain away charges when appropriate."

He pulled a slip of paper from his coat pocket and handed it to the Commissioner.

It contained the case citation of 007-SC-000399-KB (Ky. 8/23/2007) (Ky., 2007).

"In this case the Supreme Court permitted the filing of a Verified Motion for Consensual Discipline pursuant to SCR 3.480(2). The Court went on to allow the lawyer's 'attendance at remedial ethics education.' The court specifically said the Bar Counsel could create 'a formal ethics and professional enhancement program to which the lawyer could be probated'.

The only guideline for creation of such a program by the Bar Counsel was the statement, "It must be appropriate for the remedial education of the movant regarding their ethical obligation to clients, third parties, and the public."

"So" he continued, "We are willing to create an Ethics LLC which will provide a program to reeducate offending lawyers. Someone has to pay for that program, and we suggest it is entirely proper that the offending lawyer should pay for the costs of his retraining."

He presented the Commissioner with a copy of SCR 3.480 and read to her Section (2), "Any member who is under investigation pursuant to SCR 3.160(2) or who has a complaint or charge pending in this jurisdiction, and who desires to terminate such investigation or disciplinary proceedings at any stage of it may request Bar Counsel to consider a negotiated sanction."

Without taking a breath, he concluded, "We are aware of the great numbers of ethics complaints you are handling these days, and if the Ethics LLC charged each probationer $2000, this would easily raise a sufficient amount to justify our creation of a private educational program. The legislature has allowed a similar structure for DUI schools and commercial probation programs for years, and most importantly the Supreme Court has approved these programs.

"A subsidiary of our company will create and operate the remedial ethics education program. You won't have to use any of your staff to operate the program, and you won't be burdened with collection of fees. If you agree to refer clients to us, we then can justify adding you to our list of people whom we advise. We will provide you a complimentary weekly report. All the Ministry has to do is to refer eight to ten students a month to our classes."

Commissioner Hart did not reveal her elation at the potential of such a plan. She immediately loved the idea, but being cautious, committed herself to a review of all the steps required.

"Mr. Cheshire," she concluded as they approached his waiting car, "We will look at this and get back to you."

Cheshire congratulated himself, as he was sure she had swallowed the hook. He left the Castle in a very good mood. His driver whisked him away to Valhalla Golf Course near Louisville. He was pleased that he had just earned more than his $70,000 initiation fee into the state's most exclusive golf club. "Life is good!" he mumbled to himself.

Chapter Thirty-Six

Commissioner Hart read the legal research prepared by her staff on the question of the Ministry referring attorneys to a non-profit ethics rehabilitation program as a part of a negotiated plea bargain. She had not informed them of the quid pro quo offered by Cheshire. The staff report concluded that such a program was consistent with the Supreme Court Rules and more importantly consistent with the recommendations the Supreme Court made in 2009 to encourage alternatives to suspension. The staff, not knowing of the special services being offered by Cheshire, of course had no ability to provide an informed legal opinion on that issue.

The Commissioner composed a note to Cheshire. The note was terse and lacking in any incriminating detail, it read: The Ministry of Ethics has accepted the recommendation of the Supreme Court to implement a ethics diversion program, and will be glad to make referrals to your proposed program."

Three days later she received a Fed Ex message addressed to her personally. When she opened the shipping envelope she found a post office box key and a brief message.

"Box 3412 St. Matthews Branch Post Office on Shelbyville Road, Louisville—Fridays between 5 and 7 p.m."

The following Friday the Commissioner visited the post office box and had picked up the first report. The delivery method was convenient and allowed her to pick up the reports on her way home and to spend the weekend reviewing them. After reading the first report she realized the material had to have been obtained by questionable means. After reading the weekly intelligence reports she burned them in her fire place.

Within the first month a dozen attorneys had accepted the recommendation of the Ministry prosecutors to request a Negotiated Plea Settlement under SCR 3.160(2). They eagerly agreed to pay the $2,000 program fee to the Ethics Education LLC, which conducted a two day educational program once a month in a rented office in Lexington,

Kentucky. In exchange they escaped public disclosure and further prosecution of their minor but embarrassing acts.

The Commissioner was never informed that a real estate trust owned by Big Cat Cheshire was the owner of the office building where the classes were conducted. The monthly rent for the three room office suite was an unbelievable $9,000. The Ethics Education classes were conducted by one paralegal who was listed as the owner of the LLC. She was quite happy to be paid $1000 a month for two days work. Her classes consisted mostly of playing DVD's purchased by the LLC.

In exchange for the plea agreement, the attorneys kept their law licenses and their ethics violations were successfully diverted. No attorney complained about the size of the fee charged for the ethics classes. The fee was far less than the financial ruin that would occur if they lost their license to practice law. Having just escaped the ethics machine, they were not very likely to risk going through that again by being critical of the Ministry. The diversion program kept them on probation for five years.

The Commissioner had informed her staff of prosecutors of the existence of the educational program, but limited the referrals to no more than fifteen a month. She regularly made a scene of rejecting several requests a month to impress upon her staff their goal of increasing the overall number of complaints. The increasingly overworked staff were favorable to the referrals. Even though the number of cases plea bargained out were small, it did reduce their workloads and allowed them to claim success on their most doubtful complaints.

The diversion program, which had been quickly approved by the Supreme Court, was just another step in treating lawyers like criminals who also were eligible for diversion programs.

The new rule to license attorneys practicing before the KBA was effective. It didn't take long before a good deal of institutional good will was established between the defense attorneys licensed to practice before the Ministry and the prosecutors. The defense lawyers who were in good standing with a prosecutor were usually more successful in obtaining referrals to the program.

The attorneys who were licensed to practice before the Ministry boosted their fees in recognition of their new status. They no longer had competition from attorneys who were not licensed by the Ministry. The fact that they had to suck up to the Ministry to preserve their license was never mentioned.

Cheshire was pleased that his money laundering scheme was not subject to examination under open records laws since the ethics school was not a state agency. No paper trail tied him directly to Commissioner Hart.

Cheshire justified his scheme on the theory that the only victims were the attorneys charged with ethics complaints. He once justified the program to a friend. "And who gives a damn about anything happening to attorneys?"

Attorney's were treated like tethered prey with fat wallets. They were eager and willing to pay dearly to secure their safe release from the Ministry slaughter house.

As with any successful con, the victims once released were highly motivated to keep quiet about their close call. The admission that they had been required to obtain remedial ethics education was not a fact that would engender respect from their peers, or confidence from their clients.

Chapter Thirty-Seven

Commissioner Hart soon developed an addiction to Cheshire's weekly reports. He wired her into information sources she could never have obtained by any other means. While she correctly concluded that the reports were almost surely obtained by illegal means, she weighed the value of that knowledge against the priceless value of the information, and her own self-interest prevailed.

She convinced herself that no one could connect her to these reports.

She faithfully destroyed the messages in her fireplace after reading them. It never occurred to her that this might be the basis for a criminal charge of obstruction of justice.

Cheshire, a natural con man, never trusted anyone. Once a week he sent Tweedledee and Tweedledum to Louisville to place the reports in the Commissioners' post office box at the Shelbyville Road post office branch. This prevented problems that might have occurred if the weekly package of information had been trusted to the vagaries of the U.S. mail.

He was aware of post office errors where they sometimes placed letters in the wrong Post Office box, and that would not be a good thing. His plan provided a perfect drop of his material and the post office personnel never handled the material. They never noticed that 'mail' was being placed in the boxes.

Tweedledee and Tweedledum were instructed to place the package in the mailbox using a duplicate key. For several weeks they waited around in their van and videotaped her weekly visits.

As instructed, they obtained close up video of her repeatedly entering P.O. Box 3412, removing the material and placing the post office box key back in her purse. Cheshire believed one should always set his traps well. One never knew when such video tapes might be useful.

Chapter Thirty-Eight

The report that most concerned the Commissioner concerned the meeting between Williston Stafford and Justice Alice Boone. From the report she understand the nature of the attack that Alice was planning against the Ministry of Ethics.

She had directed her staff to go slow in preparing and advancing the complaint against Justice Boone after it was first filed. She frequently delayed investigations so the victim attorney could be subjected to the maximum stress. But now it was time to speed things up.

If Justice Alice Boone was going to submit rules amendments to the full Supreme Court which could eviscerate the Ministry, it was essential that the Ministry strike first. If she waited until Alice Boone's attack was disclosed, the Ministry would appear to be retaliating. "Better" she thought, "to sanction the Justice first and her reaction would be discredited".

She called in Liz Fisher, the young prosecutor she had assigned to the Alice Boone complaint, and received an update.

The complaint against Justice Boone was assigned by the Scrutiny Clerk to a panel of the Board of Scrutiny months ago, after the Commissioner had approved its advancement.

The panel which was assigned the complaint, spent all of fifteen minutes in finding probable cause that the allegations in the complaint supported a charge of violation of the Supreme Court Rules.

The Ministry prosecutor, being confident of the outcome, had taken the liberty of preparing in advance all the paperwork needed to evidence a finding by the Board of Scrutiny panel which would advance the complaint towards the hearing before the Trial Commissioner. The members of the panel quickly used their rubber stamp vote to place their signatures on the findings.

If Justice Boone had been charged with shoplifting, she would have been entitled to a independent grand jury and a jury trial, made up of citizens randomly selected by lot. But by design of the Ministry of Ethics mechanism, she got a hearing that was conducted by representatives of the Chief Justice. Since the Chief Justice was the so-called party injured by Justice Boone's comments, the impartiality of the panel chosen by the Chief Justice, was less than reassuring to Justice Boone and her attorneys. To top it off, the public was excluded from the Board of Scrutiny meeting, and everything was veiled in secrecy. Even Justice Boone was excluded from the Board of Scrutiny session.

No one who benefited from the ethics machine saw anything wrong with its procedures. They felt it was a necessary but effective tool to control the conduct of lawyers.

Those Ministry staffers who were forced to participate in the process, and thus closely viewed its operation, found the ethics mechanism to be something less than a due process proceeding.

One victim of the Ministry of Ethics had foolishly dared to raise a question about Ministry misdeeds to the Board of Governors to whom he had appealed his conviction. He had argued passionately:

"We have two thousand years of history and jurisprudence invested in the development of our civil and criminal justice system. Lawyers are the ministers of the justice system. Yet if a secret ethics claim is made against a lawyer or a judge, he is not protected by the very system he has defended for everyone else. The homeless, the poor and the insane are all entitled to a public trial where their guilt or innocence is determined in public view. They are judged by their peers who are impartially selected by lot and not by the Chief Administrator of the Ministry of Ethics. Lawyers and judges are treated like the hired help at a private club. They are not allowed to enter the big courtroom in their own defense. Lawyer's are only allowed to enter a real courtroom for the for the purpose of serving and defending others."

The Board of Governors ignored the lawyer's argument as it appeared to call for reform and all reform had to come from the Supreme Court.

Liz Fisher reported to the Queen, that the case against Justice Boone was ready for a hearing. "We can send out notices announcing the hearing date immediately."

She described her take on the case, "It's a very simple case. We have the quotes she made to the *Courier-Journal*, and it appears to be a per se violation of SCR 3.130 (8.2). The only problem we have is that the case law citing the rule suggests that we must prove that the subject's statement was false, that it was knowingly made, and that it was intended to affect a pending case.

"The U.S. Supreme Court has been expanding the free speech rights of judges, and it is possible that these free speech rulings might be interpreted to apply to attorneys."

Commissioner Hart was not pleased with the legal conclusions, and scolded the prosecutor, "You let the defendant worry about changing the law, we are prosecutors, and we'll worry about an appeal later. The Board of Scrutiny has ruled. Now your job is to be an advocate for the Ministry!"

The young prosecutor was too frightened to point out to the Queen that under the Code of Professional Conduct definition, she was also a 'Minister of Justice', and was supposed to seek justice and not just seek a conviction. She was under an ethical obligation not to let unfounded claims be prosecuted.

The Commissioner directed Liz Fisher in no uncertain terms, "Make this case a priority and get it set for a hearing immediately! Don't come back in here complaining that the Boone's attorneys want a continuance to prepare their case. There won't be any continuances."

Liz Fisher felt an ominous black cloud over her head. She didn't know how she could prevent the Trial Commissioner from allowing Boone the time to prepare her defense. She had never practiced a case in a courtroom. She was appreciative of the fact that she wouldn't have to pick a jury or write instructions.

While her best legal analysis suggested that this case was not justified, she was not going to risk her monthly paycheck by going rogue on the Queen. She had to prosecute the case and she knew she had better win!

She met with the Trial Commissioner and got his approval on the date of the hearing. She then had the clerk send out the hearing notices. It never occurred to her that the defendant had a right to be a part of the process in selecting a hearing date.

Ex parte meetings by prosecutors and the Trial Commissioner were common at the Ministry. The Trial Commissioners had an office at the Ministry Castle, and prosecutors ran into them all the time. Access to that part of the building was forbidden to defense attorneys.

In thirty days she would prosecute her first case against a skilled defense lawyer in a contested proceeding. She mentioned her fears over lunch to Bunny White, the most experienced employee of the Ministry.

Bunny gave the best advice the young prosecutor would ever receive. In her best John Lovett voice she said, "Just remember, *it's acting!*"

For the next month she experienced a roller coaster of depression and excitement. Some days she felt that she would surely win conviction and obtain a sanction against a sitting Supreme Court Justice. Her name would be made! On other days she realized that if she took a shot at Justice Alice Boone and missed, then she would forever be linked to an embarrassing failure.

Her career concerns were not alleviated by other staffers who warned her to be careful because if she failed she would have to suffer the wrath of the Queen. They all cited examples of how they had been dressed down by the Queen when they had not achieved the result desired.

She spent evening after evening during the next month reading and rereading the Rules of Evidence and going over the questions she had written down for her witnesses, and reviewing her opening and closing statements.

Two weeks before the hearing she had a subpoena served on the *Courier-Journal* reporter. The subpoena ordered his attendance and demanded his notes of the interview. She would use the reporter and his notes to offer proof of the statement made by Justice Boone. She was hoping that his notes might reveal other statements which weren't published in the newspaper and broadcast in the media.

Within four hours of the receipt of the subpoena the *Courier-Journal* had filed a motion to quash the subpoena for the reporter and his notes. They had it served on the Trial Commissioner assigned to hear the case.

A copy was placed in the mail to Justice Boone's attorney.

The Trial Commissioner assigned to the Boone complaint was an attorney who practiced law for a large firm in Louisville. He had been nominated by one of his partners who just happened to be a member of the Board of Governors. He was not foolish enough to underestimate the power of the press to ridicule him. His ruling quashed the demand for the reporter's notes but found no reason to quash the subpoena for the personal appearance of the reporter.

Commissioner Hart called the Trial Commissioner as soon as she heard of the newspaper's motion to quash the reporter's subpoena. The Trial Commissioner was well aware that Commissioner Hart's ex parte call to discuss the pending case was improper. He also realized that if his services as a Trial Commissioner were unpopular with the Ministry that he might be removed from future assignments, and he rather liked playing the role of a judge. The Trial Commissioner was after all a team player, and his services for the Ministry helped provide his firm with a degree of immunity from Ethics complaints that only an inside voice can provide.

The Trial Commissioner did not conduct a hearing on the newspapers motion. He simply issued an order. The order required the reporter to appear and testify about his interview with Justice Boone. He alleviated some of the concerns of the newspaper by stating in his order that the only purpose of the reporter's presence at the hearing was to confirm or deny that Justice Boone made the statements which were published.

No examination of any other statements or of the reporter's notes would be allowed.

The *Courier-Journal* was not comfortable with one of their reporters being used as a witness, but being aware of dozens of reporters who had been held in contempt for failing to testify, they accepted the compromise.

Kentucky law protecting journalists from disclosing their sources was one of the weakest laws in the nation.

Alice Boone did not learn of the filing of the motion to quash the reporter's subpoena until her attorney called her the next morning to tell her of a news story about the Trial Commissioner's ruling. By then the Trial Commissioner had issued his ruling and she was denied any input.

Justice Boone's formal copy of the notice for the motion to quash the subpoena of the reporter arrived at her attorney's office two days after the ruling of the Trial Commissioner had been issued.

Justice Boone was livid about the ex parte proceedings to which they had been effectively excluded. "This was a denial of due process!" Justice Boone protested to her attorney.

However, since the ruling itself appeared consistent with the law, they decided to merely file a motion for reconsideration which was also disposed of by the Trial Commissioner without a hearing. While the filing of Justice Boone's motion was overruled, it at least made a record on a denial of due process claim which would be useful in the event of an appeal.

Chapter Thirty-Nine

The Tea Party "Trial" from Alice In Wonderland by Lewis Carroll—1865

The twelve jurors were all writing very busily on slates. "What are they doing?" Alice whispered to the Gryphon. "They can't have anything to put down yet, before the trial's begun."

Alice could see that . . . all the jurors were writing down "stupid things!" on their slates, and she could even make out that one of them didn't know how to spell "stupid", and that he had to ask his neighbor to tell him.

"Herald, read the accusation!" said the King.

The White Rabbit read:

"The Queen of Hearts, she made some tarts,

All on a summer day,

The Knave of Hearts, he stole those tarts, and took them quite away!"

"Consider the verdict," the King said to the jury.

"Not yet, not yet!" the Rabbit hastily interrupted.

"There's more evidence to come yet, please, your Majesty," said the White Rabbit

"Give your evidence," said the King, "and don't be nervous, or I'll have you executed on the spot."

"Call the first witness," said the King.

The first witness was the Hatter. He came in with a teacup in one hand, and a piece of bread and butter in the other. "I beg your pardon Majesty," he began "for bringing these in; but I hadn't quite finished my tea when I was sent for."

The King said, "When did you begin?"

The Hatter looked at the March Hare, who had followed him into the court, arm in arm with the Dormouse.

"Fourteenth of March, I think it was, "he said.

"Fifteenth", said the March Hare.

"Sixteenth," added the Dormouse.

"Write that down," the King said to the jury, and the jury eagerly wrote down all three dates on their slates, and then added them up, and reduced the answer to shillings and pence.

At this moment the King, who had been for some time busily writing in his notebook, called out "Silence." and read out from his book, "Rule Forty-two. All persons more than a mile high to leave the court."

Everybody looked at Alice.

"I'm not a mile high," said Alice.

"Nearly two miles high," added the Queen.

"You are!," said the King.

"Well, I shan't go, at any rate, "said Alice; "besides that's not a regular rule in the book, you invented it just now."

"It's the oldest rule in the book," said the King.

"Then it ought to Number One, "said Alice.

The King turned pale, and shut his notebook hastily. "Consider your verdict, he said to the jury in a low trembling voice.

"Let the jury consider their verdict, "the King said, for about the twentieth time that day.

"No, no!" said the Queen. "Sentence first—verdict afterward."

JUSTICE ALICE BOONE'S HEARING

The hearing was held in a rented conference room of the Lexington Marriott Hotel. The Trial Commissioner's seat was flanked by a Deputy Inquisition Clerk and a court stenographer. Two tables were arranged at a right angle to the Trial Commissioner's table so that the prosecutor and the defendant faced each other.

A witness chair in the middle of the room faced the Trial Commissioner. A podium was provided facing the Trial Commissioner for the convenience of the attorneys.

An armed bailiff from the Ministry of Ethics opened the makeshift courtroom at 9:45 and checked off the names of all those he admitted from the list provided to him by the Ministry. When he concluded that everyone authorized to attend this secret meeting was in the room, he closed the door and took a seat inside the room next to the door. He had directed that the other witnesses remain in a meeting room next to the courtroom so that they could quickly be called when needed.

The witnesses were not allowed to hear any testimony other than their own.

Promptly at 10 a.m., Parrish Patterson, the Trial Commissioner, called the hearing to order as the court stenographer turned on her recording device.

The Trial Commissioner welcomed all parties, then read the official charge issued by the Board of Scrutiny. He asked the prosecutor, Liz Fisher, if the Ministry of Ethics had entered into any plea negotiations.

Fisher replied, "No your Honor, the Ministry believes the seriousness of these charges does not warrant any type of negotiation or mediation."

He then asked Justice Alice Boone to enter her plea.

Alice stood facing the Trial Commissioner, and firmly stated "I plead not guilty."

The Trial Commissioner, the court Stenographer and the Inquisition Clerk all made a note of the plea.

Frank Marciano, Justice Boone's attorney asked the Trial Commissioner if he could approach the bench. The Trial Commissioner nodded his approval.

Marciano then handed the Trial Commissioner and the prosecutor a brief. The brief argued that under Supreme Court Rule 4.020 the jurisdiction of the Judicial Conduct Commission was the proper body to hear any complaints of misconduct by a judge, and that it was beyond the jurisdiction of the Bar Association and the Ministry of Ethics to hear charges against a judge or justice.

Marciano explained, "Your Honor, we have previously contested the jurisdiction of this body to hear this complaint against Justice Boone. Before we proceed we would appreciate a ruling on this motion to stay this proceeding until such time as the Judicial Conduct Commission may intervene.

"We submit that this question of jurisdiction should be ruled on before the irreparable injury that this proceeding would impose on Justice Boone is inflicted on her. We submit that only the Judicial Conduct Commission has jurisdiction to hear this complaint and the Ministry of Ethics has no such jurisdiction."

Marciano then handed a second motion to the Trial Commissioner. This motion sought the recusal of the Trial Commissioner and the findings of the Board of Scrutiny, since they were appointed by the Chief Justice, and the Chief Justice was the aggrieved party to this action.

The Trial Commissioner was not pleased. He responded "Mr. Marciano, your motions are under advisement and I will rule on them in due time."

This meant that the hearing would continue without a ruling. Marciano doubted if the Trial Commissioner would ever rule on the motions. It was their common practice to just ignore troubling legal arguments.

The Trial Commissioner then looked at Fisher and said "You may begin, and please keep it brief."

Justice Boone took a pen and wrote on her yellow pad, "Appeal error number one!!"

The young prosecutor's mouth was dry as she placed her typed opening statement on the podium and nervously adjusted the papers. Every eye in the makeshift courtroom was fastened on her.

After reading two pages of her ten page opening statement it occurred to her that a ten page typed statement was anything but brief.

As she edited her lengthy prepared opening statement in her mind, she lost her train of thought for a second and had to pause as she shuffled her notes looking for a checklist she had prepared. The ten seconds seemed like ten minutes.

She read a paragraph and then immediately decided it was not working She then recklessly started another line of thought which wasn't written in the typed opening statement which had been approved by Commissioner Hart herself.

"We believe that Justice Boone was motivated by personal political ambition when she accused the Chief Justice of unethical conduct."

Before she could finish her sentence, Justice Boone's attorney, Frank Marciano, shouted out "Objection Your Honor, Argumentative."

Before Fisher could protest or answer the objection, the Trial Commissioner answered firmly, "Sustained."

Liz Fisher found herself in the dilemma inexperienced attorneys often find themselves. She had no idea what she had done wrong. She asked herself, "How could the conclusion that everyone at the Ministry had made about the motivation for Justice Boone's statements be speculative?"

She looked desperately at Justice Boone's attorney but he was not going to assist her out of the hole she had dug for herself by explaining the grounds of his objection further.

The Trial Commissioner disappointed Fisher by his ruling and by his failure to explain his ruling to her.

She quickly concluded that if she asked the Trial Commissioner what she had done wrong then she would simply confirm everyone's conclusion that she in fact didn't know what she had done wrong.

The delusion she had nurtured that the Trial Commissioner was going to be her assistant and guide in this hearing died a quick death. Her mind was not paralyzed. Her mind was in turbo charged fuel-injected overdrive examining and instantly considering and disposing of dozens of explanations for what just happened. Her light speed review of all options failed to provide a solution.

The color on the back of her neck now matched the crimson cashmere sweater she was wearing. She tried again, "Justice Boone is clearly guilty of . . . ." Before she could finish the sentence the opposing attorney once again shouted, "Objection your Honor, Argumentative."

Before she could take in enough air to protest, the Trial Commissioner once again firmly ruled, "Sustained!"

This time the Trial Commissioner looked directly to the nervous prosecutor and said derisively, "Ms. Fisher, an opening statement is not the place to speculate or to argue your case. Just tell us what you intend to prove in your case. We don't care about your personal conclusions or arguments in your opening statement. Let's move this along."

At that moment, she ever so slightly wet her panties. Although she was certainly not the first attorney so affected in their first trial, it would be thirty years before she admitted this to another person.

Finally as her hands shuffled her papers, she found the checklist, and read from it.

"The Ministry intends to prove, that Justice Boone violated the Ethics Rules by accusing Madison Hatter, the Chief Justice of the Kentucky Supreme Court, of a lack of integrity when he assigned her to duty in another court and appointed a Special Justice to take her place for one session of the Supreme Court. We will prove that this violated SCR 3.130 (8.2)."

She then sat down relieved that she would now have a brief respite to regain her composure as Frank Marciano, made his opening statement for the defense. The delusion that she would have a few minutes to collect her thoughts while Marciano made his opening argument was evaporated when the defense counsel announced to the Trial Commissioner that he would reserve his opening statement. This shifted the floor back to the prosecutor, forcing her to begin her introduction of evidence immediately.

Fisher again shuffled her six inches thick file looking for her trial outline for the first witness. The outline listed the name and personal information for each witness she intended to call along with the suggested questions of the witness and the justification for calling the witness.

Her outline was a thing of beauty. The only problem with it was that it was two hundred pages long and thus virtually useless for a fast moving trial.

An experienced lawyer would have had that rookie mistake worked out of his system, and would have kept his notes far briefer or would have had a paralegal or co-counsel handle the paperwork for him. It is hard to command the attention of the court while your head is stuck in your briefcase like an Ostrich looking for an egg you had previously hidden.

After a minute of confused inaction by Fisher, the Trial Commissioner said impatiently, "Ms. Fisher, please call your first witness."

She stood up and announced to the court that she would call Mr. Ryan Wolfenheimer, the reporter for the *Herald-Leader*.

Eva Wakefield, the bailiff, left the courtroom and shortly returned with Wolfenheimer in tow.

The Trial Commissioner sworn in the witness and directed him to the witness chair.

Fisher, then asked his name and occupation. She then proceeded to ask him, "Isn't it true that on May 15, 2015 you interviewed Justice . . . ." Again Marciano objected and was sustained by the Trial Commissioner.

Fisher was beyond embarrassed. She was now embarrassed and one inch from foaming at the mouth angry.

The Trial Commissioner could readily see her anger and asked derisively, "You should not ask leading questions Ms. Fisher. Do you know what a leading question is?"

Before she could lie and say that she knew what a leading question was, the Trial Commissioner continued, "My interpretation of a leading question usually includes any question asked on direct examination which begins with the phrase 'Isn't it true?' Such a question suggests to the witness what his answer should be. You aren't trying to lead Mr. Wolfenheimer are you?"

She took a drink of warm bottled water, and replied, "No you honor."

In the back of her mind she recalled plenty of situations where she had heard questions framed with the preface "Isn't it true?"

After the trial the Trial Commissioner explained to her that a witness can be lead only if they are declared a hostile witness who refuses to give full answers. The court can then grant permission for the cross-examining attorney to ask leading questions.

She then rephrased the question. "Mr. Wolfenheimer, did you interview Justice Alice Boone in May of 2013?"

Wolfenheimer, who had twenty more years of courtroom experience than the prosecutor, paused to see if there were any more objections before answering succinctly, "Yes." She handed the witness a newspaper and continued, "Mr. Wolfenheimer, do you recognize this document?"

The defense attorney smiled and said, "Objection your Honor. May we take a look at that first?"

The Trial Commissioner nodded his head, and Fisher showed the newspaper to Frank Marciano. He took his time reading it and delayed things even further by handing it to Justice Boone for her review. She leisurely read it and nodded her head, and gave it back to her attorney who handed it to the bailiff who then took it to the Trial Commissioner.

The Trial Commissioner briefly examined the newspaper and returned it to the bailiff who handed it back to Fisher with a nod of approval.

Fisher then handed the newspaper back to the reporter, and once again asked,

"Do you recognize this paper, and specifically do you recognize the news story which is highlighted?"

The reporter took his time and read the entire story before answering, "Yes."

She then reviewed her checklist and asked him, "Did you write that story?"

"Some of it."

His response rattled her for a moment as she recognized that she must prove the authenticity of the entire statement made by Justice Boone and his response suggested that someone else may have written part of the news story.

She asked, "Do you mean that someone else helped write this story?"

He smiled and answered, "I am just a reporter, the editor can rewrite news stories, and of course the editor writes the headline."

"Did you write the headline?"

"No," he replied.

Taking a deep breath she tried again, "But did you write the body of the story?"

She audibly exhaled in relief when he replied, "Yes, but I didn't write the headline."

"Do the statements in the story attributed to Justice Alice Boone correctly reflect what she said to you?"

The reporter of course knew what Justice Boone had said, but enjoying a chance to make news instead of just reporting it, took his time and reread the entire news story, before answering, "Yes."

There were a dozen other questions that she had planned to ask this witness, but she wisely concluded that she had achieved the essential evidence from the witness, and turned to the Trial Commissioner and asked, "Your Honor, I move that this newspaper be identified as Ministry Exhibit No. 1, and that it be admitted into evidence."

Marciano moved to have the Court mark out the headline of the story since it was hearsay. The Trial Commissioner granted the motion, and the newspaper was handed to the Deputy Inquisition Clerk who placed a stick-on note on the exhibit and wrote on it, Ministry #1.

Fisher then turned to the defense table and said dramatically, "Your witness."

Marciano rose from his chair, and walked around to stand behind the witness allowing him to face the Trial Commissioner.

"Mr. Wolfenheimer," he began, "In your job as a reporter have you had any experience in covering the Supreme Court?"

Wolfenheimer answered, "Yes Sir, I have been on the Supreme Court beat for the last nine years. During that time I have attended many Supreme Court hearings."

"Mr. Wolfenheimer, have you ever witnessed an occasion where a Chief Justice assigned another Justice of the Court to duty in another court so that he could appoint a replacement Justice?"

Before he could answer, Fisher sensing that something wasn't right about that question jumped to her feet, "Objection."

The Trial Commissioner looked at her for a moment and looked at the defense counsel, and then asked, "Ms. Fisher, what is the basis for your objection?"

"It's improper.".

"How is it improper Ms. Fisher?" the Trial Commissioner asked quietly.

"Well" she answered, "the Kentucky Constitution at Section 110 (4)(b) permits the Chief Justice to assign any judge or justice to court anywhere in the state. There is nothing improper about his application of the Constitution."

"Ms. Fisher," the Trial Commissioner replied, "I don't recall the question asking the witness if the use of that constitutional provision was improper or proper. Counsel merely asked the witness if he was aware of any other occasion when this provision had been used by a Chief Justice."

The prosecutor started to respond but was cut off by the Trial Commissioner, "Mr. Wolfenheimer, you may answer the question."

The reporter quickly answered, "I have never heard of that provision being used by any Chief Justice so as to prevent another member of the court from voting on a pending issue or case."

The defense counsel turned the witness back to the prosecutor.

Fisher started to ask another question but saw the Trial Commissioner raise his eyebrows and she thought better of proceeding. She replied, "No further questions your Honor."

The reporter stood and asked the Trial Commissioner, "Your honor, may I have permission to remain in the courtroom?"

The Trial Commissioner broke into a broad smile, and said, "I have no objection but I suspect that Ms. Fisher just might."

The prosecutor stood and rattled off a rambling citation of confidentiality rules, but the Trial Commissioner once again cut her off and said, "I'm sorry Mr. Wolfenheimer, the Ministry of Ethics obviously objects, so I must deny your request."

The prosecutor then called Bryce Cunningham, an Ethics professor from Duke Law School.

The professor detailed a list of law journal articles, two books, and several other papers he had published regarding legal ethics. After laying a proper foundation Fisher asked that he be declared an expert witness on legal ethics.

The defense counsel rose, "Your Honor, I am well acquitted with Professor Cunningham, I have read many of his articles and books, and I concede that he is well qualified to speak on legal ethics questions. While I do not waive any future objection to specific questions. I concede he is certainly an expert in this field."

Fisher proceeded to question the professor about the statement made by Justice Boone.

"After having read the statement in Exhibit #1, do you have an opinion about whether or not Justice Boone's statement charged Chief Justice Hatter with unethical behavior?"

The professor answered briefly, "Assuming that Justice Boone made such a statement, then I would conclude that she indeed accused him of an unethical act."

With all the drama of a maitre' d showing a guest to his table, Liz Fisher bowed and opened her hands palm up and pointed towards the professor and said to the defense counsel, "Your witness!"

Marciano rose and stood next to the witness with a book in his hand and began, "Professor, I have been a fan of yours for years."

Marciano was speaking to the witness, but was looking directly at the prosecutor as if each question was an accusation against her.

"I particularly appreciated your article on the Duke Lacrosse rape case. Everyone I know, agreed with your timely criticism of the improprieties of the local prosecutor who withheld evidence, stymied the investigation, and sought to benefit his re-election by playing to the voters who were crying for blood."

The defense counsel turned to the Trial Commissioner and politely asked the court, "Your Honor, please forgive me for a moment, I would like to ask the learned professor to autograph his book."

The Trial Commissioner shook his head in mock frustration, but said, "Make it quick."

The professor took the ink pen which the defense counsel offered him and quickly autographed the book.

The cross-examination begin with Marciano asking the court to permit him to show a copy of SCR 3.130 (8.2)(a) to the expert witness. After the paper was shown to the prosecutor, and the court had agreed, the Clerk marked it as Defense Exhibit #1.

"Professor," he began, "this is the ethics rule which Justice Alice Boone is charged with having violated. Would you please read it aloud?"

The professor complied. "SCR 3.130 8.2(a) A lawyer shall not make a statement that the lawyer knows to be false or with reckless disregard as to its truth or falsity concerning the qualifications or integrity of a judge, adjudicatory officer or public legal officer, or of a candidate for election or appointment to judicial or legal office."

"Now professor," he continued, "When I read this rule, the rule which is the basis for the charge against Justice Boone, I personally interpret the rule to require that an allegation which questions the integrity of a judge, to be a violation, must be known by the lawyer to be false or with reckless disregard as to its truth or falsity.

The witness replied, "Yes that is correct. The statement must be false to be actionable."

"Professor, you have been found by this court, and by the prosecutor to be an expert on legal ethics, and I certainly agree with that finding, so I would respectfully ask if you agree that a true statement which questions the integrity of a judge is not a violation?"

Professor Cunningham emphatically replied, "Certainly, the rule clearly permits a lawyer to accuse a judge of a lack of integrity if the statement is true."

Without being asked, the professor continued, "This same rule is part of the Model Rules of the American Bar Association. Most if not all other states follow this rule and have included it in their rules of conduct for lawyers.

The ethical rules are merely rules adopted by the various courts. They cannot override the free speech rights guaranteed to every citizen, under the First Amendment. This rule as stated in SCR 3.130 (8.2)(a) should be understood as being based on the libel or defamation exceptions to free speech rights. Without the requirement that the statement be false then the rule would clearly be unconstitutional."

"So clearly," he finished without being asked, "any prosecution under this rule must bear the burden of proving that the statement was "knowingly or recklessly false."

The professor was surprised that no one objected to his speech, so he continued,

"This rule has been justified in limiting the free speech of lawyers as "a reasonable sacrifice for attorneys to make in order to uphold public confidence in the administration of justice."

He pulled a paper from his note book and explained, "The commentary to SCR 3.130 8.2(a) limits the broad application of this rule. That limitation is sometimes ignored, and I must say it is ignored at the peril of a constitutional challenge. It says, and I quote:

"(1) Assessments by lawyers are relied on in evaluating the professional or personal fitness of persons being considered for election or appointment to judicial office and to public legal offices, such as attorney general, prosecuting attorney and public defender. Expressing honest and candid opinions on such matters contributes to improving the administration of justice: Conversely, "false statements by a lawyer can unfairly undermine public confidence in the administration of justice."

Marciano took a chance and asked, "Professor in your expert opinion would it be a legitimate question of a Chief Justice's integrity if he used his authority in such a way as to disenfranchise half a million voters who elected Justice Boone to the Supreme Court and expected her to be the Justice to represent their Supreme Court District by assigning her to an inferior court for duty?"

Fisher exploded from her chair and entered an objection. The Trial Commissioner for the first time sustained an objection in her favor.

Marciano turned to the Trial Commissioner and asked, "Your Honor I respectfully take exception to your ruling and I move that the court be recessed long enough for Professor Cunningham to answer the question in an avowal to preserve the record."

The Trial Commissioner quickly responded, "I can't see how that would be relevant to these proceedings, your motion to submit an avowal is denied."

Justice Boone recognizing the Trial Commissioner's clear error in refusing to allow an attorney to submit an avowal to preserve the omitted testimony for review on appeal, wrote on her pad, "Appeal error No. 2!!"

Marciano politely responded, "Your Honor, the Rules of Procedure require that I preserve the record, and I respectfully suggest that I have a right to enter this avowal, and I respectfully object to your ruling."

The Trial Commissioner stated, "Your objection is noted but my ruling stands." He then said, "we will take a two hour lunch break. Let's all be back here ready to commence at 1:00 o'clock."

Marciano interjected, "Your Honor I just have one more question for the witness, and perhaps he would appreciate being released so as not to have to return this afternoon."

Fisher, said she had no objection, and the Trial Commissioner reluctantly allowed the defense counsel to proceed, "One question only!" he warned.

"Professor Cunningham, I respect your right to be compensated for your appearance here, but I must ask for the record, how much did the Ministry of Ethics pay you for your testimony in this case?"

Fisher objected and was quickly overruled.

The professor responded, "My standard fee is $5,000 a day plus travel expenses. So if I am discharged now, I will only bill the Ministry for one day. My travel expenses are about $600. That's in addition to my basic fee."

Marciano ended his cross-examination with a statement made in a tone that half of those present interpreted as a compliment and the other half of the room read as a backhanded insult, "Thank you professor. I'm sure the members of the Bar Association whose dues pay your bill will appreciate what a good value you have been to them."

Marciano concluded," . . . And thank you so very much for your valuable autograph which I shall treasure forever."

Justice Boone wrote on her legal pad as the room cleared, "Good point for appeal to Board of Governors and Supreme Court!!!"

Professor Cunningham wrote a short note before he rose from the witness chair. He then handed it to Frank Marciano and shook his hand before leaving for his flight back to Charlotte.

The note said, "My avowal would have said, the removal of Justice Boone by Chief Justice Hatter, for the purpose of cancelling her vote, was in my opinion a violation of Canon 1 Rule 1.2 of the Judicial Code of Conduct." He had signed and dated his note.

At lunch Marciano used his I-pad to call up LawReader.com and looked up the Canon of Judicial Ethics cited by Professor Cunningham.

"A judge shall act at all times in a manner that promotes public confidence in the independence, integrity, and impartiality of the judiciary, and shall avoid impropriety and the appearance of impropriety."

During the lunch break Fisher called the war room at the Ministry of Ethics and updated the attorneys who were on duty to back her up.

She recited the evidence she had been able to introduce and reported the motion regarding jurisdiction raised by Marciano.

The phone call was placed on the speaker phone, and a discussion of what to introduce in the Ministry's case for the afternoon session was discussed.

Commissioner Hart spoke last. "We have only one remaining issue in doubt, and that is whether or not Justice Alice's statement was false. All the other required elements are in the record. The question as to whether or not the statement was "false" or "knowingly or recklessly made" comes down to a question of law. Does everyone agree?"

The war room staff remained silent in the face of the Queen's declaration.

Commissioner Hart then ordered. "Ms. Fisher, when the afternoon session begins I want you to introduce Chief Justice Hatter's affidavit then rest your case."

After the Trial Commissioner called the afternoon session to order, Fisher approached the bench and presented the affidavit of Chief Justice Hatter and moved that it be introduced into the record.

Marciano demanded, "Your Honor I haven't seen that affidavit."

Fisher handed him a copy and the court allowed him time to read it.

The affidavit was a statement by the Chief Justice that important court business required his presence elsewhere, and stated, "My act in assigning Justice Boone to duty elsewhere was an exercise of the administrative powers granted my office by the Constitution of Kentucky, by Section 110 (4)(b) and therefore could not be unethical. The exercise of my clear constitutional powers could not by definition have been unethical or demonstrative of a lack of integrity. Justice Boone is quite familiar with the Supreme Court rules."

Marciano objected, "Your Honor, this affidavit was not provided to us prior to this very moment. The name of the Chief Justice was not on the witness list provided us by the Ministry.

This affidavit is nothing more than rank hearsay. Even the Chief Justice is not immune from the Rules of Evidence. The introduction of this affidavit would deny Justice Boone the right to confront and cross-examine her accusers."

Before Marciano could complete his heated protest, the Trial Commissioner raised his hand and ruled without explanation, "The affidavit will be admitted!"

"Objection your honor!"

Fisher then announced, "Your Honor, the Ministry rests."

Marciano's face was red with rage at the ruling, as he asked for a brief recess to consult with his client.

The motion was granted and the Trial Commissioner said, "Ten minute recess" and left the room.

Justice Boone scribbled vigorously on her pad, "Appeal error No. 3!!!"

Justice Boone and Marciano walked down the hallway of the hotel until they found a private room.

They discussed the ruling and concluded that the only good thing about the court's rulings was that he had presented them with numerous appellate issues.

Marciano concluded, "Justice, I see no benefit in your taking the stand. The record without the affidavit is void of the required element that your statement must have been false. Without the affidavit they have failed to present a case against you.

If we put you on, they'll try to get you to admit the statement was false. Your testimony risks that they'll get lucky and you help them. You have nothing to gain and everything to lose."

Justice Boone agreed although she had looked forward to a chance to take the stand and express her outrage over the actions of Madison Hatter.

They returned to the court room and the Trial Commissioner called the hearing to order.

Marciano gave a brief opening statement detailing that the Ministry had failed to prove that anything that Justice Boone was alleged to have said was false.

Marciano then moved for a directed verdict on the grounds that the Ministry had not proven an essential element of the offense as charged. He pointed out that no evidence was introduced regarding the falsity of the statement of Justice Boone.

The Trial Commissioner denied the motion and ordered the hearing to proceed.

"Your Honor", Marciano announced, we will call one witness.

He then turned to the bailiff and asked him, "Would you please call Chief Justice D. Wayne Chappell to the courtroom."

Fisher and the Trial Commissioner both dove into their files to see if Chappell's name had been included in their pre-trial witness list. Fisher found the list and saw that the name of the former Chief Justice had been properly disclosed by Marciano. The Trial Commissioner frowned but said nothing as the retired Chief Justice took the stand and was sworn.

Marciano got right to the point. "Chief Justice Chappell are you familiar with Section 110 (4)(b) of the Constitution of Kentucky?"

Chief Justice Chappell needed no prodding, "Yes, I wrote that provision as part of the Judicial Amendments approved by the voters of this Commonwealth in 1976. It was intended to permit Supreme Court Justices and other judges to be assigned around the state to help alleviate heavy caseloads in some districts. "It was never envisioned to be construed to permit a sitting Chief Justice to nullify the vote of a elected Justice of the Supreme Court.

"I admit that after Chief Justice Hatter used this provision to cancel out the voice of Justice Boone and Justice Allgood, I was shocked to see the terrible loophole that we created. It says what it says, but it was never intended to give the Chief Justice extra votes by assigning elected Justices elsewhere in order to manufacture a majority."

Marciano then asked the former Chief Justice the essential question, "When Chief Justice Hatter assigned Justices' Boone and Allgood to Small Claims Court, and called a special meeting of the Court to consider the Rabbit Hole Amendments, did he act in a manner that promoted public confidence in the independence, integrity and impartiality of the judiciary?"

Fisher objected to the question and the Trial Commissioner sustained her objection.

"Exception your Honor" Marciano responded.

The Trial Commissioner replied, "Exception noted."

Marciano then asked Chief Justice Chappell, "Justice did the actions of Chief Justice Hatter provide the appearance of impropriety?"

Fisher again objected to the question and the Trial Commissioner again sustained her object without further explanation.

"Exception your Honor" Marciano responded.

The Trial Commissioner replied, "Exception noted."

Marciano tried once again, "Justice Chappell, could you define the word "integrity" for us?"

The patrician judge was a commanding presence in the courtroom. He was in his 80's. He was a tall man with only a hint of a slight stoop in his posture. He still had a full head of white hair. His contempt with the Trial Commissioner's rulings was palpable.

He asked for a glass of water which was quickly retrieved by the bailiff.

He then replied, "Integrity is not a legal term. There is no definition in the Rules for this word. Therefore, I rely on the dictionary definition which defines the word."

He took a paper from his coat pocket, and read slowly: "Firm adherence to a code of especially moral or artistic values : incorruptibility."

He paused and looked directly at the Trial Commissioner before continuing, "The definition of 'moral' is reported by Merriam Webster as, "of or relating to principles of right and wrong in behavior."

He continued, "Therefore in common English as reported since the 1400's, 'Integrity' means doing the right thing. When an official uses a law in the wrong way or for an improper purpose then it is immoral and evidences a lack of integrity."

Marciano, surprised that the prosecutor did not object, continued quickly, "Is it the proper use of the assignment rule to remove two justices to keep them from voting on an issue before the court?"

The prosecutor shouted "Objection!" Justice Chappell ignored the objection and answered the question. "It's clearly unethical and shows a lack of integrity."

He continued his answer over the voice of the Trail Commissioner who was sustaining the objection.

"The only proper use of the assignment rule is to help alleviate a heavy case load in the inferior courts, and I have seen nothing 'necessary' about the case loads of these two small counties requiring the personal attendance of a member of the Supreme Court."

The Trial Commissioner for a second time ruled, "Objection sustained." He then angrily turned to Ron, the court reporter, and ordered him to strike the witnesses answer from the record.

The court reporter, in complying with his oath to fully and correctly make a record of the proceeding, did not strike anything. He said nothing. He quietly wrote "Court ordered reporter to strike the witnesses answer."

Justice Chappell's answer was also recorded on the court stenographer's tape recorder.

Marciano stated his objections to the court's ruling and the Trial Commissioner noted his objection.

Fisher announced that she had no questions for Chief Justice Chappell, and he was dismssed.

The Trial Commissioner announced that he saw no need for closing arguments as he was the fact finder and fully understood all the issues.

Marciano then moved the court. "Your Honor I move for a mistrial."

The Trial Commissioner simply said, "Motion denied."

Marciano without pausing, made his final motion, "Your Honor I restate my motion for a directed verdict. The Ministry has not presented any evidence that the statement alleged to have been made by Justice Boone was false or concerned a pending case. Once the Supreme Court voted on the issue before them, the ruling was final.

We submit that on constitutional grounds that any lawyer, and any judge, is assured his right to free speech, and the right to petition their government for the redress of their grievances, and just as importantly, anyone brought before the Ministry is entitled to due process of law, and that has been denied to Justice Boone."

Marciano detailed a laundry list of other reasons why a directed verdict should be granted in favor of Justice Boone. This was for the purpose of making a record for the appeal which would certainly follow. He had no delusion that the Trial Commissioner would grant the requested relief.

The Trial Commissioner did not address any of the issues raised. He simply declared, "Motion denied and this hearing is adjourned."

The Trial Commissioner was the finder of fact for such a hearing, and he would issue a written verdict at his leisure.

Justice Boone held out no hope for a dismissal of the complaint. It was apparent to her, and everyone in the room, how the Trial Commissioner would rule.

She agreed to meet with Marciano to plan their appeal to the Board of Governors as soon as the written verdict was released by the Trial Commissioner.

After thanking Frank Marciano for his hard work, Justice Boone drove herself home to Salyersville.

When she entered the Mountain Parkway just north of Winchester, she soon saw the green Appalachian foothills. Her return to the safety of her mountains gave her the only comfort she had had this week.

CHAPTER FORTY

Parrish Patterson had been appointed as a Trial Commissioner by the Chief Justice with the approval of the other members of the Supreme Court. It was unusual for the other Justices to vigorously contest the nominees for the Trial Commissioner position. The same appointment process produced the members of the Board of Scrutiny panels who acted as the Grand Jury.

The appointment process was an administrative job of the Supreme Court, and it was a tradition to defer to the Chief Justice. Most members of the court were so busy writing opinions that they had little interest in such minor matters. After all the Chief Justice was paid a few thousand dollars extra in salary to handle such matters.

For Justice Alice Boone the awful price of this lack of oversight soon became evident. The neglect of the Justices of the Supreme Court to closely monitor the nominations made by the Chief Justice vastly increased his ability to control the Ministry of Ethics and indeed the Bar Association.

Patterson, like many appointees, was regularly employed by a large law firm. Most nominees viewed the appointment as a public service.

One managing partner had justified the loss of billable hours by their junior lawyers serving in such positions by quoting Lyndon Johnson, "It's better to be inside the tent pissing out, then being on the outside pissing in."

Attorneys cited by the ethics machine knew far less about the Trial Commissioner assigned to their prosecution than they knew about the judges they appeared before in the civil and criminal courts.

There were no set standards or requirements of any judicial experience for the Trial Commissioners. They were nonetheless called Judge and were protected by the same broad immunity of judges. This immunity was granted, not by law or constitutional provision, but by a rule adopted by the Supreme Court.

No one had ever contested the court's rule granting immunity to Trial Commissioners and prosecutors of the Ministry of Ethics, from civil suits. Their immunity sprang up like Topsy. It was granted without much thought to the constitutionality of such a rule. Regardless of any malice or ulterior motivation, anyone wronged by immune officials might as well go pound salt because they would have no remedy in the civil courts.

This appointment system worked reasonable well for many years but under Madison Hatter the appointment process was molded into a lethal weapon at the disposal of the Chief Justice.

No actual accommodation was ever discussed between Madison Hatter and the Trial Commissioners he appointed, that would have been a bush league tactic rife with danger.

A far more subtle and unspoken understanding came in the fact that all of his impartial Trial Commissioner appointees worked for law firms who frequently appeared before Hatter's court on behalf of wealthy corporate clients.

It didn't take a Gypsy with Tarot Cards to see that keeping the Chief Justice a friend might pay real dividends in the future.

Hearing officers in the Executive Branch were appointed by the Governor with the approval of the State Senate. They were full time employees and protected by the merit system from political influence. But the Trial Commissioners working for the Bar Association had no job security, no merit system protection, and had little experience in the duties of a judge.

No one met with Patterson and attempted to influence his decision in Alice Boone's case.

He was selected because he was known as a team player. He understood without being told, that if he strayed too far from the Ministry's line, he would never be assigned another hearing.

One of the requirements for due process rights, was "the right to have your case heard by an impartial magistrate." This right was protected by the Fourteenth Amendment to the United States Constitution, and was even part of the Supreme Court Rules regarding the disciplinary process. In practice it was just another classroom theory that should be ignored in the real world.

Trial Commissioner Patterson used a simple form in writing his findings of fact and verdict.

He waited a month before getting around to writing his decision and delivering it to the Inquisition Clerk. His decision of course had been made before the hearing commenced.

He found that Supreme Court Justice Alice Boone had violated the Supreme Court Rules by challenging the "integrity" of Chief Justice Madison Hatter in violation of SCR 3.130 (8.2)(a).

He proposed a sanction of a 180 day suspension of her license to practice law.

If the suspension was upheld, it would have the effect of imposing on Alice Boone a loss of six month's salary and six months retirement benefits. The monetary value of this suspension was about $75,000.

Marciano and Justice Boone reviewed the decision and the consequences. It was not clear if this proposed suspension would result in her removal from the Supreme Court.

Marciano concluded, "I find no authority for removal of a Justice other than by impeachment or by action of the Judicial Conduct Commission. Impeachment power is granted only to the Legislature and the Judicial Conduct Commission."

Patterson's decision did not mention any of the objections made by Frank Marciano.

It did not explain why he allowed the hearsay affidavit of Madison Hatter to be introduced but refused to allow the testimony of Justice D. Wayne Chappell. He did not respond to the prosecution's use of a witness whose name had not been disclosed to the defense prior to trial.

Most importantly the Trial Commissioner's decision did not bother to explain his finding that the statement made by Alice Boone was false.

Justice Boone noted, "I can't believe that Patterson even neglected to issue a final ruling on the jurisdiction issue. If the Ministry is upheld on this point, then they have repealed all the law regarding the powers of the Judicial Conduct Commission. They might as well dissolve that body.

"If this ruling stands, the Judicial Conduct Commission will be totally at the mercy of the Ministry of Ethics and the special procedures created to deal with misconduct by Judges would be effectively voided."

She told Marciano, "The Judicial Conduct Commission is structurally set up much more fairly than the Ministry. After a formal charge is issued, all proceedings automatically become public.

"There is no politically appointed Trial Commissioner at the Judicial Conduct Commission.

The entire Judicial Conduct Commission hears the case. One member is elected by the District Court judges, one by the Circuit Court judges, one by the Court of Appeals, and one by the Bar Association. Two citizen members are appointed by the Governor. This structure virtually eliminates the influence of the Chief Justice.

"I have never understood why the Supreme Court came up with the unwieldy Ministry of Ethics when they had such a successful model in the Judicial Conduct Commission."

Before his meeting with Justice Boone, Marciano had prepared the notice of appeal to the Board of Governors of the Bar Association. The appeal was filed immediately.

The Appeal requested a De Novo hearing by the Board of Governors. The Board of Governors had the authority to rule on the Trial Commissioner's proposal from the record or to conduct a complete new hearing in which they could make their own factual finding.

They were not required to accept the finding or the sanctions proposed by the Trial Commissioner.

Chapter Forty-One

The Board of Governors brought up the appeal at their next meeting. The Board of Governors members were elected by the membership of the Bar Association. Two members were elected from each of the states seven Supreme Court electoral districts.

A copy of the Trial Commissioner's findings and penalty recommendation, and Marciano's appeal brief were presented to each member of the Board of Governors.

William Mathis, the President of the Bar Association, presided over the closed meeting. He began, "I suggest that we advance this appeal to the top of the list. Important issues are raised in this appeal."

That was the only thing the President said that was unanimously agreed upon.

For more than an hour the members argued about the sufficiency of the Trial Commissioner's findings, the lack of evidence of the "falsity" of her statement, the admission of the Chief Justices hearsay affidavit, the recusal motion, denial of the avowal, and the jurisdiction of the Ministry to intervene and bypass the Judicial Conduct Commission.

Finally, the Bar President intervened and suggested, "First we need to select a date. Secondly we need to determine if we are going to rule on this from the record or grant a De Novo hearing."

Betsy Adams from Owensboro, moved that the hearing be set for the afternoon of their next monthly meeting. The motion was approved.

Tim Stein from Louisville, having thought a great deal about this appeal, stood up and moved for a dismissal hearing. He argued, "Let's all be very clear about this. This is a test case. The Chief Justice and the Ministry are using this case to warn all of us to remain silent in the face of their genocidal plan to reduce the number of lawyers.

"Today they are going after Alice Boone. Tomorrow it will be you. We have allowed the Ministry to become the Chief Justice's Gestapo. Don't forget the Commissioner of the Ministry of Ethics works for us! SCR 3.130 (8.2)(a) has been misused time and time again for improper purposes. And this so-called hearing they conducted has no relationship to any Due Process proceeding I have ever seen.

"We should review this from the record and dismiss it once and for all. We shouldn't stop there, we should call in the 'Queen' and give her the opportunity to go back to practicing law before real courts. I move we dismiss this complaint right now!"

Tony Monk spoke out in his most demeaning manner, "Now Tim, don't get carried away. We are now acting as an appellate court, and we shouldn't go postal here."

Several others offered comments in line with Monk's.

President Mathis wasn't sure that Stein's motion was proper but he nevertheless called a vote. The Board voted eight to six to defeat Stein's motion to dismiss the charges against Alice Boone.

Stein then stood up again and moved for a De Novo hearing. That motion passed by a vote of eight to six without further argument.

Chapter Forty-Two

Cheshire's report of the meeting of the Board of Governors was retrieved from the mail box drop by Commissioner Hart within a week. The report contained the minutes of the meeting of the Board.

She was impressed by Cheshire's' access, and concluded he must have some connection inside the KBA or the Board of Governors.

Her attention focused on the six members of the Board who voted to dismiss the Alice Boone complaint. She wrote down the names of the six dissenters before destroying the report in her fireplace.

The following day, when she got back to her office in the Castle, she called Lizarde to her office and assigned him to begin an investigation on all six dissenters on the Board. She directed him, "I want a credit check, CLE files, and I also want you to do a docket search on each of them.

"Use the docket search to find out what cases they may have appeared in, and interview their opposing counsel. That is the quickest way to discover potential ethical situations that may have been otherwise overlooked. And Lizarde, you are authorized to offer anyone who has interesting information immunity for any violations of the squeal rule if necessary." She concluded, "And get Walrus to assist you. I need this double quick."

Chapter Forty-Three

The Board of Governors heard the appeal of Justice Boone at their next meeting. The parties both argued about the function of the Board in a De Novo appeal. The Ministry argued that the Board could only review the record and then could reconsider the factual issues. Frank Marciano asserted that under the case of Brady v. Pettit, 586 S.W.2d 29 (Ky., 1979) the person appealing could call additional witnesses.

Marciano proposed to call former Chief Justice D. Wayne Chappell as a witness for the Board's hearing.

Marciano explained to Alice, "While we have the essential testimony of Justice Chappell in the original record, which will be read by the Board, I believe that it would be prudent to recall the Justice and once again attempt to get into the record the portions of his testimony that had been stricken by the Trial Commissioner at the first hearing. In case the Board doesn't admit the testimony which was stricken by Patterson, we could try again to get his testimony into the record."

Alice agreed with this plan, "Justice Chappell is highly credible, and a second bite at the apple is a good idea."

Marciano had another trick in his bag. "Alice, I want you to prepare to present a closing argument to the Board. The courts have frequently allowed defendants to make their own closing argument without surrendering their Fifth Amendment right not to testify."

Justice Boone, overlooking his underestimate of her knowledge of such matters, smiled at Marciano, "Frank, that's beautiful. I love it. I can't wait to address the Board!"

As the Bar President called the hearing to order, Marciano and Fisher approached him and argued their motions. President Mathis ruled quickly that the Board would review the entire record, and that the defense could call additional witnesses to supplement the record. He granted the motion of the Ministry to impose on Justice Boone the burden of proof to overcome the ruling of the Trial Commissioner. The President also announced that the findings of fact by the Trial Commissioner were subject to review by the Board.

Marciano and Fisher began by both moving for introduction of the record from the first hearing. That motion was granted.

Marciano then moved that the Board rule as a matter of law, that the testimony of Chief Justice Chappell that was stricken by the Trial Commissioner be admitted into the record and introduced as evidence that could be considered by the Board. The President granted the motion without comment and directed the parties to begin.

Since the appeal had been filed by Justice Boone, she was required to go first in the presentation of evidence. On her behalf Marciano called former Chief Justice D. Wayne Chappell as a witness.

After Chappell was sworn, Marciano restated the same questions he had previously asked the witness in the first hearing.

Justice Chappell gave the same answers, but added without being asked, "The Ministry of Ethics has failed to introduce any evidence that the alleged statement made by Justice Boone was false. That's the bottom line."

Fisher quickly objected to the comments of Justice Chappell, and just as quickly was overruled by the President.

He looked at Fisher and firmly stated, "Justice Chappell is an expert on the legal issues raised on this appeal. He served for many years as the Chief Justice of the Supreme Court. He was one of the original authors of the Supreme Court Rule which Justice Boone has been alleged to have violated. This Board is privileged to hear his thoughts on the issues we must consider, and we all may just learn something if we listen to him."

The President then said to Fisher, "For the record we note your objection to anything that Justice Chappell may say. The Board will consider your continuing objections to his testimony and if something should be stricken we will strike it. But there is no need to interrupt him."

Marciano, realized that continuing objections of this type had recently been found by the appellate courts to be insufficient to preserve the record, but he kept his opinion about this to himself.

Mathis then turned to Justice Chappell, "Justice you may continue."

The octogenarian asked for a bottle of water which was provided to him by the bailiff.

"It is rumored that I am so old that I played golf with Isaac Shelby, our first governor. Well that's not true, but I do confess to being old enough to have witnessed the growth of the Kentucky Bar for more years than most of the members of the Board of Governor were around.

In those years I have seen the number of lawyers grow from less than 2,000 to the current level in excess of 17,000. I recall the brotherhood that we used to have. We took care of one another. We would beat our heads against each other in the courtroom then go to dinner together in the evening.

"If there was a lawyer that broke the rules we all knew about it, and the local Circuit Judge could quickly do something about it. The local prosecutor was charged with pursuing violations of Ethics Rules.

"I concede that there was some 'Home Cookin' in this process, but it wasn't all bad. Everything was done in public and in the courtroom. While a local attorney who was respected may have been cut some slack, I had no problem with a lawyer's lifetime of distinguished conduct being a factor in considering an ethics allegation.

"Under the prior ethics review process the judge and prosecutor who heard their cases were subject to public sanction if they were not fair.

"There were no secret investigations and no anonymous squealers. The poison pen letter was treated with opprobrium and given little weight. If you had a complaint against a lawyer, you stood up in a public courtroom like a man and said so.

"Today it is too easy for a lawyer to have his integrity attacked and never know the motive or the identity of his accuser. The Ministry of Ethics has demonstrated a willingness, even an eagerness, to be the hatchet man for jealous lawyers who attack other lawyers out of envy and spite, and I'm sure they many ethics complaints are filed so the complainant can achieve a competitive advantage over other lawyers.

"I am sorry to say that our current disciplinary process has not done away with the 'Home Cookin' problem, it has just created an even greater problem, which I call 'Frankfort cookin'."

"One example of 'Frankfort cookin' occurs when one lawyer is sanctioned while another lawyer who has done far worse is left to benefit from their wrong. There is a widespread belief among members of the Bar that the Ministry takes care of those they like, and goes out of their way to punish those they don't. This favoritism is able to exist due to the secrecy rules.

"When the Supreme Court created the secrecy rules for disciplinary prosecutions they thought they were protecting honest lawyers from the embarrassment of frivolous and unfounded complaints. But secret investigations, secret hearings, and secret witnesses are anathema to a democratic society.

"The one safety valve for a democratic society is the right of citizens to stand on their soapbox and scream "Foul!" when they perceive a wrong. This right to speak one's mind is enshrined in the U.S. Constitution and the Kentucky Constitution.

"Yet somewhere along the way, someone thought it was a good idea to take from lawyers the constitutional right of free speech that even the lowest criminal enjoys. I do not believe that the interests of our society have been advanced by the denial of free speech rights to those who are best able to witness and identify a miscarriage of justice. Why shouldn't a lawyer who witnesses a flagrant foul, be able to publically shout "Foul"!

"I understand the need for decorum in our courtrooms. No lawyer and no citizen should be allowed to disrupt an ongoing trial. But once that trial is over, lawyers and citizens should not be punished if they climb on their soapboxes in the town square.

"I have spent most of my adult life as a judge. I have had my feelings hurt by ill-advised comments challenging the wisdom of my obviously wise rulings."

Everyone in the courtroom smiled as he continued.

"On the reflection of old age and time, I have concluded that on a few rare occasions I did in fact make a bad ruling. But I didn't need the Ministry of Ethics to protect me. The result of criticism of my actions didn't prevent me from doing my job. It merely toughened my hide a bit.

"This criticism served as a moral tripwire warning me when I got near the line of improper conduct or fallacious reasoning.

"If I made a mistake, the absence of criticism did not make it any more correct. If I was unjustly criticized my maker and the public were allowed to be the ultimate judges of my actions.

"I didn't need a Super Nanny with the power of sanctions to come to my aid. I allowed my rulings to be tested in the market place of public opinion and if the public disagreed with me they could vote me out of office at the next election. This is what our Founding Fathers intended when they wrote the First Amendment.

"When SCR 3.130 (8.2)(a) was adopted, it was thought that the language limiting its application to "knowing false statements about the integrity of a judge or prosecutor" was a clear message that *all* speech was not prohibited. Only *false* statements were prohibited.

"If a lawyer said a judge was a liar and a thief, and if the judge was in fact a liar and a thief then there was no violation. Subsequent court rulings limited the application of this rule to pending cases.

"I see no proof in this case that the statement of Justice Boone was made during a pending case. Her statement was made after the Supreme Court had adopted the Rabbit Hole amendments.

"When I see this pending charge against Justice Boone, I see that the Supreme Court meddled with the First Amendment. When they thought they were wiser than our Founding Fathers, they made a serious mistake of hubris.

"I would submit that I have never known of a more sinister application of the law then the disenfranchisement of two sitting Supreme Court Judges in order to manipulate a majority on an issue before the Court. This type of action would not be condoned on the basketball court. It would not be condoned or tolerated on the sandlot where young men and women play baseball and build character. It would not be tolerated on the golf course where personal ethics are the essence of the game.

"All laws must be considered in relation to other laws. The law requiring that Justices be elected implies that Justices shall have one vote per judge on all cases or issues coming before the court.

"When the Chief Justice used the assignment rule to disenfranchise the voters of two Supreme Court Districts he voided the democratic election process and eviscerated the votes of the citizens of two Supreme Court Districts.

"And I submit this type of conduct should not never be tolerated on our Supreme Court.

"The sense of Fair Play is deeply ingrained in our society. When someone bends a rule out of all reasonable interpretation in order to achieve an unjust result, someone should cry Foul!

"Justice Boone stood up and cried 'Foul!' In doing so she merely exercised her constitutional right to speak out to an injustice. The resulting complaint against her is an outrageous abuse of her First Amendment rights. She only spoke the truth.

'This body is charged with the duty of determining if the statement Alice Boone made was 'false.' The Ministry has not introduced one iota of proof that her statement was false. I know they have no such proof because her statement was, on its face, true in every respect.

"I ask you to consider that if you personally have a doubt that Justice Boone's statement was true, then the Ministry has not borne its burden of proving her guilt by a preponderance of the evidence. If you believe that Chief Justice Hatter's reassignment was proper, then I question your knowledge of the law.

"You may justifiable ignore the ramblings of an old Judge. But don't ignore that beating drum in your heart that is shouting at you that this abominable charge against Justice Boone should be dismissed immediately.

"This Board of Governors represents the 17,000 members of the Bar. You are their only voice. You can stop this Alice in Wonderland Tea Party right here!

He concluded his testimony which had become a speech by paraphrasing General Patton's movie speech by asking, "What will you say thirty years from now, when you have white hair, and are sitting on the porch with your grandchild on your knee, and when that innocent faced child looks you in the eye and says, Grandfather when the First Amendment was under attack, when the great battle for justice was in doubt, which side where you on?"

As Justice Chappell struggled to rise from his witness chair, the Board of Governors broke into applause.

The President announced that the hearing would be recessed for ten minutes.

When the hearing was called back to order, Liz Fisher rose and entered an objection,

"President Mathis, I respectfully object to the speech of Chief Justice Chappell and move it be stricken from the record. While he is entitled to express his personal views outside this hearing, I believe it is improper in the format of this appeal being heard by the Board of Governors, and it certainly should not be entered as evidence."

Frank Marciano rose to respond but President Mathis motioned for him to sit down. The President dismissed the objection.

"Ms. Fisher, my reading of SCR 3.800 (F) (ii) forces me to conclude that strict application of the Rules of Evidence are not required in these proceedings. I believe if you will take time to read these rules you will surely agree."

Fisher sat down without comment. She missed the favoritism shown her by the Trial Commissioner in the prior hearing.

Marciano then called Justice Boone to make her closing statement.

Justice Boone began a brief presentation, "Since I was notified of the complaint filed against me, I have looked forward to this opportunity. I have been eager to place my trust in my peers.

"Like me, you all have taken an oath to defend the Constitution of Kentucky and the Constitution of the United States. I have faith that you hold the First Amendment as sacred as I do.

"I feel confident that you will quickly dispose of these unjust charges.

"Let me clearly state, one thing. Chief Justice Madison Hatter was wrong to use the assignment section of the Kentucky Constitution for the unjust purpose of creating a majority to adopt the Rabbit Hole Plan Rules. The assignment section was never intended to repeal the democratic election where the voters placed Justice Allgood and myself on the Supreme Court bench. Without this maneuver, the Rabbit Hole rules would never have been adopted.

"My concern however, is not just on the improper adoption of the Rabbit Holes rules, my concern is about the future. If you allow the Chief Justice's power grab to stand, then the assignment section may well be used in the future on other issues of greater importance.

"Will he or some future Chief Justice use the assignment section to end jury trials? The right to remain silent? Will they tamper with the Rules of Evidence and allow police hearsay in prosecutions?

"My defense is obvious. I saw a wrongful use of the constitution assignment section, and I cried out. The First Amendment assures free speech for all citizens. I have read the First Amendment a thousand times, and I have never found an exception that denies the right of free speech to lawyers or to judges as is argued in this prosecution. Everything I said was protected by the First Amendment, and just as importantly, since everything I said was true, it is even protected by the language of 3.130 (8.2), the rule I am accused of having violated."

Justice Boone scanned the eyes of the members of the Board of Governors for a minute, before concluding, "Today I am in the dock. Tomorrow you may stand here accused of the same offense."

She paused briefly to let that thought sink in before finishing. "I will conclude by asking this Board to go and do justice."

Marciano then announced that he felt that the testimony of Chief Justice Chappell and the statement of Justice Boone were a sufficient basis for the Board to consider the case and justified dismissal of the charges.

He rested the case of Justice Alice Boone and waived a closing argument. "Chief Justice Chappell's testimony is the only closing argument we need."

The President looked at Fisher and asked if she intended to call any witnesses. Fisher hesitated before quietly answering, "The Ministry rests and submits the case on the record."

President Mathis rose from his chair and announced that the Board would announce its decision within 60 days.

Chapter Forty-Four

Jack Kenton received a call from a secretary at the Ministry of Ethics requesting a meeting to discuss his pending ethics complaint. He was asked to come to the Ministry's Wonderland Castle on Versailles Road. After calling his attorney, he called the Ministry and confirmed the meeting for the following day. He informed them he was bringing his attorney.

He didn't comment on their improper call to him which violated their duty to only communicate through his attorney.

At 4:00 p.m. Kenton and his attorney pulled off US 60 and drove up a gentle hill to the west entrance of the Castle. They drove through the twenty foot tall wooden gates and parked in a paved lot inside the Castle walls.

Kenton's attorney, Barbara Popplewell, smiled at him as they exited the car and looked up at the high stone walls and giant minarets that shielded the buildings from public view.

"Jack, some people call this place 'The Place de la Concorde'. That's the public square in Paris where the Guillotine was placed during the French Revolution. As you know it was used to separate thousands of the aristocracy from their heads. That period of history was called, 'The Great Terror' in France."

"Barbara, I get your point. You have a really dark sense of humor bringing that up."

Kenton did not speak his thoughts. He was very aware of the history of the 'Great Terror', and he now felt, in some small way, the apprehension the victims of the blade must have felt as they were driven in ox carts to the place of their public humiliation and impending death.

He realized that the Ministry used fear to intimidate those caught in their web. Their lease of office space in the Wonderland Castle was a masterful stroke on their part. He could not erase his fear, but he refused to allow his face to reveal those inner thoughts. He would not allow his fears to control his actions.

Popplewell, unaware of his hidden thoughts, continued her effort to lighten the mood with dark humor. "If they ask you to go to the basement, be careful that's where the dungeon is."

Kenton joined the jest. "I've heard stories that the Queen conducts her interrogations while wearing a red latex body suit, and that she has dozens of whips hanging on the walls next to the Iron Maiden and the Rack. I want to warn you, Barbara, if you let them put me on the rack I will rat you out as JFK's assassin."

Popplewell countered, "I checked out our attorney client contract and it doesn't say I have to go to the dungeon with you."

They walked to an imposing door made of massive wood planks, with a large metal doorknocker in the image of a gargoyle with wings.

Kenton, took the door knocker and loudly pounded it against the door. An electronic voice came from an unseen speaker. "The door is unlocked."

Popplewell whispered, "What, no hunchbacked Igor to open the door?"

They opened the door and walked up a short flight of stairs to a waiting room. A tall woman wearing the female version of a man's suit was waiting for them.

"Mr. Kenton, Ms. Popplewell, please come this way. You will be meeting with Mr. Terrapin."

They were escorted to an elevator where the female suit pushed a button that said "Level D."

Popplewell raised her eyebrows and suppressed the belly laugh that cried to be released. They both interpreted the elevator button marked 'Level D' to refer to the Dungeon.

After leaving the elevator their host took a large iron key from her pocket and opened a door to a hallway leading from the elevator. As they were guided down the long hallway the only sound they heard was the clicking of the escorts high heels striking the bare concrete floor.

The walls of the long hallway were unpainted cinder blocks. None of the doors had names on them, only numbers. Finally they arrived at door marked 'D-13'. The door opened for them before they could knock.

A small bald headed man in his late 30's welcomed them in. He showed them to a steel table that was bolted to the floor. The table was empty save for a large telephone console.

The steel seats he invited them to sit on, were bolted to the floor. Both attorneys recognized a police interrogation room. There was even a one-way mirror on the wall.

Both Kenton and Popplewell sensed that they were being observed and assumed they were being videotaped.

They both instinctively looked for the microphones and cameras, but none were discernable, although they both knew they were there somewhere.

He began, "My name is Phillip Terrapin. I've been assigned to your case." He explained that he was sorry to be meeting them under such unfortunate circumstances, but he was hopeful that the issues could be speedily resolved.

He had a large file in front of him. He opened it and Kenton recognized a photograph of himself that was published in the *Lexington Herald-Leader* some two years ago when he had received an award from the Bar Association as Attorney of the Year. Popplewell recognized this as a standard investigator's ploy to imply to Kenton that they knew everything about him.

"The reason I asked you to come here today is to see if we can't reach a settlement of the complaint against you for violation of SCR 3.130 (8.2) regarding your letter to the Legislative Ethics Commission.

"We are ready to submit the complaint to the Board of Scrutiny, but before we take that step, we wanted to see if we could work this out."

Popplewell interjected, "And I assume that will be a complete dismissal?"

Terrapin eyed her with the contempt that prosecutors often express towards defense attorneys when they try to place themselves between the interrogator and their targeted prey. He responded, "No, but we have a very fair offer.

"As you surely know the possible sanctions for a violation of this type can include anything from a warning letter to a permanent disbarment. We propose that you plead guilty to a violation and we will recommend a Public Reprimand and completion of an Ethics Rehabilitation Program."

Kenton asked, "And if I don't accept this offer, what happens?"

Terrapin set back in his chair and exhaled in disgust as if he was imposed upon by such a silly question, "Well, you understand that the Board of Scrutiny can add any additional charges that are warranted."

The threat was clearly understood by Popplewell and Kenton.

Kenton pressed, "Why a public reprimand, why not a private reprimand? Why not a dismissal?"

"Mr. Kenton," Terrapin relied with great seriousness, "The Ministry has reviewed the complaint against you, and it was decided that there must be some penalty due to the seriousness of your offense. We don't see any benefit from a private reprimand. It is important that other members of the Bar learn that the Rules must be complied with."

At that moment they heard a door slam loudly, and could make out the screams of someone outside their door apparently being dragged down the hallway. The male voice couldn't be understood except for the words, "You've ruined me! You've ruined me!"

Popplewell instinctively reached over to Kenton and placed her hand tightly on his wrist, having failed in her impossible attempt to move her steel chair closer to his.

Terrapin ignored the screams. He pulled a form from the file in front of him, and continued, "I have a plea agreement prepared, just sign this and the matter is over."

Popplewell said, "Phil, we have some questions for you first."

Terrapin, rose from his chair and folded his file in an attempt to express his ending of the meeting and to suggest a withdrawal of the offer.

He looked Popplewell in the eye and coldly responded, "Ms. Popplewell, you don't get to ask questions. Only the Ministry asks questions!"

He handed the plea form along with his business card to Popplewell. "You have 24 hours to accept our generous offer. If you agree please call me and place the signed agreement in the mail. If we don't hear from you by tomorrow then we will submit all outstanding issues to the Board of Scrutiny on Monday."

Popplewell said, "What are the "other issues" you are referring too?"

Terrapin ignored the question and opened the door. "Thank you for dropping by. Just go to the door at the end of the hall and someone will show you out." He remained in the room and closed the door as they left.

They waited at the exit door at the end of the hallway for ten minutes. It seemed like an hour. Both attorneys felt the heavy weight on their chest that visitors have when they leave a jail or prison and have a brief fear that they may not be let out.

Kenton, started to speak to Popplewell but she placed her finger against her lips silencing him.

After they were shown out by the female suit, they walked silently to the car before deeply inhaling the fresh air.

Once in the car Kenton said, "I can't believe we pay dues to fund this Bluegrass-Guantanamo. They treated me like a common criminal. All I did was write one letter!"

Popplewell asked, "So are you going to accept their offer?"

"Hell no!" Kenton relied, "They can threaten me all they want. The suggestion that there are other charges they may conjure up is crap!"

He looked at Popplewell and said derisively, "You know me better than that!"

Popplewell raised her hands in defense and said, "Calm down, calm down, I had to ask."

The occupants of the car were silent as they drove past the prestigious horse barns lining US 60 on their way back to Frankfort. The horse barns were better than the homes of most Kentucky families.

Popplewell broke the silence, "I'll wait until tomorrow to call them. The very fact they made you an offer suggests they are not really comfortable with this prosecution."

Kenton was clearly angry. "These ethics prosecutions as supposed to be civil matters. There is supposed to be due process but they deny me discovery rights. Even the standard of proof is a civil standard. But they treat everything like a criminal prosecution. That is so wrong. When he said 'We ask the questions here!' I wanted to rip that chair out of the floor and hit him over his pointy head!"

Popplewell had never seen the normally controlled Kenton express such emotion. She changed the subject. "Well don't forget Jack, we still have Stafford's Plan B!"

He turned to her and smiled, "Yes, we certainly have Plan B. When the time is right!"

Chapter Forty-Five

The following morning Jack Kenton read the *Courier-Journal* as he drank a cup of black coffee in the study of Kenton Farm. His eyes fell on a report of a suspected suicide. The man was a lawyer named Bubba Bensinger. He had met Bensinger some years ago and they tried a case in Jefferson Circuit Court over some issue that he could no longer remember. His impression of Bensinger was that he was a straight up guy, and a pretty good litigator.

The story reported, "Bubba Bensinger, a lawyer from Louisville, drove his car into a bridge abutment near Shelby County at a speed estimated by witnesses at over 100 miles per hour. The collision occurred at 5:30 p.m. Motorists who stopped to render aid reported that he was decapitated in the collision.

His law office in Louisville reported that he had been in a meeting with the Ministry of Ethics near Versailles, but they would not disclose the purpose of his meeting.

"A witness, H. Douglas Rouse, said he was driving west bound on I-64 at about 70 miles an hour when Bensinger's Mercedes passed him like Dale Earnhardt was driving. For no apparent reason he drove into the concrete bridge abutment near the Waddy-Paytona exit. He didn't put his brakes on and didn't skid. He just drove that Mercedes right into the wall like he meant to do it."

The story reported that Bensinger was 57, married, the father of two surviving sons, and was a member of the Jewish Temple in Louisville. The story continued, "The Ministry of Ethics refused to confirm or deny if Bensinger had been at the Ministry headquarters prior to the collision. "All actions of the Ministry are confidential," the media rep added.

Kenton's hands began to tremble as he realized that the screaming voice he had heard at the Ministry of Ethics dungeon must have been Bensinger.

He muttered to himself, "Those bastards!"

Chapter Forty-Six

Matt Simons was working on a faulty server in the Cheshire electronics hideaway when Tweedledee and Tweedledum came in. Tweedledee sat at one of the terminals, and printed out a report. Tweedledee closed the computer file, and removed the printed report from the printer before placing it in a large manila envelope.

Being curious, Simons asked them what they were doing. Tweedledum removed a toothpick from his mouth and said, "Just making our weekly Friday trip to Louisville." Simons asked himself, "To whom would they be delivering wiretap information to Louisville every week?"

In minutes Simons was in his car and rushing to keep the Tweedle brothers' van in sight as he followed them west on I-64 to Louisville. In less than an hour, they exited the Watterson Expressway and turned west on Shelbyville Road. He remained half a block behind them until he saw them pull into the Shelbyville Road Plaza Mall. He passed the Mall entrance and drove another block before circling back to the Mall parking lot.

He saw Tweedledee had parked near the entrance to the St. Matthews Branch of the Post Office. Tweedledum was walking into the Post Office as Simons parked several rows back. Through the window of the Post Office he could clearly see Tweedledum walk to a post office box, open it with a key, and place the envelope inside.

Tweedledum returned to the car but did not immediately leave. Simon took out a set of binoculars and saw that Tweedledee had a camera and was apparently waiting to take a picture of something or someone. Fifteen minutes later he saw Commissioner Heather Hart drive into the parking lot in her state car, and after parking, enter the Post Office. She immediately went to the same post office box that the envelope had been placed in, and removed it. She briskly walked to her car and left the parking lot. He smiled to himself, "So Tweedledum has a key to a post office box and The Queen of Hearts also has a key to the same box. Not a bad dead drop procedure."

He mentally patted himself on the back. His suspicion about the Tweedle brothers delivery was confirmed.

He added the Queen of Hearts to his potential blackmail list.

Chapter Forty-Seven

Supreme Court Justice Anderson had been invited to join several lawyers to play a round of Golf at the Idle Hour Golf Course on Richmond Road in Lexington. He couldn't afford a membership in this exclusive club on a judge's salary.

He appreciated the opportunity to see how the other half lived. After the round they adjourned to the Grill room and drinks were ordered by Mark Ogle, the host member.

The score card revealed that Justice Anderson, even though having a score of 15 strokes over par, had with his partner's assistance, won the $5 Nassau match. He was unaware that the golfers he had just beaten all had single digit handicaps. He enthusiastically accepted a hundred dollar bill for his share of his team's victory.

After the Justice had finished off his second round of Bourbon, the attorney who had carried him on the team, casually asked, "Justice, what's all this stuff about new Rules being proposed by Justice Alice Boone to rein in the Ministry of Ethics?"

Before Anderson could respond, a second attorney joined in, "Seems to me that Commissioner Hart has really crossed the line. Hell, she is trying to nail Jack Kenton for writing a letter."

Justice Anderson, started to respond but the third lawyer interjected with the comment. "Can't the other members of the court control the Chief Justice on issues relating to the adoption of Rules?"

The three separate questions confused him. Justice Anderson realized that he was surrounded by supporters of Alice Boone and Jack Kenton. He detected a thinly veiled hostile attitude in the tone of their questions.

He responded with a rambling answer. "Frankly we try to respect the Chief Justice's administrative role in running the courts. We aren't all that happy with the recent Rabbit Hole Rules he supported, but we recognize the public needs to be protected from the misdeeds of unethical lawyers."

He paused before adding, "I have heard that Justice Boone is going to propose new Ethics Rules, but I haven't seen them yet."

One of the lawyers, who was well aware that Justice Anderson had voted for the Rabbit Hole Rules responded in a conciliatory tone, "I would have thought that Justice Boone would have copied you on her new rules. I have a copy and will be glad to send it to you." The host of the golf outing said, "Justice I don't want to put you on the spot." He then proceeded to put the Justice on the spot.

"We believe that there is a ground swell of opposition among members of the Bar. Some are calling it 'The Lawyers Revolution'. I hear that Williston Stafford and a group he calls the "Eunuchs" are giving speeches all over the state in support of Justice Boone's proposal to clean up the Ministry of Ethics power grab. Hell there is even talk that they are soliciting candidates to run for the Supreme Court."

Ogle, the host, continued with a sweep of his hand indicating that the others were with him, "We all think you are a great Justice, and you know we would never lift a finger to solicit opposition, but we have no control over Stafford and his group. We hear that he has raised over half a million dollars to fund judicial races."

Justice Anderson's face involuntarily turned crimson.

One of the golfers added to Anderson's misery, "I hate to say this, but I was told by someone close to Stafford that he held a meeting in your district and over seventy lawyers attended and every one of them pledged at least five hundred dollars, to support the candidacy of someone to run against you."

The host held out an olive branch, "Is there anything we could say to them to back them off ? The only issue seems to be those damn Rabbit Hole rules, and the out-of-control Ministry."

The third golfer, Jeffrey Smith, had remained silent till now, but spoke up with a suggested escape route for Justice Anderson, "I know Stafford pretty well. I believe I can talk with him. If you have anything that I can pass on to him to get him off your back, I will be glad to intervene. If you are supportive of Justice Boone's rules, let us know and I think we can help you."

Justice Anderson's right hand began to shake so much that he spilled some of his drink.

He did not look forward to having to raise money for his empty campaign fund. He particularly dreaded the thought of having to actively campaign in the upcoming Supreme Court elections. He needed another ten years on the court to fully fund his Judicial retirement program.

This conversation took him from the high of a victory on an exclusive golf course, and joy in being recognized by several of the club members as a Justice of the Supreme Court, to the low of a discussion of potential opposition in the next election. His spirits plunged, and he suddenly wished he was somewhere else.

The Justice repeated his lie, "I haven't seen the rules you say are being proposed by Alice Boone, but I will be glad to read a copy if you will send them to me."

The Chief Justice had given him an outline of Alice's proposed rules weeks ago, but he wasn't going to admit that and encourage a discussion of the merits of the proposed rules.

Anderson paused for a moment to see if his response had cooled their passions. After their faces indicated that he had not done so, he continued. "I'm aware that some members of the Bar are upset with the Ministry.

"I believe that Heather Hart has possibly stepped over the line in some cases. Chief Justice Hatter seems to be strongly supportive of her. I just have one vote on this, but I assure you that I will take a very close look at Alice's new rules."

At that moment Justice Anderson's cell phone rang. After ending the call, he said he would have to reject their invitation for dinner, as he had to return home immediately.

They all stood up, and collectively invited him to join them again in the near future. He left quickly and pledged to himself that he would never again let himself be surrounded by these damn lawyers.

After the Justice left the Grill, the host called Williston Stafford and gave him a report. "We made it pretty clear that he was going to have opposition if he didn't get his mind right. He turned about six shades of red and damn near wet his shorts." The other guests could hear Stafford chuckling over the phone.

After a brief discussion with Stafford, the host reported to the others, "Williston says this was about the same reaction of the other Justices they had reached out to over the last two days."

One of the losing golfers mock whispered, "Ask Williston if we can get reimbursed for the greens fees and our share of the hundred dollars we lost by throwing the match?"

Chapter Forty-Eight

The President of the Bar Association called the meeting of the Board of Governors to order. The Board of Governors consists of fourteen lawyers two of which are elected from each of the states seven Supreme Court Districts. In Disciplinary Hearings, the Board is expanded by four citizen members appointed by the Chief Justice. (SCR 3.375). Additional members include the President, Vice-President and President-Elect.

All 21 members answered the roll call by the clerk. As usual the Commissioner of the Ministry of Ethics was in attendance and took a seat in a chair along the wall behind the Bar Association President.

Martin Huelson, one of the members of the Board of Governors stood up and said, "Mr. President I have a point of order".

The President was slightly taken aback by a point of order being raised. He nodded his head signaling Heulson to proceed.

"Mr. President, I object to the attendance at this hearing of Commissioner Hart. I know that by the Supreme Court Rules she is the legal counsel for the Board of Governors. I know she usually attends our meetings, but I see a basic conflict of interest here. She is also the Chief Prosecutor. She has prosecuted the complaint against Justice Boone, her agency seeks a conviction of Justice Boone, but she is also supposed to provide this Board independent legal advice when we ask for it."

Most everyone in the room appeared amused by this novel but obvious claim of a conflict of interest. It simply had never occurred to them that the dual offices of Bar Counsel and Commissioner of the Ministry of Ethics presented a conflict of interest for Heather Hart.

Huelson continued, "Why haven't we invited Justice Boone to sit here during our deliberations? Alice Boone is a party, and Ms. Hart is a party. Neither of them should be here when we deliberate."

The President started to answer the question but realized there was only one reasonable answer. He merely smiled at Heulson and nodded his head in agreement.

Huelson charged on. "This hearing is not a public hearing. This is akin to the jury going to the privacy of the jury room to deliberate a verdict. The prosecutor shouldn't be allowed into this 'jury room?"

Silence fell upon the room like a wet fog.

Commissioner Hart raised her hand and rose to defend herself, but President Mathis ignored her.

Huelson continued, "Is Commissioner Hart here to take names? Is she here to influence our decision by her mere presence? Or is she here to answer legal questions that members of the Board may have about SCR 3.130 (8.2)? She can't do both!"

Commissioner Hart was not used to being in the dock as a defendant, and her face revealed her displeasure.

The attack continued, "Any legal opinion she gives us as our legal counsel is tainted by the fact that she is also a prosecutor of this action. We regularly sanction attorneys who involve themselves in such blatant conflicts of interest."

No member of the Board spoke up in defense of Commissioner Hart.

President Mathis turned to Commissioner Hart, and ruled, "Commissioner would you please remove yourself from the room. Please wait outside the hearing of these deliberations. We will call you if we need any input from you."

Commissioner Hart meekly inquired, "Don't I get to defend myself?"

The President ignored her request, "Please just wait outside the hearing room."

After the Queen of Hearts left the room and quietly closed the door, the meeting continued.

President Mathis suggested that since all members had heard the testimony provided at the hearing of Justice Alice Boone, and had read the record, that they begin by a show of hands. He called on everyone who would dismiss the charge to raise their right hand. Ten members all sitting on the right side of the long conference table did so.

He then asked everyone who wished to sustain the uphold the Trial Commissioner's recommendations to raise their hands. Ten members, including the four citizen members appointed by the Chief Justice, voted for the Trial Commissioner's findings against Justice Boone to be upheld.

They were all sitting together on the left side of the conference table. He noted that the members had taken seats consistent with their vote.

President Mathis could declare the complaint as having failed since the ten votes against Justice Boone did not equal the required three-fourths of the voting members necessary to uphold the Trial Commissioner's decision. Instead he asked for discussion and explained, "This vote is going to be controversial. I believe we owe it to the parties to explore the opportunity for a unanimous vote one way or another.

He turned to the members who had voted to uphold the charge against Justice Boone and invited them to justify their votes.

Jane Austen from Owensboro was the first to speak. "The charge against Justice Boone is minor in nature. I personally am in favor of nothing more than a public reprimand. She will still be on the court and in a month everything will blow over and be forgotten.

"On the other hand, whatever happens to Alice Boone, we are still stuck with the Chief Justice. If we acquit her our working relationship with Hatter will be destroyed."

She did not disclose, nor did four of the other members who had voted for conviction, that she had been visited by representatives of the Ministry of Ethics. None had been directly threatened, and none had been asked to vote one way or another on the Alice Boone complaint, but the message was clear. A vote against the Ministry would not be welcomed, and their actions were being monitored by the Ministry.

President Mathis was disappointed by the blatant self-interest so easily admitted by Austen but he did not attempt to respond to her selfish argument.

Thomas Wakefield from Ashland was concerned about a complaint pending against his law partner over a dispute regarding a fee. He did not disclose this to the Board. He stood up and spoke his piece, "The bottom line as I see it is that the Chief Justice was clearly justified in applying the Assignment Section of the Constitution in assigning Justice Boone to special duty in another court. She should have taken her assignment like a trooper and kept her mouth shut."

President Mathis, looked sternly at Wakefield and Austen and concluded, "We are here to decide the facts and law of this charge against Justice Boone. We are not here to serve our own convenience or to be politically expedient. The standard of proof is a 'preponderance of the evidence,' not which decision will benefit this Board."

No one else from the left side of the table spoke up.

President Mathis then turned to the right side of the table. Instantly ten hands were raised as they all seemed to want to explain their vote on behalf of Justice Boone.

Joe Gilbert from Bowling Green spoke first.

"Mr. President, I will never be elected as a judge. I have no desire to assume the great responsibility that office bears. But today as a member of this board, I must play that role in a minor way. In fulfilling my duty as a member of this board, I must judge Alice Boone.

"I see our job here as not just deciding whether or not it was wise for Alice Boone to speak up. What we all are here to do is to decide if she had the First Amendment right to speak up. Our ruling may or may not silence Alice Boone, but if we convict her we will surely be silencing every other member of the legal profession in this state.

"We must consider the plight of other lawyers who in the future feel the need to speak up about an injustice. They should not be placed in fear of losing their license to practice law. If we convict her for mere words of protest, then we will forever forfeit for ourselves the moral right to speak out at injustice. We will be sending a message to everyone to speak out only at their own peril."

Martin Huelson took another tack in his opposition to a conviction of Alice Boone. "We need to send a message alright. We need to send a message to the Ministry of Ethics and the Queen of Hearts."

Several members chuckled at his mocking and inappropriate description of Commissioner Hart, a term they had all used in private.

"Let's all remember one thing. The Commissioner of Ethics works for this Board. She is paid to be our advisor and counsel. We approve her budget. Her dual assignment as Commissioner of the Ministry of Ethics and Bar Counsel is a direct conflict of interest.

"While wearing one hat she gives us legal advice about our duties and powers. Then she puts on her crown as Commissioner of the Ministry and tells us everything she does in that role is confidential and she refuses to answer our questions. Let's stop this nonsense. She is double-dipping the system and we have allowed this to happen."

He then pounded his hand on the conference table and shouted, "I for one believe that the Ministry of Ethics has no damn business trying to punish anyone for mere words. At least for words outside the courtroom.

Further, I don't see any reason why we should be carrying water for the Legislative Ethics Commission. They aren't a judicial body.

"We've allowed her to get out of hand. She is misusing the authority the court has given her for her personal advancement. It's our job to monitor her conduct, and we haven't been doing such a good job."

Douglas Milbern joined in, "The underlying charge wasn't proven by the Ministry. They have not offered proof that the statements Alice Boone made were false as required by the black letter language of SCR 3.130 (8.2). She had every right to call for an impeachment. Impeachment is a constitutional procedure.

"If the Chief Justice was justified in citing the constitution's assignment section as a defense for his actions, she is entitled to call for the application of the impeachment section of the constitution?

"And, let's not forget one of the first things we learned in law school that all rules and statutes are inferior to constitutional rights. The Supreme Court can adopt all the rules they want, but they can't repeal sections of the constitution. Supreme Court Rule 3.130 (8.2) clearly violates the First Amendment of the constitution when it attempts to limit free speech."

Tim Stein added a simple but concise statement in favor of acquittal. "We should acquit Justice Boone, and then fire Commissioner Hart for having allowed this ridiculous charge to get as far as the Board."

After a moment President Mathis called for another vote. It was a tie like the first vote. No minds where changed. No heart was moved. No soul was saved.

He then spoke in a low voice, "It is my duty to find that the charges against Justice Alice Boone have failed to be approved by the required three-quarters vote. Therefore, I will report to the Supreme Court that all charges against Justice Boone have been dismissed."

All twenty members of the Board of Governors remained silent.

Mathis adjourned the meeting, and asked the clerk to go with him to his office where he immediately dictated a finding.

When he left the hearing room Commissioner Hart was nowhere in sight.

After the formal findings were typed and printed, he signed the document and directed that it be formally entered. Copies were sent to Justice Boone and to Commissioner Hart and the Trial Commissioner.

After the clerk left, Mathis closed the door behind her and called Williston Stafford.

He described the exclusion of Commissioner Hart, and the self-serving statements of Austen and Wakefield.

He advised Stafford, that the Board's decision could be appealed to the Supreme Court. He explained that Supreme Court Rule—(SCR 3.370(8)) allowed the Ministry to appeal from a ruling by the Board of Governors.

Stafford asked him if he thought that the Ministry of Ethics would appeal the ruling.

He responded, "I have no idea if Commissioner Hart will file an appeal". He speculated however, "but if she does, she will complicate things for herself. That would surely anger those ten members who voted for dismissal. Everyone on the Board was glad to be rid of this complaint, even those who supported it.

"Huelson's argument about the duties of the Commissioner of the Ministry of Ethics having a conflict of interest with her duties as the legal counsel to the Bar Association appear to have legal merit."

Mathis went on to mention the fact that none of the four citizen members who were appointed by the Chief Justice recused themselves.

Mathis explained to Stafford how some members of the Board of Governors were influenced by the Chief Justice. "While the Board of Governors could hire and fire the Commissioner of the Ministry of Ethics, the influence and lobbying of the Chief Justice was felt when he sent the Board his recommendation without having been asked to do so.

When the Board was considering the hiring of Heather Hart as Commissioner of the Ministry, the Chief Justice had spoken personally to at least seventeen members of the Board of Governors and strongly expressed his opinion that she should be hired. While the members of the Board rarely spoke about the Chief Justice's influence. At one time or another they all thought about the consequences of crossing him."

Williston asked President Mathis about a rumor he had known of for years. "Is there any truth to the rumor that every board member has a member of the Supreme Court as their alter ego? I've heard that for years. I've heard Board members call their alter ego and get their marching orders in advance of important votes."

"I've heard that old gossip myself. But I have never seen any evidence of such a relationship. I can't say that any individual member would allow himself to be influenced in that manner, but I have never seen any evidence of that practice. I assure you that no one from the court has ever sought me out except to explain how they would prefer our Board works. I would think that there might be one or two Board Members who might suck up to a court member, but that surely comes from the member and not from the Justice."

After his discussion with President Mathis, Williston Stafford called Justice Boone, Jack Kenton, and the seven Eunuch leaders who each had a phone call list of the members in their district. They each passed the news down the phone list chains. Within three hours over 500 lawyers were aware of the Board's Ruling.

The next morning the *Courier-Journal*, the *Lexington Herald-Leader*, the *Kentucky Enquirer* and half a dozen other papers, published an Associated Press story credited to "a source close to the Board."

The headline of the *AP* story read, "JUSTICE ALICE BOONE ACQUITTED OF ETHICS VIOLATION. Free speech of lawyers upheld."

The body of the story quoted the Commissioner of the Ministry of Ethics as saying, "We will immediately file an appeal to the Supreme Court."

All who could read the tea leaves knew that the hearing of the Board of Governors was mostly a sham, since the dismissal of the charges against Alice Boone could be revived by the Supreme Court if the Ministry refused to accept the Board ruling made by her managers.

Chapter Forty-Nine

A week later Williston Stafford and Spike White, a Eunuch from Gallatin County, arrived at the Law Office of William Mathis in the PNC Bank Building in Louisville shortly before 4:00 p.m.

Mathis like other presidents of the Kentucky Bar Association held a full time job. His volunteer work for the Bar Association was done in his spare time. The KBA kept their ceremonial officers on a treadmill so that they were replaced every year. This worked to shift the real power in such organizations to the full time staff who had lesser titles, but drew comfortable salaries. Only the permanent staffers knew where the bodies were buried.

Mathis has served one year on the KBA Board, then a year as President-elect, and now was serving his one year term as President, and soon, just as he was learning the ropes, he would be replaced by another ceremonial officer. Most members of the Board never served longer than two years.

The receptionist showed them into one of the half dozen conference rooms on the 22nd. floor. Large law firms don't provide offices big enough for the lawyer to meet with their clients and guests. Visitors are greeted in conference rooms which the lawyer has to book through a secretary. The secretary manning the front desk buzzed Mathis, and he shortly joined Stafford and White.

The room had a glass wall overlooking the Ohio River which was just two blocks to the north. Williston found it hard to focus on the meeting as the view was spectacular. His natural fear of heights kept him from getting too close to the floor to ceiling window that was his only protection from the 250 foot fall to the plaza below.

President Mathis offered his guests water and coffee which they declined.

Mathis thanked them for coming to Louisville and informed them that he had secured the information they were seeking. "I have never seen these numbers. They are quite interesting."

He handed them each a copy of the caseload statistics for the Ministry of Ethics.

Mathis had secured the report, at Williston's request, by visiting Commissioner Hart and personally demanding them. The report revealed that the case load being handled by each of the Ministry's lawyers was surprisingly small.

Stafford, after reviewing the one page report responded, "This is about what I feared." A minute later after he done some mental math, he continued, "Each of the lawyers for the Ministry of Ethics only carries a real caseload of 8.89 cases per year. That works out to one case per every 5.77 weeks for the Ministry lawyers. However, since the adoption of the Rabbit Hole amendments, complaints have tripled. Those increased numbers will show up in next year's fiscal report."

Stafford looked at Mathis and said, "I suspect that your firm requires you to bill at least forty five hours a week, and if the Ministry of Ethics was held to this free market workload, they would be required to have 180 to 200 billable hours a month."

Mathis smiled and said, "Yes. I'm encouraged to bill at least 180 hours a month or I get on a list I don't want to be on."

"So," Stafford continued, "The attorneys for the Ministry are in essence getting paid to only handle one case every 5.77 weeks. That means that they are billing the state for the equivalent of 259 hours of billable time for each case they handle. That's ridiculous!"

Spike White chimed in, "Some public defenders have a case load up to 50 times greater than Ministry of Ethics lawyers, and public advocates get paid about 70% less!"

Mathis said defensively, "Well last year the Ministry actually received about 1,500 complaints."

Stafford interjected, "Yes, but these numbers show that over 600 of these annual complaints are quickly disposed of since they admittedly are 'returned as insufficient.' I suspect that most of those six hundred cases are handled by one of their many paralegals in the intake review process.

"Those are the cases by angry litigants who have lost their cases or who have been incensed by a tough cross-examination, or just don't understand that merely disliking an attorney doesn't justify an ethics complaint.

"Many cases are listed in the report as being declined, or resolved through diversion or informal resolution. That still leaves less than nine cases per year per Ministry lawyer to actually litigate."

He paused for a moment and observed, "The category of 'declined' in this report is lumped in with diversion and informal resolution."

White added, "I'd sure like to see the reason that those cases in the 'declined' category are dismissed. How is that different from the category of 'returned as insufficient'? It looks to me like their numbers are padded by inflating the numerical value of crank cases, which they immediately dump in the shredder and which are never litigated. When you cull out these frivolous complaints which are readily dismissed, they really don't have that many serious complaints."

Stafford raised an eyebrow and continued, "There is no way from this report to determine if any of the dismissed cases were friends of the Ministry. The secrecy rules prevent us or the public from really seeing what's going on over at the Castle. Under their secrecy rules we have no way of identifying the persons who have complaints against them dismissed.

"I contacted the Ministry earlier this year and asked how many prosecutors have been investigated by the Ministry. They refused to give me an answer. They as expected, cited the confidentiality rules. I didn't ask for names, I just asked for numbers, and they refused my request."

He mentally compared this system with the regular court system where every defendant's name is a public record.

Mathis responded by interjecting, "As you know, it's the Supreme Court who passed the secrecy rules."

Williston smiled at Mathis. "True. But my reading of the confidentiality rules shows that they are not for the protection of the Ministry. They are solely for the protection of defendant attorneys. I'll buy you a new briefcase if you can show me a rule that prohibits the Ministry from accurately reporting their statistics."

White intervened. "So no one, not even you as the President of the Bar Association, really know the specific reason why the Ministry elects to dismiss some 1400 cases a year? And you don't know the criteria for the selection of the 100 or so attorneys who are actually prosecuted?"

Mathis merely gave a negative head shake acknowledging that he didn't know the answer to that question.

White continued his challenge of the Ministry with a comparison of judicial caseloads. "District Judges average an annual case load of 8,000 cases, and Circuit Judges average an annual case load of 800 cases, some do many more. How can those slackers at the Ministry get away with this? The entire Ministry only handles about 100 real cases a year."

Mathis did not attempt to argue the obvious.

Stafford asked Mathis, "How much are the staff lawyers paid?"

Mathis said that he didn't have the number at his fingertips, but he believed it was a minimum of $85,000 with a top salary of $135,000 for the Commissioner."

Stafford pressed on, "And the funding for the Ministry comes from dues paid by the lawyers of Kentucky?"

"Yes, almost all the funding is from lawyers' dues paid to the KBA, but there is some supplemental funding recouped from fines and costs imposed on convicted lawyers when they are ordered to pay the costs of their investigations."

Stafford said, "I understand the Board of Governors approves the budget for the Ministry, and therefore I would assume that the Board of Governors sets the salaries for the attorneys and paralegals of the Ministry?"

Mathis again nodded in the affirmative. but added, "The Chief Justice compiles the budget for the Ministry and we just basically rubber stamp it."

The room fell silent as the two visiting lawyers examined the one page list of statistics in search of any other revelations.

Stafford broke the silence, "Bill, does the Board of Governors have any interest at all in providing real oversight on the cost and operations of the Ministry?"

The President of the Board of Governors rose from his chair and walked to the window and stared at the Belle of Louisville chugging upriver with a load of conventioneers going on a two hour cruise.

Finally he conceded. "The Board members are as afraid of the Ministry as anyone else." Williston forced himself to sublimate his acrophobia and walked to the window next to President Mathis and said quietly, "There are a great number of lawyers from all walks of life, lawyers from all areas of the Commonwealth, who want some accountability for the Ministry. They are telling me they want transparency of the actions of the Ministry.

"If you asked the Board to request a rules change to allow an efficiency expert to review the Ministry's work load, and to repeal the confidentiality rules, would there be any support on the Board of Governors?"

Mathis, put his arm around Williston's shoulder and committed himself, "Will, if you have the balls to publically call for such a resolution, I will see that it is introduced to the Board. I will promise you a second of the motion, and then we can see what happens. All I can promise you is the issue will be voted on. But don't forget, the Board of Governors is merely window dressing, all resolutions of the Board are just expressions of opinion.

"The Supreme Court is the rule making body. They accept our resolutions when they like them, and they reject them or amend them out of existence whenever they don't like our resolutions. And sometimes they don't even go through the charade of asking our opinion. Virtually everything we do is just to provide political cover for the Supreme Court.

"The Board's function is to create the allusion that the 17,000 members of the Bar Association actually have representatives who can speak to the Supreme Court in their behalf.

"Back in 2010 the Board suggested a watered down version of the Squeal Rule. The Supreme Court ignored our recommendation and unilaterally imposed their own rule. And we never saw the Rabbit Hole Amendments at all."

Stafford asked Mathis, "Are you aware of the claim that the Ministry knew of complaints pending against one of the attorneys in the Fen Phen case regarding overcharging his clients, but never informed the Fen Phen trial judge to give him a heads up? The story goes that they could have given the Fen Phen litigants a warning that their attorney was involved in making excessive fee claims in other cases."

"I wasn't aware of that story. I don't know if the Ministry could have warned the public of problems that threatened innocent parties. But they certainly should be able to share such information and take any necessary step to protect the public. I agree that the Ministry has egg on its face over the Fen Phen errors.

"Even if they correctly followed the confidentiality rule in not informing the trial judge and the plaintiff's about a potential problem, there is something terribly wrong with such a rule.

"It makes sense that the Ministry would want to cover their butts by placing the blame on members of the bar for not squealing. But it is unlikely that anyone but the Fen Phen attorneys knew anything about a secret plan to steal millions. The testimony at their criminal trial revealed that they had lied to the trial judge about material issues.

"The Squeal Rule probably wouldn't have prevented the Fen Phen problem, but its adoption provided a useful public relations distraction for the Ministry and for the Supreme Court. My concern about the Squeal

Rule is that the Ministry is now using it to expand their ability to nail attorneys for not reporting rumors about which they have no personal knowledge.

"I don't see how you can justify a rule that requires a complaint to be filed by an attorney who hears a rumor when the attorney would never be allowed by the hearsay rules to testify about such a rumor.

Spike White added, "The squeal rule is now being used by the Ministry to coerce everyone. It appears that the Ministry has us all by the shorthairs. Mark my word, the Supreme Court will come to regret they adopted this rule. After all, it applies to members of the Supreme Court.

None of us benefit with a discipline system based on gossip and rumors and secret investigations."

Stafford asked President Mathis how the Squeal Rule came to be. Mathis began by citing the rule, "SCR 3.130(8.3) was studied by the Board of Governors. We felt that it should be limited only to criminal acts or conduct involving fraud, dishonesty or deceit by a lawyer.

"The Supreme Court ignored our recommendations and broadened the rule to include any question of a lawyer's 'honesty, trustworthiness or fitness as a lawyer'. This broad language added by the Court, allows anyone who pisses someone off, to be subject to an ethics investigation."

White shook his head, "Once again the Supreme Court expresses their contempt for the opinions of the elected representatives of the Bar members!"

Chapter Fifty

After Jack Kenton read the ruling of the Board of Governors and saw that the Ministry was appealing the acquittal of Justice Boone to the Supreme Court, he immediately called his attorney, and authorized the implementation of Plan B. Four days after the filing of the Ministry's appeal in the Boone case, Kenton asked Barbara Popplewell to come to his office to prepare for Plan B.

Barbara Popplewell arrived ten minutes early at Jack Kenton's law office off Nicholasville Road in Lexington. The purpose of the meeting was to go over the facts which lead to the ethics investigation against Kenton. She needed to be sure of all the facts before she drafted and filed a complaint against the Ministry of Ethics and the Board of Scrutiny in Federal Court.

She was escorted to a conference room where she was immediately joined by Kenton. From the window Popplewell could see the nearby Jockey Club offices.

She greeted Kenton with a question, "Is that where you go to hire the jockey who rides your horses?"

He smiled, and told her that the Jockey Club had very little to do with the small men and women who ride horses. "The Jockey Club is the breed Registry for Thoroughbred horses." He pointed at the building, "That's the national headquarters."

Popplewell spread out her notes and legal pad and began questioning her client about the communications that inspired the Ministry of Ethics to make him the focus of an investigation.

They discussed Kenton's appearance at the Legislative Ethics Commission hearing. He explained that he and two friends wanted to see how the Commission dealt with the complaint against the State Senator who was accused of violating fund raising rules. He laid out in chronological order all of the events.

Popplewell made notes and asked questions for an hour before taking a comfort break. Upon returning she began, "One of the main issues we will raise in the Federal lawsuit is the denial of due process rights in violation of the 14th. Amendment of the U.S. Constitution.

Let's go over their proceedings."

Kenton, had anticipated this question ever since he had received the Notice of Investigation from the Ministry. His response followed the list he had prepared which outlined his concerns.

"I had no right to know or confront my accuser. His identity has been kept confidential under the Ministry's rules. I still haven't been provided with the name of my accuser.

"The Ministry mailed me a letter styled, 'Notice of Investigation', and after that, they just left me hanging. I was never interviewed or contacted by the Ministry prosecutors. No one from the Ministry has contacted me personally to this date.

"In fact, the notice letter warned me not to contact any member of the Ministry or any officer or director of the Bar Association, or any member of the Supreme Court. I was effectively prevented from preparing my own defense.

"I was ordered in the Notice to submit a written response within fifteen days. I was denied the right to know the evidence against me other than the letter I wrote to the Legislative Ethics Commission. In their letter they claimed to have 'other evidence' besides my letter. But I was never told what that 'other evidence' was to which I was required to respond.

"As you know I was not given an opportunity to appear before the Ministry or to file a brief in my own defense.

"Under their directions, I was under the mandatory duty to keep everything confidential during the investigation. The investigation ends when the Board of Scrutiny issues a formal complaint or decides not to issue a complaint.

"The rules of the ethics procedures provide that the confidentiality requirement doesn't end until the Ministry takes formal action on the complaint. In my case the Board of Scrutiny decided not to issue a formal complaint. This would have ended everything there, but they just couldn't close the matter. Having drawn their sword, the Ministry concluded it had to taste blood.

"They issued a Warning Letter in which they informed me that I was guilty of violating the Ethics Rules. They explained to me in their letter, that this meant that the matter would die if I didn't get in trouble again during the next calendar year. So in effect I was found guilty without a hearing or trial, and placed on probation for one year.

"I never got to testify, and had no opportunity to call witnesses in my behalf, and I was never allowed to know the nature of the evidence against me.

"If they had issued a formal complaint, they could have sought my disbarment or could have imposed a suspension or reprimand. But if they had done that, I could have appealed their finding. I could have had at least the semblance of a Due Process hearing before the Trial Commissioner. They notified me that, under a rule adopted in 2008, that there was no right to appeal from their issuance of a formal Warning Letter issued by the Board of Scrutiny.

"To this day they have never revealed the evidence considered by the Board in finding me to be in violation of the Supreme Court Rule.

"I was entirely excluded from the matter and left without any recourse to appeal their finding.

"I've researched the consequence of having such a Warning Letter issued. That means that if another complaint is filed against me, that they can enhance the penalty since I already have a warning letter in my file. They said that after a year they would destroy the Warning Letter.

The explicit message was, 'Keep your mouth shut for the next year!' "However, I believe the real message was "Don't ever criticize our friends or we will come after you again. Next time you won't get off with a mere Warning Letter."

Popplewell arranged her notes, and gave Kenton a summary of the research she had done on the issue of Due Process rights under the l4th. Amendment.

"The U.S. Supreme Court has emphasized in recent years that procedural due process requires the right of confrontation and cross-examination of those whose testimony deprives a person of his livelihood.

"That view has been taken by several state courts who upheld due process rights of persons who was denied admission to practice law. The courts have held that the government, even in a quasi-judicial proceedings, has to allow confrontation of the accusers they rely upon to deny a law license to an applicant. I found that law in a U.S. Supreme Court case.

"In Willner v. Committee On Character and Fitness, the U.S. Sup. Ct. said "'A State cannot exclude a person from the practice of law or from any other occupation in a manner or for reasons that contravene the Due Process or Equal Protection Clause of the Fourteenth Amendment."

"Jack, In my opinion this is a strong defense. I believe this language is broad enough to cover your situation. They took action against you in a secret hearing from which you were excluded. They apparently received evidence from a person whom you did not get to confront. They even concealed the identity of your accuser from you. You didn't get a chance to cross-examine anyone who made allegations against you.

"The very basis for Due Process Rights is protection against arbitrary government action. There is a requirement of basic fairness in any hearing conducted by the government, and I can't wait to see how they argue otherwise.

"In placing a warning letter in your file, they have found you guilty, and imposed a small but potentially serious penalty. This procedure denies you an appeal. A basic rule of the 1976 Judicial Article Amendments to the constitution was to assure every citizen of at least one appeal."

Kenton, agreed with Popplewell's statement and changed the issue.

"We also have the First Amendment free speech issue. I believe that is one of our strongest arguments.

Popplewell responded with a caveat. "This is a strong argument, but there is troublesome language in a number of court decisions which place attorneys in a special category and hold that lawyers, and particularly judges, waive some of their free speech rights.

"These decisions seem to be focused on cases where an attorney attempted to influence the outcome of a pending case.

"The problem the Ministry has in getting the Federal Court to uphold the rule they cited against you, is that it's language requires that the attorney's statement must be false in order to be a violation. Truth appears to be a defense.

"I believe it's impossible for them to prove your letter contained a false statement. The Kentucky rule also requires that the offending statement must specifically question the integrity or qualifications for office of the Legislative Ethics Committee. There simply is no such allegation in your letter."

Popplewell, thanked Kenton for his assistance. "I'm feeling pretty good about the case law. We should have the lawsuit ready for filing by next week. Can you come to my office and sign the complaint?"

Kenton ended the meeting with an assurance that he would be glad to meet her whenever she was ready to file the Federal law suit.

The following week Kenton placed his signature on multiple copies of a Federal civil rights lawsuit to be filed in the Federal Court for the Eastern District of Kentucky at Lexington.

Barbara Popplewell added her certification to the copies, and then handed them to one of her paralegals with instructions to immediately drive to the Federal Court Building in Lexington and file them.

As she handed the papers to the paralegal she instructed him to have them served personally on the members of the Board of Scrutiny and Commissioner Heather Hart. She said to her client, "I wish I could order the Bailiff serving these to take a picture of each of them as they read the complaint."

The lawsuit sought a permanent Federal injunction against the Ministry of Ethics. If the Court granted this relief, the Ministry couldn't use the speech limitation rule to silence attorney's truthful comments made outside the courtroom in future cases. The injunction motion was based on a claim that the punishment, even in the form of a Warning Letter, based on SCR 3.130 (8.2) violated the First Amendment rights of Jack Kenton and all other lawyers by punishing him for expressing his personal opinion about the official actions of a public official.

Kenton sought no damages for himself, but the complaint asked that his legal expenses be awarded. Since this was a claim regarding a constitutional civil rights violation, it was almost certain that any favorable ruling would require the Bar Association to reimburse Kenton's legal expenses incurred in the Federal Civil Rights action.

Plan B, if successful, would probably provide a result in less than a year, and had the potential for a Federal Court ruling that any use of the Supreme Court Rule restricting the free speech of lawyers was unconstitutional.

The Federal Civil Rights suit provided a chance that Kenton's legal bills would have to be paid by the Bar. That made Plan B very attractive.

Kenton, feeling in high spirits for the first time in the two years since the Ministry had taken up the complaint against him, put his feet on Popplewell's desk and lit a hand rolled (and illegally imported) Cuban cigar that had been given to him by Williston Stafford.

He suddenly felt that for the first time since this matter had been pursued by the Ministry, that he had taken control of his future. From somewhere in the midst of an enormous white cloud of expensive smoke, he shouted to the absent Queen and the Ministry in general, "Take that, you S.O.B's!"

Popplewell, was not a smoker, but she readily accepted Kenton's offer of a cigar, and joined him in enlarging the white cloud in her smoke free office.

Chapter Fifty-One

Within days a copy of the Federal complaint made its way through the system and landed on Commissioner Hart's desk. She had already been called by a dozen news reporters for comments on the lawsuit even before she had seen a copy of the complaint. She had refused any comment, incorrectly citing the rules of confidentiality, which clearly did not apply to a Federal lawsuit.

Every member of the Board of Scrutiny had called her to seek her advice on whether the Bar would pay their attorney's fees. She had lied and told them that she was certain that the lawsuit would be quickly dismissed, and there 'was nothing to worry about' since they were protected by 'sovereign immunity' for their official acts.

She hoped the Bar would pay for the Ministry's defense of the federal lawsuit. She knew the Bar would have to pay any award of costs and attorney fees that might be awarded by the Federal Court, but she hid her concerns from her fellow travelers.

This was unplowed ground. The Ministry had never had to defend against a Federal Civil Rights claim

When she was served, Commissioner Hart made a scene for her staff and angrily threw the complaint in her trash can. Later, realizing the futility of that action, and when she was sure no one was watching, she fished it out. She realized that she had the unpleasant task of delivering a copy to the President of the Bar Association. He had to be informed immediately.

She had Bunny White make an appointment for her to see President Mathis on an urgent matter. She then called in three attorneys and had them begin researching who would be responsible for filing an answer to the complaint and whether or not the Ministry would be authorized to do so.

She wasn't sure if she could represent the Board of Scrutiny who was the actual defendant in the federal suit.

"Get me an answer by noon," she warned them.

That afternoon she drove from the Castle to Louisville to meet with President Mathis. He was not happy.

"Commissioner why haven't you informed the Board that you were prosecuting a complaint against a lawyer for expressing his opinion?"

She meekly tried to explain. "The confidentiality rules," before he cut her off.

"Don't cite that drivel to me. I have already read the complaint, a reporter gave me a copy. You are our legal counsel and you withheld this from the Board!

"In case you were unaware of it, our firm has filed numerous civil rights claims and I have a good idea of what is going to happen. If Kenton gets even a sliver of relief from the Federal Court, the Bar will be hit with $20,000, maybe $30,000 in attorney fees and costs."

He didn't pause for her response, and hit her with, "Who filed the Ethics complaint against Kenton?"

The Queen of Hearts, was taken aback. The truth would be embarrassing. She righteously refused to answer the question, "That information is confidential."

It occurred her that he might be setting her up. "Does he know that it was handed to me by Cheshire? Did Cheshire set me up?"

"Commissioner Hart," he bellowed, "I'm certain you are aware that there is a serious discussion on the Board of Governors about the conflict of interest in your serving as the Board's legal counsel and also serving as the Commissioner of the Ministry of Ethics. Just where does your heart belong? Do you see your job as the Board's legal advisor, with a duty to keep us informed on all legal issues affecting us, or are you merely the administrator of the Ministry with the duty to slavishly obey the confidentiality rules and treat us like mushrooms?"

She knew she must deflect the question. "The Board hired me and assigned my duties pursuant to Supreme Court Rules. I didn't create the Ministry, the Supreme Court did."

Mathis, was aware of the rationale of her defense, but he would not give her the satisfaction of his agreement.

She tried to take control of the confrontation by changing the subject. "Our research indicates that as the legal counsel for the Board of Governors our office can defend the Board of Scrutiny in this lawsuit. That will keep our costs down."

"I can't interfere with you in your handling of this lawsuit, and don't intend too, but I suggest that you had better fix this before it gets out of control. When this is done you had better be ready to explain your actions to the Board of Governors. I'm not sure the Board of Governors will want you to defend this lawsuit. We may hire outside counsel. After all we will get stuck with the bill! You got us in this mess, and I'm not sure you're the right person to get us out of it."

He picked up a file he had laid on the table, and before leaving her without the courtesy of showing her out, said over his shoulder as he stalked out of the conference room, "When you talk to the press, and I know you will, I suggest that you make it clear that the Board knew nothing of your complaint being filed against Jack Kenton, and that we had nothing to do with it. You created this problem. Now take ownership of it."

The Queen of Hearts quickly left the Mathis law firm tower and drove to her condo in downtown Louisville near the Louisville Bats Baseball Field. After she got home she kicked off her high heels and called Bunny White. She instructed Bunny to call Barbara Popplewell and set up a meeting, and to tell her that she would be glad to come to Popplewell's office first thing in the morning.

Chapter Fifty-Two

Popplewell was surprised to hear from the Ministry so quickly after the filing of the lawsuit. "Of course," she told Bunny White, "I would be glad to see Commissioner Hart, but I am busy until 10:30. I can work her in then if that's alright." She immediately called Kenton and informed him of the call.

From the tone of Commissioner Hart's orders, Bunny determined that anytime would be convenient, and she readily agreed to the 10:30 meeting.

Promptly at 10:25 the following morning, Commissioner Hart entered the small reception room of the Popplewell law office located in an office tower fronting on Fourth Street Live. The receptionist as instructed, kept her waiting for fifteen minutes before showing her into Popplewell's personal office.

At the meeting Commissioner Hart began with a tap dance with her thoughts of how unfortunate that these matters are, and how distasteful she thought the prosecution of Jack Kenton was, before getting to the point of her pitch.

"After reviewing this complaint against Jack Kenton, which was only brought to my attention after you went to Federal court, I have determined that some of our people may have been a little over eager. I am willing to dismiss the ethics complaint and withdraw the warning letter. We just ask that you dismiss the Federal lawsuit."

Popplewell was amazed at the audacity of the Queen.

"Let me understand your offer," she replied, "We surrender our only chance at vindication and you get a free pass. Kenton has spent a small fortune in defending himself against your complaint, you have kept him twisting in the wind for most of two years, and your best offer is that he remains stuck with his legal expenses, and never gets a public vindication.

The Queen nodded her head in agreement with that analysis and said, "Yes, we dismiss our complaint and you dismiss your lawsuit."

Popplewell, looked the Queen in the eye and said, "I have known Jack Kenton for almost twenty years. He has an unblemished record as a lawyer. I can't believe that he would ever agree to your offer which is too little too late. How would your dismissal restore his reputation in the eyes of the public? I know that he's strongly committed to stopping the use of the speech rule against other lawyers in the future."

She paused before adding, "But of course I will ask him, it's his case not mine."

Before leaving, the Queen requested a response from Kenton as soon as possible, "We would like to put this matter behind us." She gave Popplewell her personal cell phone number.

The Queen at first felt that Popplewell was supportive of a possible compromise, but while driving back to Frankfort, she felt less sure that Kenton would be tempted.

Chapter Fifty-Three

As soon as the Queen left her office, Popplewell called Jack Kenton. She presented the offer without emotion and did not attempt to influence his decision one way or the other.

Kenton did not hesitate to reject the offer. "That offer is ridiculous. I'm impressed with how quickly the filing of a Federal lawsuit can get a Queen out of her Castle.

He added sarcastically, "That was very nice of her to drop by to see you. I know how shocked she must have been to learn that one of the dunces in her office was negligent in accepting the complaint against me.

"There is no telling how many lawyers have been victimized by 'her underlings' mistakes. Many of her victims can't afford an attorney as good as you. I think that this puts a moral burden on us to join this fight and to right this wrong. We have the means and the opportunity to stand up and protect the First Amendment rights of all lawyers.

"Barbara, I think you are the greatest. I have so much confidence in your legal skills that I have to reject the Queen's offer. I want my day in a court. I want to hear a Federal Judge say that I, and every lawyer in the country, have free speech rights. And if he rules against me, I want the public to know that under the rules of the Kentucky Supreme Court, lawyers are second class citizens. Even that admission will be a step towards fixing this problem. This is the only way to let the public know that Madison Hatter and the Queen of Hearts are running a Dog and Pony show over there in Frankfort."

Popplewell asked, "So you are telling me to reject her offer?"

"Yes, Barbara, how clear do I have to be?"

"Calm down Jack, you know I have to hear the magic words from you."

Popplewell probed, "Would you want me to make a counteroffer where we dismiss everything if they dismiss everything. They ditch the Warning Letter, and the Ministry issues you a public apology and pays your attorney fees?"

Kenton laughed out loud, "Barbara, that's tempting but I'm afraid she would accept it. I want a published opinion from a Federal Court holding the Speech Rule unconstitutional. Nothing less. Just tell her thanks, but no thanks, and leave any future offers to the Ministry."

In order to show that Kenton wasn't desperate to cut a deal, Popplewell waited 24 hours before calling the Queen to reject the offer.

The next day Popplewell informed the Queen that the Ministry's offer to settle was rejected and advised her there were no counter offers.

The Queen of Hearts read the handwriting on the wall. Kenton was going to pursue his claim for a permanent injunction against the Ministry's use of SCR 3.130 (8.2). She called Bunny White into her office and directed her to prepare an order withdrawing the warning letter against Jack Kenton.

Bunny White recognized that the Commissioner didn't have the authority to dismiss a warning letter issued by the Board of Scrutiny, but her opinion has not been sought, she had merely received an order. She was not eager to challenge her frightened and angry boss.

The Queen theorized that this maneuver might give the Ministry a basis to seek dismissal of the Federal lawsuit as being moot. She had done enough research to understand that mootness of a claim is sometimes used by courts to dismiss claims that no longer exist.

She had used a strategic dismissal in other cases in which she wanted to prevent a lawyer from availing himself of the internal appeals process provided in disciplinary matters. The Board of Governors and the Supreme Court could not hear an appeal if no complaint was pending. She theorized that the Federal Court might buy into this legal defense.

She hoped that if the claim was dismissed this might take some fire out of the Board of Governors' belly.

She signed the dismissal letter and filed it with the Ministry clerk. She then dictated a single sentence letter to Kenton. The letter simply informed Kenton that "the complaint has been dismissed and the warning letter has been removed from your personnel file and destroyed."

She could now report to President Mathis that the matter had been dismissed and there would be no further action on the matter by the Ministry of Ethics. Technically she was not allowed to report the dismissal to President Mathis, as it was confidential, but she nevertheless wrote him a brief letter reporting the dismissal.

When Mathis received the letter, he shook his head in disbelief. He was aware that the Board of Scrutiny had ordered the warning letter to be placed in Kenton's file, and only the Board of Scrutiny could order its destruction.

Chapter Fifty-Four

The weak attention provided to the administrative functions of the Supreme Court was evident in the court's failure to recognize significant problems in security. Any Chief Justice would have his hands full in just managing the judicial functions of the Supreme Court, but when he was also expected to manage all the administrative functions of the court system, the task was almost impossible.

Big Cat Cheshire and others took advantage of these neglected administrative functions of the Chief Justice. An example of this neglect was evidenced in the Kinman case.

The Goliath Insurance Company was the tenth largest casualty insurance company in America. It sold homeowner's insurance, automobile insurance, and half a dozen other insurance products. They were ranked tenth in amount of coverage sold, but were a respectable third in profitability.

They pumped up their sales by having some of the lowest prices in the industry. Their unusual level of profitability is credited to their parsimonious payment of claims. Their claims adjustors were the toughest in the business. They litigated a higher percentage of claims than any other insurance company in America, and delayed any settlement as long as possible.

Their lawyers, accountants and actuaries have developed a claims adjustment program that kept the money they rightfully owed on legitimate claims in their hands for years.

They know that by merely delaying the payment of the average claim by four months, they can annually boost their overall profits by $3.7 million dollars. They have developed a generous incentive plan for their adjustors to encourage them to hold on to every penny of company money and to delay settlements until the last moment before trial.

They were known in the industry as experts at evaluating claims. Their statistics reveal the propensity of jurors in every county in the country for awarding verdicts to plaintiffs. If you had a $10,000 damage claim in a county that usually didn't award large verdicts. Goliath would offer a policy holder a maximum of $5000 in settlement.

If the same claim was in a county that awarded high verdicts then they might go as far as $8000. They weren't afraid to litigate, because on the average they won over half their cases that went to trial. Even in cases where they lost, they almost automatically appealed every claim.

Goliath's bosses considered any adjuster that settled a claim for the legitimate value as a slacker. Slackers didn't last long at Goliath.

The case of Rebecca Kinman involved a claim against Kyota Motors for negligently manufacturing a car which caused a collision. She had lost a leg in the resulting automobile accident. A fire after the collision had left scars on her face.

The collision was alleged by Kinman to have been caused by the rapid and uncontrollable acceleration of her Japanese SUV. Kyota's experts predictably blamed the acceleration on the driver. The insurer was Goliath. The claims evaluation committee at Goliath noted that Rebecca Kinman was a 65 year old widow. Her home was paid for, and she lived on her retirement benefits as a school teacher which were supplemented by her deceased husband's retirement benefits. She attended church and had a clean driving record. Her three children were all adults.

The adjustor didn't note in his report that she looked much younger than her true age and that she had an engaging personality which made her potentially popular with a jury.

Kinman had over $100,000 in medical expenses most of which had been paid by Medicare. Medicare retained a lien on their medical payments to be paid out of any award she received by reason of her claim. She had actively accepted the required rehabilitation and had been given an artificial leg that she had not yet fully mastered. She still required a crutch to get around.

Even with the scaring on her face, and the artificial leg, she remained a beautiful woman.

The claims evaluation committee of Goliath, never met with Rebecca Kinman. They never saw her struggle in going up the stairs at night to her bedroom. They never saw her cry at night from the pain she still felt from the injuries. They ignored the pain of her physical rehabilitation exercises. They never witnessed the indignity she endured when she lost her balance and fell down in public. These personal issues were of no concern to the corporation and its shareholders.

Insurance companies have a great advantage over their policy holders. They have the checkbook and the claimant is usually in dire financial straits. This makes it easy for them to settle claims for less than their true value.

The Goliath insurance company only concerned itself with the facts that Kinman was from Lexington, Kentucky and that the juries there issued favorable insurance company verdicts in 70% of all cases sent to a jury.

In medical malpractice claims, juries in Fayette County found for the insurance company 95% of the time. In those verdicts in which the juries actually awarded something to the plaintiff, it was usually much less than the damages claimed.

Fayette county was notorious for small jury verdicts in personal injury claims.

Unfortunately for Rebecca Kinman she lived in Fayette County.

The Goliath Insurance Company used its software to evaluate Kinman's claim. The insurance company biased software called 'Colossus' valued her claim at $50,000. The adjustor offered her $10,000 to start. After six months without additional efforts to settle the case by Goliath, the plaintiff filed her civil suit in Fayette Circuit Court. Goliath then agreed to a mediation and upped their offer to $35,000. Mrs. Kinman demanded $250,000. This offer included her medical expenses and pain and suffering. She had no loss of income as she was retired.

In Kentucky the courts hold that retired people don't have to be compensated for their injuries wrongfully caused by others, to the degree that employed people are. Since retired people have no monthly salary, they can't claim a loss of wages.

Mrs. Kinman had a competent attorney. His name was Ward Bourne. His fee agreement granted him one-third of any award received by his client as a result of this claim. If the matter was appealed the fee would increase to forty percent.

The defense counsel was authorized to offer $50,000 to the plaintiff but only if she was able to survive the preliminary motions which they would file seeking to deny the right of her expert medical and automotive witnesses to testify, and if she could survive a motion for summary judgment dismissing the claim.

Mrs. Kinman was required to advance $12,500 for the two expert witnesses her attorney had recommended. Without an expert it is almost impossible to survive a motion for summary judgment in tort cases, especially when the plaintiff claims an engineering defect or physical injuries.

The Circuit Court judge denied Goliath's motions to exclude her expert witnesses, and their motion for summary judgment was likewise denied. Thereafter the court set a trial date.

The defendant gave notice to Mrs. Kinman that she would have to present herself to a physician selected by the insurance company. Such evaluations are called an IME. (Independent Medical Exam.) These physicians didn't treat a patient, they just allow the insurance carrier and their insured to make the plaintiff be examined by a physician that was highly reliable in finding that all medical problems where either non-existent are simply caused by the natural aging process. They were highly paid for their biased diagnosis which was conducted solely for the purpose of influencing the jury that would decide the case. Every large city had two or three doctors who made a substantial part of their income from insurance company referrals for IME's.

After the IME report was filed by the insurance company friendly physician, Goliath upped their offer to $50,000.

Kinman's attorney had advised her of the risks of going to trial, and asked her to seriously consider their offer of $50,000.

She told him, "This case is more important than my claim. I want to find justice for all those other motorists who have been injured or killed by those defective cars." The fact that a settlement of $50,000 wouldn't even pay off the Medicare lien made her rejection an easy decision.

The trial was set for the first week of October. The outlook was not promising. But in the last week of September there was a fiery wreck on the Mountain Parkway near Salyersville in which it was claimed that the Kyota driven by a school librarian had suddenly accelerated. The librarian and her two children died in the flames caused by the collision.

Three days after the Salyersville wreck, Mrs. Kinman's attorney received an anonymous letter which contained an engineering report which detailed possible design flaws in the accelerator software used in that model Kyota. The report revealed accelerator design flaws in the same model driven by Kinman and the model involved in the Salyersville wreck.

Ward Bourne instantly recognized that the report had not been included in the discovery provided him by the automaker. He had formally sought such data in his discovery motions. He issued a subpoena and this time included the date of publication and the name of the engineer who authored the study. The attorney hired by Goliath moved to quash the subpoena as the time for discovery had expired in compliance with the court's trial order.

The trial court recognized the value of the engineering report, and held a hearing on whether or not the automaker had violated the Civil Rules regarding their discovery duties. The Judge granted Mrs. Kinman the right to subpoena the engineer who wrote the report. It turned out that the engineer was conveniently vacationing somewhere in Europe and could not be found.

The trial judge ruled that the report could be used in cross-examination of the automaker's experts if they testified on the issue of rapid acceleration. The trial Judge said that at the end of the case he would consider a Rule 11 motion, which would allow him to sanction the automaker for not turning over the report. This would be in the nature of a monetary award.

The defense lawyers objected to his ruling, moved for a mistrial and filed a interlocutory motion for a Writ of Prohibition with the Court of Appeals.

The motion for a Writ of Prohibition was heard by a three judge panel of the Court of Appeals. In record time they denied the motion and upheld the ruling of the trial judge. Goliath responded by upping their offer of settlement to $100,000. This offer was rejected by Kinman.

Goliath and Kyota were faced with the dilemma of not being able to contest the claims of rapid acceleration without calling their expert to the stand. If they called him he would face difficult questions about the plaintiff's engineering report which had not been shared in discovery. They really had no choice, but to call him to the stand.

Kinman's attorney skillfully attacked the expert's credibility and suggested that the automaker had willfully withheld an engineering report which contradicted their own expert witness. When the jury was sent out to deliberate, Goliath increased their offer of settlement to $200,000 but Kinman had Bourne reject it out of hand.

The jury came back with a plaintiff's verdict of $4,000, 000 for pain and suffering, $100,000 for past medical expenses, $250,000 for future medical expenses, and $8,000,000 in punitive damages. The plaintiff's attorney added the numbers up on a yellow legal pad as they were read to the near empty courtroom. $12,350,000!

He quickly calculated that his 40% would be just under $5 million dollars. He calculated his fee at 40% because it was obvious that an appeal was in the future with such a large verdict. He was correct, Kyota appealed the verdict.

Goliath's post verdict offer was $2,000,000 to settle the claim and prevent an appeal. The offer was rejected by Mrs. Kinman.

It took thirteen months for the Court of Appeals to issue a ruling upholding the verdict. Goliath then upped their offer to $4,000,000 which was again rejected by Mrs. Kinman even though Bourne almost got on his knees and pleaded with her to take the cash.

Goliath and the automaker filed a motion for discretionary review with the Kentucky Supreme Court. It took eleven months for the Supreme Court to grant the motion for discretionary review.

All judgments in Kentucky bear interest on unpaid verdicts at the rate of 12% per year. By the time the Supreme Court agreed to accept an appeal in the case, the interest had accrued to $988,000, which would be added to the jury verdict if the Court upheld the award.

Six months after each party submitted briefs to the Supreme Court, the matter was set for argument behind the closed doors of the Supreme Court conference room on the second floor of the State Capitol Building in Frankfort.

The Kyota defense team had argued in their appeal brief, that under the facts the punitive damage claim should not have been submitted to the jury. They also argued in their appeal brief that the trial court's ruling allowing the non-disclosed engineering study to be used on cross-examination was improperly decided.

Kyota's appellate team, which had been selected by Goliath, made an impressive argument on the auto maker's behalf.

On the day set for considering the appeal, the Supreme Court members marched into the conference room and the heavy doors were closed behind them and guarded by an armed bailiff to assure the confidentiality of the deliberations of the seven justices. They were not alone in this hearing.

Big Cat Cheshire's laser beam acoustic listening device was delivering every word spoken in the conference room to his recording devices aimed at the single pane unprotected windows of the Supreme Court Conference room.

Cheshire had been hired by Goliath, without the knowledge of the defense attorneys, to advise Goliath's corporate managers on the possible outcome of the appeal. The contract between Cheshire and Goliath did not mention the means by which Cheshire was to predict the Supreme Court's final verdict. The fee however was spelled out in detail. The fee was $250,000 if an accurate report was delivered at least two days before publication of the court's decision.

It was made obvious to Cheshire, that Goliath expected something more than an educated guess when they agreed to pay $250,000 to Cheshire, half in advance. He would have to produce real evidence. They were aware of the possibility that Cheshire might just take a 50-50 guess. They demanded real proof or the fee would have to be returned.

The Supreme Court had never considered in any great detail their susceptibility to security breaches. They had a few armed guards around the Capitol Building, and had a bailiff stationed outside the door of the conference room.

Their security practices hadn't been changed much in the last hundred years. This lack of knowledge of advances in spying technology was not a mistake made by Big Cat Cheshire. He had long been waiting for a case involving a lot of money to come before the court. He had set his traps well. His only error was that he had underestimated the ambition of his electronics technician Matt Simons.

The Supreme Court panel discussed the case among themselves briefly as all Justices had previously submitted their opinions. When the Chief Justice read the ballots of each Justice's vote he noted four voted for upholding the plaintiff's verdict and three for granting a new trial. The decision would be kept secret until such time as the Justice assigned to write the opinion had completed the work and it was signed off on by all the other Justices in attendance. That might take anywhere from two months to six months.

Cheshire personally listened to the discussions at the Supreme Court hearing and then typed out his report. His entire report contained only nine words. He earned $27,777 for each word of the nine word report.

"Four to uphold the plaintiff's award, and three against."

Cheshire personally delivered the report as directed to Goliath's corporate representative who had been monitoring the case from his hotel room at the Lexington Hyatt Regency Hotel.

In the history of the Kentucky Appellate courts there is no known instance of any Justice leaking the vote on a case prior to its public release.

If that had ever happened it had never been disclosed. This fidelity by the Court made Cheshire's spying all that more valuable.

The next morning the original trial team for Goliath visited the office of Kinman's attorney and made their final offer of settlement. The tall bald headed attorney in a black Brooks Brothers suit spoke for Goliath. "We would like to close this case out. There is a value to the insured to have this case settled. I'm authorized to make a final offer of settlement with standard confidentiality clauses, to Mrs. Kinman, of $10,000,000. If this is accepted, we'll require you to join in a motion to the Supreme Court to dismiss the appeal."

The offer was accompanied by a settlement agreement already signed by Goliath. A check for $10,000,000 was shown to Bourne. If accepted, payment would be made immediately and any further consideration of appeal through the Federal courts would be dropped.

All the widow Kinman had to do to claim the prize, was to sign her name to the settlement agreement. The insurance company was well aware of the difficulty that most plaintiffs had in refusing a settlement after actually seeing the settlement check laying on the table before them, only a signature away from their possession.

Bourne did his best to not show any emotion. He thanked them for the offer. He told them he'd call them before noon the next day. They left him a cell phone number to call.

Bourne's first thoughts were that a settlement of $10 million would guarantee him $4 million dollars. Visions of sports cars and Ft. Lauderdale condos, danced through his head.

He had made up a chart on his computer showing the daily interest which was accumulating. Interest on the original judgment had accumulated to almost $3,000,000. If the offer of $10,000,000 was accepted, Goliath would save themselves $5,350,000.

If the Supreme Court ruled against Rebecca Kinman, they could totally dismiss the case, or reduce the punitive damages as they sometimes did, or they could order a new trial. All of these possibilities made the offer of $10,000,000 a very serious offer considering the risk involved in a bad decision coming from the Supreme Court.

Bourne didn't want to risk the four million dollar fee he would receive from the tendered settlement. But holding out for the larger fee he would receive if the court upheld the jury verdict was enticing. He could earn several more millions if the jury verdict was upheld on appeal.

He put the dreams of a profligate new life style out of mind. He realized that he didn't get to make this decision. The widow made the decision, and he was afraid that he knew what her decision would be. As he was dialing her number, he thought to himself, "I will jump off the tallest building in the Commonwealth if she rejects this offer and the Supreme Court tosses her case."

He arranged to meet the widow at her home. She sat in her chair and continued calmly embroidering a napkin as he explained the numbers and the options to her. He showed her the signature of Goliath Insurance Company on the settlement papers and emphasized that the settlement would be paid immediately.

He pointed out that they had shown him the settlement check which had already been prepared.

Her only question was, "If I sign this, then no one else will ever learn of the jury verdict that Kyota designed a dangerous car. Will they?"

Bourne shook his head negatively and said, "Well that is a standard requirement in most insurance settlements." He quickly added, "These settlements often are leaked to the press, and as long as you aren't the one doing the leaking, you still keep the settlement."

She continued with her fine hand work in silence.

He had one more card to play. He pulled out a paper he had prepared which showed the breakdown of all her court costs, the sums owed to Medicare, the amount of the award, the amount he would receive and the net amount she would receive. He completed this final ploy by advising her that "everything she would receive would be tax free."

She ended the meeting by telling him. "Mr. Bourne you have done a good job. I appreciate that. But I want to think about this and I want to pray about it. Leave your papers here. Call me at ten o'clock tomorrow morning and I'll have an answer".

He responded, "No need to call me. I'll be back to see you sharply at 10 A.M."

Bourne drove himself to a bar. He realized that it wouldn't be possible for him to sleep that night if he was sober. He couldn't get the thought out of his mind, "I'll be richer than god."

Chapter Fifty-Five

An hour after her attorney left her to ponder the acceptance or rejection of the $10 million dollar offer from the automaker and Goliath, Kinman received a phone call from a former student, Matthew Simons.

She had known Matt since he was a student in a class she taught at Henry Clay High School on Richmond Road. He had recently installed a new flat screen television for her. It had been a birthday gift from a group of her former students.

Matt told her that there was an important matter that he needed to talk with her about and asked if he could drop by. He didn't tell her that he had discovered the facts of her case when he was reviewing Cheshire's intelligence tapes.

She said that she was on her way to her parish church, but if he could come right over she would be glad to see him.

Matt got quickly to the point after she seated him in the living room. "I've been following your lawsuit in the newspapers. I know that you have appealed the jury verdict to the Supreme Court. That's all public knowledge.

"I have reason to believe that the insurance company may be trying to take advantage of you. Please confirm one thing for me. Isn't it true that the automaker or their insurance company made you a final offer in the last 24 hours?"

She was surprised and asked him, "'Matt, how did you know that? I just learned about the new offer two hours ago."

"It doesn't matter how, but I have been approached by two people who appear to be close to the automaker and they say they want to help you. They said they thought it was only right that you be fairly compensated for your injuries. They have asked me to make you an offer.

"They claim to have information about how the Supreme Court is going to rule in your case. They assure me there is no bribery involved, and that no bribes have been, or will be offered to any judge. They are willing to share that information with you but they want a fee."

Simons continued, "They told me to tell you that if you get more than the automaker's final offer, they want 10% of whatever the excess is that you actually receive. They aren't asking for a penny up front. They guarantee their information. If you agree, they will provide you immediately with proof of the outcome of your appeal. This information will allow you to accept or reject automaker's offer based on actual proof. Right now you don't know how the court will rule. The automaker doesn't know. The lawyers don't know. But if you agree to pay the source 10% of anything you get over and above the final offer the defendant makes, then proof of the outcome of your appeal will be given to you immediately."

"Matt, you are pulling my one good leg aren't you?"

"No, Mrs. Kinman, I'm not. This is not a trick. I fear these people. I wish they had never approached me. I don't even know how they knew that I know you."

She pressed, "Will I meet these people?"

"No, they gave me a sealed envelope, I have it with me. I assume it contains the proof they mention. If you accept the deal then they trust you to pay them. They said there is a overseas bank account number in the sealed envelope. You are to wire the money to that account exactly three days after your receive the judgment money being paid to you by the defendant company.

"They said you can back out of the offer by not opening the envelope. It's wrapped in duct tape and it appears that it would be impossible to open the envelope and view their evidence without destroying the envelope. If I return the envelope unopened tonight, there is no deal. But if you open the envelope or return it in a damaged condition then they will hold you to the deal. These are people that I wouldn't want to cross."

She asked, "So how will they know what the final offer was that the automaker made to me today?"

Simons sat up straight in his chair, and replied, "They knew about the settlement offer before you did. They seem to know everything".

"So if the final offer is, say $5 million, then I would owe them 10% of everything over $5 million and nothing more?"

"Yes, Nothing more. And you will never have to deal with them. They say you will never hear from them, unless of course you open the envelope and don't pay them."

"And they say the proof is unassailable?"

"Yes, they claim it will be absolutely convincing."

"If they are wrong, and I reject the defendant's final offer, I may lose everything. The court may dismiss my appeal, and I might get nothing."

Simons agreed, "That's true, but they didn't create that risk, the insurance company and Kyota did."

Rebecca Kinman didn't like the risk, but she was intrigued to see what was in the envelope.

Simons sensing her reticence, fired his last shot, "They told me that if you weren't convinced, I should give you a second envelope. There is no obligation if you open the second envelope.

He pulled both envelopes from his windbreaker, and placed them on the sofa next to her.

She gently picked up the plain envelope, and after holding it to the light to see if she could read anything, opened it.

She read to herself: "The defendant automaker today offered a final settlement to Rebecca Kinman for the sum of $10,000,000. The settlement is subject to a confidentiality agreement, and must be accepted prior to the release to the public of the Supreme Court's ruling in the Kinman vs. Kyota civil claim which is pending before the Kentucky Supreme Court".

Kinman was impressed. "They know the amount of the offer. I haven't told anyone. And you are telling me that the second envelope, the one with the duct tape all over it, contains absolute proof of the Court's ruling."

"Yes" he replied, "If the court grants you less than $10,000,000 you don't pay these people anything. If the court grants you more than $10,000,000 then you wire them 10% of the excess over $10 million, including any accrued interest you receive due to their appeal."

She thought to herself, "Ten per cent to take a peek at the future!"

Simons nodded his head and added, "They told me that I had to bring the envelope and all its contents back to them tonight regardless if the deal is accepted or rejected. I was told not to allow you to make any photo copies."

Rebecca Kinman realized that the difference between the $10 million offer that was on the table and the trial court verdict, plus accrued interest, would be over $5 million dollars. If the envelope revealed that the Court had dismissed her case, then she could still accept the automaker's offer and receive $10 million.

She knew there was something wrong about this, but there was also something terribly unjust about Kyota's faulty accelerator costing her a leg and then hiding the engineering report from her attorney.

She was rightfully angry with the automaker. They denied their liability and made her sue them and forced her to fight for three years to get to this point. A part of her felt that they deserved the disloyalty of their own people who were telling her the future.

She picked up the envelope and felt it. It appeared to contain several pieces of paper and perhaps a DVD disc.

"Matthew, would you please fetch my sewing box off the sideboard over there?"

She took the scissors from the sewing box and carefully cut through the duct tape on one end of the envelope. She spread the envelope open, and removed two sheets of paper and a DVD disc. The first piece of paper reported the good news:

"By a vote of 4 to 3 the Kentucky Supreme Court voted to uphold the jury verdict, and to sustain the affirmation of the Court of Appeals, and the trial court, on all issues in the case of Rebecca Kinman vs. Kyota."

She then laid the first paper on the sofa next to her good leg, and picked up the second piece of paper. It was a photo copy of a black and white photograph of seven Justices of the Supreme Court sitting around a long conference table. She recognized Chief Justice Madison Hatter. She had attended a UK Alumni party several years ago and had been introduced to him.

She gave the DVD disc to Matt and asked him to play it on the DVD player he had installed with her television.

Simons soon had the TV displaying a slightly grainey video of the seven Justices sitting around a long conference table. She heard the Chief Justice read off his tally of the votes.

The video was only about two minutes long. She asked Simons to play it again. She had heard the ruling correctly the first time. The vote was reassuringly still 4 to 3 in her favor when it was played the second time.

She was disappointed to learn from the video that Madison Hatter had voted against her.

She asked Simons, "Can I show this to my lawyer?" Simons had a very troubled look on his face as he quietly but firmly replied, "Mrs. Kinman, we can't do that. This has to remain a secret. These may be dangerous people, and you would just be getting your lawyer in trouble with the Bar

Association. If he sees this, he has to report it to the court, and that might be disastrous to your case."

She picked up the envelope and once again opened it and looked inside to see if it had any other contents. She found a business card sized piece of paper. It provided the number of what she assumed was a bank account number and the name of a Bank.

It read, "Wire exactly at noon on the third day after you receive payment. Wire to the bank and account number provided. "

Simons rose to leave and gathered up the disc, the paper and the photograph and said, "Congratulations Mrs. Kinman, I guess you really have been vindicated. You deserve every penny."

The next morning she told Ward Bourne that she was rejecting the offer of $10,000, 000. He lost all color in his face. He took a very deep breath before commenting, "Mrs. Kinman, you are the strongest willed woman I have ever met. I pray to God that you are right."

While sitting in her living room, her attorney used his cell phone and called the Goliath attorney and told him of her decision to reject their offer. They immediately upped the offer to twelve million dollars, but she also rejected that offer.

There are two Catholic churches in Lexington, St. Peter's and St. Paul's. While she attended Mass at both churches from time to time, today she chose St. Paul's on Short Street. After her lawyer left, she got her crutch, and hobbled to her car, and drove to the church where she gave her confession and prayed for forgiveness.

When the final decision of the Kentucky Supreme Court was released, it was reported in the on a Thursday by LawReader.com and on Friday was reported in both local and national news outlets. Within thirty days seventy-eight additional civil suits and two class actions were filed against Kyota by people with rapid acceleration claims.

Seven days after the release of the decision, Rebecca Kinman's lawyer received a cashier's check for $15,350,000 dollars from the Goliath insurance company.

Her lawyer gleefully withheld his 40% fee which came to $6,140,000. Kinman paid off the Medicare lien of $100,000 for her past medical expenses, wired $535,000 to the overseas bank account, mailed a check to St. Paul's for $75,000, mailed a check to St. Peter's for $125,000, and in appreciation for his efforts she mailed a check to Matt Simons for

$100,000. She retained $8,270,000 tax free dollars in her personal bank account.

She granted more money to St. Peter's because he was the saint Christ had designated as the "rock upon which I build my church". She gave the smaller amount to St. Paul's, as she believed him to have been a bit of a misogynist.

She never heard further from the source close to the automaker who had given her an accurate peek at the future.

Rebecca Kinman never knew that Matt Simons had been working for himself or that he had never been contacted by anyone close to the manufacturer. She never knew or really cared that he was the owner of the overseas bank account to which she had wired a small fortune. She never concerned herself with how those 'dangerous people' learned of the final offer.

The wire transfer of $535,000 went to the Caribbean bank selected by Simons, then was transferred to another bank account in the Cayman Islands, and then transferred to the Simons Software Consultants, LLC account in a Fayette County bank. Simons explained the money as having been derived from the sale of his share of a software program he had written for a software development company.

He instructed his accountant to duly list the income in his next tax return. He certainly didn't want the IRS to come snooping around. He was more than willing to pay the 15% capital gains tax, in order to be able to sleep at night.

Six months later Rebecca was on a Mediterranean cruise. She had invited her cousin Jeri Boyd from Carrollton, to be her guest. They were traveling first class to Venice, Italy and the Greek Isles.

One night at dinner, having the honor of being invited to be seated at the Captain's table, Rebecca ordered two bottles of Dom Perignon at $175 a bottle, for her table mates. Jeri scolded her for being so extravagant.

The rich widow laughed off the friendly admonition and said in her defense, "I'm just borrowing from Goliath to pay Peter and Paul." Jeri Boyd never really understood the pun.

A month after Rebecca Kinman returned from her vacation she was visited by Art Petrov. He gave her a business card which identified him as a Consumer Protection Representative of the Bar Association's Ministry of Ethics. He explained that the Ministry was aware of her lawsuit and merely wanted to be sure that she was satisfied with her attorney's services.

He asked her if her attorney had obtained a signed fee contract from her, and inquired about how the expert witness fees and trial consultant fees were handled.

She had retained all of her papers and showed Petrov the fee contract, the disbursement accounting, and the agreement with the trial consultant. He asked several more questions about her satisfaction with her attorney's services. She assured him that she was quite satisfied with her attorney's services and had no complaints.

As soon as Petrov left, Kinman called Ward Bourne and told him of the visit from Petrov. He was not happy. He felt insulted that the Ministry would be interviewing his client without informing him. He lied and told his client that this was normal in large cases.

Bourne had worked hard to earn his fee. He had worked for three years on this case and had been at risk of not receiving a penny if the case had not been successful. He had invested his own money to pay for depositions and medical reports. His client was happy. He couldn't discern any reason the Bar Association could have come up with to question his work. Nevertheless, he saw no benefit from getting into a dispute with the Ministry. He, like most attorneys, feared the Ministry and decided to let the matter drop.

Later he followed a suggestion from another lawyer and anonymously sent a story to LawReader.com about the post trial interview of his client by the Ministry.

Chapter Fifty-Six

Most lawyers believed that Kenton and Justice Boone's challenge to the system were courageous acts. But they refrained from any public comment to avoid being drawn into the affair. Taking a position against the Ministry was a risky endeavor.

Williston Stafford had explained to the Eunuchs why he avoided enlisting younger lawyers in their group to oppose the Ministry. "Young lawyers are still actively practicing law and have financial obligations. They fear the loss of their careers if they became to vocal."

Stafford didn't publically fault them for their prudence, but privately he was disappointed in their lack of interest in the defense of the profession. Stafford recognized the old saying that, 'there are times to stand tall, and then there are other times'. When given a chance to publically support their fellow lawyers, most attorneys concluded that this was 'the other time'.

He told Kenton, "I don't see lawyers writing letters to the editor, I don't see them marching in the streets. Whenever the Ministry goes after an attorney most other attorneys just put their heads in the sand and brush it off with the conclusion that he was probably guilty anyway. The potion served by the Queen of Hearts made most lawyers small in stature."

Kenton responded, "Lawyers remind me of the Eloi in H.G. Wells novel *The Time Machine*. The innocent Eloi lacked curiosity or discipline. They played in the sun all day, and ate the low hanging fruit on the trees. But at night the brutish light-fearing Morlocks came out of their underground tunnels and took some Eloi back underground, where they were butchered and eaten. They ate just enough of the Eloi to keep them from becoming extinct."

Stafford, completed the anecdote, "Exactly! The Morlocks at the Ministry fear the light. We need to expose them to all the daylight that's possible!"

CHAPTER FIFTY-SEVEN

Williston Stafford was asked to speak to members of the Muhlenberg County Bar Association at the courthouse in Greenville, Kentucky. They wanted to learn more about the operation of the Ministry of Ethics and wanted suggestions on what they could do to help the Eunuchs.

The host of the meeting, Julie Thompson, was the President of the Muhlenberg County Bar Association.

When she called Stafford to invite him to the meeting, she specifically asked him to address the ethics proceedings pending against Judge Natrona Clay. "Judge Clay was raised near Drakesboro. He's got a large number of family members that still live around here. Natrona was valedictorian of his High School class at Muhlenberg Central. He left here to attend law school at U of L and like so many of our best students, he never came home. We've never really understood what went on with his case. I know you'll get some questions on this subject."

Stafford knew little of the Clay investigation but agreed to do his best for the group.

A month before his trip to Muhlenberg County, Stafford searched the internet and found that Natrona Clay was the first of several African-American Judges appointed by Governor Beshear in 2008. Stafford's questioning around Louisville lead him to conclude that Clay was likely to be the first judge disbarred by action of the Ministry of Ethics without a recommendation from the Judicial Conduct Commission.

Natrona Clay had served as a Circuit Court Judge in Louisville for eight years before the complaint was filed against him. His work ethic and knowledge of the law earned him the respect of his peers in the Louisville bar. However, like most judges he made enemies as a result of some of his decisions. He was never one to suffer fools or to tolerate frivolous legal arguments.

While Stafford knew that the Bar Association and the Ministry of Ethics had records regarding the Clay disbarment proceedings, he knew from experience that the records were hidden behind the curtain of secrecy. It was almost impossible to review the conduct of the Ministry.

Stafford had on several occasions contacted the Bar Association requesting information, and had never been successful in receiving anything but a brush off. He concluded that they must have a training session in Frankfort, where everyone from the janitor to the Commissioner of the Ministry of Ethics were taught that the only comment they could ever make to the public about any topic was 'that's confidential'.

Stafford concluded the since he couldn't go through the front door of the Ministry, he would try to go through the back door.

In late November, Stafford drove to Lexington for a Continuing Legal Education class at the Convention Center next to Rupp Arena. He speculated that since this program was the closest one to the Ministry of Ethics office, that some of their staffers might be in attendance. Like every other lawyer, they had to attend a minimum number of classes each year to maintain their law license. Since this program was one of the few CLE programs that was provided for free, it drew a large crowd. Usually around a thousand lawyers attended the annual Lexington meeting.

After signing in, and receiving his program folder, Stafford entered the large hall. The first class of the day was titled 'Ethics Update'. Surely members of the Ministry would be in attendance.

He walked slowly around the edges of the hall for ten minutes looking for a familiar face.

He saw a lot of familiar faces, but he was looking for one of the few people he knew that worked at the Ministry.

Finally, he spotted Bunny White who had entered the room just as the speaker was being introduced. She appeared to be by herself. He followed her up an aisle until she took a seat. He then sat down next to her and placed his program folder on the table.

When she turned to see who was sitting next to her, he greeted her. "Good morning Bunny, I had hoped you might be here."

She nodded to him but avoided speaking. A few minutes later he saw her writing something on her legal pad. She slipped the paper in front of him.

"Be careful," the note said, "cameras are everywhere."

Stafford kept his head down for a few moments before slowly searching the walls for cameras and indeed spotted at least half a dozen security cameras focused on the group. Fifteen minutes into the session, he wrote a note to her and carefully slid it towards her.

"Can we talk?"

Shortly before the end of the ninety minute class, she returned his message with the addition, "5:30 at room 314 Hyatt Regency." She left him standing by his chair as she left the room.

Promptly at 5:30 he knocked on the door to Room 314 and it opened immediately. She looked up and down the hallway to see if anyone saw him.

"Did anyone see you?" she asked.

"No, of course not."

She motioned him to a seat and apologized for having nothing to drink but tap water.

"Williston, it's not wise for me to be seen talking with you. You are not exactly a friend of my people. I'll give you ten minutes and then you've got to go. What is it that you want to talk about?" She had turned the television on and it was very loud.

He explained over the noise that he was curious about the attempt to disbar Judge Clay. "I can't find anything but some news reports. What really is happening?"

She sat on the King sized bed with her legs crossed. "To tell you the truth, what happened is that he pissed off the wrong people."

"That's not a disbarment offense," he countered.

"Why do you want to know? Shouldn't you just let sleeping dogs lie?"

Williston Stafford looked her in the eye and asked, "Bunny, I've always thought a lot of you. You're one of the brightest people in Frankfort. You could do a lot better than selling your soul to the Queen of Hearts."

Defensively, she answered, "It's a job. While we have our dark moments. Most of what we do is necessary."

Both lawyers sat silent for a moment.

Stafford, changed his direction and got to the point. "I always thought that the Judicial Conduct Commission had exclusive authority to sanction Judges, but in this case the Ministry is ignoring the jurisdiction of the Judicial Conduct Commission and going after a judge without the JCC having requested their intervention. It appears that the Ministry is seeking to punish Judge Clay over a ruling he issued."

Bunny White smiled, "Williston, put your reading glasses on. Read the rule regarding the jurisdiction of the JCC. I know it by heart. It says, 'Any erroneous decision made in good faith shall not be subject to the jurisdiction of the Commission.' She placed a heavy emphasis on the word 'Commission'.

He said, "I don't understand. That Rule says to me that a judge can't be sanctioned for a bad ruling. Every judge makes a bad ruling from time to time. That's what we have appellate courts for."

"Williston, sometimes you have to look closer at a law. That Rule doesn't say the Ministry of Ethics can't sanction a judge for a bad ruling. It says the *Judicial Conduct Commission* can't sanction a judge for a bad ruling."

Stafford was dumbfounded. "But the whole purpose of the Judicial Conduct Commission's existence is to remove judges from regulation by the Bar!"

She leaned towards him and asked him almost in a whisper, "Where in the Rules does it say that?"

"Are you saying that the Ministry takes the position that while the Judicial Conduct Code says a judge can't be removed from office for a bad ruling, that his license can be suspended to practice law, thereby removing him from office, if he happens to make a bad ruling?"

"Williston, that's exactly what's happening to Judge Clay. I admit this interpretation of the law is a bit of a stretch, but the JCC didn't bat an eyelash when we did this. No one from the JCC protested or sought to intervene. Clay's attorneys raised this defense, but Commissioner Hart ordered us to just ignore it. Judge Clay's only hope is that the Supreme Court will reject this expansion of the Ministry's jurisdiction if they get the case on appeal.

"We debated this issue for weeks at the Ministry. I was against this expansion of the Ministry's jurisdiction, but I lost the argument, and Judge Clay will be soon selling insurance in the west end of Louisville."

"But what did he do that was so serious?"

"I told you he pissed off the wrong people!"

"Can you tell me who 'the wrong people' are?"

He noticed a flash of fear in her face. She pulled out a pad and scribbled a note which she handed him. It read, "Are you wearing a wire?"

He took the pen from her and wrote "NO!"

He stood up and whispered, "You can frisk me for a wire if you wish."

She paused for a moment and whispered, "Williston, do me a favor. Take your cell phone and jacket and put them in the bathroom, turn on the faucet to the sink and the tub and then close the door behind you."

He thought this was silly, but hoping this would convince her to open up, he complied with her bizarre request. When he returned, he pulled out his pockets and demonstrated they were empty. She wasn't the least bit embarrassed by his drama.

"Williston, I've tried to tip you off. You and Jack Kenton are the only people who seem to want to do anything about the Ministry. Don't think for a minute that they don't keep a close eye on you. They have heard of your Lawyer's Revolution and are watching you closely."

Stafford concluded that her previous comment about trying to "tip him off" meant she was the whistleblower who had been sending him unsigned letters about the Ministry's plans.

He allowed her to continue and didn't press her on this admission.

"Since Heather Hart became Commissioner things have gotten curiouser and curiouser.

"She starts investigations and we are never told who filed the complaint. The whole office is frightened of her. Even the Board of Governors gives her a wide berth. She has developed a group of snitches whom she protects from sanctions in return for their spying on other lawyers.

The whole set up is a complete disaster waiting to happen.

"No one monitors our conduct. She is always screaming at the staff to produce numbers. She seems immune to staff protests that many weak claims are being prosecuted by the Ministry.

"When someone raises a question, we are told to hide behind the confidentiality rules. The Board of Governors has allowed us to do this. They are supposed to supervise Heather Hart and the Ministry, but everyone over there must have some secret in their past that they fear might be exposed. They don't mess with Heather Hart and the Ministry. I don't suspect this is a surprise since the Board of Governors are volunteers who only meet once a month. There is no institutional knowledge built up at the Board of Governors since by rule no one can serve on the board for more than two brief terms.

"You and Jack Kenton, and Justice Boone are the only people who are interested enough to start asking questions. She is very aware of what you are doing, and don't be surprised if she doesn't come after you.

"I believe she even has a spy among your Eunuchs."

"Who would that be?" Stafford asked.

"I don't know, but I saw some hand written notes on her desk recently, and it had a report about your meeting with Justice Boone at the Metropolitan Club in Covington. I would assume that one of the other guests at your meeting was the leak."

"That can't be, Bunny. There was no one else at that meeting but Justice Boone and myself."

They both sat silent for a moment measuring the consequences of their interlocking revelations.

"She had to have bugged the room!" Stafford concluded.

"Williston, I wouldn't put that past Commissioner Hart, but she couldn't have used anyone from the Ministry. We don't have any staffers with that capability. I really don't think that any of our people would do that. It would be a felony. Our people would never go to prison for Heather Hart."

Williston pressed the growing trust he detected, "Is there a possibility that I might be able to see the investigation file on Judge Clay?"

"I don't know if I could do that. It's clearly against the rules. It's an ongoing case and it would be improper. That would be risky."

Stafford restrained himself from rebutting her comment with the observation that the Ministry always seems to leak case details to the press when it serves their purpose.

He only commented, "I'm told that Judge Clay has formally waived confidentiality in his case, and under my reading of the rules, that allows public disclosure of the facts of the case."

Bunny looked at her wrist watch, and said, "You've had more than your ten minutes. You've got to go."

Stafford opened the door and cautiously looked up and down the hall before making a clean get-a-way.

Ten days after the meeting with Bunny White, Stafford received a package delivered by FedEx. The return address was listed to a company he had never heard of located in Louisville.

When he opened the package, he discovered a copy of the case file regarding the Ministry's investigation of Judge Natrona Clay.

Stafford called AT&T information but they had no listing for Universal Import Export Ltd., the company whose name was the return address on the package. He then used LawReader to check the corporate name filings in the Secretary of State's business office.

Nothing was listed under the name of Universal Import and Export, Ltd. He then did a search on the internet. He laughed out loud when he found a reference to Ian Fleming's James Bond novels. It seems that secret agent James Bond's cover employer was Universal Import and Export, Ltd. He would forever after refer to Bunny White as "007."

The investigative report told a story of a civil case which had been heard by Judge Clay.

Judge Clay approved a settlement in a class action. The award was in the millions. The record revealed pleadings where the attorneys had informed Judge Clay that all class plaintiffs approved of the settlement. He was told that each member of the class had physically signed off on the settlement. After approving the settlement, he approved the attorney fees to be deducted from the award by the plaintiff's attorneys.

Stafford stopped reading the file and researched the law on settlement procedures. He called a respected mediator and asked them if they were aware of any court anywhere refusing to accept a settlement which was agreed to by all the plaintiff's and the defendant. No source searched by Stafford revealed any precedent for a court refusing to accept settlement of a civil lawsuit when all the parties wanted to settle and had actually agreed upon the terms of the settlement.

Several years after the plaintiff's were paid their money, an attorney named Melanie Hancock wrote all of the plaintiff's and suggested to them that they had been swindled by their attorneys who had conspired with the judge to hide from them the true size of the settlement. The total amount of the settlement was kept confidential. Many civil cases are settled and confidentiality agreements are common. Some states have outlawed confidentiality clauses in settlements but the Kentucky Supreme Court has so far refused to adopt this reform.

Judge Clay ruled that nothing in the Class Action Rules required that every plaintiff know what every other plaintiff received in a settlement when there was a mutually agreed upon confidentiality agreement. Each only had to know what they were to receive and to approve or reject the offer.

Each of the plaintiff's had claimed different degrees of personal injury as the result of the defendant's product. Some actually died as a result of the injury. The vast majority of the 500 plaintiffs suffered no injury at all, but still received a settlement check.

Stafford learned that in class actions where physical injuries are claimed, a special Master Commissioner is appointed to evaluate the injury of each of the 500 plaintiffs. Such a Master Commissioner met with each plaintiff, reviewed their claims of injury, and assigned a dollar value to each claim.

All 500 plaintiffs signed their individual settlement letter approving the Master's award to them. This procedure prevented the courts having to conduct 500 separate jury trials, and by doing so saved the defendant the cost of litigation and encouraged the defendant to be liberal in its settlement offer. Such a time saving procedure was the reason justifying class actions.

In the process, Judge Clay allowed the costs of the experts and consultants, and all other court costs to be paid from the settlement funds. Without trial consultants, it was unlikely that the settlement offer would have been half as big as was finally offered.

The final attorney's fees of the plaintiff's lawyers came out to one-third of the settlement. The law does not require the trial judge to limit the attorney fees to the amount contracted for with the client, since the conversion of the lawsuit from 500 individual lawsuits into a class action changes the basis for a fee determination. The trial court handling a class action has the authority to award more or less than the fee contract requires.

Melanie Hancock, signed up hundreds of the original plaintiffs on the promise of additional money to be paid to them. The dispute arose over a claim that the court costs should have been paid out of the portion of the settlement going to the plaintiff's attorneys. Such a finding would mean that they plaintiff's did not have to pay their own court costs.

The original plaintiffs, having been told by their new attorney that the court costs and consultant fees awarded by Judge Clay were excessive, bought into Hancock's claim that that they had been cheated.

All 500 plaintiff's, many of whom had already spent their settlement checks, were heavily solicited to join in a lawsuit against their class action attorneys. The promise of recovering large sums enticed many of them to join. About 300 of the original plaintiffs joined in the lawsuit against the attorneys, but 200 refused to do so.

Stafford found notes in the file from a Ministry attorney's research that indicated that the only way the suit against the plaintiff's attorneys could be successful was if it could be proven that they had illegally bribed the judge to keep the original plaintiff's in the dark.

The file contained briefs of Judge Clay's attorneys where they cited examples in other class action lawsuits where such a confidentiality ruling was upheld. However, these other cases were from other states, and technically the Kentucky Courts were not bound by these foreign rulings.

Examples were shown of a Kentucky case by the Court of Appeals where class action attorneys were allowed a fee of 50% of the settlement amount. The attorney fees awarded by Judge Clay only came to 33 1/3%. Nevertheless, the argument raised was one of excessive attorney fees being approved by Judge Clay.

The conspiracy theory, without which the claimant's would be lost, alleged that the Judge approved the confidentiality provision, and that the Judge had a close personal relationship with the plaintiff's attorneys.

Affidavits were filed alleging that Judge Clay, after the case was closed, and before the new dispute was raised, attended a golf trip with some of the plaintiff's lawyers. Clay countered with an affidavit and receipts showing he had paid his own way on the trip.

Another claim was that the Judge improperly accepted an appointment to a Charitable Trust. The trust had been set up by the plaintiff's attorneys out of Cy Pres funds left over from the settlement.

Cy Pres funds are funds left over in a class action lawsuit after all the Master Commissioner's awards court costs and attorney fees had been paid.

Stafford read a brief filed in behalf of Judge Clay, which explained that the Master Commissioner had evaluated all of the claims and that several million dollars were left over. Authorities were cited where the Federal Courts had approved of excess funds in class action cases being donated to charitable causes having some relation to the wrong caused by the defendant. Several Federal class action rulings expressly ruled that it would be improper for the excess funds to be divided among the class action members, since the 500 members of the class had already received the fair amount of their claim.

This theory acknowledged that the defendant's medical product had been used by over 50,000 persons. The extra funds were to be used in some manner to benefit the 49,500 potential plaintiff's who had not joined the class action law suit.

In such cases, the Federal courts had frequently approved the excess funds being placed in a charity set up to benefit the consumers of the product who had not joined the class action. Judge Clay accepted this precedent from the Federal courts and approved the charitable trust.

A year after the conclusion of the class action lawsuit, Judge Clay was invited to sit on the board of the charitable trust.

In the records, Stafford found an affidavit from Judge Clay. It cited Canon 4-C-3, a provision of the Code of Judicial Conduct that permitted sitting judges to serve on the boards of charitable organizations. He also had submitted an ethics opinion he had obtained from a lawyer who practiced Ethics Law which said there was no ethical violation of the Code of Judicial Conduct in Judge Clay accepting the position on the charitable trust.

The press picked up on the lawsuit against the class action attorneys, and the allegations of a conspiracy with Judge Clay. A complaint against Judge Clay found its way to the Judicial Conduct Commission. He defended himself by citing the provision of the Code that forbade sanctioning of a Judge for making an "erroneous" ruling. The Judicial Conduct Commission reviewed all claims and settled the matter with Judge Clay.

In the settlement he agreed to accept a public reprimand, to resign from the Trust, and to repay the salary he had earned while a Trustee of the Trust. The Judicial Conduct Commission had the option to refer the matter to the Bar Association for consideration of disbarment or other sanction, but they did not make such a referral.

The public reprimand was reported in the newspapers. Headlines screamed of "Greedy lawyers scam millions from injured citizens in a conspiracy with Judge Clay."

Stafford thought that the public reprimand by the Judicial Conduct Commission should have closed the matter. The doctrine of double jeopardy holds that a person shall not be punished twice for the same offense. That constitutional doctrine appeared to prevent the Ministry of Ethics from proceeding against Judge Clay after he was sanctioned by the Judicial Conduct Commission.

After an unexplainable delay of four years, the Ministry of Ethics launched an investigation of Judge Clay.

The file revealed that an unsigned complaint against Judge Clay was stamped, "HRH".

That suggested that the Queen had ordered the investigation on her own volition.

The Board of Scrutiny promptly approved the complaint and the matter was assigned to a Trial Commissioner for trial.

Judge Clay reached by a reporter, made a critical comment about the Ministry of Ethics.

He said, "We have a system of ethics enforcement that is, skewed toward conviction, infected with politics and tinged with hysteria."

Chief Justice Madison Hatter read the comment in his newspaper and immediately sent word to the Queen of Hearts that he was 'very unhappy' about this allegation by Judge Clay.

The hearing before the Trial Commissioner, who had been selected by the Supreme Court, resulted in a polemic ten page finding against Judge Clay. The finding failed to clearly state what rule Judge Clay had violated, only that his conduct was "inappropriate".

The matter was now on appeal to the Board of Governors.

After Stafford finished reading the file, he wrote down his observations of the issues raised by the Ministry against Judge Clay. These legal issues, upon which the courts had never ruled, seemed to bring into question the jurisdiction of the Bar to prosecute such a complaint.

His notes listed the problems with the Ministry's case:

"Lack of jurisdiction of the Judicial Conduct Commission to sanction a judge for an erroneous ruling.

Lack of jurisdiction of Ministry of Ethics to sanction a judge for an erroneous ruling.

Lack of a specific charge under the Code of Professional Conduct.

Hearing by the Ministry of a rule under the exclusive jurisdiction of the Judicial Conduct Commission.

Double jeopardy. Punishment by the JCC and punishment for the same thing by the Ministry."

Stafford concluded that the handwriting was on the wall. The lynch mob was doing a real job on Judge Natrona Clay, and only the Supreme Court could right this wrong.

CHAPTER FIFTY-EIGHT

Williston Stafford could not share the files he had been sent by agent 007. This risked involving any attorney who viewed the file in an ethics investigation. While it was unlikely that he had broken some rule in reading the case file sent to him, he didn't take any risks. After he had read everything twice, he started a fire in his fire place and burnt to a crisp every paper and even the box in which the files were delivered.

Stafford made some calls and located Judge Natrona Clay. He had met Judge Clay on some prior occasion. He was pleased when Judge Clay accepted his phone call.

They arranged to meet two days later in Louisville at Captain's Quarters, a popular watering hole which fronted on Harrod's Creek where it flows into the Ohio River.

Stafford arrived first and was seated outside under a tall sycamore tree. He had a spectacular view of the Ohio River which was full of tow boats, motor boats, and fishing boats.

There was a slow but steady parade of boats of all sizes easing by the restaurant. The boaters eyed the guests at the restaurant, and the guests eyed the barely clad boaters. A large white yacht, large enough to host a wedding, was parked at the boat slip twenty yards from Stafford's table. Stafford wondered where people got the money to afford those large yachts.

The waitress brought Williston an unsweetened ice tea. Shortly the tall handsome Clay showed himself to the table. They shook hands as Williston thanked the Judge for meeting with him. "I've been trying to uncover the methods of the Ministry in pursuing their claims. I hope you can give me some background. I want to assure you that I will not quote you on anything you say."

"What in particular are you wanting to know?"

"Well, I admit I have read all the newspaper articles on your case, and I have talked to a few people who have filled me in on what they knew of the case. It appears to me that there is a serious jurisdictional issue. Has that been raised by your attorneys?"

Judge Clay took a drink from the low calorie Miller 64 beer he had ordered. "Yes, that's one of many issues raised. But the Board of Scrutiny and the Trial Commissioner brushed that issue aside. It's frustrating to raise a valid legal issue and have the judge simply ignore it. We have preserved the issue and perhaps the Supreme Court will look at in the future. I admit I am not optimistic. I don't mean to sound defeatist but things don't look good."

Williston said nothing and after a moment of silence the Judge pressed ahead. "You know hindsight is far more accurate than foresight. I believe that is where I failed. I did everything in good faith, and only in hindsight saw how the facts could be interpreted quite differently than the way things actually happened. Class action cases are pretty complex. The Civil Rules provide a section for the conduct of class action cases, but they provide almost no guidance to the judge.

"The rules say nothing about a judge's duty regarding the approval of fees, his duties for double checking settlements, or the award of expert witness fees. I was presented with a settlement where all the plaintiff's and the defendant stated in writing that they were happy with everything.

"The Cy Pres trust I approved was novel to me, but the plaintiff's lawyers showed me Federal cases where the courts had encouraged the distribution of excess settlement funds into a Cy Pres charitable trust. The Federal rulings recognize that after each claim is evaluated, if there are excess funds, it is improper to split the excess funds among the plaintiffs. This theory recognizes that while 500 people joined the class action, the number of people who were eligible to join the class claiming injury by the defendant's product numbered in the thousands. Most of the eligible parties didn't bother to join the class action.

"So the Cy Pres doctrine holds that it is the better practice to set up a charity and allow the excess funds to benefit the people who didn't join in the class action lawsuit. I saw the logic in that, and approved the charitable trust.

"The Ministry and the press simply ignored the Cy Pres doctrine and made it sound like a scam. Had this class action been in Federal Court instead of state court, this trust would never have been an issue.

The waitress brought another round of drinks. Williston took a cell phone call before Judge Clay continued.

"The Master Commissioner had evaluated each of the 500 plaintiff's claims, and each plaintiff had approved their award in writing. It is not uncommon in a class action for excess funds to be left over after all the individual claims are evaluated and paid. Everybody who objected to my final ruling had the right to appeal but no one did. It was several years later before any complaint was raised. As you surely know Williston, I lost all jurisdiction to amend my ruling ten days after it was entered. So years later when the plaintiff's became unhappy, there was nothing I could do about it.

"None of this would have involved me were it not for my acceptance of the offer to be a Trustee of the Cy Pres trust, two years after my final ruling. That position as Trustee of the Trust did not influence my decision in anyway, but I admit with the hindsight I now have, it was a mistake in a political sense. That's why I admitted the charges before the Judicial Conduct Commission and accepted the penalty of a public reprimand."

Williston, sipped his tea, and remained silent.

Judge Clay continued, "Don't think I didn't research the issue of whether a sitting judge could sit on the board of a charitable trust. There is a rule in the Judicial Code of Conduct, that says specifically that judges can serve on such boards.

"I also obtained two ethics opinions saying it was not a conflict of interest. Later when this issue became an accusation on my lack of integrity, I immediately resigned from the Trust and repaid all the salary I had been paid."

Williston nodded in agreement, "Judge, it appears that they are saying that your approval of the settlement was in consideration of a future appointment to the charitable trust board. Even though a year passed before you were offered the position, the Ministry assumes it was a quid pro quo arrangement. Do they have any proof of that?"

"Of course not. There is no proof of any sort. It's just their conclusion. They added up 2 plus 2 and got 5. There is no presumption of innocence. I am just presumed guilty. I am left with the impossible task of proving my innocent thoughts to a Ministry that has already presumed my guilty intent. If this was heard before a criminal court it would be dismissed immediately.

"The bottom line as I see it, is that the orders I signed all stand by themselves. No one has alleged that any order I signed was improper or not within the bounds of the law. The whole claim against me is their presumption that I signed the fee orders and approval of the settlement with the idea that years later I would be invited to serve on the board of the trust."

Williston agreed, "Judge, the thing that bothers me is that if this charge against you is allowed to stand that every judge in the future can have any decision he has made in his entire judicial career subject to "hindsight" review. Forget about the finality of judgments, forget about a litigant's duty to file an appeal within thirty days of a ruling. Forget about statutes of limitation.

"They have now created a precedent that any case ruled on by a judge can be reviewed and he can be sanctioned on facts that didn't exist at the time of the offending ruling."

"My only hope for vindication is the Supreme Court. Will they apply the law, or will they sacrifice me to the mob? I admit I'm pretty depressed by all this."

Williston asked, "Judge what has this done to you personally?"

Judge Clay responded quietly, "It's ruined my life. Even if I'm acquitted, my chances of ever being a judge again are zilch. That isn't enough. They now want to take the one thing that is the most important achievement in my life. They want to take my license to practice law. People who I thought were friends have stopped calling me.

"Even my relatives have their doubts about me. For nine years I was a good judge. I was never overruled on any decision I made. I was invited to speak at CLE events. My children looked up to me. Now even my son has doubts about me. I had just been re-elected to a new term by a comfortable margin. But after the Ministry and the press attacked me, I doubt if I'd be approved for a new Visa card. Even if I'm acquitted, I'm ruined."

Stafford asked Clay where he thought the Ministry was going with their investigation of his judicial ruling.

"The power move of the Ministry to interfere with the duties of the Judicial Conduct Commission by assuming the power to sanction judges for 'erroneous rulings' bodes ill for the future independence of the judiciary.

"I'm not sure, but it sure looks to me that most of the Trial Commissioners that hear Ethics cases come from the large law firms in Louisville and Lexington. Some actually come from large Ohio firms which have branch offices in Kentucky.

"The large law firms don't represent many plaintiff's in personal injury cases. Those firms represent large corporate interests. In insurance cases they always represent the insurer. I believe these corporate lawyers have a bias against any judge who from time to time rules against the big corporations and insurance companies

"Now Trial Commissioners who regularly represent large corporate interests are being placed in charge of ethics regulation of judges. This is like putting the U.S. Chamber of Commerce in charge of reviewing the rulings of judges.

"These appointment are made by the Chief Justice and the Supreme Court. One wonders if they appoint Trial Commissioners from the large law firms because they anticipate that in the future they may retire from the court and seek employment from one of the big firms. That's the reasoning that gave rise to the charge against me.

"If they can read my mind about what I thought might happen in the future, why can't we read their minds and conclude that their appointments are made in order to curry favor from the big law firms?

"Those Trial Commissioners are allowed to impose their personal standards on rulings. If their law firm does something one way, they tend to ignore any other way of doing business. They have little respect for lawyers from small firms. They have even less respect for trial judges who make less money than they do, and who often issue rulings that are against their corporate clients interests.

"The American Bar Association has adopted a Model Code of Conduct, most of which has been adopted by this state and most other states. Those rules bear little resemblance to a real code. The rules are vague, and the commentary had to be added to explain what the rule means. The commentary is only advisory. That means that the Ministry gets to interpret the rules anyway they want. Many of the ethics rules are completely subjective.

"I have looked up the definition of the word "erroneous" which is used in the Judicial Conduct Code. It means "any ruling not in agreement with established law." That means that a judge could never overrule a prior ruling. Any judge who rules that an established doctrine or statute is unconstitutional violates this rule. That's just one example of how poorly the Code of Conduct is written.

"A fee charged by a small law firm might be found to be exorbitant, while the fee charged by large law firms for the same service, might be ten times higher, but is rarely found to be exorbitant. I truly believe there is a strong bias by the Ministry and indeed the entire Bar Association in favor of large law firms over single practitioners.

"The Squeal Rule now requires that even the lawyer members of the Judicial Conduct Commission must inform the Ministry of any hint of an ethical violation by a judge

"Any judge who cooperates with the Judicial Conduct Commission is now on notice that any admission he or she makes to them will find its way to the Ministry for a second investigation. Any judge who decides to enter into a settlement with the Judicial Conduct Commission is just asking for trouble now that the Ministry is taking charge of judicial ethics regulation.

"I hope the Supreme Court comes to their senses and establish a doctrine that limits the Ministry of Ethics from further gutting the Judicial Conduct Commission. If that isn't done, then my case will provide a precedent that will someday threaten every judge's independence. That includes appellate judges."

"Judge, I'm sorry that all of this has happened to you. Is there anything that I can do for you?"

"Just one thing Stafford. You keep those Eunuchs of yours working. They've just about ruined me, but if you do a good enough job, perhaps this will never happen to another judge."

Whenever Williston thought of Judge Clay, he always remembered the forlorn look in his eyes.

A month after his meeting with Natrona Clay Stafford learned of a ruling by the Court of Appeals which appeared to uphold Judge Clay's original ruling at least in part. That ruling had taken six years. Considering the potential for a retrial and further appeals, it would be another half-a-dozen years before the courts would finally dispose of the case which got Judge Clay in the gun sights of the Ministry. This didn't seem to bother the Ministry, they chose to continue to go after Judge Clay even though the Court of Appeals had substantially upheld his original ruling.

Chapter Fifty-Nine

Members of The Supreme Court met behind closed doors to decide if they would hear the Ministry's appeal of the Board of Governors' decision dismissing the Boone complaint. This meeting came three months after the filing of the Appeal by the Ministry of Ethics. They asked the Supreme Court to accept the appeal, and hoped to obtain a reversal of the Board of Governors ruling in favor of Justice Alice Boone.

Pursuant to SCR 3.370 the Supreme Court had the discretion to accept the appeal or to reject it.

Justice Boone had properly recused herself from the hearing. Anyone who thought the Chief Justice would recuse himself, since he was the supposed victim of Justice Boone's comments, were wrong. He refused to surrender control of the hearing to anyone else, and there was no one who could do anything about his refusal to recuse himself.

There is no provision in the Rules or the Constitution which provide a method to appeal the refusal of the Chief Justice to recuse himself, even when he is a party to the action before the court.

The absence of Justice Boone did not require the Chief Justice to seek appointment of a Special Justice by the Governor. Only when two vacancies on the court exist is the Chief Justice required to seek appointment of a replacement. The Chief Justice needed his vote and three others to prevail against Justice Boone.

Hatter had been warned by Cheshire that the Governor was apparently hostile to the attack on Justice Boone. While he could have asked for the appointment of one Special Justice he no longer trusted the Governor to accept his recommendations. The Dribble Drive option was not going to work this time. He would just have to build a coalition with the remaining Justices.

He assumed that Justice Anderson would be with him. He needed two additional votes but Justices Allgood, Zevely and Collins refused to discuss the issue with him.

Shortly before the vote, Hatter saw the handwriting on the wall and concluded that he simply couldn't get the votes to accept the appeal filed by the Ministry of Ethics.

When the vote was taken Anderson abandoned him. The Lawyer's Revolution, the Eunuchs, and Williston Stafford's fund raising, had proven effective.

The Chief Justice voted last. Seeing the vote was lost, he made a tactical decision and joined in voting to reject the appeal, making the vote unanimous.

By voting with the majority he reserved the right to appoint the Justice who wrote the actual decision. Seizing a final opportunity to assert his influence on the matter, he chose to personally write the decision.

The decision of Chief Justice Madison Hatter was published two months after the actual vote. In his decision he stated that the court had denied the appeal "out of a desire to exercise comity with the Board of Governors and out of respect for everyone's free speech rights, *even when their comments were clearly wrong.*"

He ordered that the decision be formally published. A hundred years in the future some scholar would read this and might incorrectly conclude that Justice Boone was acquitted of the ethics complaint only on the grounds of the court's mercy.

Justice Boone read the decision later and shouted to Scout, her German Shepherd, "That son-of-a-bitch!" Scout barked his agreement.

Chief Justice Hatter felt he had prevailed in the matter. He had forced Justice Boone to pay a high price for making comments about him in public. Others would think twice before criticizing him in the future.

The following week Justice Boone went back to work at the Court and never brought the subject up with any staff members or other Justices. One would have thought that she had forgotten all about the matter, but they would have been wrong. Justice Boone reconciled herself to work even harder to amend the Supreme Court rules.

While she never discussed the case again, she never forgot it.

Chapter Sixty

The Federal Judge's decision was handed down eleven months after it was submitted to him. His ruling shocked almost everyone.

He upheld the Ministry of Ethics prosecution by side stepping the issue. He ruled that the Federal Courts had no jurisdiction to consider the constitutionality of the State Bar Association rules. He ignored the fact that Federal Courts had frequently held otherwise. A ruling of the U.S. Supreme Court in the Feldman case had clearly recognized the jurisdiction of Federal Courts to review bar rules which infringed upon lawyer's constitutional rights.

Kenton quickly called his attorney's office and spoke to her law partner Les Houston. He authorized an appeal to the Sixth Circuit Court of Appeals.

Houston said he had concluded that "the ruling was full of holes and improper interpretation of precedent rulings, and that it would be almost be fun to write the appeal."

The judge's decision detailed the first amendment rights of free speech and discussed the history of ethics regulation by Bar Associations around the country. His decision then concluded that the First Amendment didn't apply to lawyers speech.

The District Judge reasoned that the Bar Associations under SCR 3.130 (8.2) could sanction a lawyer even for "truthful" statements. He cited the language of the SCR which mentioned a prohibition against a lawyer making a statement that was "true but reckless". He didn't explain or discuss who got to determine if a statement was "reckless". Kenton concluded that if anyone was offended by a statement made by a lawyer about a member of the protected class of public officials, that he was subject to an ethics sanction.

Jack Kenton faxed a copy of the ruling to Williston Stafford and an hour later called him to discuss the surprising ruling.

"Williston, if this crazy ruling holds up, then every lawyer will be forever be a second class citizen."

Williston responded, "He didn't cite the U.S. Supreme Court's ruling contrary to his theories. He didn't discuss the fact that the Ministry's prosecution failed to point out the fact that your letter didn't question anyone's integrity or qualifications for office and those were material requirements of the SCR.

"He held that the Federal Courts have no jurisdiction over Bar rules but he totally ignored dozens of rulings by the Federal Courts to the contrary. He also totally failed to discuss the complete denial of due process of law. You were sanctioned but had no hearing and no right to an appeal. Those are the basic requirements of Due Process!!"

"Jack", he continued, "even the Kentucky Supreme Court Commentary, says that lawyers are permitted to make statements "Expressing honest and candid opinions on such matters which contribute to improving the administration of justice."

"We are left with a situation where appellate judges can criticize lawyers and inferior judges, but if anyone else questions their legal theories they can be sanctioned, regardless of the truth of the statement."

Kenton chuckled and replied, "I guess you have just violated the rule by discussing the weakness of this ruling."

Williston Stafford did not laugh. "He actually wrote that there was a 'significant state interest' in suppressing a lawyer's comments made even after the conclusion of a trial.

"I wonder if law professors can even discuss the historic Marbury v. Madison decision issued in 1803 which was the first court ruling that held the court could find an action by another branch of government unconstitutional?"

Kenton as usual was more constrained than Stafford. "We still have our work cut out for us. This is only a small defeat. There is one positive aspect to this ruling. When we win at the Sixth Circuit Court of Appeals, and I believe we will, the ruling will have far more national significance."

Stafford acknowledged the work to be done, "We have the right to an appeal but we also have the political option available. The Kentucky Supreme Court elections come up in less than a year and Justice Boone's reform rules need to be adopted."

A reporter called Kenton and asked for his response to the ruling. Kenton refused to criticize the ruling other than to say that he would be filing an appeal.

He added, "If the Federal courts uphold this rule against free speech, then we will still have the right to go to the ballot box and change the faces on the Kentucky Supreme Court. We will work to elect some justices who are committed to upholding the Bill of Rights adopted by our founding fathers."

Stafford passed news of the ruling along to the Eunuchs.

In the morning papers, the Queen of Hearts said she was not surprised by the ruling. She was quoted in the AP news story as predicting the Sixth Circuit would surely uphold the ruling of the District Judge. She added, "We will defeat any appeal even if it goes all the way to the U.S. Supreme Court."

When Chief Justice Hatter read that Kenton was going to launch a political campaign against the Supreme Court, he clearly understood that he would be the main target of the Lawyer's Revolution. He was livid. He called his secretary and told her to get Heather Hart in his office immediately.

Chapter Sixty-One

At ten o'clock, Commissioner Hart was shown into Madison Hatter's office in the state capitol building. He wasted no time in setting her straight about an appeal. "I read that you are going to fight Kenton all the way to the U.S. Supreme Court. Have you thought about the consequences of such an appeal?"

She started to defend herself but he didn't give her the chance.

"Do you realize that Kenton might just win on his appeal? Have you given any thought on what a ruling by the U.S. Supreme Court would do if it ruled that the Rules of Professional Conduct were vague and overly broad? Have you thought about the cost of such an appeal?"

He did not wait for her response.

"Have you thought about the damage an appeal could do if it resulted in a complete rewriting of the Code of Professional Conduct? Don't forget the Federal Courts and even the U.S. Supreme Court have been on a thirty year campaign to weaken the State Bar Associations' control over judges and lawyers.

"First there was the ruling which outlawed a minimum fee schedule regulating lawyer's fees. They have upheld the free speech of judges in that Minnesota case, and several Federal courts have struck blows at the Code of Professional Conduct.

"Do you really want to give the Supreme Court another chance to further restrict state control of lawyer's conduct?"

He finally added the real objection he had to an appeal. "Are you aware that Alice Boone has drafted numerous amendments to the Supreme Court Rules, and that if they are adopted you will be out of a job? Your appeal will just inflame Boone and the so called Lawyers Revolution.

"Don't you realize that the Lawyer's Revolution is aimed directly at you? You ordered these roses to be painted red! Because of you half the Supreme Court is in danger of being voted out in next year's election!"

Chief Justice Hatter made the hardest cut of all by adding, "Why did you go after Jack Kenton for criticizing the Legislative Ethics Commission?

Why should the judicial branch carry water for the legislative branch. We can hardly regulate ourselves. This was a stupid prosecution."

The Chief Justice sat down at his desk and picked up the telephone to demonstrate he was finished with her, but added, "I would suggest that you find a way to work out this problem with Kenton and prevent more appeals. Appeals are expensive, and ultimately may destroy the attorney discipline mechanism."

She wanted to defend herself by telling the Chief Justice that it had been his idea to go after Jack Kenton, but she realized she couldn't prove that. She had only assumed that Cheshire's request came from the Chief Justice. Either Hatter was lying or she had been duped by Cheshire. She realized that she had fallen into her own little Rabbit Hole. She would be more embarrassed by telling the truth then she would be by just hunkering down until it all blew over. She chose to just hunker down.

It was obvious to the Queen that the Chief Justice cared little about the attorney discipline machine in light of Kenton's threat to go to the ballot box. Madison Hatter was obviously frightened by Kenton's threat to recruit an opponent to run against him.

The chastised Queen left the Capitol Building and sulked all the way back to the Ministry Castle. When she got back to the protection of the high stone walls, she called Big Cat Cheshire and asked why she wasn't informed of the details of Justice Boone's proposed rules amendments.

Cheshire pled ignorance, which was a lie, he knew everything. He promised he would check this out and get back to her.

Over the long weekend, the Queen finally reached an obvious conclusion, "Cheshire has been playing me just like he plays everyone else." There was nothing she could do. For once she did not have control of the situation.

The sweet taste of victory in the Federal District Court had quickly turned to ashes in her mouth.

Chapter Sixty-Two

Williston Stafford, Jack Kenton and Justice Alice Boone met at the rural home of a Eunuch friend near Stanton, Kentucky. The road up the hill to the one level ranch style home was accessed through a locked security gate. The rear of the house was guarded by a steep hill and dense woods. The hostess had at least five dogs which patrolled the five acre area around the home.

Justice Boone and her guests were unaware they had been followed by Tweedledee and Tweedledum. She was unaware that a GPS unit they had placed on her car months ago, and transmitted to Cheshire a record of all her travels.

Stafford had unknowingly selected a home for this meeting that could not be bugged by Cheshire's portable laser mike due to the dense row of trees protecting the home from the front. Only the roof of the home was visible from the road.

Tweedledee tried unsuccessfully to access the cell phones of their subjects. They finally concluded the closest cell phone tower was fifteen miles to the west. Even if it had been closer, the steep hills between the home, and the nearest cell phone tower, made signal reception impossible.

The van Cheshire's henchmen were driving, was soon spotted by the hostess's dogs when it parked just off the roadway, near the fence encircling the home. The barking dogs scared Cheshire's spies away. They realized that their white van parked by the side of the road in a rural area was highly suspicious.

Rural people in the area were familiar with the local cars and are on alert when they see a strange car or truck cruising their road. They are very aware of potential burglars and troublemaking strangers.

Tweedledee moved the van up the road a quarter mile to avoid the dogs. He told Tweedledum that he was going to have to go in on foot.

In minutes Tweedledum had put on a back pack which contained a mobile laser mike, a pair of night vision goggles, a compass and a walkie talkie. Tweedledee said, "When you are finished call me, and I'll meet you back here. I'll be close by."

Tweedledee drove two miles up the road and pulled over at a wide spot. He then removed the vehicles jack, and proceeded to appear to be changing a flat tire. Several cars came by and one motorist stopped and offered to help him, but he waved them off.

Tweedledum worked his way on foot up a ravine parallel to the target house. He hiked toward the steep hill at the rear of the house where the meeting was underway. He was fortunately downwind of the dogs. He was looking for a location where he could have line of sight with a window that was not shielded by the trees and brush.

It was hard climbing along the ravine which ran up a steep hill through a wooded area. The sun sets early in East Kentucky and this night was no exception. Soon it was pitch black in the woods. He would have been totally lost without his compass and night vision goggles.

Twenty minutes later Tweedledee heard a series of screams over the walkie talkie. "Help! Help! Dear God help!"

Tweedledee shouted back, "What's going on, what's going on?" He heard nothing but silence for ten minutes. Tweedledee didn't know if he should drive back to the pick-up point or abandon his brother and make an escape back to Frankfort.

Finally a winded voice full of fear, came back to him. "Pick me up, come quick." Tweedledee radioed back that he was on the way.

Five minutes later he saw his rotund twin brother running down the road towards him. He had lost his back pack and was missing one shoe and half his jacket was missing. As the van pulled up next to him he jumped in, and slammed and locked the door. He had nasty scratches on his hands and forearms and his nose was bleeding profusely.

"What in the world happened to you?" Tweedledee demanded.

All Tweedledum could say as his lungs screamed for air, was "Black Bear . . . Black Bear, BIG FUCKING BLACK BEAR!"

In the tension of the moment Tweedledee began laughing so hard his ribs hurt.

The essence of all comedy is seeing someone else barely escaping a life-threatening event. The mental picture of a Black Bear jumping out from behind a tree, growling, with his nostrils flaring, and his fangs and teeth bared, at Tweedledum, was the funniest thing Tweedledee had ever heard.

The Tweedle brothers surrendered the surveillance and drove back to Frankfort. They stopped briefly in Winchester to buy some bandages and disinfectant for Tweedeldum.

Tweedledee finally stifled his hysterical laughter as they turned on the Mountain Parkway and headed towards Lexington. He asked his brother where the laser mike and night goggles were.

"They cost over $5,000 and Cheshire will be mad as hell."

Tweedledum looked at Tweedledee as if he were an idiot. "You are welcome to go look for them if you want, but I'm sure as hell never coming back to these mountains without a machine gun and a couple of hand grenades."

Tweedledee rejected the offer to recover the equipment himself, and once again began laughing uncontrollably. He laughed so hard on the way home that he twice ran the van into the emergency lane.

Tweedledum angrily stated that he didn't see the humor in being chased by a bear. This set Tweedledee off again.

The next morning they had to explain the loss of the equipment to Cheshire. They blamed Tweedledum's encounter with a Black Bear. Cheshire laughed so hard he nearly fell out of his chair.

"You damn fools, didn't you know those mountains are full of bears?"

He didn't have the heart to dock their pay.

The following summer a grounds man was bush hogging in the area where the bear attack occurred. He found the eavesdropping equipment, but never told the property owner. He could use them in deer hunting when the season opened in the fall.

Chapter Sixty-Three

Inside the home where the Eunuch's meeting was being held, the guests were unaware of the Tweedle brothers drama.

After dinner Justice Boone distributed copies of her draft of proposed amendments to the Supreme Court Rules. The report contained a general description of the 25 rules amendments she was promoting. The Boone Rules Amendment addressed in detail the reforms needed to make the discipline process fair.

(Author's note: The Boone Rules Amendments are found in the appendix to this book.)

Stafford and Kenton discussed each amendment with Justice Boone. She presented a credible justification for each proposal. After three hours everyone had bought into her plan.

Stafford sat back in his chair and held up his glass of scotch in appreciation of the hostess.

"This glass of fine whisky was worth the long drive to the mountains."

Kenton teased him, "Do you value your scotch more than the historic reforms of the discipline system you have just endorsed?"

Stafford, drained the last dregs of the imported gold and replied, "It's a close call Jack, a very close call."

Kenton asked Alice what was her plan for getting these reforms actually adopted.

"We have two options. We can submit them now and see what the vote might be. I believe we have three votes right now. Hatter will have his vote and maybe two others."

Stafford asked her who the seventh vote was.

She explained, "Justice Anderson was for the original Rabbit Hole amendments, and has been under Hatter's influence for a long time. But I understand that someone took him out on a golf course and scared him with a threat of a well funded opponent in next year's election. He described it to me as a 'near religious experience'. He has actually been quite friendly to me recently."

Stafford wasn't so sure. "I believe that Anderson is basically spineless. He is friendly to you today, but if Hatter really squeezes him hard, he'll stay in Hatter's fold."

Kenton agreed, "He will go in the direction the wind is blowing. We've got to point a wind machine in his direction to keep him from tacking off course."

Alice Boone didn't argue with their analysis. She went on to option two.

"We could wait until after the election next year and hope to remove two or three of Hatter's flock from the court. This would take the drama out of the equation."

Stafford ran the two options through his mind for a moment, and provided a third option.

"It's just a thought, but what if you submitted your 25 amendments just before next year's election. We will have the 17,000 members of the Bar motivated. We can inspire a couple of truck loads of hostile mail to be delivered to the Justices' offices. Then we release polls to the press which express the outrage of the voters with the Rabbit Hole Amendments. We then waive our campaign checkbook under their noses, and I believe they will follow us anywhere we want them to go."

The three sat in silence and pondered the options.

Their hostess who had not spoken on the plan, broke her silence and suggested, "If you go with option one and don't get the fourth vote then you are toast. It will be hard to submit the amendments twice. But if you proceed with option two for recruiting candidates to replace recalcitrant Justices, you reserve the option to implement option three if the tide turns in your favor."

Alice Boone, Williston Stafford and Jack Kenton all looked at one another and virtually in unison said they liked it.

The hostess asked Alice if she was going to seek the approval of the Board of Governors for her amendments before presenting them to the Court.

Alice explained, "That of course has been the practice but the Supreme Court has frequently ignored the recommendations of the Board on Rules Amendments. It's just a courtesy to permit them to express their opinion. The current makeup of the Board is about evenly divided. If we submit the amendments to the Board we are just likely to give the opposition a chance to muddy the water. A loss there would hurt us more than a victory would help us. I see no benefit in giving the opposition two bites at the apple."

Stafford added, "Next year we have Supreme Court elections. After the Supreme Court elections the newly elected Court will select the Chief Justice. Hatter's term as Chief Justice will be up. This presents two chances to minimize his influence."

Kenton added, "Don't forget the Board of Governors will also have an election. This presents an opportunity for the state's lawyers to remove people like Austen and Wakefield.

If we could remove those two, then the progressives on the Board would have a majority."

He concluded, "Don't forget there is one power that the Board of Governors does have, and it's important. They can fire the Queen of Hearts!"

Stafford expanded on Kenton's comments, "We have candidates lined up to run against five of the six Ministry dupes on the Board of Governors. We believe most of them will be vulnerable when word gets out about their support for the Rabbit Hole Amendments. Our polling shows the Bar members oppose the Rabbit Hole Amendments by a margin of five to one . . ."

The hostess asked, "Do you have any polling on Madison Hatter?"

Stafford responded, "We have three potential candidates. In a Hatter versus Jack Kenton race, Kenton has a 4% edge. That's within the margin of error. Shelly Chappell is the granddaughter of the former Chief Justice, she trails by 6%. Judge Berta Bingington trails by 12%. All of these numbers are very much in play. The primary is eight months from now.

The run-off is 14 months from now. A lot of things can change from now until the general election."

Alice Boone turned to Kenton and asked, "Jack are you going to file?"

Everyone looked at Kenton for his response, "I really don't want the job. But we have two or three more months before the filing date. Let's see how the others are doing in the polls. I think it's important that someone challenges Hatter, and if I have the best chance, I may do it. But I really would prefer that someone else take him on."

Stafford, remembering the speech Kenton gave to his children in front of the Kenton Farms fireplace, leaned over to Kenton and in a stage whisper said, "Ask not what your country can do for you."

Kenton grinned "Quit it, that's not fair!"

Chapter Sixty-Four

Williston Stafford spent the next four months traveling the Commonwealth organizing campaigns for those who had agreed to oppose the 'Mad Court' members aligned with Chief Justice Hatter. He delegated to a committee of Eunuchs the job of recruiting and assisting candidates for the Board of Governors elections.

For possibly the first time in the history of the Board of Governors, the lawyers who elected the Board Members actually interviewed the candidates to find out their views about the Ministry and the Queen of Hearts conduct.

Stafford spent some of the funds raised by the Eunuchs to lobby key legislators and to educate them on the necessity for those portions of the Boone Amendments that required legislative action. He was able to assure that at least the desired legislation would be introduced. He spent a great deal on polling of potential candidate matchups for the Supreme Court and on the public's opinion of the proposed Boone Amendments.

Kentucky law requires that all candidates for judicial offices file their candidacy papers by late January in the year of the election. The May primary race for judges determines the top two candidates who would face a runoff in the November general election.

A week before the filing date, he met with Jack Kenton at Kenton Farms. Stafford showed the current polls to Kenton. The poll revealed that Kenton had a seven point advantage over Madison Hatter.

He explained to Kenton that Chappell was leading Hatter by four per cent and Berta Bingington had closed the margin a bit but was still trailing Hatter by ten per cent.

He explained to Kenton, "This poll suggests that Hatter is vulnerable to being knocked off in the primary. It's possible that you and Chappell would win the primary and Hatter would be a lame duck with only seven months before his term would expire."

Stafford reported that the Eunuchs Committee had approved a budget for the election cycle.

"We will heavily finance candidates who oppose the three "Mad Court" members. We have budgeted adequate funding to help the Supreme Court incumbents loyal to Justice Boone. Some Justices will need more support than others.

"We have set aside $20,000 for the Board of Governors races and plan to spend heavily on a direct mail campaign to the 17,000 lawyers who elect the Board. We have at least one candidate in each race who are with us."

Kenton approved the planning and discussed his involvement in the election.

"Williston, I really don't want the job, but I am committed to the effort to remove Hatter from office. I'll make this commitment to you. I'll file and will work hard to get elected, but I don't promise I will serve out a full term if I'm elected. If we are lucky enough to knock off Hatter in the primary, I reserve the right to withdraw from the general election if Chappell and I are the two candidates for the November run-off. That would assure her election. Chappell is reliable and would make a great judge. Our goal would be achieved."

Stafford pulled out the filing papers and placed them in front of Kenton. Kenton signed his name and Stafford placed the papers back in his briefcase.

"I already have the required nominating signatures and I will personally file these. The Committee will pay your filing fee."

Stafford swore Kenton to keep his future plan to possibly withdraw to himself. "That is between you and me."

Kenton agreed.

Over the next week, Stafford repeated this scene across the state as he finalized the commitments of the selected candidates and shepherded them through the filing process.

One day before the filing deadline, Stafford received a call from Justice Anderson requesting a meeting. Stafford tried to avoid the meeting, which had all the earmarks of a confrontation, but when Anderson said he would drive to Carrollton immediately, he couldn't refuse the meeting.

Two hours later Stafford's doorbell rang and he showed Justice Anderson into his home. Stafford directed him to the formal dining room where they sat around at large walnut table.

The anxious Justice began, "Williston, I know that your group has been upset with me in the past."

Stafford's face revealed his agreement and not wanting to be prolong the meeting by being coy replied firmly, "You got that right!"

"But," the Justice continued, ignoring Stafford's bold reply, "Things have changed. I have given a lot of thought to the way that Hatter has been running things. He was wrong to use the assignment section to remove Alice Boone from the vote on the Rabbit Hole Amendments. I want you to know that I knew nothing about that before it happened. I had never heard of his damn Rabbit Hole Amendments. I wish I had paid attention. I was wrong.

"You must understand, most of us on the court defer to the Chief Justice in administrative matters. He is assigned the role of administrator by the constitution, and while the rest of the court have a vote on some administrative issues, it just creates dissension on more important issues if we interfere with his duties. I know that's not a good excuse, but that's the truth. We should have paid more attention and we definitely should have stood up to him."

Stafford thought about making a reply but preferred that the Justice be given all the rope that he wanted.

Anderson continued with the hint of a tear in his eye, "I know that your group has recruited a circuit judge to run against me. Is there anything you could do to give me a break?"

Stafford was careful not to say anything that might cross the thin line between hard campaigning and illegality.

"Justice, I appreciate your comments. I wish you had stood up to Chief Justice Hatter. I sympathize with your situation. But there are larger issues on the table than my sympathy. You don't have an opponent because we don't personally like you. You have an opponent because you facilitated Hatter's rampage against the members of the legal profession. More importantly you are not trusted by those who want to institute the rules reform we think are necessary to bring fairness to the disciplinary process."

Anderson perceiving a small opening interjected, "I have read Justice Boone's Amendments. I want you to know that I'm ready to make up for my mistake on the Rabbit Hole fiasco and I will publically commit to voting for adoption of the Boone Amendments and repeal of the Rabbit Hole Amendments. Believe me I have studied them in detail. I'm 100% in favor of Alice's reforms. You can count on me."

Stafford knew that if Anderson was being honest that they would have the necessary four votes to adopt Boone's Amendments and clean up the mess created by Hatter and the Ministry of Ethics.

The fact that Anderson might be violating the Judicial Ethics Code by promising his vote in favor of an issue that was surely going to come before him, did not escape Stafford. He didn't know if that rule applied to administrative matters or just to cases before the court.

He cautiously explained his limitations to Justice Anderson. He wouldn't put it past Anderson to be wearing a hidden microphone.

"Justice, I am just a member of a private Committee. I am not authorized to promise you anything. You said that you were willing to make a public announcement supporting the Boone Amendments. If you were to do that, then I can only promise to call a meeting of the committee and seek their advice.

"If they are convinced that you will be in favor of reform and not against it, a lot of their passion against you might be directed elsewhere."

He continued for the benefit of the potential hidden microphone.

"I want to be honest with you and not mislead you. I don't have the power to make a candidate drop out of a race. I have no influence over your opponent or what he does. I can only say that if you make a public call for adoption of the Boone Amendments, I will speak to the committee. I'm sure that they want to focus their efforts on the Justices that oppose their goals, and if you are no longer on that list, they may have a change of heart. They will put their money and influence where its most effective.

"The burden is on you to convince them you can be counted on. I can't make any deal and I can't make any promises other than a promise to call a meeting of the committee and to discuss your public announcement."

Justice Anderson pulled a speech from his jacket pocket and offered it to Stafford. "I already have my announcement prepared".

Stafford refused to touch the speech. "Justice I feel uncomfortable in reading your speech. I trust you to say the right thing, but I don't want to put myself in a position where I suggest or influence what you say. The public announcement is your project not mine."

Anderson ignored the rebuff and tried another tack, "I am speaking to the Frankfort Rotary Club tonight at 7 p.m. I have already sent copies of my speech to the *Courier-Journal* and the *Herald-Leader*."

Stafford said, "Justice, I'm impressed. I'll look forward to reading your statement in the newspaper tomorrow morning." And he added, "Could you fax me a copy after you give the speech?"

"'Of course," Anderson replied, "I will fax it to you tonight by 9 p.m."

Stafford wanted the speech from Anderson to have the date and hour stamp and number of the fax machine from which it was sent. This would distance him from having seen a copy before it was given and minimize any potential claim that he had influenced the wording of the speech if the matter ever came up."

Stafford showed Justice Anderson out, and returned to the dining room where he turned off his pin hole video camera concealed in a flower arrangement in the middle of the dining room table. If Anderson was playing him, he would find his face on YouTube and Facebook.

As soon as Anderson's car left, Stafford called Jack Kenton and reported the amazing conversion. "Jack, Do you think this is enough for us to go to Option Three?"

"I don't know. I can't see any way he could back out of a public promise. If he gives the speech, and then he is given an opportunity to vote on the amendments, it would be totally disastrous to his campaign for him to back out. He would be totally discredited if he broke his word to the public."

Stafford agreed, "I think you have it right. I'll call Alice and pass on the news."

She was delighted with the news, "Fine! Williston, that is 1000% fine!

"If we call the vote right away this will be a total embarrassment to the Chief Justice".

Stafford cautioned, "Justice, let's not forget that Anderson might be setting us up. If he has lied to me and if he repudiates his public announcement and votes against the Amendments this could actually help the Chief Justice. It would demonstrate to everyone his absolute power."

Justice Boone brushed aside this concern. "Williston, if he makes the speech and if it's reported in the morning papers, then I'm going to submit the Amendments on the 15th. That's the next court meeting date and administrative issues can be raised by any Justice.

"Now Williston, don't fall a victim to approach avoidance syndrome. We have worked for a long time to get to this point. Now is the time to strike. Sure there's a risk, but it's an acceptable risk. If he double crosses us, he will surely lose his re-election bid, and we will still have our fourth vote. We'll just have to wait a few more months to resubmit it."

After hanging up the telephone Williston called up the definition for "approach avoidance crisis syndrome" on the internet. After reading the definition he laughed out loud and said in the general direction of Justice Boone's office in Frankfort, "Honey, you got that right!"

Chapter Sixty-Five

On February 15th. at 1:00 pm sharp, the Chief Justice called the Supreme Court to order in the court's conference room. While he sat as the head of the conference table and held the gavel, the real person in charge of the meeting was Alice Boone.

When the time came for new business to be considered, Justice Boone moved for adoption of what the members of the court now knew were the Boone Amendments.

She explained that she had forwarded copies of the 72 pages of proposed Supreme Court Rules amendments with explanatory commentary to all court members and then, without further comment, made a formal motion for their adoption by the full court.

Justice Anderson and Justice Zevely both seconded the motion for adoption at the same time and it quickly was adopted.

Before the meeting of the Supreme Court the Chief Justice was informed by Cheshire that the amendments would pass by a vote of five to two. Cheshire was wrong.

At the last minute the Chief Justice was abandoned by his last supporter, who had correctly determined it was not in his best interest to oppose the reforms. He had felt the heat of the Lawyer's Revolution against the court. The final vote was six to one. Only the Chief Justice stood his ground.

After the vote, the meeting was adjourned.

The Chief Justice walked alone back to his office and slammed the door shut. The loud noise reverberated like a gun shot throughout the three floors of the marble capitol building. Later he issued a press release with a vigorous dissent opposing the amendments. Few people were moved by this loser's vitriol.

CHAPTER SIXTY-SIX

The Boone Amendments could not all be effected by merely amending the Supreme Court Rules of the Code of Professional Conduct. Several of the reforms called for legislative action.

An amendment to the Kentucky Constitution to eliminate the ability of the Chief Justice to use the Assignment Section to reassign Justices of the Supreme Court against their will was introduced in the Legislature and passed the House.

However, like so many bills and resolutions, it failed to be approved by the State Senate.

The Assignment Section continues to remain in the Kentucky Constitution threatening future generations.

Justice Alice Boone and her coalition on the Supreme Court publically pledged they would do their best in trying to prevent any further misuse of the Assignment Section. She obtained approval of a Supreme Court Rule that specified that no Justice of the Supreme Court could be assigned to another court by the Chief Justice if the assignment interfered with a scheduled vote on cases or administrative issues.

While the constitutionality of this Supreme Court Rule was doubtful, it at least meant that any Chief Justice who attempted to abuse the rule would be buying himself a lawsuit.

Chapter Sixty-Seven

The Queen of Hearts saw the handwriting on the wall, but she refused to move on. It was obvious to everyone that her days were numbered. She defiantly told Bunny White that "I will never surrender voluntarily. They'll have to carry me out of here on a stretcher."

The Boone Amendments provided for splitting up the office of Bar Counsel into an Office of the Bar Counsel, whose only duty was to act as legal counsel to the Board of Governors. The ethics prosecution duties of the Ministry of Ethics where assigned to another person.

At the first meeting of the newly elected Board of Governors, they dealt with Heather Hart.

Lawrence Dillon, the newly elected President of the Bar Association advised the Board that as an employee of the Judicial Branch of Government, Commissioner Hart was not protected by the state Merit System. Since she served at the pleasure of the Board of Governors, she could be fired immediately.

He opined that while her firing did not require 'good cause' there certainly was plenty of 'good cause'. The overriding justification for her removal was her prosecution of Jack Kenton.

As the first official action of the newly reconstituted Board, the members voted unanimously to fire Heather Regina Hart.

Dillon personally delivered the pink slip to Commissioner Hart at her office in the Wonderland Castle. He was accompanied by an armed Deputy Sheriff.

President Dillon informed Commissioner Hart that she had ten minutes to clean out personal items from her desk, to surrender her electronic key card to the Ministry Castle, and to surrender the keys to her state automobile. He gave her $100 cash for cab fare from his own pocket and informed her a taxi was waiting for her in the Castle's parking lot.

Without saying a word, and without making eye contact with any of the stunned employees, she filled up one cardboard box with her personal belongings, including her autographed Rand Paul photo, and walked out of the Wonderland Castle for the last time.

President Dillon and Ministry staffers watched through windows in the Castle towers as the Queen of Hearts climbed into the Yellow Cab and was driven away.

Dillon then called a meeting of all Ministry staff members and informed them that the Heather Hart had been discharged, and that Bunny White would be the acting Commissioner.

He warned the staffers that they were to have no official contact with Heather Hart and any communications she made with them was to be immediately reported to Bunny White.

Mathis then left without further explanation for the firing of the Queen or their future fates.

After Dillon left the Castle, Claudia Smithson grabbed Art Petrov and began dancing around the room singing a chorus from the Wizard of Oz, "Ding Dong, the Witch is Dead. Which old witch? The wicked witch!"

Bunny White did not join in the dancing but she had a broad smile on her face.

Everyone at the Ministry for Ethics had reason to suspect that they might be fired next, but they nevertheless felt a heavy burden had been lifted from their shoulders.

The firing of the Queen of Hearts had been recorded on the office security cameras including her getting into a Yellow Cab with a frown on her face and a card board box in her lap. Within minutes the video was posted on YouTube.

The castle in which the Ministry of Ethics offices were located was damaged by a fire two days after the firing of the Queen of Hearts. All the computer files and records of the Ministry were destroyed. This loss of records was speculated by many to have saved Heather Hart's law license.

One witness reported seeing a white van in the area shortly before the fire was discovered. Authorities found evidence of arson but no one was ever prosecuted.

Bunny White accepted the offer of the Board of Governors to become their legal counsel, which under Justice Boone's new rules, was separated from the Ministry of Ethics. She was directed in writing by the Board of Governors to closely monitor the activities of the Ministry of Ethics and to serve as an Ombudsman to review complaints of Ministry abuses.

The offices of the Ministry of Ethics were moved back to Frankfort, into a renovated distillery warehouse, several miles distant from the Kentucky Bar Association headquarters. The full time staff members of the Bar Association had been pleased when they found that the Ministry people would not be coming back to their building.

The new Commissioner of the Ministry of Ethics who replaced the Queen was Jim Robke. In his hiring, the mold of hiring ex-prosecutors was broken. Robke had served for ten years as a Public Defender. He brought a sense of fair play and due process to the discipline process.

Commissioner Robke placed an engraving on his office wall to inspire the staff.

It read:

"Of all tyrannies, a tyranny exercised for the good of its victims may be the most oppressive. It would be better to live under robber barons than under omnipotent moral busybodies. The robber baron's cruelty may sometimes sleep, his cupidity may at some point be satiated; but those who torment us for our own good will torment us without end, for they do so with the approval of their consciences."—C.S. Lewis

Chapter Sixty-Eight

Over 100 Eunuchs and 200 others met on the evening of the Primary election in a meeting room at the Marriott Hotel in Lexington to learn of the results of the judicial elections.

The election results trickled in and by eleven o'clock it was clear that Zevely and Collins had received the highest number of votes in their respective districts and where heavily favored to win in the November run-offs. Justice Boone was unopposed in the primary and thus was guaranteed re-election in November.

Justice Anderson barely made the top two in his race but was still alive. Since he had supported the Boone Amendments the Eunuchs had stayed out of his race. On election night Stafford assured him that the Eunuchs would help him financially in the November election in appreciation of his new reform minded attitude.

By midnight it was soon evident that the Boone coalition of reformers would clearly take control of the Supreme Court in January

Shelly Chappell, the granddaughter of former Chief Justice Chappell came in 514 votes ahead of Jack Kenton. Madison Hatter came in last in his race and was therefore eliminated from the November run-off. His term would expire in January, and therefore he was a lame duck within only seven more months to serve on the Supreme Court.

Jack Kenton was delighted that he had finished in second place behind Chappell. He was honest when he had told Williston Stafford that he really didn't want the job. His candidacy was important in eliminating Madison Hatter from the runoff election.

Having served that function and having come in second in the race, he felt he could properly withdraw from the November runoff without embarrassment.

After all the returns for the Lexington Supreme Court District were completed, he took the podium with Shelly Chappell congratulated her and made his announcement. He explained that he had long been a fan of the fine work Chappell had done as a Circuit Judge in Fayette County, and that he was impressed with her credentials.

He discussed that at his age he would not be able to serve for any great length of time on the Supreme Court, and that the public would benefit by having a younger member on the court who would be able to devote many years to the job.

Finally he said, "I defer to the wishes of the voters who gave the greatest number of votes to Judge Chappell, and I hereby wish to announce that I will officially file my withdrawal affidavit with the Secretary of State tomorrow morning. I rejoice that the voters have selected her as the next member of the Supreme Court from the Fifth Supreme Court District".

He took Judge Chappell's hand in his and held her arm high in a victory celebration.

The crowd applauded wildly. Champagne corks were popped throughout the room. Justice-elect Chappell gave Kenton a bear hug and a kiss on the cheek. This inspired the crowd to even more cheers and celebration.

A week later Kenton and Stafford met for breakfast at Welch's riverside restaurant in Carrollton. Stafford looked wearily out the picture window at the Ohio River and commented. "Jack we have won a battle, but we haven't won the war. If an ambitious Chief Justice cuts a deal with a sitting Governor, they can send the entire Supreme Court out of town and take absolute control of the judiciary. If they control the judiciary, they control the entire state. The next time we may not be so lucky."

In January the Supreme Court elected Alice Boone as Chief Justice. She was the first female in Kentucky history to serve as Chief Justice.

GLOSSARY

"BAR"—The Kentucky Bar Association. Membership in the Kentucky Bar Association is mandatory for all lawyers. Some states do not mandate membership in their Bar Association.

"BAR COUNSEL"—Attorney hired by the Board of Governors to provide legal advice. This office has been expanded to assign the Bar Counsel to be administrator of the Ministry of Ethics.

"BOARD OF GOVERNORS"—The 14 lawyers who are elected by members of the Bar Association to represent lawyers. The Board has limited control over the Ministry of Ethics or the Bar Association. It often studies issues but its recommendations are only advisory.

"COMPARATIVE NEGLIGENCE"—Rule that an award to a plaintiff based on negligence should be reduced by the per cent of the plaintiff's on negligence. Previously if a plaintiff was 1% negligent and the defendant was 99% negligent the plaintiff recovered nothing.

"DE NOVO HEARING"—a hearing where an appellate court considers facts as well as law

"EX PARTE DISCUSSIONS"—Discussion between a judge and a lawyer or party conducted in the absence of the opposing attorney or party. Such discussions are improper.

"HARMLESS ERROR RULE"—A minor error that does not affect the outcome of the trial and thus does not justify a new trial.

"IOLTA"—Interest on Lawyer' Trust Account. When a client advances a fee to a lawyer, the lawyer must keep these unearned funds in trust, and the interest earned on that money goes to the Bar Association. This only applies to small trusts.

"JUDICIAL CONDUCT COMMISSION" (JCC) Commission assigned to enforce Judicial Code of Conduct for Judges. They can sanction or remove judges who violate the Code of Conduct for Judges. They are separate from the Bar Association.

"MINISTRY OF ETHICS"—Agency of the Bar Association which conducts ethics investigations and prosecutions against lawyers. The Commissioner is also the Bar Counsel. Supreme Court Rules encourage the Ministry to conceal their actions from the Board of Governors. The Board of Governors is charged with the responsibility to monitor the actions of the Ministry. This conflict violates the duty of the Bar Counsel to keep her client(the Board of Governors) informed.

"MOOTNESS"—When an alleged wrong has been settled, the courts sometimes dismiss the pending lawsuit as there is no longer any real issue before the court, since. If there is no relief for the court to give, then the existing lawsuit is said to be "moot."

"RECUSE"—Removal of a judicial officer from a trial or hearing due to some personal bias or ethical disqualification. The Chief Justice is directed by statute to "immediately review the facts" of all recusal motions filed with him. A judicial officer may remove himself, or may be removed by the Chief Justice. The Chief Justice has absolute discretion in recusal motions.

"RULE 11 AWARD"—A monetary award given by the court against a party or attorney who has violated the Rules of Procedure by filing frivolous pleadings, and using delaying or other improper tactics which cause the innocent party to incur unnecessary expenses in prosecuting their claim

"THE BOARD OF SCRUTINY" consists of three panels of three persons each. This Board acts like a grand jury to issue the "indictment" against an attorney. Two of the members of each panel are required to be an attorney. The remaining member was required to be a non-attorney.

The appointment of a citizen member was justified as a person who would represent the public and who would prevent the legal profession from taking care of its own. In practice the citizen members rarely understood the underlying legal principles and merely went along with the Ministry's recommendations. After an "indictment" is issued approving the complaint against the lawyer, he is entitled to a fact hearing before the Trial Commissioner.

"SCRUNTINEERS" are members of the "Board of Scrutiny"—the investigative body of the Ministry of Ethics. They meet in secret to consider the approval or denial of a formal complaint against lawyers. An attorney against whom a complaint has been filed, does not get to look the members of this body in the eye. They can only submit written answers to the complaint filed against them by the Ministry investigators. They are appointed by the Supreme Court and the Chief Justice. If the Supreme Court defers appointment powers to the Chief Justice his power to control the committee is enhanced.

"STATUTE OF LIMITATION" Laws passed by the legislature which limit the time in which a offense may be filed. If a violation of a law is not brought within the statutory period it is tolled and may never be brought.

"**SUMMARY JUDGMENT"**—An order by a court dismissing a complaint due to a lack of a genuine legal issue in dispute. If a civil case is dismissed, the plaintiff never gets to the jury.

Appendix-I

(The Rabbit Hole Plan)

CONFIDENTIAL WORKING DOCUMENT

THIS DOCUMENT IS NOT FOR PUBLICATION AND MAY NOT BE COPIED OR DISTRIBUTED WITHOUT EXPRESS WRITTEN AUTHORIZATION OF THE MINISTRY OF ETHICS, BY ORDER 2017-52 ISSUED BY THE CHIEF JUSTICE.

KENTUCKY MINISTRY OF ETHICS

U.S. 60

Versailles, Ky.

MEMO

TO: CHIEF JUSTICE MADISON HATTER—***HIS EYES ONLY***

FROM: HEATHER REGINA HART, COMMISSIONER OF THE MINISTRY OF ETHICS

DATE: July 1, 2017.

RE: PROPOSED AMENDMENTS TO THE CODE OF PROFESSIONAL CONDUCT

Pursuant to your Order of March 4, 2017, the Ministry of Ethics has reviewed the laws regulating the speech and conduct of licensed attorneys, and the following recommendations for remedial action are provided.

It is the finding of the Ministry of Ethics that some members of the bar have inappropriately criticized rulings of the Ministry of Ethics, actions taken by the Legislative Ethics Commission, rulings of the Executive Branch Ethics Commission, appellate and trial court judges, and prosecutors in general. These loose comments by licensed attorneys have besmirched and challenged the integrity of institutions upon which our criminal justice system is founded.

In order to assure and effectuate the desired level of institutional integrity of the criminal justice system, the following recommendations are offered here as a remedial program to bring under control those who would besmirch the integrity of the protected class of officials identified in SCR 3.130 (8.2)(a).

The Ministry of Ethics recommends adoption of the following Enlightened Reforms:

1. Absolute Immunity should be expanded to cover all actions of prosecutors and officials of the Ministry of Ethics. The current limits of the absolute immunity doctrine currently enjoyed by prosecutors for actions taken only during the conduct of their "prosecutorial phase" are found to be inadequate to assure the expeditious enforcement of the criminal and ethical requirements of the law. Absolute Immunity should be expanded to cover all investigative actions of prosecutors.

Prosecutors must be allowed to conduct their official duties without the impending restraint of a potential civil action currently protected by absolute immunity during the prosecutorial phase, but only protected by a qualified immunity during the investigatory phase.

This expansion of absolute immunity to cover all conduct of prosecutors during the "investigative phase" of their work can be achieved by a timely court ruling. We recommend that this ruling be retroactive in order to allow immediate dismissal of all current civil suits pending against prosecutors.

2. The Kentucky Penal Code statutes, KRS 522.020 Official Misconduct in the first degree, KRS 522.030 Official Misconduct in the second degree, and KRS 519.060 Tampering With Official Records, should be

interpreted by a timely ruling of the Supreme Court to exclude actions of any official otherwise protected by the doctrine of absolute immunity. A more difficult alternative is to seek legislative amendment of these statutes so as to add absolute immunity prosecutors.

3. Supreme Court Preamble Rule XII should be repealed. Rule XII currently states:

> *"An independent legal profession is an important force in preserving government under law, for abuse of legal authority is more readily challenged by a profession whose members are not dependent on government for the right to practice."*

The Ministry of Ethics suggests that this rule as currently written provides a defense to lawyers to publically question decisions and practices of prosecutors and the judiciary and others within the protected class identified in SCR 3.130 8.2(a). Preamble Rule XII has encouraged disrespect for the proper and efficient enforcement of the law. Membership in the Bar is a privilege, and any abuse of that privilege by licensed lawyers should be discouraged by a clear policy that unruly and disruptive public comments concerning members of the protected class are forbidden. Several court rulings have upheld the right of the Supreme Court to limit comments by licensed lawyers about the qualification and integrity of judges, candidates for judicial office, prosecutors, candidates for the office of prosecutor, administrative judicial officers, and legal officers. (We suggest that these rulings include prosecutors employed by the Ministry of Ethics.)

The objectives sought by this report can only be effectively implemented when all doubt is removed from the minds of licensed attorneys that they depend on the state for the privilege to practice law.

We recommend a new rule which allows all complaints by licensed lawyers regarding the conduct of administrative agencies of state government, against judges, against prosecutors, against detectives employed by prosecutors, and public advocates to be filed in a Suggestion Box to be maintained by the Ministry of Ethics. This will preserve their first amendment right of lawyers to express their complaints, but will allow a proper regulation of such comments in order to maintain the respect for the judicial branch of government and the criminal justice system.

4. The Supreme Court in 2009 made membership in IOLTA mandatory. The funds generated by the interest on lawyers' trust accounts is currently dedicated to programs providing civil claim representation to indigents, and to reimburse clients who have had financial losses caused by improper acts of their attorney. We recommend that 10% of these funds be awarded to the Ministry of Justice to finance the expansion of the staff of the Ministry which will be required by the implementation of RABBIT HOLE.

We further recommend that the right of the Ministry of Justice to audit lawyers' trust accounts be granted to allow proper review of lawyers' handling and timely disbursement of IOLTA funds. This audit authority is necessary to assure that these funds are properly collected and forwarded to the Ministry. To assure proper enforcement of this program every licensed lawyer shall be required under the proposed audit program to disclose the amount and source of all funds held by them in trust. The Ministry shall be authorized to share this information with local prosecutors to assist in the proper enforcement.

5. We recommend that the Supreme Court repeal the official commentary to SCR 3.130 (3.8) which states:

"A prosecutor has the responsibility of a minister of justice and not simply that of an advocate . . ."

This language is currently only advisory but has been cited by the courts on occasion to limit the prosecutorial functions of prosecutors. The concept of a prosecutor having any role but that of a fierce and dedicated advocate is an outdated concept, and being merely advisory, will not be missed.

6. We recommend amendment of language in the Judicial Code of Conduct which has been argued in a recent case to limit the jurisdiction of the Ministry of Ethics to sanction judges for improper rulings after the Judicial Conduct Commission has issued a formal ruling.

The Judicial Conduct Commission would be preserved but the language in the Judicial Code of Conduct which allows the Judicial Conduct Commission the discretion to refer cases to the Ministry of Ethics for additional sanctions should be made mandatory, and every complaint heard by the Judicial Conduct Commission should be automatically referred to the Ministry.

We recommend that the Judicial Conduct Commission be mandated to forward the official record of all private reprimands, all public reprimands, and all actions imposing sanctions against Judges to the Ministry of Ethics for their consideration. The amendment should clarify once and for all that actions of the Judicial Conduct Commission do not limit the jurisdiction of the Ministry of Ethics, and that the Doctrine of Double Jeopardy does not apply to Judges tried by the Judicial Conduct Commission and who are subsequently sanctioned by the Ministry of Ethics for the same offense.

7. We recommend creation of a new Supreme Court Rule which allows the Ministry of Ethics to immediately inform all trial judges of any complaint filed against any attorney who resides in the trial court's jurisdiction or regularly or currently practices in their court upon the decision of the Ministry of Ethics to institute an investigation of said lawyer. The trial court receiving such information shall be subject to all confidentiality rules.

8. We recommend a new rule that requires that all lawyers who represent other lawyers in proceedings before the Ministry of Justice and the Board of Scrutiny be registered and licensed by the Ministry of Ethics, and that said special license be subject to revocation by the Ministry if it is found by the Ministry of Ethics that said attorney representing another attorney has improperly advanced legal arguments found not to be supported by the law or which question the authority or jurisdiction of the Ministry of Ethics or of the Board of Scrutiny.

9. We recommend repeal of current Supreme Court Rules, which allow respondent attorneys being investigated or prosecuted by the Ministry of Ethics, to waive the rules regarding confidentiality without the prior written authorization of the Ministry of Ethics.

10. We recommend legislative amendment of KRS 15.753 which currently provides that civil judgments against prosecutors shall be paid by the state but which currently limits compensation to those instances where the prosecutor has acted within the scope of his official duties. The recommended language would clarify that any jury award for civil

damages or attorney fees, against a prosecutor would be reimbursed by the state treasury within the dangerous requirement that the prosecutor be acting within their official scope of duties.

11. Current Supreme Court Rule **SCR 3.180** requires that all investigations and ethics prosecutions against attorneys be concluded "promptly". The Ministry recommends deletion of all time limits for conclusion of prosecutions as they hinder the Ministry in the careful development of their claims. Further we find that once an attorney has been notified of a pending ethics investigation by the Ministry that the ethical conduct of the attorney during the investigation is usually within the approved rules. Therefore, the mere initiation of an investigation serves a valid state interest and provides an efficient and cost effective tool for regulation of the conduct of attorneys. A prompt termination of an investigation or a prompt resolution of a charge is usually only beneficial in instances where the charge is easily proven or readily admitted. We do not believe that an errant attorney should be able to hide behind any artificial Statute of Limitations or speedy trial requirement.

12. We recommend that the Supreme Court vigorously oppose any attempt to adopt the ABA Model Rules for Prosecutorial Conduct provisions regarding the duty to report and correct improper convictions.

In 2008 the American Bar Association adopted a suggested rule that requires a prosecutor to report knowledge of the improper conviction of innocent persons. Kentucky amended its Rules for Prosecutorial Conduct in 2009 and wisely eliminated that provision.

It remains our belief that the finality of judgments, and the finality of ethics findings should not be easily overturned at the expense of judicial economy and efficiency.

13. It is the finding of the Ministry of Ethics that the so-called Squeal Rule adopted by the Supreme Court in 2009, which required all attorneys to report ethics violations of other attorneys, while certainly beneficial, stopped short of providing any tool by which the Ministry of Ethics could keep track of the good faith of attorneys who failed to comply with the squeal rule.

The Ministry recommends that all attorneys be required to annually file with the Ministry of Ethics an affidavit reporting any unethical conduct they had observed or heard concerning another lawyer or judge. They should also be required to make required reports within seven days of having observed such anti-institutional conduct. A failure to comply with the reporting requirement of this rule would itself be an ethical violation which could result in suspension of the lawyer's license.

This report will provide a basis for sanctions against those licensed attorneys who have not taken the squeal rule seriously. To accommodate members of the bar and to save mailing costs, this affidavit should be made a part of the annual bar association dues billing forms.

14. The Ministry proposes a new Supreme Court Rule which allows the KBA to develop dress code standards for attorneys. While our committee considered proposals for all attorneys appearing in court to wear horsehair wigs and waistcoats, the expense was not justified.

In order to establish the proper decorum and professionalism owed to the courtroom we propose the following guidelines for attorneys appearing in any court facility or during the taking of depositions:

We propose that all male attorneys should be required to wear dark suits, white shirts, and neckties without ornamentation. Sport coats with khaki pants are to be strictly forbidden.

Female attorneys should be restrained from wearing dresses or blouses which unduly display cleavage. No heels should exceed one inch. No open-toed shoes should be tolerated. Female attorneys should be restricted from wearing pants without a matching jacket of the same color and fabric. All shirts, tops or blouses should be white. Makeup should be muted and bright lipstick or painted fingernails are not conducive to the required decorum of the courtroom.

Any attorney should be forbidden to display a tattoo, or piercing which is viewable in any public place.

The Ministry proposes that the Chief Justice appoint a Dress Code Sub-Committee as an adjunct of the Advertising Committee, to monitor and to approve all styles and colors to be implemented in the Dress Code.

15. Since all court facilities are now smoke-free, we propose a Supreme Court Rule strictly forbid the use of tobacco in any form by any attorney at anytime.

Respectfully submitted,

/Hon. Heather Regina Hart/

Commissioner Ministry of Ethics

Appendix-2

JUSTICE BOONE'S NOTES ON HER AMENDMENTS FOR SUPREME COURT REFORM

1. **Repeal of the Rabbit Hole Amendments.**
2. **Repeal of the attorney dress code and the no smoking rule**.
3. **Discharge the Bailiffs hired by the Ministry.**
4. **Create a sliding scale of punishments to fit the crime following the model of the Penal Code** and classifying ethical offenses into three classes. The most severe offenses would be designated as Class A offenses, mandating Suspension of five years or permanent expulsion.

Class B offenses would allow suspensions of from 1 month to 5 years.

Class C offenses would allow private or public reprimands.

The purpose of this classification system is to prevent the Ministry from threatening attorneys charged with minor violations with permanent suspension.

5. **Mandate a statute of limitations on ethical complaints**. There shall be a ten year statute of limitations for a Class A ethical offense, a five year statute of a Class B ethical offense, and a one year statute for a Class C ethical offense. Currently it is possible that the Ministry can pursue a complaint for a violation which occurred years before and which was not easily defended after such a passage of time. The current system allows the Ministry to review an attorney's entire career looking for ancient violations to harass them.
6. **Impose transparency to the discipline process.** Outlaw the use of secrecy rules. No right for government secrecy is authorized by the constitution. Government secrecy is the fig leaf of tyrants. Mandate that all complaints filed with the Ministry be public records. Make the

names of persons filing complaints public. This will better alert the public and allow them to protect themselves from bad lawyers. Just as criminal charges are public records, ethics complaints accepted by the Ministry for prosecution shall be made public records. Our judicial system must be transparent. Transparency is a means of holding all judicial branch officials accountable. It is effective in helping to prevent corruption. Court actions including civil settlements should be available for review by anyone. The only confidentiality should be in cases involving minors who are victims, and divorce property settlements and division order if approved by the court. When rules, decisions and proceedings by ethics enforcers are open to public view, there is less opportunity for them to abuse the system in their own interest. We should let the sun shine upon all ethics proceedings against attorneys and judges.

We should also mandate that a complete listing of all Supreme Court Rules and Codes of Conduct for lawyers and judges should be accurately and completely published by the Bar Association's website. She noted that the website was poorly maintained and didn't accurately list the Supreme Court Rules. (She also expressed her concern about the accuracy of CLE records posted on the KBA's website.)

The Kentucky Supreme Court has ruled that open-records acts don't apply to the courts, Florida's high court has adopted a rule specifically saying the same principles apply to every judicial branch, including those entities that regulate lawyers and judges. We propose that the Supreme Court adopt the Florida rule and impose Open Records rights to the Ministry of Ethics, and for all administrative acts of the judiciary.

"7. **Limit restrictions against lawyer's free speech** to statements which are libelous of slanderous regarding judges and prosecutors and public officials except during a pending trial.

Forbid any free speech limitations in the Code to be used to protect comments regarding actions of the Executive or Legislative branch officials short of libel or slander.

"8. **Repeal the rules regarding absolute immunity of complainants who recklessly make false claims.** The highest degree of immunity granted to complainants or Ministry officials shall be a qualified immunity. An ethics violation which is maliciously prosecuted should only enjoy qualified immunity. This should allow the victim to pursue civil damages if the prosecution was malicious. Prosecutors should have no more immunity than a police officer enjoys.

"9. **Apply of the 5th. Amendment of the Constitution to ethics proceedings**. Establish that any attorney who is charged with an ethical violation has the right to remain silent. The burden to prove a charge should always remain on the state. There should be a presumption of innocence in all Ministry of Ethics disciplinary proceedings.

"10. **Application of the 4th. Amendment of the Constitution to Ethics investigations.** Require that all search warrants sought by the Ministry must be approved by a sitting Circuit Judge or other impartial magistrate, having no connection to the Ministry of Ethics. Require probable cause to be a material requirement of all search warrants.

"11. **Establish specific due process rights of all lawyers being prosecuted.** All ethics complaints shall be heard within 90 days. Any complaints held longer than that without a hearing should be dismissed. Federal and State criminal law places a similar speedy trial requirement on the government, and there is no justification for failing to impose this same standard on the Ministry of Ethics.

"12. **Outlaw the Bar's overreaching of the Judicial Conduct Commission** and require that any ethics prosecutions or disbarment actions against Judges by the Ministry, must first be recommended by the Judicial Conduct Commission. The only exception should be situations where the complaint involves criminal charges against the judge.

Expand the rule adopted for the Judicial Conduct Commission and outlaw any prosecution of a judge by the Ministry regarding a ruling later deemed to be incorrect or erroneous.

"13. **Separate the jobs of Bar Counsel to the Board of Governors from the prosecutorial function of the Ministry of Ethics** The Bar Counsel and the Commissioner of the Ministry of Ethics shall be separate persons with separate duties. Limit the influence of the Chief Justice in selecting the Bar Counsel.

"14. **Strike the power of the Chief Justice to appoint four citizen members to the Board of Governors to assist in hearing ethics cases**. If citizen members are deemed necessary or advisable they should be selected by the Governor, in the manner that the citizen members of the Judicial Conduct Commission are appointed.

"15. **Provide the Board of Governors with a monthly case report on all investigations so they can properly perform their administrative oversight role of the Ministry.** The Board of Governors shall annually report all case load statistics to the Supreme Court and these reports shall be published as a public record on the Bar's website. We can't administer the Ministry if they are allowed to keep all their work secret from the Board of Governors and the public.

"16. **Adopt a rule which would authorize Rule 11 sanctions allowing reimbursement for legal fees and court costs to those who are wrongfully prosecuted by the Ministry.** Rule 11 as found in the civil rules provides the template for this rule. This rule should clearly include frivolous prosecutions by the Ministry of Ethics.

"17. **Eliminate the Trial Commissioner**. The trial of all ethics complaints will be heard by a panel of three retired judges nominated by the Chief Justice and approved by the Supreme Court. One of the three judges shall be from the defendant lawyers Supreme Court District.

"18. **Qualify all Ministry of Ethics employees assigned to prosecute complaints.** All who actually prosecute complaints will have to have the qualifications of a Circuit Judge which consists of the requirement that all have a law license, and eight years of legal experience. The eight years of legal experience must include at least two years in private practice.

"19. **Adopt a rule where ethics complaints against the President of the Bar or the Vice President or the President-Elect** shall be heard directly by the Supreme Court and shall be subject to the speedy trial rule.

"20. **Adopt a rule that requires that all ethics re-education programs shall be operated by the Administrative Office of the Courts**, and all fees paid shall be paid to the Clerk of the Supreme Court and kept in the judicial budget. This would generate an estimated $2 million dollars to the income to be administered through the judicial budget. This rule should also bring DUI schools under the umbrella of the Administrative Office of the Courts as is done in Nevada.

"21. **Rewrite the Squeal Rule** to limit it to a duty to report any act which would constitute probable cause to believe that a crime has been committed or is about to be committed by an attorney. A failure to comply with the squeal rule shall be limited to a Class C violation and only punished by a private or public reprimand for the first offense, and by a fine not to exceed $500 on subsequent offenses. However, if the unreported crime results in bodily harm or financial harm greater than $500, a violation could be elevated to the highest classification.

"22. **Adoption of the provision of the ABA Code of Professional Conduct Rules regarding duties of prosecutors to report to the appropriate court any evidence that tends to support a claim of innocence by a person convicted of a crime.** Kentucky has failed to adopt these recommendations which are in the ABA model code.

"23. **Adopt a Supreme Court rule mandating punishment for prosecutorial misconduct**. Any finding by a trial or appellate judge that a prosecutor has improperly lied to the court about material issues, or who has knowingly withheld exculpatory evidence, shall be reported by the presiding judge to the Ministry of Ethics for investigation and said report shall be part of the public record. This rule shall apply to Ministry prosecutors, and also to criminal prosecutors.

"The penalty for a prosecutor improperly withholding exculpatory evidence shall result in a minimum loss of the prosecutors law license for not less than 30 days. It may include permanent expulsion from the Bar. Failure of a prosecutor who violates the squeal rule and fails to report a violation of the Code of Professional Conduct by another prosecutor shall result in a finding that they are conspirators and both shall be subject to a penalty equal to the sentence imposed on the defendant who was wrongfully convicted. The burden of proof shall be upon an prosecutor on the issue of whether or not the information withheld was exculpatory. Withholding exculpatory evidence may not be excused by the Harmless Error Rule.

"The Criminal Rules should be amended to require that any exculpatory evidence required to be provided to the defendant shall be provided within two business days of it becoming subject to the control of the police or the prosecutor. Any such evidence coming into the knowledge of the prosecutor or those under his control, within two weeks prior to trial shall result in the right of the defendant to obtain an automatic continuance of at least two weeks.

"U.S. District Judge Emmet Sullivan, who dismissed the Federal prosecution against Alaska Senator Ted Stevens, has urged a change in the national judicial rules to establish consequences for prosecutors who don't follow the rules on turning over evidence to defendants. Current rules leave it up to the Justice Department to deal with prosecutors' actions.

"24. **Adopt an "open file" discovery policy** for all prosecutors in Kentucky, including the Ministry of Ethics prosecutors. This shall not include a duty to allow discovery on those items currently protected from discovery by the Criminal Rules or the Rules of Evidence.

"25. **Adopt Public financing of Judicial Elections.** The recent decision of the U.S. Supreme Court in Citizen United, allows corporations to directly contribute to elections. In 2000 the Chamber of Commerce spent $5 million dollars in the election of an Ohio Appellate Judge. Three states have subsequently adopted public financing of judicial elections to protect the independence of the judiciary from the influence of groups like the Chamber of Commerce and Insurance companies. This might require an act of the legislature, but the Judiciary should adopt a resolution in support of public financing."